D1826551

Picking Murphys

❖

Enjoy My Nightmare

James A Summers

2-15-16

James Summers

Copyright © 2016 by James Summers.

Library of Congress Control Number:		2016902146
ISBN:	Hardcover	978-1-5144-5861-7
	Softcover	978-1-5144-5860-0
	eBook	978-1-5144-5859-4

All rights reserved. No part of this book may be reproduced or transmitted in any form or by any means, electronic or mechanical, including photocopying, recording, or by any information storage and retrieval system, without permission in writing from the copyright owner.

This is a work of fiction. Names, characters, places and incidents either are the product of the author's imagination or are used fictitiously, and any resemblance to any actual persons, living or dead, events, or locales is entirely coincidental.

Any people depicted in stock imagery provided by Thinkstock are models, and such images are being used for illustrative purposes only.
Certain stock imagery © Thinkstock.

Print information available on the last page.

Rev. date: 02/15/2016

To order additional copies of this book, contact:
Xlibris
1-888-795-4274
www.Xlibris.com
Orders@Xlibris.com
723373

To my little Naturegirl2: Stay in school and study hard. You too can be an Author!

Mad: Come back to the states and spend time with us.

ADBM: I can't wait for our camping trip!

CONTENTS

CHAPTER ONE

Life Transitions

Kent, Connecticut

Deirdre was only six when the headaches started to alter her life, resulting in the loss of family and friends. Being a child, she could not accurately articulate her pain. Although her experiences were somewhat debilitating, she managed to have an average childhood. She lived with her mother and father in a small community west of Hartford, Connecticut. Their modest two-bedroom red brick house was centered on half an acre and surrounded by a traditional white picket fence.

The backyard had a small play set with ladders and ropes complete with sand underneath. Deirdre could not easily count the number of times that she had fallen and been comforted by that sand. As a family, they never had pets in the traditional sense, although she did have a frog from time to time. Green was her favorite color and it was the color of her playground. It was also the main color of her bedroom, which, thanks to a local high-school artist, was painted into a dense coniferous forest.

The forest located on the walls of Deirdre's bedroom was completely different from that of her backyard and surrounding community. The leaves on her trees were thin and narrow needles of all lengths with some even having cones. Outside her window, the trees had large flat leaves in every color and size imaginable, but they were much smaller than what she had on her walls. She enjoyed long walks through the woods with her parents, who often took her to Bigelow Hollow State Park. No matter how hard she tried, she could never find a tree that matched the height or the leaves of hers. She made her mom promise one day to take her to a place where she could enjoy those trees in nature.

It took her mom, Mattie, over a week to locate that artist that had painted Deirdre's bedroom. After several unanswered e-mails, she finally had her response—redwood trees. The artist had painted a redwood forest like the ones that existed in California. Mattie smiled from ear to ear at the thought of telling Deirdre about those trees one evening over dinner. Arnold would be happy too; although he was a very loving and caring father, he tired easily when the discussion turned to trees.

Six years ago

Mattie was a forty-something, married, stay-at-home woman with a daughter that she had late in life. When Arnold and Mattie found out that they were pregnant, their good news was overshadowed by the bad. Complications were inevitable, and their doctor gave her a fifty-fifty chance of carrying their baby girl full term and only a 10 percent chance of that child being healthy. Mattie had high blood pressure, diabetes, and heart disease. Those potential complications together generally meant that most would not reach the age of fifty, let alone birth a child.

As their baby continued to grow inside Mattie, Arnold worried more than she did. Before he knew it, he had put on about ten unwanted pounds during their pregnancy. Mattie actually felt better after the first trimester. She worked hard at her diet and remained moderately active throughout her pregnancy. Mattie's latest doctor visit gave her a clean bill of health for her and her baby. "It was a miracle," Mattie would say.

On the longest day of the year, toward the end of the month of June, on one of the darkest nights Arnold could remember, baby Deirdre Elizabeth Anne Daly was born. On the outskirts of town in the county general hospital shortly after midnight, several nurses scrambled to give baby Deirdre a fighting chance. It was the summer solstice, the beginning of summer in the Northern Hemisphere. Today's date went unnoticed by most, but it did not escape Lucinda.

Lucinda gently cleaned up baby Deirdre and then wrapped her up so they could show her mother. Mattie was weak and tired, but having Arnold close to her gave her strength. The pain from her birth was managed wonderfully, and Mattie had no complaints about any portion of the delivery. Smiling at her little baby girl, she looked up at Arnold and blew him a soft kiss before she closed her eyes and fell asleep.

Arnold looked on as Lucinda moved the baby into another room and placed her with the others. He read the little armband as she took her away:

DEAD, 12:02 a.m., 6 pounds, 0 ounces baby girl

Arnold found her initials a little disturbing and made a point not to mention them to Mattie or Deirdre—ever. With all of the health issues that were overcome, Mattie and Arnold treated every moment as something special. They treasured every day that they had with their little girl.

Present time

Christmas came and went, and as with all past holidays, family portraits were taken. Mattie would look at them and always wonder about Deirdre's long blond hair. There she was, sitting between them in various poses over the years, sporting her long blond hair. Arnold and Mattie had thick brown hair. They were both Native Americans mixed with European blood.

The two met years ago at a tribal event that their grandparents had taken them to. As it would turn out, Arnold was a third Schaghticoke and Mattie was half. Their relatives had met Polish and Irish settlers and then started their own families. It was a small world indeed. What were the odds of moving around the United States growing up as children, only to settle back down as adults where your ancestors hunted and fished, *and* finding the one you love?

It was Deirdre's sixth birthday, and as a surprise, her parents were taking a trip to Murphys, California. More specifically, they were to visit Calaveras County and participate in their annual frog jumping contest. When Deirdre was dropped off from school and came into the kitchen for milk and cookies, she was greeted by Mattie and Arnold.

"Get changed, quick! Put on jeans and your favorite green shirt. We are taking a trip!" Mattie said excitedly.

Deirdre didn't know what to think. She was halfway into her second bite of her cookie when she turned on her heels and ran for her bedroom. Deirdre left a trail of cookie crumbs that any dog would have loved to have cleaned up, but that responsibility went to her mom. Before Deirdre had come back out of her room, the floor was swept up and Arnold had packed their suitcases into their small SUV. A few moments later, Mattie walked Deirdre out the front door to start her vacation.

Union, Connecticut

A trip to California was just what Susan wanted. She'd been planning it for over a year now, and with the money that she and Matthew saved, the timing was right. It was Christmas in September, and they were excited. They planned out their money well, although it didn't go far enough nowadays with two kids and a stay-at-home mom. Susan would always say that she did her part. She saved for their future and any vacations that they might take by using her thriftiness. Saving money was something she did in her sleep. She cut coupons, waited for sales, and even bargain shopped when time allowed. These things coupled with her husband's income from doing IT support for a

Fortune 500 company worked out nicely for them. Matthew even worked an occasional job on the side to add to their coffers.

Susan stared into the mirror, making a few facial gestures as she turned her head from side to side. This she did anytime she checked herself out in any mirrored surface. She looked for wrinkles, blemishes, flaws, and any other imperfections that she could correct with tomorrow's beauty creams. She smiled and told herself that she still had it, and turning her head again to the side, she checked out her smile before leaving the bathroom.

Susan boasted short black hair with a light sun-free complexion and stood at an impressive six feet two inches. She loved the fact that even after having two kids and being a stay-at-home mom, she maintained a healthy 145-pound weight. It wasn't the fact that she drew men's glances when walking around in public. It was quite beneficial to be strong and to have a height advantage when Black Friday came around. She laughed at the thought of dropping an elbow on an unsuspecting line jumper.

Having taken only one step out of the door, she heard her husband yell that he was taking Robbie out for his meeting. Susan yelled in response that she was coming and told them not to leave before she said good-bye. She smiled at what she had recently said and then ran down the hallway. Taking a sharp left turn, she slid into the wall, laughing. She caught her footing and continued running, wondering why she had her white socks on. She knew better, soon those lovely white socks would be very dirty on the bottom.

Robbie smiled and ran to his mom, hugging her good-bye. Matthew told them both that it was only for two weeks. After this last trip, he would be certified, capable of being in the woods and surviving with a rock and a stick. Matthew just loved the YSDB organization. He supported all outings and even worked on their website and performed general computer work for free. Robbie had been a member of the Young Sons of Daniel Boone for two years now. His dad signed him up as soon as he hit eight, which was the earliest that they accepted members.

"You take care, Robbie. Remember to always do your best and to treat others like you would have them treat you," Susan told him.

"Yes, Mom, I will," Robbie replied.

Susan watched as her little freckled ten-year-old walked out the front door. He was on his way to his yearly camp, and as always, he was in the best of spirits when he left. When Robbie came home, however, she noticed that it took him a few days to get back into the scheme of things. Robbie really loved the outdoors, and it was his love of nature that helped him stay active and fit. He was slightly taller than the kids in his class, but he had a physical build that was too small for football and too large for track. Robbie joked that someday he would have to try out for the chess club.

"Come on, Robbie, let us go. We need to make haste if you want to make it there on time," Matthew said.

Robbie hit the door, laughing as his dad gave him his rock and stick. It was a joke that his dad did each year. Each year he would get that rock and stick to take to camp. And each year he forgot them and had to find others on the way home to bring back for his dad. It was something that his dad pretended he did not notice they were different and something that his son pretended that his dad did not notice that they were.

Matthew kissed his wife and told her he would be back in an hour or two. She reminded him that she was dropping Thomas off at day care and that they were going to an auction today. They would also try to hit a couple of small antique thrift stores if they had enough time. He didn't look forward to this, but it's something that he did because he needed to support her hobbies. She loved antiques, and he had to admit, their house looked very nicely decorated.

"Back in an hour, hon," he told her.

"I can't wait," she said.

Leaving on a jet plane

Matthew found himself staring out the small portal window of his plane over his right shoulder. It had been three weeks since he last had Susan in his life; it felt so foreign for her to not be with them. Robbie was on his left, sitting motionless, looking at the back of the seat in front of him, almost catatonic. Turbulence jolted the plane to and fro, up and down. At times even Matthew thought he was to be thrown out of his seat. The only time that he knew that his son was alive was when the plane bounced him slightly upward and he struggled to stay attached to his seat. There were times where Matthew bounced up and his son did not move at all. This was explained by Robbie's white knuckles that held tightly on to the armrests and his feet that were wedged under his chair.

"We are almost there, son. Hang in there," he told Robbie as he rubbed his head.

Robbie didn't speak at all, but his dad did see him nod an acknowledgment. Robbie found it difficult to breathe on the plane. He had barely slept in over a week, and now his dad was taking him to California; he was not a happy camper. His grades were suffering and he was barely approved for his trip during the middle of the school year. How his dad had done that was beyond his imagination, but he loved him for it. This entire trip was a last-minute endeavor. Matthew didn't even know that Robbie would be able to legally go until the day before last. He was hoping that it would help to relax them and give them a way to get back to their normal lives.

A woman's voice crackled from above, stating that they would be preparing for landing. Matthew and Robbie were told that they were expected to be on the ground within twenty-six minutes. Robbie smiled at his dad as he turned back to face the tray that was attached to the chair in front of him. Matthew thought that they were early and he was already planning on getting through the gates as soon as possible so they could pick out their rental car.

Robbie had never been to California before. He was told by his friends at school who had gone there that he would have fun. His teacher Mrs. Belthood said where they were going offered lots of outdoor activities, including several national parks with very large trees. His mom and dad were going to taste wine and then they would part ways where she would shop and he would prospect for gold. Robbie was to spend some time with both, and then before he knew it, it would be time to go back home and their vacation would be over.

This was never to be; it was not possible, not anymore. He was alone with his dad on this trip, and it was more of a scouting trip than a vacation, his dad had told him. It was not a true vacation, not in Robbie's eyes. This trip was to look at some property with open fields, hills, and valleys that hid treasures in the ground that he could unearth. They would also check out the local school system and determine if it was a good fit for their new family.

Matthew watched as the flight attendant moved up and down the aisle, collecting any remaining trash from outstretched arms. She was a young brown-haired woman who wore her uniform with pride. Her name tag said Flight Professional Christy in bright red letters, and she believed in every word. It showed in the way she moved and how she smiled and in the requests that she loved fulfilling. She had passed up the aisle twice now, and each time her smile was larger than before, if that was even possible. Matthew noticed that smile. He had not smiled in quite some time now and he wasn't sure if he would feel like doing so again anytime soon.

Christy made her way from the middle of the plane to the rear, slowly checking seat belts. She also paid attention to the trays and seat backs, making sure they were in their original upright positions. As she made her way further toward the back, she noticed how the seats were smaller and the passengers were larger than they used to be. She thought of herself being older and hoped that she never got that way, God willing. She made a mental note to work out tonight to take better care of her health.

Walking steadily, she looked left and right, scanning the seats as she went along. When she passed the passenger sitting in 34D, an older woman firmly grabbed her elbow, stopping her dead in her tracks. They made eye contact, and Christy looked at the old woman closely. She wore at least three sweaters of various dark colors and sizes, her hair was done up, and she sported faded blue jeans.

"Be a dear and get me a coffee, will you please?" she asked.

"Sure. I'll be right back with it," Christy said as she continued to feel pain in her elbow.

The woman let go of Christy's arm and sat back, relaxing in her seat as best she could. Smiling and slightly confused at her interaction with the flight attendant, she watched her walk away equally confused. Christy continued walking to the back of the plane but no longer checked for seat belts, trays, or tables.

"OK, everyone, please stay in your seats no matter what happens, as we are soon to be on the ground. That is all," she said with a scowl as she eyed a heavyset man who had no sooner finished listening to her instructions than he got up and walked to the restroom.

Matthew noticed the woman start to walk straight for them before stopping to the side to look at his son.

"Your seat belt, please," the attendant said as she reached down to tug on the boy's belt.

"It's snug," Matthew said to her. Matthew looked on as the woman pulled on the loose end, tightening it even further.

"And you, sir?" Christy said as she reached for his belt. Her hand pulled up on it one time, checking the buckle, and then strayed as she cupped his balls tightly, pulling them upward. Matthew was caught off guard and just looked at her, not knowing what to do or say.

"Nice. Yes, this one's good," she said as she released her grip. Matthew looked away and then toward his son as she continued moving to the back of the plane, but she had lost her smile.

Christy made a beeline for the restroom as she saw the occupied light turn off. She met the man at the entrance as he opened the door and slid in against him. Pushing him back inside, she closed the folding door behind them. The plane hit turbulence and shook violently, pushing her forward and into the man. She threw her hands against the man's stomach and her breasts against his chest. She smiled as she leaned in to kiss him. Christy moved her hands lower and pushed both inside his open zipper.

"Your barn door's open," she said, smiling, as she leaned in harder against him and kissed the large man.

The man kissed her sloppily as he reached for her breasts, and pressing them hard, he rubbed his thumbs over her nipples. Christy took his penis in her hands and stretched downward, looking into his eyes as she kissed him again. He closed his eyes, enjoying her attention, and returning a favor, he squeezed her breasts and pulled them upward toward her neck. Another kiss, and Christy bit down on his lip, drawing blood. He instantly let go as she dug her claws into his member with her right hand. She then slammed her left into his face and bloodied his nose.

The man tried to scream, but he was quickly silenced by both of her hands closing around his windpipe. He reached his hands upward in an attempt to break her hold as knee after knee met him in his stomach. The look in her eyes horrified the man. He could not break her hold and he could not get free. The large man continued to struggle to get free and to breathe. He heard cracking bone noises and then ceased to resist her, sliding backward with a smile that slowly faded into a lack of expression.

Christy led the man to the toilet and sat him down, lowering his pants to his ankles. She left him there fully erect and half naked as she turned to face the door. She opened it and looked back at him one more time before pulling up his shirt to his neck to hide the bruises. She stepped out and closed the door. Christy took a few steps and sat down in the adjacent flight attendant seat and stared forward.

Matthew looked over his left shoulder again and noticed the woman sitting in the chair, smiling at him. She mouthed the words "Later, I'll catch you later." He was puzzled by this and turned back to Robbie, who was still concentrating on attaching himself to his seat for all eternity. He was talking to Robbie, telling him that everything was fine as he saw the flight attendant walk up the main aisle and turn left of the cabin door. She pushed some buttons on a control panel and then turned the top and left levers, opening the door.

The cabin pressure dropped, and chaos erupted all around them. Masks fell from their holders, alarms were going off, and anything not secured was soon on its way out of the door. The first thing Matthew saw sucked out of the open door was the flight attendant, but if he didn't know better, he thought she had jumped. The noises from the people around him coupled with the vacuum sucking noises from the open door made it damn near impossible to hear the instructions from the captain. He remembered "Your mask first, place your mask on first before helping others." Reaching up, he grabbed the mask, pulled down like he was instructed to, and placed it on his face. Matthew secured the elastic band over the back of his head just like the others around him were doing.

The plane was to land sooner than expected; that much he knew for sure. Matthew felt the nose of the plane reaching for a sharp angle of descent as he looked out the window for reassurance. Matthew finished placing the other mask over Robbie's face as he looked around the plane. To Robbie, it seemed that the lower the nose was pointing toward the ground, the faster they travelled. The noise from the open door grew louder, which muffled most of the shouts for help around them. All manner of loose paper, hats, and any remaining trash from this afternoon's snacks became debris that whirled and spun through the air at an incredible speed before exiting the plane.

Matthew heard a loud noise from behind him. He saw the fear on Robbie's face, so he ignored it and held on to Robbie tightly to comfort him. He was glad his son's unduly tightened seat belt kept him firmly in place. Robbie held on as if his life depended on it. He tried not to, but he looked around the plane, somehow managing to peel his eyes from the seat in front of him. He screamed as the next series of bumps jolted the plane. This caused his dad to hold on to him even harder, pulling him over against his shoulder. Robbie watched as a woman tried to leave her seat and make it to the restroom in the front of the plane. Matthew tried to cover Robbie's eyes before the lady was picked up and lifted into the air, but he was too late. She traveled headfirst out the window like she was able to fly.

He knew that Robbie had watched her disappear, and Matthew thought that he would have to figure a way to explain today's events, if they survived. More messages attempted to reach the passengers and flight attendants, but very little was heard; there was just too much noise. Matthew felt that now the plane was under control. Although he knew it was traveling at a high rate of speed and that their elevation was dropping very rapidly, he still thought the captain had control of the plane. Looking around, he saw more and more people start to settle in, staying safely in their seats and even calming down.

Robbie was crying less at this point, Matthew noticed. Although Robbie resumed staring at the back of the chair in front of him and breathed normally, he was again white-knuckling the armrests. This was a good thing, Matthew would soon find out as he slowly turned his head to his left and saw a very large man lying on the floor. He was slowly sliding his way toward the exit, an exit that Matthew did not want to go out of until the plane was safely stopped on the ground. The plane jumped a few times, and the man was actually bouncing forward. His head tossed around to his left, displaying a very large pair of bruised handprints around his neck. His eyes were emotionless and open. His eyes stared at Matthew briefly before the large man continued traveling to the front of the plane on his back.

As the plane shook from turbulence, somewhat violently at times, the dead man continued to bounce forward. Each time his body came back down, his head made an audible thump when it hit the floor. The large man was on his way toward the open door at the front of the cabin. He had traveled half the distance already, and with each bounce, people screamed in horror as he passed. Lucky were the ones that were sitting on the left side, as they never made eye contact with the dead man.

Robbie watched as the dead man bounced forward and out of sight. His dad ensured that he did not make eye contact as he passed; it was the least he could do for him. Heavy turbulence again shook the plane, dislodging the beverage cart. Robbie looked around the plane and concentrated on the cart as it tried to follow everything else and exit through the loud open door. Crackling could once again be heard, but it was faint. The man's voice said something on the lines of "Stay seated" and "Prepare for," and then the plane slammed into the ground.

The plane rose back into the air and then hit the ground one more time. The impact was enough to throw the cart on top of the dead man, wedging him in the doorway. Matthew held on to Robbie as best he could and watched as others around him did the same. *Wow,* he thought, *these masks do provide oxygen,* as he had almost forgotten it was on his face.

After bouncing a few more times, the plane began to slow. It was now easier to hear communications from the crew, and Matthew listened closely when the captain spoke.

"Almost made it. Everyone, please stay seated as we come to a complete stop," he heard from the captain as the plane continued to slow down.

The captain was of medium build and he carried it well. He would work out each time he went to a hotel for an overnight stay. It was soon time to retire, and the last plane he would ever be on would take him to Prague. It was there that he was to spend the last of his days with Raphael, his lover of ten years to the day. He could not wait for this to be over so he could get started on his new life.

Looking through the portal window, Matthew saw trees, houses, and land; it was such a relief for him. One could easily tell from looking at anyone's faces that all was well. Cheers of joy erupted as other passengers came to the same realization that they were safely on the ground. Although the mood of adjacent passengers was generally good, Matthew was concerned that they were still moving at a pretty fast speed. He looked around and could not help but notice the open door and the cart. It was on still on top of the man, and only his legs were sticking out. It was a scene straight out of the classic movie *The Wizard of Oz*, only gorier. It was more disturbing and personal because he was a human being. What had occurred here happened to a real person; the man was obviously murdered.

Robbie looked over at his dad and smiled. He felt relieved that they were slowing down and that they were on the ground. He released his grip on the armrests ever so slightly and he too looked out the window.

"Are we on a road, Dad?" he asked.

"Yes, we appear to be," Matthew said.

"Cool" was Robbie's reply.

There's something to be said about being in the middle of nowhere, Matthew thought. They were on a road, and that much was for certain; it didn't matter how remote they were. The houses on the side were far apart from each other and also a good distance from the road. There were no mailboxes, trees, or bushes at the sides of the road. It was just a road cutting through the land, which was sparsely populated. The plane continued to slow down, although there were potholes and rocks that made things difficult. Any bumps that they did hit minimally affected the plane, as they were still safely in their seats. Matthew looked around and saw that others were still secured just like they were. If they had been safe on the tarmac, everyone would have already been loosening their seat belts. Some would have already been standing, but not on this road.

The captain initiated the brakes and reversed the engines just enough to feel comfortable. He focused on slowing the plane safely enough to stop short of what he saw straight ahead of him. There was a road crew with stopped traffic dead center of the only road he saw for miles. He made a calculated guess on how fast he was going and how much distance he had before he would crush through the stopped traffic. It wasn't long now, he thought; soon everybody would know if this would work out or if it wasn't meant to be. At almost the same time, everyone seated found themselves leaning forward, seat belt or not. The brakes were being applied; that was what the experienced flyers thought. For those who weren't as experienced, the looks on their faces that they shared with all present were that of panic and fear.

"Country roads have bumps—what do you do?" the captain said to the woman on his right.

She smiled back, nodding in his direction and then turned to monitor her half of the instruments. She thought the lights were pretty, but she really didn't understand them. They had patterns, she thought; some flashed green, yellow, and some were solid green. A few were red, but they meant nothing to her. She looked over at the man beside her; he looked absolutely lovely in his uniform. He had a large smile on his face, and his eyes darted around, checking this gauge and that button with passion as he continued to speak.

"I'll be able to get around most of them," he told her.

"Won't we be stopped by then?" she asked.

"Most assuredly not," he replied.

Why does it always have to be the women, she asked herself, *always the women . . .*

"You picked the wrong flight," she said, smiling to the captain.

He glanced at his copilot and witnessed her pressing random buttons, changing dials, and moving sliders their opposite directions. He quickly took control and overrode her controls, disabling the effects from her button pushing.

"What the fuck, Elliott! We have landed. It's going to be all right. We're almost stopped!" he shouted.

"I guess it's just not your day, Mitch," she said as she turned her head to face him.

"How did you know my middle name?" he asked her.

"Well, Mitch, I know as much about you as I care to know. I'm afraid that you are not going to make it out of this—it's just not in the cards," she said, smiling.

Mitch looked at the road in front of them and decided that they were going to be fine. They were slowing nicely, and there was plenty of room as he gave more power to the engines that were already working hard to reverse their forward progress. Several more bumps lie ahead of them, and there were areas that were just too dangerous to avoid. He would have to hit them at an angle or slightly head-on. All was well, he thought; he didn't know what the hell she was talking about. He wondered how she would know anyway; she's much less experienced than he was.

Matthew was watching their progress and he smiled to Robbie as they bounced in their seats a few times. Robbie found that comforting and he too felt that soon they would be walking on the ground, talking about their unusual flight. There was a loud noise that seemed to come from just outside their window, followed by smoke and screeching metal noises before the plane veered sharply right and left the paved road. They were now heading for a lovely farmhouse, which they had just passed only seconds ago as they seemed to be making a wide arc to the right. It was obvious to all that they had blown a tire.

Matthew continued watching and began to count. He went over his math and did it again. He looked at the very old trees that were slowly moving toward them. If he was correct, they had to change seats. To Matthew, it looked as if the plane was going to hit them on the right side. The right side of the plane was going to lose its wing along with half of the seats on that side. Hell, both wings would be ripped off if he was right, and everyone and everything seven seats forward and rear from that wing were toast.

"Robbie! Get up!" he yelled as he struggled to undo his own belt.

It would not release no matter how hard he pulled on it. If he didn't know better, he thought it looked melted. The edges looked uneven, possibly welded, and upon closer inspection, it looked to be a single piece of metal with no lever to pull at all.

"Dad, it won't budge. It's stuck. It won't open," Robbie squeaked frantically.

"I know. Mine too. One second," Matthew replied.

Matthew pulled with all his might, but he could not free himself. He then focused on his son. His belt was the same way, almost melted around the edges. How they both could have failed on the same trip, he wasn't sure, but he was going to play the lottery this week, especially if they made it out of this. The ground they were traveling over bounced them around in their seats with a vengeance. It was probably a good thing they were still sitting, but he would have loved to have had a choice.

Matthew saw them both dead within a few minutes' time. He was sure those trees would do the job; their course was true. They were arcing right toward them, although their speed was slowing. With another slight turn to the right, they were on a course to reach the trees head-on, dead center if you will. They were heading straight for the small gap between two large growths of trees as if being guided there.

Mitch continued to fight their present course as he attempted to steer the plane away from the house. He was trying to make it through the hole in the trees. He knew it would be tight and that he would lose the right wing or both, but the main body of the plane would escape destruction. Looking over at his copilot, he noticed she was gone; she was of no use to him at all. The woman was staring out the cockpit window at the farmhouse, smiling. She continued pressing buttons, although they were already disabled.

Robbie had feelings of sadness and helplessness creep over him. Where only minutes ago Robbie had seen himself walking on the ground with his dad after they had exited the plane, he now saw everything good start to slip away. He looked at his dad and smiled anyway.

"It's OK, Dad. It will be all right," Robbie said as he turned to look out the portal.

"It's not over yet, son," Matthew said between grunts as he attempted to raise himself upward in his seat.

That part of superhuman strength, where one was capable of extreme acts of courage and power in extreme situations—well, it failed him, and apparently for the last time. Those around him were running around the plane, being bounced around at times, and every few seconds, one or two passengers jumped out the door. Matthew screamed for assistance as they ran past him, but no one stopped to help.

An older man and woman were walking toward the front of the plane and asked them if they were OK and why they were staying seated. Matthew asked them for help and mentioned the stuck seat belt buckles. The old man reached down, smiling, and released the lever on Matthew's buckle. Matthew looked up in astonishment and watched as the old man reached over to Robbie's and did the same.

"You have to have faith, son," the old man said as he turned and walked toward the door with his wife.

Looking down, he saw that the buckle looked normal now, but he didn't know why. He stood and grabbed his son up in his arms, moving to the front of the cabin and just out of reach from the door. The old man and woman held hands and jumped out the door. Matthew watched out of the left portal windows as they tumbled out of sight. Matthew looked around and then turned back to his son.

"We were just shown the way out. Let's get out of here," he told Robbie.

"Really?" Robbie asked.

"Now how many opportunities will one have to jump out of a perfectly damaged airplane heading straight for an old farmhouse with several very large trees?" he asked, laughing.

The copilot looked agitated. She moved her eyes to the left and waited for the confrontation to ensue, but it never came. As soon as she felt it, the feeling was gone. It was her fight-or-flight reflex, and there were several warning signs, the first of which was nausea. She never made it to the second one, as she always chose flight. She would always live to fight another day, she thought; no one stays on this earth as long as she has without being cautious and running away. The copilot wasn't sure that a human could confront her to that end anyway, but she wasn't taking any chances today.

She wondered who it had been, who had visited her today. The only thing she knew for sure was it had left very quickly, probably when it too felt nausea, if they felt that warning like she did. The battle would be wonderful when it happened. She felt that this time she would fight to ensure her plan would end the way she wanted it to.

The time had come, Matthew thought; they weren't showing any signs of slowing down. If anything, they were speeding up, he was sure of it. He looked down at his son, and as Robbie spoke, he gathered him up and jumped out of the noisy cabin door.

The copilot rubbed her bottom against Mitch's lap. She made small circular movements as she smiled, looking forward and holding his stick. The plane bounced roughly over the uneven ground as it abruptly changed course. Mitch's head rolled to the left, and his lifeless expression could be seen in the reflection of the window.

The minute she felt them leave the plane, she lost interest in her current course of action. She sighed and let go of his stick, sliding back into her seat. A minute later, the plane attempted to squeeze between the small copse of trees, slicing off both wings at the same time. The middle trees rocked against the plane's movement, and as Matthew watched on, he saw the right side of the plane peel away, leaving many sections of the right side on the ground and against the trees. His calculations were spot on, and if they had remained sitting, they would have not survived.

The plane showed signs of slowing; the wind had been taken from its sails, but it was not to be stopped, not just yet. The copilot stared out the cockpit and counted down from three, and upon reaching one, she witnessed the nose of the plane dig into the ground and flip end over end into the trees. Matthew watched as the plane twisted midair and the tail end wedged itself between two sparsely leaved trees.

Matthew felt rough for sure. He had lost count of the number of times that he tumbled head over heel before stopping abruptly in the sitting position. Robbie had not rolled as much as him and at first glance looked OK. Matthew got up and started checking his son out for injuries. Robbie told him that was the most fun that he had on the entire plane ride.

"Honestly, Dad, I'm all right," Robbie said with his eyes aglow.

"OK then, let's go and have a look around here and see if we can help out," Matthew said.

Robbie walked with his dad toward the old farmhouse as stragglers walked this direction and that. Sirens could be heard coming closer from both ends of the road that they had earlier landed on. Passersby were now stopping to render aid and help out as best they could. Robbie kept up a fast pace, and it was all Matthew could do to keep up. He examined the house more closely now that they were heading straight for it; it looked abandoned, empty.

There was a large wraparound porch with a swing immediately to the left side of the front door. The building seemed to have been painted three or four times with various shades of white and was adorned with unusually shaped peeling paint chips. It had wooden shingles, and even the glass on the windows looked old and thin. Getting closer, he noticed the numbers on the side of the building: four five six seven.

"Damn, we're home, Robbie," Matthew said.

Looking around, he took in the view around him and double-checked the address.

"Yup, this is the place that we were going to buy—that's the address all right," Matthew told Robbie.

"Cool!" Robbie yelled as he broke out in an all-out run for the front porch.

He found distraction in the house, in the thought of living here. He forgot about his bumps and bruises, the recent events, and even the plane crash. The plane crash—he had been in a plane crash, he thought. Looking around, he saw stragglers being attended to; most had been sat down on the ground and were being checked over. Some former passengers were still walking around, generally in crooked lines that could be seen as paths through the tall summer grass.

No one thinks clearly at times like this; most don't even recognize that they are close to being in shock, let alone recognizing when it happens. Matthew felt nausea overtake him. He felt dizzy and thought it was better to sit down lest he lost his balance and fall over. Sitting down gave him an entirely different perspective of the farmhouse. It was a single-floor ranch; well, he wasn't sure if it had a basement or cellar, but neither was visible.

Turning his head back to the road, he saw police cruisers and a fire truck park along where he thought the road was. The house was a good distance from there, with no lane or driveway that went to the street; it was all grass. Looking back at the house, he saw a road that went behind the house with some paths and trails and, yes, plenty of hills with trees. All country places had hills and trees; it was part of having character the realtor had told him.

Hills and trees were on both sides of the house, and this property held two hundred acres of lovely land, nestled somewhere northeast between the cities of Arnold and Murphys, California. That was the selling point—a large amount of land—but most of all was the potential for minerals. On this property alone, there were supposedly four mines, of which only three had been recorded and submitted by the prior property owner.

More pain rocked his body; his stomach contracted, and he leaned over to throw up. The timing was as perfect as any special effects company in Hollywood could have ever hoped for. Two quick explosions rocked the plane, throwing a few stragglers through the air and scattering them about. A very large ball of fire erupted into the sky and licked at the tree limbs that still held the plane vertical and firmly in place.

The earlier two explosions caused all caregivers to immediately charge the plane to render assistance. Matthew heard screams and yells, and it appeared that they all were charging him as opposed to the plane. He felt pain in his head, his left leg, and possibly his left arm, but he needed to get to Robbie, who was still sitting on the front porch swing. He stood up and scanned the very large piece of land that was his front yard and saw movement to the right. He turned his head and watched a thin figure walking toward him.

The copilot was very mad now. She had grown tired of this and wanted it all to come to an end. She too saw people around walking toward the house and a large group of individuals about six hundred yards away running in her general direction. She cared not for them; no one mattered here except the man who had just stood up and was staring at her.

Matthew changed his mind and took off after the person so he could help. His strides were long, covering much more ground that he knew as he ran. Not only was he closer than the first responders, but also he was carrying less weight and moving faster as a whole. He had traveled about ten or so long strides when he started to realize that she was burning. Matthew didn't notice it before, but from all the shouts from the others running closer meant that they did. A few more steps and then he knew for sure that she was not burning; she was on fire.

The flames followed the woman as if she was their fuel. They licked at her hair and rose in varying heights from her elbows, her shoulders, and her hands. At times he could see through them as if the flames had parted, or maybe they were burning only certain locations on her body, he wasn't sure. Matthew noticed her speed up and her direction turn to meet him. She was coming straight for him now, he was sure of it.

The first responders were closing the gap between them as quick as they could. They continued to run at a good pace to reach the plane before another explosion occurred. Something didn't feel right as Matthew kept watching the person walking toward him. He was not wearing a uniform, but Matthew thought he was the captain. From the way he walked, his gait looked unusual. It wasn't a man at all; it had long brown hair. It was a woman! He didn't remember seeing her on the plane before, and from the lack of discernible clothing, he could not be certain who she was. Again he felt nausea overtaking him and he had to take a knee to throw up.

A third and fourth explosion rocked the plane, sending a piece of the fuselage hurling through the air in their direction.

"Aw, give me a break!" he yelled as he lunged to the left and started to run as best he could to get out of its path.

A very large piece of plane about four window seats in size spun through the air and hit the lady square in her back, effectively cutting her in two. Her lifeless body hit the ground, and the flames disappeared. He closed his eyes to shield himself from the image of death in front of him. He felt the need to nurture, to protect, and to hug. He made his way back to the house to gather up his son.

The first responders seemed to switch to a brisk walk and were no longer running toward the person that had only recently been on fire. They too saw the body fall after a large piece of plane flew into it. They thought the worse and were cautious at this point as they approached the person, knowing that the plane could explode again at any moment. Matthew had reached Robbie by this time and through the shouting in the distance heard some in the group agree to go and check on the two on the porch.

The community's finest slowed down even more as they approached the body. Matthew continued hugging Robbie as a large man and a muscular woman approached, decked out in full firefighter gear. As they asked him questions about how he was and checked them both for injuries, Matthew found himself answering them with vague replies. He was more focused on the old man and woman who had first saved them and then jumped out of the plane. He answered yes a few times and then paused as the couple disappeared into the trees to the left of the plane.

"What a shame, she's beautiful," said the policeman.

"Why, she's totally naked—she's not burned at all," commented another.

"Damn, damn," the third responder said.

She watched them with disdain. *What a backwoods fucking redneck place this is—and no women,* she thought as she plotted a course to town.

"What a way to spend a Wednesday, hey, Dad?" Robbie asked.

"Sure, right. Rather uneventful and boring, wasn't it?" Matthew asked, laughing.

The two looked at each other and just sat on the front porch, sharing the swing. Matthew rocked it gently, thinking that they have had enough excitement for one day and he didn't know how strong it was. For hours, they watched the crews put out the fire and cordon off the wreckage. It would be months, he thought, before they would be finished with that investigation. He hoped they would carry the wreckage off to a nearby warehouse to finish it on their own time. *That plane ride—man, it was something,* Matthew thought. Both Matthew and Robbie knew they were lucky to have survived.

They had survived for sure, but they only had the clothes on their backs and whatever they had in their pockets. The luggage had surely been destroyed, but things could be replaced. He knew they were very lucky to have lost only their luggage. Matthew was sure that there were people who had died. That brought back images of the woman burning alive as she made her way to him as if to give him a message. He wasn't sure, but he thought he had heard her say, "I'll catch you later."

Looking back at the house to get his mind off of today's recent events, he looked at the front door. It looked a bit rough and worse for wear, almost different from the pictures that he had been shown by his realtor. *Oh well,* he thought, *time to check it out.*

"Robbie, are you with me? I want to go and check out the house," he asked.

"Well, I think I'll sit here while you go check it out. I seem to have lost my survival rock," Robbie snickered as he said that.

"Funny. Yeah, I'll go check it out, and later on I'll send you to find your own rock. You're old enough now," Matthew said matter-of-factly.

He took the keys out of his left pocket and walked for the front door. The lock turned easily enough, and it appeared not to have mattered. If he pushed hard enough on it, the door would have given way under the pressure and opened without it. Matthew would add that to his list of things to do.

The door swung wide, and the dark room beyond called out to him: "Clean me." Looking around for a light switch, he placed his hands on something sticking out of the wall and moved it upward. The lights turned on, and the room came to life. It was a lovely room devoid of furniture of any kind and it had been recently dusted. *Yup, a nice clean fixer-upper, just like they told me.* Matthew laughed.

There was a breeze brushing past him as if the air conditioning was turned on, but it was warm. Walking small circles around the room, he determined that it was a draft and that the windows needed to be looked at. He hoped that it wasn't from holes in the walls, but who knows—he would have to go over the entire house room by room and check everything out to be certain. First things first: he would change the locks, shore up the doors, and then check the windows. He had months to go before he had to worry about it getting colder. It was already getting hot here, but that didn't bother him much as the cold would.

A cursory walk through the house was necessary. Matthew had to check the kitchen and the bathroom out at a minimum. The kitchen was dated, with Formica countertops, bluish tiled floor, and an old stove and fridge that did not match. That would have made Susan mad, and she would have gutted out the entire kitchen to make it her own. He would have gladly helped in that process, but she was no longer here.

Making his way into the bathroom, the lights did not work, but the water turned on when he tried it. *Damn, I forgot to check the water in the kitchen*, he thought. Flushing the toilet seemed to work as expected; the water drained and refilled quickly. Overall, the house did not smell, had free air conditioning, and offered a lovely '70s lifestyle ranch with easily accessible living space. Matthew laughed as he went back into the kitchen to turn on the kitchen sink faucet, ensuring that it worked.

Matthew thought about what else had to be done immediately; he tried to remember his mental checklist:

1. *Have local mattress dealer deliver king-size and twin-size beds. Check.*
2. *Have furniture store deliver general living room furniture that he picked out from the Internet. Check.*
3. *Find local woman to babysit and help plan some meals until he can find a girlfriend. Damn, behind on that one, need to check the local papers this weekend.*
4. *Refer to items 1 to 3.*

Not bad; he had to add a few more entries to his list of things to do as he thought about the doors, getting some groceries and checking out the general store in Murphys.

Stepping out onto the porch, he watched a fireman slowly walking up to his house.

"Robbie, we'll have to go into town and get a few things this afternoon. It will be sort of like camping, son, but I promise I'll check on the status of those deliveries tomorrow," Matthew said.

"No problem, Dad. I'm ready to go when you are," Robbie said, smiling.

The fireman had just made it up to the porch when his radio went off.

"Fourteen dead. A few body parts here and there. Still can't tell if it's the same person or not—oh, and there's the one that was on fire walking through the field, sir," the man's voice said.

"Sorry about that. Bad timing, 'tis all," the man told them as he scratched his head.

"I came to ask you if you needed a ride into town—it's the least that I can do. We are taking the other survivors into town on a bus. It should be here in a few minutes, and I didn't want you to miss it," the fireman said.

"Very cool of you. Yes, we might just stay in town for the night and try to get a vehicle and some necessities for the house," Matthew told him.

"All right, follow me then. Is your son all right? Oh, I'm sorry, I never introduced myself—Fire Chief Mary Lewis at your service, sir," he told Matthew.

"I'm sorry. Matthew, my name's Matthew, and my son over there is Robbie," Matthew replied.

Robbie nodded as he stood up from the swing. He was ready to take the bus and go to town. Robbie had not truly slept in hours and he was exhausted. He didn't care if it was a small hotel room in town or a sleeping bag in his new room; he just wanted sleep.

Matthew closed the door but didn't bother locking it. It wouldn't have helped anyway, and besides, nothing of value was in the house. The three walked across the field and arrived just in time. An old faded yellow school bus drove up, and people queued up to gain access. Robbie didn't mind getting on a school bus and not having a chance for the backseat; he was just happy for the ride. From what he was told by his dad, he wouldn't be taking one anyway; he had to walk over a few hills and down a path to get to school. He hoped his new friends would be fun.

The door opened, and people filed inside the bus with little struggle. Everyone was quiet, mainly keeping to themselves or just being preoccupied with what to do next. Most were not staying in this community from what he remembered during the conversations on the plane. Now that he and his son were not hurt, he could laugh about being dropped off at his doorstep without their luggage. Most of the times that he flew, his luggage arrived after he did. Matthew thought that of all the times for his luggage to arrive late; this time would have been fortuitous.

"One can only hope," he said as he sat next beside Robbie and waited for their turn to leave.

CHAPTER TWO

Uneventful:
U N E V E N T F U L, Uneventful

A quiet ride into town was just what the doctor ordered. Robbie attempted to doze off, and Matthew found it hard to stay awake himself. There were others around him that slept too. The ride into town took about twenty minutes at the slow speed that they were traveling, but it was very relaxing. After several minutes of sitting for Matthew and sleeping for Robbie, they could hardly take it any longer. It appeared to them that each person took their time and waited for the other people around them to exit before they even stood up and gathered their stuff. It was a very painful ride indeed, and as he looked at his dad in frustration, Matthew told him that he would make it up to him soon. He apologized for the situation and then looked Robbie in the eyes.

"I'll do my best to ensure that you have some fun and freedom, son. It will get better, I promise," Matthew told him.

"OK, Dad" was all Robbie said.

Checking into a room was the last thing that Matthew wanted to do when he had just purchased a house, but it was the right thing to do in their current situation. It was convenient and offered a bit of time to unwind before starting on the chores of preparing a new house for living. He needed a vehicle—period; they had to have one. He needed to get Robbie some supplies for school just as soon as he figured out what was necessary. They needed basics for daily living, and he even tried to rationalize dropping by the general store to see what they had for mining supplies. Matthew didn't know it yet, but he was going to be busy!

Matthew told Robbie that they had to stay here until they had all the initial tasks scratched off of his to-do list and that they would get started on that tomorrow. Robbie was OK with that and offered little resistance as he fell asleep to Matthew, telling him the contents of said list. Matthew looked over for acknowledgement on his school supplies and saw that Robbie was out cold. *Oh well,* Matthew thought as he settled in for his rest.

Two days turned into four as Matthew diligently worked through his list. The touristy town of Murphys was small after all and, well, touristy. You had to go off the beaten path by a few streets left and right of their main street to find the buildings with the services that he required, including but not limited to school lists, signing up for Internet, and finding a trustworthy vehicle. Stopped at a red light on the outskirts of Main Street, he saw a light-gray colored Toyota Sienna packed with smiling people. The side of the van read Court Wood Wine Tasting Tours, and as they passed him, three young happy women with very large smiles blew him kisses. He saw them turn down a side street and figured they were on their way back from a winery.

It was a nice pickup, an older 2005 model, but it was still worth having. *Can't go wrong with a Chevy,* he thought as he drove back to the hotel to get his son. There was about a fifty-fifty chance of having him in the room watching movies or down the street at one of the numerous shops. He thought he would just keep an eye out for him when he drove past and possibly save himself a trip back.

There was no sign of him as he slowly drove the main drag in his shiny new gunmetal-gray Chevy S10 pickup. *Oh well, maybe he was in the room,* he thought again as he parked across the street and walked toward the hotel. It took all of a few minutes to determine that Robbie was shopping somewhere in town. He made a note to himself to purchase a cell phone plan and get updated phones.

Thinking back, Matthew tried to remember the shops that Robbie liked the most here. There was a shop that catered to pet lovers, an ice cream shop, a place that made world-famous cupcakes—oh, and another offered tours where one could find gold! He hoped his son had an interest, and even if he did, he wasn't sure that he wasn't having ice cream at this moment in time. *Ice cream shop it was,* he thought as he took a left and hit the side walk.

Halfway up the street, Robbie was walking toward Matthew with an ice cream cone in hand.

"Strawberry flavor, seriously? Won't you ever try any other flavor?" Matthew said, laughing.

"Why change when it works for me?" Robbie asked as he played a game of Missile Command with his drippy cone.

"I'm sorry about making us move. It was the right thing to do, I promise. I know you will like it here, and the friends that you will meet will be incredible," Matthew said.

Robbie nodded agreement between making repeated attempts to save his base. They turned around for the hotel and kept walking. Matthew looked around at the businesses on this street, at the amount of street traffic that was present, and at the numbers of people walking, and he absolutely loved it!

Robbie packed up his stuff, which wasn't much. Matthew noticed him looking around and thought that "all things kids" were gone.

"It's in the budget, you know," Matthew said to him.

"Yeah, what is, Dad?" Robbie replied.

"Your stuff, things that you like, such as games, comics, books, and we're going to replace our movies. You'll see, it will be normal, better than normal, soon." Matthew smiled as he grabbed Robbie up and swung him through the air.

He didn't do this long, as he didn't want to spread melted strawberry ice cream all over the room. Still holding Robbie up in the air, he raised him over his head and smiled at him.

"Oh no, not the double bed rope twister, no, it can't be!" Matthew said loudly.

"Come on, Dad," Robbie said, laughing.

"And here's the bed, there's the twist," Matthew said as he risked all by spinning him again one more time.

In one fell swoop, Matthew jumped on the bed, turning his body so he landed on his back, while he held Robbie high above him the entire time. Robbie loved that, and although he knew it was not a sanctioned wrestling move, it was still fun. Matthew knew that wrestling kept him involved with his son, and after all, he loved wrestling too!

It was now off for some supplies, and then they would go back to the house. He would take a few days to clean up and stock up the pantry, and then it was off to explore the surrounding hills. Matthew could not wait to hard rock mine, although he had no equipment here yet; he had some packages arriving in a few days. Thinking back on all of this, he was extremely happy and thought himself wise for not placing all his eggs in the same basket. Instead, he had them shipped separately so they could hopefully arrive when he was getting the house organized.

They arrived home to a few large moving trucks in their front yard. Their drivers had taken the closest path to the house, and since there was no noticeable driveway, they cut straight through the front yard. Robbie was excited and looked at his dad to ask a single question: "Do I have a bed tonight?" Robbie smirked.

"Looks like we both do, son," Matthew replied.

Matthew saw the excitement Robbie was holding in; he felt it too. He hoped that everything was in stock . . .

The drivers were preparing to unload the furniture and leave it on the porch, as no one had answered the door. They were rather disappointed when Matthew arrived, as it meant that they had to carry it all inside.

"Sorry about that, I was stuck in traffic," Matthew said.

They were not amused and nodded as they motioned for him to open the door.

"Yeah, I know what you mean. Can you hurry up so we can beat the after-brunch rush, sir?" the closest driver said with a smile.

Matthew and the men all laughed as he opened the door and walked inside. He told them the bedrooms were to the left and to put the bigger bed in the bigger room and the smaller in the smaller room. He pointed to walls in the main room and gave some simple directions.

"Please place the couch over there, and the two chairs here and here," Matthew said, pointing.

"Yes, sir, will do. The other stuff is easy. We'll place the kitchen table and microwave in there," the driver said.

"Dad, I'm going for a walk. I want to check out the backyard and the paths," Robbie said as he bolted for the door.

Matthew never heard him as Robbie left the house and made a path through the tall grass. Robbie looked around and saw green and brown colors as far as the eye could see. Trees were scattered in small groups here and there, and there were so many hills that they could not be easily counted. The trees blocked out what was past them, and with some of them being on hills, it looked not unlike a forest in some directions. There were a few paths, but he didn't want to check them out at this time; he just chose a few hills to climb to check out what was hidden behind them.

More trees, more hills, and a path going out of sight up and to the left were visible. He would go down them later, and just so he wouldn't get lost, he turned around and headed back toward the house. Robbie could only think how bad this place would look at night without a moon and with the local wild life trying to eat him. As he walked down the hill, he imagined wolves baying, sticks breaking, and the wind rustling through the leaves; Robbie loved to be scared! He thought about sneaking out tonight to check out the same hill he had just climbed, full moon or not.

Matthew watched as the last of the pieces of furniture were assembled in the kitchen and the microwave was tested. *Sheets, damn, I forgot to get sheets,* he thought. No doubt there would be other things that were neglected or forgotten; he would have to make a list after all. He looked through the kitchen window and noticed that he didn't have curtains either. He never did this kind of stuff before; it was always done by Susan. He longed for those days, but as much as they were part of his past, they were still a distraction from daily life at the moment. He had to move forward, to adapt and overcome. It was also time to start looking for gold.

Now *that* was a distraction—gold. He was very excited to have a large piece of property in which to prospect and to grow a family. Susan was no longer a part of their lives, nor was his youngest son, Thomas, but he still had a family; he still had Robbie. Matthew was still staring out the window when Robbie crossed the grass from one side of the path to the other and kept walking. Matthew thought back to when things were different; he thought about the box . . .

Robbie played for hours in the backyard. He was aware of the fact that the movers had left a long time ago, and still he kept playing. This place was huge, he thought. There was no other way to figure it out; he had to walk the area or see it from the air. He didn't want to go back up in an airplane for quite some time. Robbie laughed at the idea of having to fly anywhere. He wanted no part of that process, not anytime soon at least.

He picked up rocks for the number of hills he climbed over so he could keep track of distance. They would only be helpful if he didn't lose them and if he went back the way he came. He opened his left hand and counted four small rocks. *Time to go back,* he thought. He had to see if anything was needed to be done around the house to get it ready for tonight's rest. He smiled when he thought about sleeping in his own bed in their new house. His pace quickened as he started climbing the hills back toward his new home.

Matthew was on the second page of his list when the front door opened, and in strode Robbie, smiling from ear to ear. He told him he loved this place, that it's very large, and that he had climbed over four hills before turning around and coming back home.

"Do you need anything, Dad?" Robbie asked.

"Nope, just finishing up a list of what we're getting from the stores. I seem to be missing some things from you. What do you need, Robbie?" he asked.

"Well, now, sir, I've given this a lot of thought," Robbie said as he put his hands together and rubbed them very loudly.

"Go on," Matthew said.

"Comics, a few books, several movies, many marbles, snacks, a new flat-screen TV, the Cartoon Network cable channel, soda, more snacks—oh, and a computer so I can get my homework done and play the newest games," Robbie said, laughing.

"Yes, sure, of course, possibly, maybe, not sure, probably—if available, nope, too much already, and of course," he said, laughing.

Robbie took off running and made it to the kitchen before he was snatched up and flown around the house on a grand tour.

"This is my bedroom, vroooooom," Matthew said as he turned Robbie around and ran out into the hallway.

"And this one is yours," he told him as he prepared to launch his son onto the bed.

Robbie loved it, his own room. He had never had one before by himself. This was the first time that he had thought about his brother in weeks. He didn't know how to feel, and blocking those thoughts out of his head as best he could, he asked his dad when they were going to go shopping for that list of his.

"So are we going into town again soon to work on that list?" Robbie asked.

"Yes, this weekend, if all goes as planned. I need a few days to look around this property first, as I'll have to buy some stuff from the general store for mining too," he replied.

Matthew thought about dinner and planned a simple meal for the two of them consisting of cheeseburgers and macaroni and cheese. It wouldn't take too long, and then they could unwind and take a closer look at the house. Lists, Matthew hated them, but it kept him organized.

Dinner went off without a hitch, and soon after that, they parted ways. Matthew went about creating another list, and Robbie explored each room and then went outside to walk around the house in the darkness.

"Don't be out there too long, Robbie. We still don't know the area," he told his son.

"Dad, you know it's almost dark outside and the lights work. I can find the house. I promise I won't go too far," Robbie said as he bolted from the door and closed it before his dad could say anything else.

Matthew finished up his list as best he could and then looked it over, reading it out loud.

"Kitchen: one table, four chairs, and a microwave, check. Bathroom: basic toiletries, toilet paper, check. Living room: end table, coffee table, TV stand. No TV or video players or game systems . . . not good," he said.

"Robbie's bedroom: new bed, nightstand, and light—damn, there's no light. I'll have to get on that tomorrow," Matthew said.

"Master bedroom: nightstand, comfy large bed, alarm clock, light—no light," Matthew mumbled his disappointment.

He began to see a trend; he didn't have lights—really none, except what happened to have been already placed into the ceilings in the rooms.

"Nosey: an interesting woman who lives nearby checking on why a neighboring house had its lights on when no one lived there, check. Hi, I'm Chloe. I live one property down the way," Chloe said, peeking through the front door.

Matthew was taken aback and almost jumped clear out of his skin.

Smiling at the woman, he said, "I really have to get that front door fixed."

"Here's an idea. You can put it on your list," Chloe said, smiling.

Chloe looked at the man standing in his living room and put his face into her memory. He stood a few inches taller than she was, as best she could guess. He looked in shape, not fat, but maybe a bit scruffy; he could probably use a shave. That would probably come after he got a few things done around his new house. *Can't fault him for that*, she thought.

He apologized for seeming weird and invited the woman inside. Chloe looked around and saw the most scantily decorated house this side of the Rockies.

"I know—it's a fixer-upper," he told her.

"No worries. Aren't they all?" she asked with a smile.

"Would you like to sit down?" he asked.

"Oh, no, thank you. I've not much time. My daughter is in the truck, and I just stopped by to make sure the area was still a safe place to live," Chloe smiled again at him.

"Ah, understandable. So you stopped by in blue jean shorts and a concert T-shirt from the '90s all by your lonesome?" he smirked.

"No, I brought six of my friends," Chloe said as she raised her .44 revolver.

"Nice. I'll have to add something like that to my list," he said.

"Oh, did you mean me or my gun? I'm sorry, I've really got to get going," Chloe said, embarrassed.

"Both, probably, time will tell. I'll see you around," he said.

"Probably, time will tell. Good evening then, Mr.?" Chloe said as she turned for the door.

"Matthew. It's Matthew," he said as his front door closed.

I have got to pull it together, he thought, laughing. *I've been married for over ten years now, or was, until recently.* Talking to woman was not awkward for Matthew, just not the best practice to flirt when one's married. He laughed when he thought about him saying that he'd add that to his list. Taking a deep breath, he stood up and turned to his left to use the restroom when Robbie burst into the room.

"Dad," Robbie repeated three times. "You have to come and see this—it's incredible!" Robbie said, short of breath.

"Calm down. Is everything all right?" he said excitedly as he followed Robbie outside.

"Look. Over there!" Robbie said, pointing to the left side of their house.

Matthew looked as a light bounced up and down slowly from left to right and then disappeared behind a hill.

"I've seen it three times now—it's totally crazy. What could it be—ghosts? Glow-in-the-dark heads roaming the forests?" Robbie asked.

"No, Robbie, those are bad people probably looking for gold on our land. You will have to be careful, son. Don't talk to or approach any strangers. Always come and get me first, you hear me?" Matthew said with a very serious tone. "Always come and get me first."

He took Robbie's hand, and they walked back into the house, and he slid his couch in front of the door to keep it closed. Matthew had Robbie sleep in his big bed tonight until they made the house more secure. He settled all in and made sure Robbie was comfortable and closed his eyes. He wondered how it would be with Chloe; she seemed fun. Matthew thought about her being beside him, with Robbie at a friend's house or away for the weekend. He wouldn't have minded even tonight, he laughed, as she had a gun and she could protect them. Smiling, he closed his eyes and drifted off to sleep.

Robbie stared at the ceiling, too excited to sleep. He so wanted to sneak outside. *It would be terribly easy,* he thought, *but not while sleeping in the same bed as your dad.* He would have to wait another night, he thought, maybe two. Soon, he too fell asleep, and both snored equally loud, with neither waking up the other.

The next few days were busy and scheduled, which involved over a dozen errands. Matthew had very little time to explore his land, not nearly as much as he would have loved to have had. He signed up Robbie for school, finished some paperwork with the recent plane crash, and fixed all windows and doors of his house, to the best of his ability anyway.

Matthew walked with Robbie to school for a few days in a row to get him used to the trek. It's only half a mile, and it hardly rains here, so they both agreed to try it and see how it goes. If he has to start driving him to school, he has the vehicle now, so it can be done. From the path that they take, Chloe's house can be seen off to the right. It's a nice single-story ranch style, just like theirs, only a little bigger. The path branches off to their house, just like it does their own, and leads to school.

Robbie learned the trail to school very quickly. He paid particular attention to the landmarks necessary to traverse the proper amount of hills along the way. It only takes two walks with his dad before Robbie's willing to try it on his own. Matthew tells him to leave about thirty minutes earlier than normal for his first trip so he can see how it's going to work out. Robbie is excited as his first day of school approaches and he's to walk there all by himself! The word for the day, if given the chance to select it himself, would have been "uneventful": "U N E V E N T F U L, uneventful," he said to himself, laughing, as he took one step in front of the other and trekked onward.

CHAPTER THREE

It's Just Marbles . . .

Time flew by for the next two weeks as both became acquainted with their new friends. If asked to sum up how his time at school was going, Robbie would say that he loves his teachers, the new friends he has met are nice, and he would speak highly or at least a lot about Thomas and Luke. They were cool; he watched them play marbles, and Robbie learned all sorts of games. Marbles were one of the few things that they were unable to find in town. Most things on the list were already purchased and being used and enjoyed in the house, save a new computer and marbles. "It would come," Matthew would tell him, and he'll find them soon in town or he would order them online.

Matthew, on the other hand, spoke just as passionately about his new friends, Mr. Pick and Mr. Axe. He used them regularly in the first mine that he found to explore its contents. His property was rumored to have four or even five mines, but only three were reported and registered. Of those three, two were close to the house and one was further away. Matthew had not brought home a single flake of gold up to this point, but he had lots of samples and new tunnels to speak of. He told Robbie that he would take him there soon and that he was not to go inside any of their mines alone. He made Robbie pinky swear and promise not to go inside unless he was in sight of him.

Robbie had snuck out four times over that initial two-week period, and his dad had only caught him once. Matthew only saw the last attempt and he just kept an eye on his son, not a leash, so he didn't address the issue immediately. He did put it on the list, though. He would tell you that he would talk to him about it eventually. For now, though, it was no harm, no foul. Matthew admitted to himself that raising a son was much harder now that Susan was gone, and he would also tell you that he was not good at it, not good at all. He would have to try harder, he thought, much harder.

The days passed more slowly now that both had responsibilities, chores, and each other to work with. Matthew set goals that were hard to achieve, even for him. Robbie took longer to get home as he hung out with his friends and even did his homework while he watched them play marbles. He told his dad that his grades were not suffering and he was learning a lot and making really good friends. In all actuality, he wasn't too far from the truth. His grades were great; he was a smart kid, smart with book senses, more to the point. Now as far as common sense went, he would tell you not so much. His friends that he had chosen had only the fact that they played marbles in common. They were much different, and if aliens came down and collected all the marbles in the world, these three kids would probably never talk to each other again.

Sunday was here before they knew it, and it was their day to go into town. For most people around the area, Sunday was a day of worship, or even one of their days, depending on their faith. But for them, it was just another day with one exception. It was their day for a scheduled bimonthly trip into town. The town of Murphys was awesome and a bit more organized for tourists, one might say. Arnold was a bit more scattered, and since Murphys was technically closer, they went there more often.

A trip to the general store, the mining tour company, an ice cream shop, the cupcake store, and, oh, possibly a bit of wine tasting was in store for them, Matthew said. Robbie watched all of these predictions come true, except the wine tasting; his dad could never go through with it. Wine tasting was one of the purposes of their initial visit to this area, Robbie remembered. Mom and Dad talked about it for months, and when those unfortunate events happened, as Dad would call them, and Mom was no longer around, he still tried to do it, but he never walked through the door.

At the general store, Matthew left a note requesting a babysitter. It was a normal sheet of handwritten paper with pieces of tape holding an address and his name. It stated that a babysitter was needed for a single-parent household. It went on to explain that it was for a ten-year-old boy and that meal preparation and some basic chores were also required. A successful applicant would be required to show up Monday through Friday, from three in the afternoon sharp to sometime early evening. He hoped that it would work out, but just to be safe, he asked for three references.

They had picked up mostly everything they needed today, even scoring a laptop and some newer movies, but still no marbles. Oh well, now it was up to him to go out and find them when he was in school or to search for it on the Internet, if and when it was working on their new laptop. Tonight's dinner was beanie weenies and iced tea, with homemade biscuits. Biscuits were one thing Robbie baked well; it was his specialty, one might say. The measuring thing did not bother him; it was just patience and knowing that even when one removes something from the oven, it's still cooking, so don't stare through the window for the proper result; think of how it would look after a few minutes of sitting on the counter.

Robbie went to bed with a full tummy and with thoughts of sneaking out tonight, but he was too tired. The more he thought about it, the more he knew he would probably just stay inside. It wasn't long before Robbie closed his eyes to relax a bit and fell asleep. Matthew pulled out a small notebook and looked at his sketches. He was working on mapping that place out as best he could; he had not found anything of value there yet, but if asked, he would say it was only a matter of time. There was always that last mine that was elusive, the one that was hidden or possibly did not exist; all he had to do was to go out and find it.

It appeared that the shopping had made him tired as well, and he followed Robbie's lead and went into his own bedroom after locking all the doors in the house. He felt safer now and more at ease knowing that the windows locked and the doors did too. He even added a dead bolt and an extra chain for the inside. Matthew thought of anything that he could add to make it harder for the honest guy to gain access. The only thing that he had on his list of home security that he had not purchased yet was a handgun. He would make an effort to get that one day when Robbie was in school. That handgun would make it more difficult for the dishonest guy, Matthew thought.

"Good night, son. I had a wonderful day today. Get some rest," he said loud enough to make it into Robbie's room.

"Thanks, Dad, I will," Robbie replied.

Robbie tossed and turned in his new bed; it was comfy, but he still could not fall asleep. He was too tired to go exploring but not enough to close his eyes and fall asleep. He was too warm now, so Robbie threw off his blankets, choosing to use only a top sheet. A few more minutes of relaxing with only a single, thin white sheet and he was out like a light. Matthew had a quite different experience. He was cold, very cold, and since there was no working air conditioner installed, he thought it must be a draft. He spent the next few minutes trying to locate said draft, to no success. He gave up and put his shirt and pants back on. He then climbed back into the bed under all the covers that he had in the room. That would go on the list, he laughed, more blankets.

Robbie awoke thirsty, and it was the middle of the night, he was sure of it. School was still to come, and he wasn't sure how much more sleep he would get; he just knew he was thirsty. He pushed the covers aside and placed his feet onto the cold wood floor. He yawned as he took steps to the door and quietly continued to walk to the bathroom for a glass of water. Listening for his dad as he went, he neither heard nor saw any signs of him stirring. Robbie thought it was a good time to sneak out, but he was still too tired, so he finished his water and then walked back to bed.

Robbie got back up into his bed and reached down for the covers to pull them back up. He noticed his feet were dirty; they were muddy actually. He had made a very big mess with the cheap white sheets that his dad had recently purchased for their new beds. Robbie looked in amazement as he could not believe they were that muddy. They were caked with moist dirt and his feet ranged in color from light brown to red clay. Robbie wondered where they could have gotten that dirty; he always remembered to clean up after returning from a late-night hike.

Looking down, Robbie saw the dirt floor rising up to meet him. It climbed higher and higher until it was even with the bed. It continued upward and the mud rolled over the bed and onto the sheets. He saw the room getting smaller, so Robbie looked for a way out. He saw the bedroom door shrinking as the mud rose even higher, attempting to block his way. He turned around and pushed open his window as the mud claimed the bottom portion of the windowsill for its own. He climbed out of the window and turned to see the mud pouring outside his bedroom window.

Robbie took off running as he was sure the mud was coming for him. He saw trees parting his way, leading him down an open path over the hills. When Robbie did take time to turn around as he was running, he saw the mud not too far behind. He thought that it would continue to grow and to turn into a sort of clay monster, a physical shape that would surely fight him.

It became darker and darker as he ran through the hills. Robbie turned to witness his fears take physical shape. As the mud flowed forward, it grew two legs and started on the middle section; it was turning into a monster right in front of his eyes. The creature seemed to move faster now having just grown two legs, Robbie thought, so he picked up the pace.

He found himself breathing very hard, and for the life of him, Robbie could not remember a time where he had ever run faster. The creature matched him step for step, and Robbie heard him right behind him, he was sure of it. The opening came upon Robbie quickly, and during one of his attempts to lose his pursuer, he turned sharply to the right. He was left with no choice but to enter the mine or smack into the side of it headfirst.

Robbie turned sharply left and headed into the mine at a full run. Rocks and debris littered the opening, and as he tried to slow down, his feet glided over all sort of rock and dirt. The ground could not have been more uneven if it were a mountain all itself, and a few steps later, he found out that he could fly. Robbie launched through the air at a slight angle being helped by a very large rock and a left step instead of a right one.

As he slowly turned from left to right, he glanced over his shoulder at the creature that had chosen not to enter the mine. He smiled as he looked forward and saw the ground quickly approaching. His breathing was calming now, and just as things were getting normal, he landed in a huge puddle. Water splashed upward and coated the walls and ceiling immediately surrounding Robbie. He could not have done a more spectacular job had he purposefully tried to do it himself.

Robbie had landed on his butt, and when the weight of his body pushed itself through the water, it made a squishing feeling as it reached up to cover the parts of his body that were below the waterline. He looked around the room and up to the ceiling and laughed. He placed his hands beside his legs and tried to push up to get out of the mud. He made a sucking noise as his arms sunk in the mud to his wrists. A little more struggling and he freed himself from the mud, and not a minute too soon, he was beginning to panic.

He looked over his shoulder toward the entrance to the mine and saw nothing, only the moonlit grass on the nearby hills. The water reflected some of the light his way and into the mine, but it provided little useful light. However little light was present, it was still better than being totally in the dark. Robbie was cold now, and although his breathing was normal now, it was still hard for him to breathe. The air stank here, badly. It wasn't this stinky before, he thought, as he walked through the water. Exploring a few more feet in, he remembered what his dad had told him about being in the mines without him.

Robbie turned around and started walking back to the entrance, hoping to get some fresh air and a peek at where that creature had gone to. Outside he heard the noises of crickets and occasionally a bat or two flying overhead. He listened for any disturbance, any sign that something was lurking, but he had nothing. He breathed in a sigh of relief and began thinking how he would explain this to dad has he took his first steps toward home.

Taking another breath, it appeared to him that he still had plenty of time to get cleaned up and sneak back into bed. If he was right thinking what time it was, he even had a few more hours of sleep after all of that was said and done; he would be fine, he thought. Robbie took another step and then found that his foot would not follow his simple instructions—it would not move; it appeared stuck. Looking down, he saw a hand of mud holding firmly onto his left foot.

As Robbie struggled, he saw the second hand come out of the ground. They looked much dryer now, not as wet or muddy as they had been before but still fully functional. He cried out for help, and as he yelled, the sounds of the night around him became louder, as if attempting to drown him out. Not even the crickets or the bats or even the night itself cared for him. The wind picked up and howled so loudly that his screams died in volume only inches away after being issued forth.

He drew in another breath, preparing to yell as he was knocked over from behind. The wind left his body, and he could not breathe, let alone attempt to speak or yell for help. If Robbie could have witnessed it, he would have seen the mud-and-rock creature appear to climb out of the ground and pull itself on top of him. It would have been horrifying to witness and it would have frightened him to his core. All he knew was that he could not move and he had been recently knocked to the ground, landing on his stomach.

Robbie began crawling through the grass and trying to pull himself out of the grasp of whatever was holding him. He wheezed and made sucking noises as his lungs tried to breath in any air that they could. At times, he could not do either at the same time. He either attempted to move forward or he attempted to breathe. Robbie looked up at the moonlit sky and closed his eyes as he began to lose consciousness. His last breath was shallow, only partially successful and not really an adequate attempt to gain fresh air; it was as if he just gave up.

The old man and woman watched curiously as they saw the young boy run out of the mine and fall to the ground. He stayed there breathing heavily and then slowly calmed down. They continued to watch from the distance as he stood up, dusted off his pajamas, and started walking back over the hill.

"Weird," the old man said.

"Yup, very weird, hon," the old woman replied.

Robbie awoke in a panic and stood straight up on his bed, almost touching the ceiling. He was covered with sweat from head to toe, and where he had been laying was soaked. *What a horrible dream,* he thought as he looked around the room. He felt safe knowing that he was in bed, in his house, and that none of that had really happened. He looked around the room again, checking out the window and the door, and found nothing amiss.

Robbie reached for the sheets, pulling them back up over his muddy ankles, and quickly fell back to sleep. He awoke almost late for school and, as usual, with his dad already mining. A note on the table told him to remember to take his lunch, to leave early due to bad weather, and to have a good day. He also mentioned a surprise for Robbie tonight, but Robbie had no idea what that might be. He showered with sleep still in his eyes. Keeping them shut, he turned around to rinse off his back, and leaning backward, he let the water rush over his face. Robbie never saw the mud rinse off and disappear into the drain; to him, it was just another day in his new house.

As Robbie started running over the hills that led him to school, he remembered his lunch that he left on the kitchen table. *Oh well,* he thought, *who has time to eat when you're playing marbles?* He laughed. It wasn't long before Robbie climbed the hill that hid Ruthie's house from view. It wasn't too far away from his house and even his window faced that direction, but that hill . . .

The place looked well kept—manicured is what his mom would call it. He missed her, often thinking of her daily comments and advice. Robbie didn't understand why they had to leave so quickly. One minute he was in camp, counting the minutes to get home, and the next thing he knew, his dad was taking him to the airport.

Robbie picked up the pace as he wanted to play a round or two before school started. As he made his way along the trail, he passed the last curve and looked at the playground area. No one was there; he was late. Oh well, he tried; it was just another day for him. Each school day was dual purposed; it moved time closer to the weekend and allowed for the playing of marbles with new friends. "The three Rs, Reading, wRiting, and aRithmetic; they should have been gRab your marbles, Run to the playground, and get Ready to play!" Robbie laughed as he said that and knew that his English teacher would have nothing to do with that silly statement.

Robbie opened the door and snuck into his chair, which was conveniently located at the rear of the classroom. This was way too early for math for him, but he always made the best of it. He understood more than most around him. His mom had spent long hours during weekends helping him with the problems that he did not grasp. *Twice in one morning,* he thought; he was thinking of his mom a lot today.

Ruthie looked back occasionally to see if Robbie was going to show today and was pleased when she peered over her shoulder to find him opening his book to catch up.

"Page 34, Robbie," Ms. Edwards stated.

"Thank you, Ms. Edwards," Robbie replied.

Thomas and Luke snickered and said something to each other under their breath. Ruthie turned back around and prepared for today's lesson on integers.

The day started off normal for Robbie. Between classes on breaks, he played marbles with the guys. Walking back from break or to his next class, he would pass Ruthie in the halls and say hi. Thomas passed Luke a note and he tossed it to Ruthie.

The note read: Please ask your boyfriend to come and play marbles during lunch, if it's OK with you—signed Thomas.

Ruthie read it and then handed it to the girl sitting in front of him, who in turn handed the note to Robbie. He read it and laughed. He had already been asked to play marbles; those guys were too funny. Robbie looked at Ruthie and shrugged his shoulders. Just as he already knew about the date for marbles, he already knew that she was his girlfriend.

The next two classes went by quickly, and before he knew it, lunch was here.

"I'll catch you later, Robbie. I know you have a lunch date," Ruthie said, laughing.

"Thanks, I promise I'll catch up and walk you home too," Robbie replied.

Ruthie smiled as she turned around and walked to the lunchroom. Robbie took off, heading for the library. He thought about when he would come here to learn, to read. He laughed at the fact that they visited the library to find a lonely dusty corner to play marbles without interruption.

Thomas and Luke were late, so Robbie just sat down in the corner and grabbed a book from the closest shelf titled Psychology. He read the title but had barely finished it before his eyes took in the entire cover. It had a woman with her hands elevated above her head, secured to a metal bar, scantily clothed, and looking muscular, defiant. The title read *Bereft*

Reality—by James Summers. Robbie cared little for anything, save the woman on the cover. The title did not matter to him, nor did he understand what "bereft" meant. He had never heard of James Summers either. The woman he understood well; he had seen pictures like that before in some of his dad's magazines. The book obviously didn't belong here, he thought as he placed it into his book bag, smiling.

It was shortly after zipping the bag closed that he heard commotion about two shelves away, and then Luke came into view. Thomas was at his side, and they were laughing and smiling as they walked toward him, not caring whether they were quiet.

"What's up, Robbie?" Luke said, smiling.

"We were just discussing your technique," followed Thomas.

"Fellas," Robbie nodded.

Robbie watched them both as they walked directly to him before turning to his left side and then sat down beside him.

"It's a different game today, son, different from now on, I'm afraid," Thomas said as he unrolled an old piece of leather onto the library floor.

The leather measured approximately two by three feet and had an outline of a snake from head to tail. It was probably done with pen at first and then etched over with a knife blade.

Robbie watched as Luke smiled at Thomas and then turned to face him.

"The holes have to be filled with marbles, son, shot marbles, in order, from the tail to head. It's OK to knock another's marbles out of the holes—if you are good enough, that is. The winner is the one that shoots his marble into the last hole in the snakes head after tail has been filled. This game is called Black Snake, and it's a winner-takes-all game, so whoever shoots the head takes all marbles," Thomas said excitedly.

Robbie looked around at the course and thought of how to best proceed.

"If your shooter gets stuck, you lose your shooter for the game and you are out," Luke said matter-of-factly.

"Are you ready to play, son?" Thomas asked Robbie.

"Sure, looks like fun," Robbie said as he set up his marbles for battle.

The game went on for a few minutes without any player having an advantage. Marbles were getting knocked out by one player and its hole refilled by another. At times, it would seem that those two worked together, and Robbie half expected them to, but mostly it was just luck. Luke was advancing nicely, and it appeared that Thomas was knocking anything he could out of the snake.

There were only a few minutes to go before lunch was over, and Robbie was still behind the others. Even though he had several marbles in holes, he was not the highest one. A minute later and Luke lost his shooter.

"Hot damn!" Robbie said excitedly. "That one's gonna be mine, and how lucky it is too."

"Not if I can help it," said Thomas.

Two more holes remained before reaching the tail. Robbie thought how cool it was to be doing so well against these guys, and now with a level playing field.

It was Robbie's shoot, and there were two holes remaining. His hope was to remove an existing one or two and put him going last, where he could take the head. His plan would involve Thomas missing, making Robbie shoot last. From a few shelves away, Ruthie saw the whole match. She loved that Robbie was beating these guys and that soon he would be back in class with her. She had some news that she wanted to share with him, and Ruthie wanted to tell him before they started their walk home.

Robbie took a breath and then made his move. The marble he was going for was hit in the seven o'clock position, sending it veering off the leather and lodging underneath the nearby shelf. Immediately afterward, his shooter rolled into an adjacent hole; it was lost. Thomas laughed as he announced to the world that Robbie's timing was perfect; it was time to go back to class.

"Thanks for playing. Bye. Bye. Ba-bye. Ba-bye," Thomas said as he started picking up all marbles in the holes and placing them in his bag.

Robbie couldn't believe it; he had planned for everything. He'd thought that shot over in his head ten times at least but never did he think that he would wind up in that hole. Robbie looked down and saw that he only had four left and no shooter. What would one do with that? He needed more . . .

Ruthie was crushed; she felt bad for Robbie. She ducked behind the shelf and made her way back to class so she could be sitting there when he passed her.

Luke didn't say much as he watched Thomas place his marbles in the bag right along with Robbie's.

"Life's hard, fellas," Thomas told them.

"Good game, Thomas. Good game, Luke," Robbie replied.

"Yeah, it *was* fun," Luke said.

The three boys packed up their things and began walking through the library to get to their class. They would be late, not by much but late nonetheless. They all knew nothing would come from it. Mrs. Lewis was a pushover and cared more for the learning aspect of the game than discipline. Robbie thought about what he would say, but it wouldn't matter. She would just tell him that "he would make it up to the class" and that "he was only hurting himself" by being late. Robbie knew the other guys wouldn't care in the slightest and that they did not plan on doing any makeup work to correct their grades.

The rest of the day went rough for Robbie. He hardly talked, answering only questions posed directly toward him by his teachers. Ruthie could not get his attention, shy of throwing something at him if the teacher had his or her back turned just long enough for her to do so. Ruthie wanted to tell Robbie how she felt about him and that she was going to spend some time with her dad, if her mother had anything to say about it. Ruthie just didn't want to not show up at school one day and then back again a week or two later. She would not tell Robbie this today, not after what happened to him. He was obviously devastated, although she didn't know exactly why; it's just marbles. *Boys,* she thought as she closed her book.

CHAPTER FOUR

MPK and SNMDs

Matthew didn't know it yet, but he was burning his candle at both ends. His full-time job, which used to be in information technology, had been replaced with his son. He wasn't taking good care of Robbie, not at the moment. He has picked up a hobby, and with the house being sold soon, he didn't have to worry about money.

Robbie was settling into school nicely. He was taking care of whatever Matthew gave him for chores and tasks and even doing extra to help out. Robbie was acting much older than he was, and he was as responsible as they come for that age. Matthew didn't really notice that he kept adding to Robbie's tasks and that his hobby, mining for gold, was taking over.

It was nothing more than a hobby before, but now that he had more time on his hands, and a smaller family, he didn't mind so much if he spent more time below ground. There was also no one to complain or push back when he proposed mining for three days straight or taking extra time to tear through a vein, not caring when he finished it. Robbie could take care of himself, he thought.

The last few days were longer and longer for him. Matthew noticed that his walks home grew darker and darker until finally his walks home required the use of a flashlight. Matthew had found no gold up to this point. Most of his time was searching the grounds in the area to find the three additional mines that were hidden. He had only found the first one and he was so sure that it was mined out that he wanted only to procure the whereabouts of the three hidden ones rumored to be close by.

The moon shone brightly overhead, so much so that Matthew didn't need the help from his flashlight tonight. He counted the hills that he passed. *Four more to go,* he thought. Matthew made various noises as he moved along through the hills, metal on metal, metal on plastic, wood on plastic. They all occurred with his rhythmic walking and fluctuated only when his pace was slow or fast.

Each trip he carried two buckets worth of supplies. Matthew did the math in his head as he traversed his property's hills. If he carried all of them at once, he would have needed thirty-six pairs of hands; too funny, he thought. Out of the corner of his eye he saw it moving. It was a very large shadow that wound its way slowly in and around some of the rocks off to his left. The locals had talked about a mountain lion having been seen nearby and to be cautious when walking alone, but this was a first for Matthew.

It wasn't easy to keep up with, and as to not draw additional attention to him, Matthew kept up his pace as he continued watching it move. It seemed to stay on his periphery and it appeared to be more concerned for its own safety than in threatening him. Matthew kept walking and looked at the hill in front of him. The hill looked different; it wasn't the one he had expected to see. In the time it had taken him to realize what a predicament he was in, Matthew found himself lost. The animal was apparently stalking him. With the possibility of it being a mountain lion that was preparing to eat him, Matthew found himself staring forward and wondering what to do next.

What kind of prepared man was he, alone at night in the wilds of California without a gun or a decent knife, brandishing only a very old, well-used pickaxe? He would have laughed if it would not have spooked the animal. Matthew had spent too much time looking in front of him and for a moment forgot about keeping one eye on the cat; it had become smaller! This meant that it was either coming straight for him, or it was moving away. Matthew was sure that it was no longer moving with him.

He scanned the darkness for the figure to ensure that he was indeed still looking at it and not something else. Matthew concentrated on the creature's last known whereabouts and he felt confident that it was coming toward him and that he was indeed looking at the large animal as it continued to approach. The shadow moved closer still and then vanished; it vanished! It took several minutes of staring for him to become convinced that the creature was gone and that nothing was coming straight for him, not anymore anyways. He sat his buckets down and held the pickaxe with both hands, waiting for it to jump out from the shadows, but it never did.

Matthew's eyes were fully adjusted to the moonlight by now, so he scanned the horizon. He wasn't sure how that creature had disappeared or where it had gone, but he had to know. He picked up his buckets and started making all sorts of noise as he headed straight for the shadow's last location. As he got closer, a few rocks turned into boulders. They were much larger in size than he thought they were from afar. One in particular was adamant on not disappearing into the hills; it was as tall as it was wide.

He continued walking toward the larger boulder, and soon it was apparent to him that there was just no other place to hide. The mountain lion was behind it, or he didn't exist; he just was not present. He placed his buckets down, gripped his pickaxe with all the strength he could muster, and then took a few steps to the left. A deep breath preceded his movement, and he had barely drawn it all in when he saw the animal. It was crouching very low to the ground as if ready to pounce. Its eyes, yes, the eyes were green and very large. They did not blink, but Matthew knew he was being sized up. He heard the creature do a much larger version of a cat's purr and then he noticed the back legs flexing several times.

Matthew was going to lose this game. He could not continue staring at the animal without blinking. He didn't want to take his eyes off of him, but they burned. His eyes were becoming watery, and he could not fight the reflex to blink any longer. In the time that it took to close and reopen them, his eyes adjusted to the image of a large cat that had launched itself in his general direction. Instinctively, he raised his hands to protect his chest and face, hoping that it would soften the blow that was inevitable. He was hit mid chest, close to his shoulders, and knocked backward on his ass. Matthew was on his way to meet his maker, he thought, but the cat bounded off of him and never hit the ground. The mountain lion never scratched or bit him. It had just knocked him backward, using that time to escape into the darkness.

Matthew scrambled backward, further pushing himself away from the large animal. He watched as he saw the last of the animal's tail disappear into the darkness, leaving not even a shadow behind. His breathing was intense now, and as he continued to move backward, he stopped panicking and sat there, motionless. The animal had entered a cave. It didn't disappear behind the rock; it went into the ground!

He waited well over a half an hour, pickaxe at the ready, staring at the hole. The cat never came out, so he just waited longer. It was daylight now, and he grew tired of waiting, so he stood up, looked around to determine his location, and headed off to the first mine for supplies. Matthew looked over his shoulder from time to time as he moved through the field. He stopped to examine where he was in relation to the mine he was previously working. He determined that he had gone two hills further than he should have. Matthew was off to the left; he was way off his mark. In his defense, it was dark, and this was still fairly new property; he laughed as he tried to defend what he had done. If Robbie had done this, he would have been really mad and would have scolded him over it. "Bad Matthew," he said to himself as he yet again looked over his shoulder.

As Matthew walked to the other mine, his mind wandered. He didn't know if both of these places would meet underground. He didn't know if they shared the same water table, mineral deposits, or if it was just coincidence. He would be happy to get in there today and start mapping this out, he thought. Soon he would know the answers to those questions, he was certain of it. There was one more question that he desired to know the answer to—would he find gold?

Matthew was shown the way to the secret mine; it was fate that he found it. It was fate that he was here in the first place. He believed in those two facts, but he didn't believe that his fate was all wrapped up in death, divorce, and destruction. Another thing that bothered him as he approached his old mine was why would a cornered animal jump onto the threat with the intention of knocking it down? Why would it escape only to seek refuge inside an old mine that might only have one way out?

Looking around, he quickly took inventory of his surroundings. He was looking for things out of place or missing. He wasn't taking any chances at this point as he scanned his belongings that he had scattered just inside the opening. Everything was just as he had left it. Grabbing a shovel, a few buckets, and a classifying screen, and ensuring that he took his pickaxe with him, Matthew headed for the new mine. Along the way, he made a mental note to purchase a handgun the next time he went into town.

The trip back to the mine was slower than his previous escape from that large cat. He was carrying more weight, of course, but he was watching everything as he slowly as he arrived. Matthew took great care to approach the entrance so he could see both it and behind the large boulder at the same time. After several minutes of waiting, he gave himself an all clear. Stopping about ten yards from the entrance and still with a good view of the side of the boulder, he made a base camp. Matthew turned one of the buckets over and used it for a seat. He took his time and continued to watch for any signs of movement.

There was nothing. Matthew looked around one last time and then took a single bucket and shovel in one hand and his pickaxe in the other. He made noises as he walked closer, and just to be clear on what his intentions were, he clanked the shovel against the pickaxe a few times for good measure. The sun was hanging low in the sky; it was still early morning here, and the wind confirmed his findings with a cool westerly breeze that was barely strong enough to be felt, unless one was sweating profusely.

Matthew had taught Robbie to use the wind when hunting, and to be honest, he had forgotten about that altogether until he smelled it; "foul," "dank," "stinky," "dead"—these were all words that Robbie would get extra credit for using in a sentence describing his approach to the mine. He could hear it now: "Well done, Robbie. Now go and help the coroner identify your dad . . ." Matthew hoped he would live through this day and that his son would never have to go through that pain, never in a million years.

This place had to be a den; it smelled that badly, which probably meant that the creature lived here. Matthew then thought that the mine probably had not been worked over— well, not recently at least. He grew more and more excited and then he went for it. Matthew picked up the pace and reached the hole. It went down. Shit, it wasn't truly a mine entrance into a hill or rock face; it went down as if it had caved in.

"Awesome!" he yelled as he sat on his bum and slid inside.

His entrance into the mine was at best a controlled slide, taking all of six seconds before his feet were on the ground. He would have to fix that with a ladder or cut in some steps, he thought.

Thinking erratically, he thought that he could attempt to find the creature and either chase it out or kill it. One thing was for certain: he knew that it was here. If he left to come back another time, he would not know if the creature was behind him or not. Moving forward this way, he thought, he could concentrate on moving forward. Matthew felt a bit safer now that he knew he would not be grabbed from behind and pulled away to be eaten!

He walked very slowly, very methodically, as he continued to look for any signs of the creature. No one except him can take refuge in his newly found mine, not on his watch. Matthew's flashlight was barely bright enough to light his path; he wasn't equipped the way he needed to be. He could tell the contrast of dirt and rock, but the flashlight did not do much more than that. He would bring more powerful lights next time and possibly even an old fuel burning lantern.

The initial entry had a few old boxes in one corner, a pile of rocks in another, and only one path stood before him, going deeper into the mine. Some work would be necessary to get this opening a bit larger so he could stage his equipment here before determining where he would carry it into the mine for use. He definitely could not just leave this stuff lying around here to be easily found by passersby. He also couldn't board up the entrance, which would draw attention to this location from a distance. One day of rain would coat the wood and make it shiny and reflective. His newly boarded up mine would turn into a beacon of hope for all would-be claim jumpers.

Shining his light down the tunnel, he saw some bones from a recently half-eaten animal. "Geez," Matthew said out loud for no one to hear, "it's like a new job down here."

It was a job that he alone was responsible for. He would be doing maintenance, electrical, construction, janitorial services, when all he wanted to do was to mine. Matthew laughed as he sat down to take a break.

There were no signs of the creature being present. There were no unduly strong smells, no noises, and no blatantly obvious paw prints. There was nothing at all; the creature had just vanished into the tunnels. Matthew began doubting what he saw, what he had experienced. He had been working hard, he's been doing as much as he could, and he hadn't had a good night's sleep in days.

Matthew would spend the next several hours examining the immediate area and mapping out this direction and that. His handy notebook, a two-inch-wide-by-four-inch-tall doodle pad that never left his side was once again very handy. If looked at from a distance, one would think that the metal loops that held the pages together at the top were rusted! From what Matthew could determine, this mine went backward toward his other mine, he was sure of it. Now whether the two mines met was yet to be determined, he could not be sure.

He mapped a few more hundred feet inward and came upon a very large, potentially deep pool of water. The smell here changed immediately from fresh, cool air to dank, stuffy, and dead. Something was in that water, stinking, decaying, he could smell it. He laughed as he knew that he was unwilling at this point to check it out. His flashlight was failing him, but he could tell that the water was extensive. Matthew could not see ground beyond the water with the lighting that he had at the moment. More disturbing, though, was the fact that he saw no other way past it, and from what he could tell, the water had not been traversed recently. So where *did* that large animal go?

Turning around to walk back to the entrance, he saw something out of the corner of his eye. He ducked and swung his body and his flashlight in that direction. Ledges, there were ledges carved into the walls of the cave like handholds. Upon closer inspection, they were longer than the width of a human hand and further apart. Matthew looked more closely at them, passing the dim beam from the flashlight over them from left to right. "Man, they are far apart," he muttered. They looked more like shelves for small candles than handholds. Maybe they were used for additional lighting, he thought.

How old was this place? That question barely had time to register before a very large black shape jumped toward him. Matthew hit the ground hard before noticing that it wasn't coming straight for him; it was bounding off of the ledges. It must have chosen every third one, he thought, as the distance traveled each time was very large. Only a few seconds had passed before the shadow was gone from sight. From the close up that almost made him soil his pants, he was sure that this thing was real. It was a dark-haired feline, a very large dark-haired feline with typical green eyes.

Matthew realized that he was screaming. Both of his hands were up in front of his face as if they would have been able to protect him from the cat's claws. His hands were clubs, his fingers tucked tightly into the balled fist position. He wasn't trying to protect himself; he had gone on the offense. Matthew was going to pummel it to death. As to why he dropped a perfectly good pickaxe, he did not know. Fear does things like that, he had read somewhere. It makes the strong man weak and gives the strength of ten to a weak man, all for its own purpose.

He felt better now that he had looked over his life in the blink of an eye. Contemplating those quick images over the course of several hours will do that to you. He looked up, barely blinking, and noticed that daylight was passing him by. Soon it would be dark, and with no flashlight to help, he was at the mercy of whatever light was given to him by the moon and stars. Matthew gathered up his pickaxe and his now dead flashlight and headed out into the sunset.

It was harder for him to get out the mine than it was for him to slide inside. He used his pickaxe to make some simple handholds and then climbed on up. He placed his feet where his hands had previously been and he steadily climbed out. Looking down into the hole, he thought that it was nicely hidden. It was dangerous for sure, but it was nicely hidden. He would lower down all of his supplies and equipment with ropes and then he would cover as much of the entrance as he could with some dead branches.

Matthew wanted to get all of his equipment over here tonight. He was a driven man; he needed results, and quick. The first mine had not given anything to him except practice. He would make several trips back and forth between the two mines and he would sleep in this one. After everything was here, he would protect this place better, but until then, he would sleep here to keep it as safe as he could.

He was nothing if not motivated as he started the first of what would be eight trips back and forth between the mines. Each leg of the trip was spent scanning the horizon for silhouettes moving over the sparse landscape. Matthew was exhausted; he had to sleep soon. It wasn't too much longer before fatigue became a factor and he would act careless or sloppy. With the last of the trips completed, he lowered the last bundle of supplies down with his rope. He loosed the end and dropped it over the edge and then climbed down into the entrance.

Carefully he placed his feet into the first and then second makeshift steps and then placed his hands on the edges of the ground. He held on tightly and searched for another place to put his left foot. He dug in with the toes of his boots and went searching for the next step to place his left hand. He followed through with his right foot, and then his right hand took hold of its first step. Matthew repeated this process two more times before reaching bottom.

Looking around, he took quick inventory of his equipment and then found what he was looking for. Matthew reached down and took a small green backpack and opened it. Pulling out his MPK 7.0, he walked down deeper into the mine, just shy of the puddle. He reached into his pocket and selected the first tool necessary for installing his MPK and opened it very slowly. He took a small amount of material out and stretched it nicely from one end of the cave wall to the other, so it would block or restrict the movement of something coming through the water. Later on he would have to make it higher for anything choosing to jump or fly, he laughed. Soon it wouldn't matter, as this mine would be more protected and secure. He used his tool to ensure an excess of material so he could attach the SNMDs.

Matthew worked on this for nearly twenty minutes before marveling at his work. *MacGyver himself would have been proud,* he thought as he looked at his fishing wire that spread across his end of the water puddle as if weaved by an aging, drunken spider. Old soda cans were suspended in various locations, close enough to make a ruckus if anyone or anything ran into it in the dark. What a lovely mine protection kit with suspended noisemaking devices, Matthew thought, smiling.

He returned to the entrance and settled into his sleeping bag, getting as comfortable as he could. It wasn't long before he was snoring. Matthew had never been told he snored, nor had he ever heard it before, but everyone in his family had. His son would refer to his snoring with a lovely variant of a *LOTR* quote: "He snores so loud, we could have shot him in the dark."

Back at the house

Robbie awoke to total and utter silence. Not a single sound was audible, yet he knew not what had awoken him this lovely evening. Looking over at the soft red glow, Robbie batted his eyes a few times before the numbers came into focus; the clock read 3:45 a.m. Sitting up, he looked outside at the moonlit grass and listened. *Another night of being by myself,* he thought as he verified that his alarm was set for school before trying to fall back to sleep.

Seven o'clock came early, and having been woken up in the middle of the night, he didn't feel rested. He rubbed his eyes and removed as many crunchies as he could before greeting the early morning. Robbie sat up and stretched to the left, and then with a small moan, he stretched to the right and turned off the alarm. Once again he was greeted by silence; no sounds, no smells, just silence. If Dad was home, he would have had coffee going, and he would have been lumbering around, making noise without trying.

Sometimes it was those noises that woke Robbie up in the mornings. Many a school day started with turning off his alarm before it was to go off. It wasn't the fact that Robbie had to make his own breakfast today. Not even the issues of getting his stuff ready and getting dressed for his day bothered him. Robbie would have loved to have had breakfast with his dad and to talk a bit before heading off to school. Robbie missed his dad.

Oh well, Robbie thought as he made his way to the bathroom. Looking out the window, he noticed that it was getting daylight; he was running out of time. Within minutes, he was soaped up and had scrubbed all the areas that he needed to. He was now looking for a towel. Robbie looked down on the toilet. The seat was down, but his towel was missing. He scanned the room for anything that could be used and thought about reaching for the hand towel. It was gone too; there was nothing that he could use, and as he looked at the sink again, he was made aware of the nature around him.

Robbie listened to songbirds through the thin glass windows of the bathroom. He was standing now, devoid of soap, and dripping wet. Staring at the window for a few minutes, trying to see the birds who were talking to him helped with that. Robbie was going to have to make a run for it. *No big deal,* he thought, *no one's here.* He placed his feet on the mat and dried them off as best he could. He was not going to run as he would surely break his neck. Robbie slowly walked toward the small sink and looked underneath it for a towel. Taking the last one, he made his way to his room to get dressed.

He tried to pick out the best clothes possible because he wanted Ruthie to like the way he dressed. Robbie looked forward to his daily talks with her. They talked on the way to school, at school, and on the way home. They had very little time in the evenings to do things together, even though they lived close enough to do so. And on the weekends, both of them found themselves spending time with their single parent, so not much time left for them. Robbie laughed. "For them," he said again as he continued to get ready for school.

"Not even officially his girlfriend yet," he said as he put on his dark-blue shirt. No sooner had he done that than he noticed that nature had left him. There were no sounds outside, no birds of prey, no chipmunks, no songbirds, nothing at all. He slid the collar over his neck and then he heard a single deep growl. It lasted several seconds and it was obviously a warning of some sort, but for whom? Robbie placed his hands on the window to the sides of his face and pressed his forehead to the glass. He looked left and right, turning his head very slowly, but saw nothing. He didn't hear another growl or sound for that matter; it was totally quiet.

"Weird," Robbie said as he pulled up his blue jeans and tightened his belt.

Checking himself out in the mirror, he rated himself acceptable and then left for the kitchen. Taking a few steps, he stopped, wiggled his toes, and turned around, heading right back into his bedroom. He had felt his right sock slide down a bit. Robbie had to feel his socks over the top of his boots. He could not stand it when he felt the sides of his boots rub his legs. He enjoyed the taller white socks the way his friends did the ankle socks. This would not take long to fix; it's just one sock, but he doubted that he could get through his day without changing it.

Sitting on the foot of his bed, he removed his boot and took off his sock, throwing it in the corner by his chair. He stared at the window again and concentrated on listening for anything he could hear. It was still quiet; there were no birds, there were no bugs, but there was also no growling. He glanced over to the clock and checked the time. *Still time for breakfast,* he thought as he tied the laces on his boots and left the room once again.

Robbie was on his way to make breakfast. He preferred bacon and eggs to cereal, hot or cold, any day. Today he made extra bacon because he was taking some to school for his lunch. His dad would have been mad at him if he knew he was using the cast iron skillet. Robbie had always promised to use the microwave to cook bacon, as it involved no potential for fire damage to Robbie or his immediate surroundings. *Sorry, Dad,* he thought, *a man's bacon had to be cooked in a cast iron skillet!*

Robbie was extra careful to clean up the pan and to put everything back the way he found it. He even ensured that any remaining grease was dissolved in hot water and a heavy concentrate of dish detergent, just to cover his tracks. Robbie would do anything for bacon, even his dad would say it was so; it was his only true vice. Given the friends that Robbie knew, it was only a matter of time before he smoked and drank, his dad had told him. "Choose your friends carefully," he often told him. Robbie laughed as he thought of Ruthie, who did not fit into his dad's theory.

If Matthew was to come in and catch Robbie right now with a strong smell of bacon lingering heavy through the air, he would still feel like his son was a success. He saw perfection, an honor student who always tried to do good as often as he could. He was a caring and intelligent individual; he was his wonderful son. It didn't matter to Matthew that he knew his son cooked bacon in the cast iron skillet when he wasn't there! He would tell this story to Robbie when he was older, probably over a beer or two with his son. Matthew would then laugh, as he knew his grandson would do the same to him.

Robbie raced around the house, getting ready for school. He had finished his bacon and eggs, cleaned up the dishes, and even sprayed air freshener around to mask the heavy bacon aroma. Looking for his book bag that he had just picked up a few minutes ago, he placed the air freshener back by the side of the TV and again checked the kitchen for completeness.

Robbie took a bottle of water and an apple along with his sandwich and placed it into his bag. He took a few steps toward the front door and threw a backward glance over his shoulder to check one more time that everything was right. As he grabbed the door handle and stepped outside, he had forgotten about the earlier encounter he experienced in the bathroom; he had forgotten about the growling.

Robbie maintained a steady pace as he covered the hills between him and Ruthie's house. As he approached the top of the last hill, he watched with anticipation for what he was sure to be Ruthie standing by her mailbox, but, alas, she was not there. He was sure that he was running a little late, but Robbie didn't know if she had already left or if she was running late herself. He called out for her a few times as he continued walking to school. Deep down inside, he knew she had started off so she would not be late, so he picked up his pace.

She had followed him ever since he had passed the house, making sure to stay a safe distance behind him. She was never too close and she went to great lengths to move quietly. She got as close as ten yards one time before backing off, just to be safe and remain hidden. She laughed in her mind, smiling as she thought that at least three or four times she could have snuck up close enough to touch his arm, or worse.

Smiling once again, she closed the distance between herself and Robbie, but this time she knew she had gone too close too fast. Robbie soon became aware that he was being followed. What had tipped him off was the fact that he had heard a woman's laugh behind him. He listened carefully as he continued walking. *Not much further now,* he thought. Robbie didn't remember what Ruthie's mom looked like; he'd only seen her once. He also didn't know why she was following him to school. Maybe Ruthie and her mom were both behind him, trying to play a joke on him.

Thinking on the woman's laugh he had heard, he couldn't tell if it was Ruthie's mom or not, but one thing was for certain: it wasn't Ruthie. A few more steps and he was going to say hello to them both. He assumed that Ruthie was with her mom and that he wasn't just being followed only by her mom.

"Ha-ha, very funny, guys." Robbie laughed as he stopped abruptly and turned to look over his left shoulder.

Nobody answered him, and when he turned further around, he saw that no one was present. Robbie thought surely he would catch someone ducking behind a tree or running this way or that, but nobody was there.

Continuing on to school, Robbie chalked it down to his imagination, and as he climbed the final two hills, he saw Ruthie walking ahead of him. He shouted her name and finally caught up to her, saying hello between heavy breaths.

"Oh, sorry," Ruthie said, "I just couldn't wait any longer."

Robbie had not stopped smiling or started breathing since he had laid eyes on her, but he managed to get out. "It's all right, Ruthie, I understand," before struggling to breathe again.

They made small talk on the way to their first class of the day, English.

CHAPTER FIVE

Your Introduction

U

nder what pretense do you think I care for you at all? It is to please the One, and in doing so, I find my thirst for knowledge and power satiated. To spread darkness and chaos is to enlighten all to that which has been previously hidden from sight. I did not start out this way; there was a time when my goals were, how do you say, much loftier. To darkness I was drawn, and closer and closer I moved around the periphery until one day I was pulled inside.

N

ever have I thought what others did around me mattered. Seeing people grow older as they live out their pathetic lives interested me, at first. Finding a mate, having children, growing their lives together; it was not that long to wait. One could sit and pass the time at a nearby fireplace and watch them all age; I am nothing if not patient. Some would achieve greatness, but most would just pass to leave their marks upon their own lawns.

H

ow I spend my time with you depends on your strength, or lack thereof. Just look at you sitting there in your chair, reading my story. You have been comfortable up to this point. When I tell you that you are wearing a blue T-shirt with jeans and that you are barefoot, you tense up. Don't worry; there is no need to be unduly frightened or to run; I have plans for you. Do me a favor, will you? Please try *not* to do good today; you will probably just piss me off.

O

pen your mind to me. It is only a matter of time before I achieve my goals; it is inevitable. You are probably thinking on stopping, but it is a wonderful read; you must carry on. Why, it is unknown how mad I would become if you never experience what I have in store for you. Whatever you choose to do, do not go to the last chapter and read from there; you will surely miss out on what I wish you to learn from me.

L

ove, what do *you* know about love? Peace, compassion, trust— throw these words out of your vocabulary; you no longer need them. Love only yourself; the ones around you, the ones who you have picked to share your life with, they care not for you. Trust no one with two or less legs. Man is inherently evil; there is bad inside you all. Take pets for a moment; it is your definition that I speak of, not mine. You do not see pets screwing each other over, do you? Now I am not talking about the predator-and-prey relationship, I love that part; I refer to two squirrels attempting to kill each other over a dispute about their nuts.

Y

esterday I spent some time with you, and to be quite honest, you bore me. Every day you try too hard, you know. Others will like you if they want to. Others will spend time with you if they want to. Others will most likely not think you are attractive, so stop trying; it's embarrassing. Oh, and let us find you another job; the one you currently try to succeed in is an endeavor in futility. Enough about you. Let us get back to me; there is so much more I want to show you.

CHAPTER SIX

Digital Diaries

Each school day in the teacher's break room, three lost souls began their days. A rather thin man slowly sipped on his coffee. The aroma of hazelnut wafted throughout the break room as he smiled and thought of today's assignments. Over to his left, in an oversized chair was Ms. Broakus. She sat frowning and was generally unhappy to be sitting in said break room. Every day she would tell anyone who would listen about her string of bad luck. Someday it would end and she would be in a bigger city getting paid more money, she would say.

Ms. Broakus filled that chair to capacity. There wasn't a day that Mr. Martinez didn't think about that chair breaking. There was a running joke going through the school that if anything was broken, it was because of Ms. Broakus. Mr. Martinez sat there, notebook in hand, doodling away. He occasionally stopped to sip his coffee, which sent more hazelnut plumes into the air. Ms. Broakus watched him closely from time to time before going back to thinking about her current situation.

He sat there in his chair, always with his left leg crossed over the right. If he was located in this break room, he had his coffee nearby. No matter where you saw him, he wore tan khakis with a colored button-up shirt with a single pocket. There was never anything in that pocket, as if it was reserved for something special. That pocket was always available; it was always empty.

Mr. Martinez closed his notepad and looked at his watch. Taking a quick sip of his coffee, he quickly straightened up and corrected his posture as it was almost ten of. He faced the door, but his eyes were down on the face of his watch. He watched as the digital numbers counted upward, and then as his eyes moved up and toward the door, it swung open wide. Ms. Sanders entered slowly and smiled at the two as she slowly turned to her left and closed the door. Turning to her right, she made her way to the kitchen sink and poured a cup of tap water into her thermos.

"I hope everyone had a wonderful weekend," she said as she sat down beside Mr. Martinez.

"Yes, great. What a wonderful weekend it was. Why, I barely had time to," Ms. Broakus barely finished before Mr. Martinez interrupted her.

"Why, yes. Yes, it was great," he said, smiling.

Ms. Broakus rolled her eyes and went back to thinking about her bad luck. Ms. Sanders smiled as she looked at Mr. Martinez to address him. It was Monday, and like planned, he wore a light-blue shirt. She always coordinated her clothing based on his shirt color of the day. She never failed to match him, and he never strayed from his habits. Smiling still, she looked away for a second and then back into his eyes.

"Any plans for next weekend or Friday actually?" she asked, already knowing the answer.

"Nope, I'm all yours. What are your plans?" he asked.

"I was hoping that we could binge on that vampire show. Maybe order some takeout perhaps?" she flirted.

It was always at this time when Ms. Broakus sighed and got up and left.

"Everyone knows you're dating, yeah, sure, whatever. You are not fooling anyone," Ms. Broakus said as she squeezed out of her chair and left the room.

A few minutes went by, and just as all hope was lost, they broke out in laughter.

"That never gets old," he said.

"I know, right!" she said.

"Maybe one of these weekends, we actually could . . . never mind," Mr. Martinez said.

"You never know, sir. You never know," she said as she got up, touched his shoulder, and left for her class.

They played this game every Monday. When Friday came around, they were done with it and they left with each one going their own way. He didn't mind the game; after all, it did get Ms. Broakus all riled up.

Ms. Sanders passed Ms. Broakus in the hallway halfway toward the lunchroom. *How does that happen*, Ms. Sanders thought, *she left first?* An annoying sigh escaped Ms. Broakus as she passed her, but, oh well, it was still funny. Ms. Sanders remarked on the size of Ms. Broakus several times a day, but she did dress nicely. Large skirts, a large blouse, and a largely negative attitude were all things worn nicely by her. Overall, her students liked her, but she wasn't friendly, not one bit.

It wasn't long before Mr. Martinez left the break room and headed down the hall. His classes were early in the day, which left the afternoon for grading papers and assignments. He would admit it to anyone; he spent a good amount of his days grading papers and correcting grammar. It wasn't as easy as turning a gas into a liquid or for checking the number ten to have a minus sign in front of it. There were many ways to say the same thing, and many of them were correctly demonstrated daily in each paragraph.

Robbie and Ruthie sat in class, on opposite ends of the room. To some that would sound very far away, but the classrooms here were very small. The local school board prided themselves on personal attention, and each class had a maximum of twelve seats. With smaller class sizes, grades were better, attendance was better, and they had a higher graduation rate than some of the larger schools in the city. None of that mattered to Robbie. He was just happy being close to Ruthie; he enjoyed her so much.

The bell rang, and as usual, Mr. Martinez was nowhere to be found. He was expected to be there on time, Robbie thought, why not him? Oh well, less time to go over their papers was fine with him. He continued to talk to those around about Mr. Martinez and occasionally found himself smiling at a not-so-distant Ruthie.

"Sorry, I'm late, all. I had an emergency come up. I'm going to have to leave and I'm afraid that I won't be back for a few days. In my absence, Ms. Sanders will be helping out. Please extend to her the same courtesy you give me," he said as he hurriedly left the room.

A few moments later, Ms. Sanders arrived to a room full of unruly kids.

"All right, everyone, please take your seats," she said to them.

Ms. Sanders looked around and took a quick roll call for those present. *All present and accounted for,* she thought. *Not a bad start, not a bad start at all.*

"OK. Let's take a thirty-minute recess while I get something planned for the rest of our time here today. I'll come outside and get you all when it's time. Go and have fun," she told them.

"Robbie, Robbie, Robbie?" Ms. Sanders called out to him several times before he responded.

"It's your turn. Please come up to the board and write your name, and next to it a single word, please and thank you," Ms. Sanders patiently said.

It was easy enough to hear Ruthie murmur the word "daydreamer" as he passed through the chuckles of his friends. Robbie made it to the board and looked at what was already written. Several words made no sense, and when read from top to bottom, it was a crazy sentence: "Four little mice chased the cat into the . . ." Robbie looked at them again and wrote his word—"mine." He smiled and walked back to his seat. *Three more to go. There were three more kids to go and that sentence would be complete,* Robbie thought. It had to be an assignment, it just had to be.

Ms. Sanders looked at everybody and gave them their assignments. They were to take each word on the board and use it in a sentence. Next they would take every three words and use them in a paragraph. And finally, they would write a nine-hundred-word short story on the initial sentence on the board. She paused as all of the kids at the same time let flies into their mouths.

"Oh, come on, it's not that bad, is it? How about I offer something else instead, how would that be?" Ms. Sanders asked.

The class erupted in cheers, and what was to have been a lynching had just turned into total buy-in. She loved that method of teaching: horror first then easy-peasy.

Once the class quieted down, she handed them a small printout of their assignments. There wasn't much on that paper actually, only a few paragraphs of instructions from what Robbie noticed.

"Read them to yourselves and raise your hands if you have any questions. I'm going to need all of those papers back, so please take notes on what you need to do," she told them.

Ruthie slowly read the paragraphs and understood immediately that this was no ordinary assignment. The instructions read something to the extent of performing a digital diary of your friends, your family, and where you resided. It consisted of a digital representation of the house you lived in, room by room. You were to also squeeze in some math and English. Each room had to be measured with a tape measure, and a paragraph had to be written about it. The last sentence of the last paragraph read: You will be given a digital camera to use for this project, and when finished, it was yours to keep. The fine print underneath that sentence stipulated that one must obtain a B minus or higher to keep the camera, or their parents would be billed $49.99 for it if not returned.

Overall, the kids were happy and moderately quiet, passersby would admit. Looking around, Ms. Sanders saw only one hand raised.

Looking at the seating chart for a brief second, she looked up and asked, "Yes, Suzie?"

"I was wondering if you were OK. Earlier I saw you and Mr. Martinez arguing and then you helped him up from the floor. Are you both sick?" asked little Suzie.

Ms. Sanders was caught off guard and quickly addressed the question with a smile.

"I'm just fine, and he's fine too. He had fallen down, and I helped him up. Mr. Martinez had some pressing details to attend to. I'm sure he'll be back soon," she said with a fading smile.

"Well, if there are no further questions on the paper that I have given you, please take the rest of the day off. Go to your homes and finish that assignment—it's due tomorrow. Please pick up the cameras from the small box at the door when you leave," she said as she scanned the room for disappointment.

There was none to be found, only excitement and loud cheers that quickly faded away as all the kids left the room. *Now that's how you teach young minds*, she said, laughing to herself. Ms. Sanders closed the door behind her and followed some of the kids down the main road back between some hills.

Robbie and Ruthie walked back toward their houses. They talked about this and that, with Ruthie mainly speaking of the digital camera project and Robbie of marbles. He had lost too many marbles to practice, and without practice, he wouldn't get any better; he needed marbles.

"Robbie, had it occurred to you that when we came into class, there was no box of digital cameras by the door? There was nothing by the door like usual," she stated.

"You know, I actually don't remember. I wasn't thinking about that. I was just waiting for my day to begin," Robbie replied.

"Well, there wasn't anything there, I'm sure of it. It's just a bit weird, that's all," Ruthie said.

"Ruthie, I've been thinking—I need more marbles, and we are off early now to go and do our assignments," he said.

"Yes," Ruthie said very slowly.

"I was thinking about going into town and shopping for marbles before the few shops there closed. I know there's time to get this assignment done, and I can do so after the shops are closed," he said confidently.

The last of the hills was coming into view as Ruthie thought about what he was asking.

"I'm sorry, but I'm going home to finish this up. I have no interest in marbles and no desire to go to town right now. I think it will take longer than you think to get this done," Ruthie said.

"Do you mind if I don't finish walking you home so I can get there quicker?" he asked.

"Not at all. Do what you need to do. Just don't forget about getting a good grade so you can keep that camera!" she said in an "I told you so" voice.

"Will do. I'll see you tomorrow," he said excitedly as he ran off in the direction of town.

She smiled as she watched Robbie start running and quickly disappear between another hill and a large boulder. A few minutes passed before she started moving again, so she thought, but it was actually only a few seconds. She turned and watched Ruthie enter her front door and close it behind her. *What a wonderful day,* she thought as she inhaled deeply and drank it all in.

Matthew spent most of his morning using his pickaxe. He worked an area that looked promising and kept at it until he had gone in about two feet. It was from this material that he sorted and sifted through to get pieces of rock and material all the same size. Damn. There were those that would make fun of him if he spoke that way in public; it was classify, classify. He would classify the material and then pan out what he could. Matthew still needed to purchase some equipment, and for that, he would have to go to town and see what they had in stock and order what he could not easily find.

It was convenient to use the local pooled water supply to wash over his material, but he still needed to get his pump set up. He had to try to get some sort of recirculation system in place so he could quickly sluice his materials. Listening to himself think on all of this, he laughed. Sometimes he sounded like a miner, and others he was a schoolgirl. A green horn was rough around the edges and wet behind the ears; these were all terms for being inexperienced.

No matter, he thought, he was learning this as he went along. There were several locals that he could learn from, he was sure of that. Swirling his gold pan in the water, he took one knee to get even closer to the ground. Matthew swirled the material and water in his pan in a circular motion in an effort to keep the heavies on the bottom and to move the lighter material to the surface. He did this over and over, and soon he was at a point where he could slide some of the top material right off into the pool. Later on, he would have a better setup where he would pan into a large trough so he would not lose any material at all, but for now, this would have to do.

More and more he sloshed the material around in the pan, and each two or three times, he repeated those steps, angling the pan just enough to allow some of the lighter material to leave. The heavy material stayed put, and the lighter made their way out of the pan. This was panning 101 oversimplified, he would say. More often than not, he found himself spending too much time moving the material around the pan and not enough on removing the lighter pieces. It wasn't long before his hands and wrist became tired and ceased cooperating in an effective manner. Matthew knew that he was by no means an expert; he needed more practice.

This would be his first results from this mine, using the smaller material from this morning's muck. There he was again, miner Matthew has showed up.

"Nice to meet you," he said, laughing.

Miner Matthew stopped the action in his pan and started moving some larger pieces toward the opposite end with his finger. Keeping the pan tilted slightly backward, he slowly tapped it from time to time to move material the way he wanted it to go. Time and time again, he moved material out of the way with his index finger and then he would take his thumb and slide them off of the pan and into the water below.

Now all he did was tap one end of the pan and look on as the lighter material hopped forward. Back at the bottom of the pan remained the majority of the water and all of the heavies. He stopped tapping the pan and slowly moved the water from left to right over them. Stopping after a few tries, he again took his index finger and moved it through the remaining material, looking for gold that would be underneath.

There was his first picker! An irregularly shaped piece of gold, one might add, but a piece of gold nonetheless. It was as if a grain of rice and a pea had fell in love and made a love child—a love child made entirely of gold! It wasn't much to look at, and everything else around it was much smaller, but there was a good amount of flour and flake gold present, along with several other small pieces. He took out a small plastic container and placed the picker into it.

Matthew then took his plastic snuffer bottle and filled it almost full and sucked up what gold he could. He took in all manner of debris and material that was located immediately around the gold pieces, but he left no gold behind. Better to have some material with the gold than no material with little gold, he thought as he removed the last of it from his pan. Sealing the top of the small vial by turning it a few times to lock it into place, he admired his new friend.

Matthew looked up toward the top of the cave wall where he was and wondered what his son was doing, what time it was, and how much longer before he would have to stop digging. Tonight was Matthew's night to make dinner for the both of them, for them to sit down to and enjoy their meal together, and he didn't want to miss that.

Robbie had cleared the last small group of boulders and then he settled into a fast walking pace as he caught his breath. Soon he would be in town and he wanted to breathe and speak to the store owners. He wasn't sure where to go to look for marbles, and once there, he wasn't sure that they would have any. It seemed like several of the boys in school played marbles, so he was sure the local selection would be small. *Oh well,* he thought, at least he was going to ask, and who knows—maybe he could order some or request that they carry them.

The first store Robbie walked into was pet themed. He didn't think that marbles were dangerous for most pets and that they could die if they ate them. Soon after entering the store, he noticed that everyone he talked to had contorted facial expressions when asked if they carried marbles. Their eyes and foreheads contributed to the scary expressions when he asked what stores around town did carry them.

Robbie was unsure of whether the stores here carried marbles at all. He did know that the people around him were unhelpful, to say the least. None of them asked him where his parents were or why he wasn't in school. He took a few more stabs at it and tried two nearby shops. None of them carried them, and each time Robbie left the shop with a frown.

"Wait," the shop keep said as he pulled open the old glass door.

Robbie turned around with excitement and looked up at the man.

"Where's your dad, son?" he asked Robbie.

Robbie pointed to the right, which would mean he was down the street toward a few more shops.

The old man pointed to the left and said, "General store. Have him try the general store."

"Thanks," he said to the man as Robbie took a step out the door and turned right.

"Arnold, the general store in Arnold," the man told Robbie.

Robbie was instantly crushed. He knew that he could not make it there without his dad's help, and that meant that no marbles for him until he did so.

"Thank you, sir" was Robbie's reply as he solemnly closed the door behind him.

The old man smiled as he reached below and looked through a large box of marbles. He had promised Thomas and his friends that they would have first dibs and that he wouldn't sell to strangers. The old man always kept his promises . . .

Robbie had just enough time to make it home and start on his assignment before his dad got there. It was a safe bet to say that dinner would be late or not come at all. Eating sometimes revolved around the outcome of what his dad would call "a good day's mining." He didn't mind, though; there was always bacon for him! Robbie's smile returned as he picked up the pace and headed for home.

Passing the last hill, Robbie looked at the house as it came into view. Their place wasn't like most, not even out here, but especially when compared to where he used to live. There wasn't a car in the driveway; hell, there wasn't even a driveway. One had to look to the ground the way the Native Americans did in the old movies to determine if anyone was home. This applied to the footsteps of man and any vehicle one might have obtained from a friend or the local store. He didn't watch much TV, but what he did occasionally watch were old reruns and local rebroadcasts.

He opened the door and looked at his dad, who was sitting on the couch, staring at him. You know the drill: start talking, and right now, mister. Robbie closed his eyes, placed a hand on the door, and took a step backward, closing it. He took a step forward and sat down on the floor.

"Dad, do you really have to make me do this again?" Robbie pleaded.

"You should be used to it by now, and it is being done for the betterment of your skills son," Matthew said.

"Now what do you have to say to me?" he asked Robbie.

Robbie found these things easy most of the time, but today was an exception. He had cut school—well, not actually *cut*, Robbie thought. He was let go for an assignment, but he had never come back home to do it. He thought about the task at hand and began to speak.

"Ah, this is easy. Is this the best you can do?" Robbie bragged.

Matthew looked on unamused and awaited his explanation.

"Bacon, that's a dead giveaway. Then there's macaroni and cheese, sharp, possibly regular and white cheddars too. Let me think on the next one. Potatoes, yes, baked, butter, sour cream, oh, sneaky. Looks like Thousand Island dressing to boot. See, I told you it was easy," Robbie said with a very large smile.

"Are you slipping, son? Is that it, nothing else then?" Matthew said quizzically.

"Oh, now that is *not fair*. Not fair at all," Robbie retorted.

While sitting still, Robbie thought about other smells, the ones that lingered or were masked by stronger ones. Even worse, he thought, something could have been cooked earlier, and that's why it wasn't predominating. Matthew looked on and told him to concentrate.

"This one's a bit harder," Robbie admitted.

"Brownies, you baked brownies earlier? What time did you get home anyway?" he asked his dad.

"Great job, Robbie!" Matthew shouted out as he charged his son to catch him.

Robbie took off toward the bathroom and seemed to almost jump two feet straight up. He ducked and hit the floor, running with both his hands and feet, helping him to keep going.

"Made it!" Robbie yelled as he turned on the water to wash his hands.

"I've got a surprise for you tonight, son. I know you'll be excited, and when I tell you all about it over dinner, we'll discuss some things that are equally important, such as coming home straight from school when released to do a project," Matthew said, laughing.

"Ah, Dad," Robbie said as he wiped his hands dry.

"Looks like I'm still the smarter one, huh?" Matthew said, trying to be cool.

Robbie nodded and got ready for dinner.

Robbie and Matthew enjoyed a dinner that was special in many ways. Everything was cooked with love; there was a wonderful collection of vegetables with his bacon, and to finish everything off, brownies! There was also the fact that there were enough for leftovers. It was the one rule that they had that they both ensured that was followed when they cooked: make enough for the next day. Cooking enough food for the next day helped a single parent make ends meet with meal preparation and time.

Fully loaded potatoes, macaroni and cheese, and brownies were a favorite of Robbie's. It had been months since they had it last; Susan didn't make it that often. The last time was with the entire family present; Robbie missed his mom.

Matthew saw Robbie playing with his food, or more to the point stop eating, as if daydreaming, and he thought that now was the right time.

"Robbie, check this out," Matthew said as he brandished a small plastic vial with a black cap.

He held on to it, making sure that Robbie knew to take great care with what he was given. Robbie looked at his dad and gave him an understanding glance as he attempted to pry it away from his dad's index finger and thumb.

"No way!" Robbie shouted. "Seriously?"

Matthew looked on as Robbie continued to turn the plastic vial this way and that.

"It's not much, really, and it won't pay the bills if I keep finding my pickers that size, but it's the first, and hopefully the first of many. What do you think?" he asked Robbie.

"Get out of here. You really found that, you dug that up?" he asked his dad.

"Yup, it was all me. I used my pickaxe and broke into a wall and went over what I could. I still need you go to into town with me and pick up a few things, probably this Saturday," Matthew said.

Robbie continued smiling, and not missing a beat, he said, "If I have to, I'll go into town if I have to."

"I'm recommending Arnold, Dad. All the kids say that it's a larger city and with more availability as far as ranch tools, digging, fencing, and home repair," Robbie said.

"Oh, sure, I also think they have lots of marbles too," he said as he looked at Robbie and extended his right hand.

Robbie handed over the plastic vial and mouthed the word "Oh."

"So let's talk about that," he continued as he looked at Robbie.

"I thought I had enough time, Dad. They let us go early for an assignment. I know I can do it well. It will be finished, I promise. How did you find out anyway?" he asked.

"I'm your dad. I know these things. I've tried most of them before you were born on my dad, and with your same success rate, I might add," Matthew replied.

Robbie smiled and nodded approval and that he understood. Matthew looked on and knew that he didn't have to say it; he knew Robbie wouldn't do that again.

"OK. Time for more rules: it's your turn to clean, my friend, as I cooked. I hope you factored in tonight's dishes in your earlier formula," Matthew said as he ducked out of the kitchen behind the living room wall with a small smile.

Robbie stacked the dishes on the table up and walked over to the sink, and everything was already cleaned up. The only dirty dishes were what he was holding in his hands, and that wouldn't take long at all.

"Thanks, Dad. I appreciate that," Robbie told him.

Matthew continued smiling as he walked over to the couch and continued to examine his picker. He took out his trusty notebook and looked at his drawings on where he found it, what time, and anything else that was important.

It didn't take long for Robbie to finish the dishes and wipe off the table. He rummaged through his book bag and pulled out the camera and began taking pictures and notes. Matthew had fallen asleep on the couch with his notebook in one hand and the vial in the other. Robbie picked both of them up and placed them on the coffee table and threw a blanket over him. He knew he would be gone when he woke up for school, and he didn't mind at all.

"Good night, Dad," Robbie said as he headed off to finish the drawing in his bedroom.

CHAPTER SEVEN

No Pets Allowed

Robbie awoke to peace and quiet, which was the norm as of late. He was sure that his dad had already left; the aroma of coffee that was present was faint. He knew something was wrong, though; he didn't smell bacon. Looks like today would be cereal, as he was not going to test his dad any further until after he obtained his marbles. Robbie laughed at that thought as he placed two feet on the ground and turned off the alarm clock before it was scheduled to wake him.

This morning went like the previous three mornings ahead of it, except he didn't have bacon. It would have to wait. It wasn't like he could hide the fact that he made it; the bacon reserves would have to be tapped to make that meal happen. He probably needed to cut down on the bacon anyway. Who knows—he probably already knew that he was making it in the cast iron skillet and that he was waiting for the right time to tell him. Another smile crept up and lingered for a few seconds until a yawn wrecked it.

With his morning ritual complete, he stopped to stare at the bathroom window and listened again for the source of that growling. Nope, nothing doing today; this was good news for Robbie. He grabbed his book bag, threw his assignment inside and the digital camera along with it, just in case. Robbie headed out for school and walked toward Ruthie's house. *What a day,* he thought, *almost Saturday.* Saturday was the day he would help his dad secure some mining equipment, but more importantly, it was the day that he would peruse marble heaven.

Robbie was on autopilot as he weaved his way into and around the hills that were between his and Ruthie's houses. It wasn't long before he saw her standing outside by her mailbox, looking in his direction. She smiled as Robbie came into view. Robbie was one of the nicer boys in school, and even her mom liked him. She sometimes wondered how their family would turn out, with her and her mom joining Robbie and his dad.

"I'm sorry that I'm on time," Robbie said.

"Oh, never mind all of that, I'm already over it. Just don't do it again, all right?" she said.

Smiling at each other, they took off for school at a brisk walk. Ruthie liked to get to school a bit early so she could review her previous day's assignments. Robbie liked getting to school early, as he played marbles anytime he could. As of late, however, all he was doing was watching; he still needed marbles to play with.

"I'm not sure why we're walking so fast today, Robbie. If I remember correctly, you're almost out of marbles, aren't you?" Ruthie said slyly.

"Oh, you are exactly correct, as always. I am still learning a lot from them. Some of those games are tricky," Robbie said seriously.

With the last hill coming into view, Ruthie told him to have a good time and not to be late for his first class.

"You never know if she will grade your assignment down if you don't turn it in on time," Ruthie stated.

"Hmm, do you mind taking mine with you just in case? I promise I'll be there, but you are making me nervous," he told her.

"Sure. Give," she said, smiling.

Robbie handed over the assignment and took off running to the boys' locker room. It was one safe place to shoot marbles, one that had not been found yet, Robbie hoped.

Thursday was to be like any other day for Robbie—walk to school with Ruthie and spend a little time with the boys on breaks and before school started. He would pay as much attention to Ruthie as possible and try to get through the day without being bored. Robbie maintained an A grade point average without trying. Sometimes he caught it up at the end of the semester; sometimes it started at an A+ and fell slightly, but it always wound up that way. He laughed as he took off running to his first class of the morning, knowing that he was going to be a little late. Good thing he turned in his assignment to Ruthie.

Ms. Sanders was just closing the door when he slid inside, smiling.

"Sorry, I'm late, Ms. Sanders," he said to her.

Nodding back an "It's all right, get going look," he smiled again and ran to his seat. Robbie kept smiling as he sat in his seat, looking forward to the chalkboard.

The board read "I will not play marbles in the boys' bathroom. I will not play marbles in the boys' locker room. I will not play marbles in the maintenance closet, and I especially will not play marbles in the girls' locker room."

It was written from top to bottom until there were no empty areas. Robbie stared at the board and tried to determine which colors were used first. It looked like white, blue, green, and red chalks were used, but he could not determine the order.

"Go ahead, Robbie. Pick a color that has not been used and walk up to the board for me, please," Ms. Sanders said.

The entire classroom hushed as Robbie slowly walked to the board and picked up the purple-colored one.

"Feel free to start at the top and work your way to the bottom. Make haste, we are all waiting eagerly to start our day's work," she told him.

Robbie shot his friends an evil glance as he turned back to the board and started his writing assignment. *They could have at least warned me,* he thought, *geez.* It took Robbie several minutes to finish, and that was with writing at a pretty good pace. He was slow enough to write legibly and fast enough to look like he was actually caring.

"I know I didn't catch you down there, Robbie, but you were late today, and I'm assuming that it was over a game of marbles," Ms. Sanders remarked.

"Yes, ma'am" was his reply.

Robbie finished writing those sentences and had just placed the chalk on the bottom rest on the board when he suddenly felt ill.

"Play marbles as much as you like, Robbie, there's no harm in it," the voice told him.

He smiled and turned back to see Ms. Sanders leaving the room, but not before mumbling over her shoulder, "I'll be right back. Please turn to page 69 and read until I return."

Mumbles and rumbles erupted just as the class thought she was far enough to not hear them. Nobody was happy to be surprised with a reading assignment, but everybody cracked open their books and began reading.

Ms. Sanders walked all the way to her office and closed the door. She began perusing the recent homework assignments. She skilled the papers and went straight for the master drawing of their houses. She separated each one and placed them on top of each paper. Smiling, she looked over the pictures and then started looking at the digital cameras that were turned back in. She had them all except Robbie's. She made a note to get that back so she could review the pictures of his house.

Slowly picking this paper over that paper, she sorted them out and placed the ones that were not interesting into the trash. Three stood out, and she couldn't wait to share them with Mr. Martinez.

"Where the fuck are you, you ass," she said.

Mr. Martinez had taken his van and driven two or so cities away to a small hardware store for supplies. He was to purchase the supplies necessary for the burglaries and then return by Friday. He should have been back by now, but he was late; he was always late. She often wondered what she saw in that man. It was almost more of a partnership than a relationship. Ms. Sanders could count on one hand the number of times that they had fooled around, and only one time that was memorable to her.

This was her last score; she was going to take her share and leave him far behind. She wasn't getting any younger, and what kind of name was Ms. Sanders anyway? She preferred Paisley Marcy Perkins; it was, after all, her true name. Hell, for all she knew, he was Mr. Sanders; she really didn't know his true name. They had hooked up just north of the Mexico border and hit it off. They had been together for six years now, traveling to four counties and working at five schools. Paisley was just plane ole tired; she wanted to settle down.

It probably wasn't much longer now before Ms. Broakus decided to kill them both over what might go down in the history books as a simple case of jealous rage. Ms. Sanders laughed. It wasn't jealously over them liking each other as much as it was that they got along. Ms. Broakus probably couldn't get along with anybody. She was very angry and negative most of the time, and it showed in everything she did. If she only knew the truth, Ms. Sanders thought. As if on cue, she looked up and saw Mr. Martinez walking down the hallway. He had a very large smile on his face and he was carrying a small box in his left hand.

She returned his smile, matching its duration and size, but her pretended excitement was short lived. Mr. Martinez was starting to slow down and he even lost his smile. He seemed to look right past her and, by now, he was totally motionless. Out of the corner of her eye, she saw something approaching very quickly. Turning her head, she found herself face-to-face with a mountain lion. Her heart skipped a beat; she was frozen with fear. She imagined herself being ripped to shreds, grabbed by her face, and dragged down the hallway, leaving a blood trail not to be believed. She thought she stopped breathing one moment and saw herself hyperventilating the next. The noise that the cat made as it came closer was that of the stereotypical clicking of claws over a hard surface, but she had not heard it until she was already aware that something was there.

It took a few more steps and stood looking at her with its mouth slightly agape. Down the hall, the action played out like an adult-rated video game. There were kids in the classroom in the rear, running this way and that, screaming loud enough to drown out the best of background singers. Resting against the outside wall was the top half of Mr. Martinez. The other half, well, she wasn't quite sure where it was. The blood trail went down the hallway to her left and disappeared out of sight to the right. She drew in a breath and held it as she leveled the shotgun just below the head of the beast.

It wore a beard of blood and it stood so stationary that she thought that if the kids had been any quieter, she could have heard the individual droplets of blood hitting the floor beneath its head. It growled once and shook its body in defiance. Blood flew against the walls, the ceiling, and the floor; there was so much blood. The scene was no different than a dog trying to dry itself after its bath, except that it was not harmless water. What it left behind were large filthy tainted red stains that slowly slid down the walls and dripped from the ceiling. It was an explosion of the remnants of two teachers that Ms. Broakus really didn't care for too much anyway. It was at this point that the kids in the classroom became silent. They were either escaping out a window or they were going into shock.

Ms. Broakus closed her eyes as she pulled both triggers. It was as if the cat didn't think she would do it, as if it didn't think she could do it. Ms. Broakus left the floor airborne, traveling backward at what felt to her as the speed of light. Her feet were rising above her head when she landed squarely on the flat of her back. The wind left her in one massive exhale that had to have changed the air pressure in the hallway, if only anyone had been there to measure it.

Bluish-gray smoke filled the hallway, and everything grew silent. She stood up and looked around to assess the situation. Mr. Martinez was bitten in half, lying there dead against the wall. Ms. Sanders was dragged away, kicking and screaming, bleeding down the hallway as she went. The large mountain lion had been shot to death with a large hole under his head that poured blood to the left of its body. The very large woman was still breathing heavily and lying on her back. She moved down the hallway and entered the classroom. Looking around, she saw nothing of interest; it was apparent to her that the half-opened window was the way they all escaped. She let out an inaudible sigh and headed out in the direction of the open window.

Robbie led the others as best he could toward the adults that would be in town. Ruthie had the idea to escape through the windows, but she lacked the strength to open them. Robbie had enough smarts to grab a nearby chair and use it to break the frame. That allowed the window to be pushed open, and a good thing too; he didn't want to be showed up by a girl. There were times where Robbie thought she was stronger; he had to squash that!

The kids took turns looking behind them as they ran. Ruthie helped to motivate the group and kept them moving at a good pace. Robbie helped to push the stragglers, and sometimes this meant calling them names and even grabbing them by their shirts to help them keep up. They had made it all the way to the last hill before they slowed down.

"Here, we start walking here," Robbie managed to say between heavy breaths.

Most of the kids were breathing heavy but walking at a good pace. That's when Robbie noticed it: most of the kids here were fit and in shape. He didn't see anybody that was heavy, except older people. This area of the country ate better; they were more physical, and some areas were more active than most of the United States. One of the newest crazes for dining was old school here; it was called from farm to table. He enjoyed the desserts when he went out to eat, but there wasn't any place locally that he could go out to eat that didn't offer their own farm-grown vegetables, beef, and sometimes seafood.

"We are almost there, everyone," Ruthie said.

"So, Mitch, sorry to see you again under these circumstances, but—" John stated.

"No worries. How are you really holding up?" the coroner asked.

John's nods were enough; he looked stressed, upset, and disappointed. Nothing in Murphys had ever happened like this on his watch. Mitch knew John loved what they referred to as "the game" very much; he was always a part of it.

"So what did you find interesting with this one, John?" Mitch asked.

John smiled and walked back to Ms. Broakus and examined the scene for a few moments before, speaking.

"Well, her body is angled one way, her head another. It's too soon for all of the details. A full investigation and autopsy are necessary, and she's cuddling the shotgun that she presumably used to fell the giant beast," he told him.

"Now that's all fine and dandy, but you missed these. Well, they weren't there before. It took time for them to appear, but check out both sides of her neck," Mitch told him.

"No shit?" John said as he examined her neck.

There were what appeared to be handprints on either side of her face. The hands were of a pretty good size too, leaving imprints that were half on the face and half on her neck. Her face had been turned wildly to the right side; somebody had physically tried to twist her head off! This place had just turned from a freakish unexplained act of grave misfortune into a murder investigation.

Mitch took the bodies away after digital pictures were taken of that portion of the crime scene. John and George would spend the next four hours documenting with pictures of everything they could see from every angle possible. Evidence was collected and bagged, including a focus on blood splatter and DNA examples. Crime scene tape was placed around the school to keep everyone out, and when darkness finally came, John and George were so exhausted that they didn't care that they had each went to bed without supper.

Robbie had been home for hours now, but all he could think about was the mountain lion. *It was huge! It was a very large animal that was found walking the hallways of my school,* Robbie thought. Robbie wondered how it got into the school in the first place; long story short, they were all very lucky. A note on the kitchen table informed him that dad would not be home tonight. He had taken some food and water to the mine and was going to maximize his time prospecting so he would have something to barter for this weekend in town. It was a good plan, Robbie thought, but it left him by himself tonight.

With dinner finished, Robbie took a few minutes to clean up the remaining mess and then sat down to do some homework. There wasn't much to do, as school today was cut short. That gave him some time to review all of the homework that was supposed to have been turned in today. *A do-over,* he thought as he laughed. Minutes later, Robbie was finished reviewing his assignments and placed everything into his book bag, preparing for bed. As he dug himself under the covers, he thought about Ruthie. She was a tough little girl, one that he enjoyed immensely. He was very happy that she didn't get eaten today. Robbie fell asleep with a large smile on his face.

CHAPTER NINE

Betty's Challenge

The shop owner drove back to her bakery after taking the kids to their houses. She couldn't remember if she had turned off the oven. Of all things, she laughed, a baker not remembering if the oven had been turned off upon leaving her own business. In her defense, she was a little rattled over the incident at the school and very concerned about the welfare of the kids involved. Pulling into one of the back parking spots that were only available for the business owners, she turned off the engine and the lights of her Jeep Cherokee. Making her way to the back door, she checked it to ensure it was locked. The shop owner pulled on the handle a few times, and when it didn't open, she walked to the front to use her key.

She didn't know why that thought had popped into her head, but she just felt that the oven was left on. The shop owner worried heavily when she turned the corner and walked behind her counter; it was unusually warm. Taking a quick look at the settings on her primary oven, she found it on and set to 450 degrees. There was a timer that was set for two minutes. She froze where she was and listened very carefully to see if someone was here. Panning left to right, she looked through her backroom for an intruder. Her eyes were coming back to the right side of the room when the oven timer beeped one time, signifying that there was one minute left.

The lady let out a piercing shriek and jumped backward away from the oven, placing a hand on the stainless steel table behind her to stop from falling over. Thinking back, she knew she hadn't used the oven recently; it had been hours since the last of the cupcakes were baked. She always baked them last because she used their cook time to clean up everything to help her close her shop on time. She was positive that she had turned it off after removing the cupcakes. Looking around, she scanned the room a second time before turning the oven off so the final timer would not sound.

She looked around and smiled and then closed her eyes a few times as if trying to clear them. The shop owner felt an all-too-familiar feeling, usually brought on by stress and sometimes outside stimuli. It was usually followed by a headache and then nausea.

"Get yourself together, Betty," she told herself as she closed her eyes a few more times.

Taking a few deep breaths, she walked over to the sink and washed her hands, looking in the mirror at herself as she did so. Turning her head to the left and right, she checked herself out. Smiling, she raised and lowered her head, examining her neckline, her cheekbones, her wrinkles.

"Not bad for several hundred years old, not bad at all," she said.

Betty did not know why she had said that or why she was cupping her breasts with wet hands. She rubbed them firmly, pressing them against each other and raising them up into more flattering positions. This she did several times while she closed her open mouth and puckered her lips a few times, blowing kisses to her mirrored self.

Several shocking pains coursed through the front of her head, making her reflexively close her eyes. When she opened them, she couldn't help to notice the handprints on her baby-blue blouse; dark blue hands covered her breasts, and they looked like they were still presently holding them in an upward raised position. Her face presently had an evil smile, and her eyebrows looked different, more pronounced, and *red?* Her hair was short cropped now and very, very red. Gone was her long, flowing blond hair. Even her complexion looked lighter, as if she were a true redhead. She didn't look like she belonged in suntan country, and if left outside, she might burn to a crisp being so white. What was going on here? She didn't know who she was looking at anymore.

She tried to raise her hands to her head to check out her hair, but they would not move. She smiled as she turned her face to the left, and then her right hand moved up to play with her curls, except she didn't tell her hand to do that. This was one of the parts that she liked—when she began to take control of an individual and they were fighting it. Most of the time, they didn't understand what was happening or they didn't know how to respond. Some have more willpower than others, but most fail very quickly and submit to her.

Betty looked on as she undressed in front of the mirror. Her eyes never left her reflection, but her hands knew exactly what to do. They unbuttoned her jeans first and then lowered the zipper forcefully in one downward motion. The jeans moved slightly down to the round of her ass in an instant and then down to her ankles with the second motion. She didn't bend her body forward for this to happen; it was apparent to her that she was having some help undressing. When she saw that thought come through, another larger smile was placed on her face and her hands went and removed her blouse. This time her hands did all of the work, and she watched on as they raised it over her short red hair and dropped it to the ground.

She blew several kisses to herself in the mirror as she rubbed her breasts. Her right hand moved lower in small circles until it focused on her nipple. Palming her right breast, she ground her hand against it and then tightened her fingers around her nipple. Squeezing it slowly several times, she made fuck faces— various expressions of pleasure, of enticement, of anger, and at times, of happiness.

Her hands again rubbed over her breasts roughly, only now with more anger. Her facial expressions were that of hate and pain as her hands moved up and down her body from her breasts to her face and back down to her breasts. She pressed firmly against her cheeks; she pulled her hair briefly, and then it was back to her breasts. More frowns and hate poses reflected back in the mirror; Betty didn't like what she saw. She began biting her lower lip now, and the first signs of blood came much after the pain had registered. Her hands now traveled up and down her body, again pulling her hair, and then when reaching her stomach, she pushed inward with great strength.

Her thumbs now were being used to push into her body, pressing deeper and deeper into her stomach. Lower and lower her hands moved, and now more smiles. The smiles would come and then go, replaced with looks of anger and more biting. Blood ran down her chin on the left side in a small trickle, making her look like a vampire. *A vampire*, she thought, *hell no, you are more powerful than that*, she heard herself say as her hands now focused on her panties. Betty pressed her thumbs downward and inward repeatedly as smiles came across her face and stayed there. Gone were her frowns, her biting, the hate; it was now all about pleasure.

She used her right hand to pleasure and her left to cause pain. Betty could not move her head or any part of her body the way she needed to. She wanted to flee, to escape, to call out for help, but she would not have it. Her hands went back to her breasts and again concentrated on mashing them up and down against her body. She took her left hand and grabbed her left thigh just below her groin and held on tightly. Her right hand turned ever slightly to allow her fingers to take over where her thumb had recently been. Slowly at first, then more rapidly, she inserted her fingers inside her. They moved as far as they were allowed to go and then slightly further when more force was applied.

More smiles visited her face between facial expressions of desire and sex. There was no pattern, and as Betty looked on, she wondered what she would see next: kisses blown to her, a frown, more biting, a smile perhaps. Betty cared less and less for this. *Just let it be done,* she thought, *kill me.*

"Oh, not for you, hon, no death for you. For you I have great plans," she heard herself say as she started moving her head up and down in sequence with her right hand.

She was close now, and as much as she didn't want to, she would soon come.

"Yes, you will, and you will not enjoy it, hon, I'm afraid it's more for me than for you, so enjoy what you can. When you awake, you will not remember any of this," she said again.

Where these thoughts came from, Betty did not know, but they did disturb her. She was hoping to awake from this dream very shortly and then she could get on with her day. Immediately following that thought, she felt the first of many explosions shoot through her body. Her left hand took it upon itself to pinch and pull and twist the meaty portion of her left thigh that it held on to; and it would not stop. All of this coupled with the orgasm she was feeling drove her crazy.

Make it stop, stop this now, what is going on. Wake up, Betty, wake up, she thought. The fucking intensified, and even as her orgasm grew, so did her pain. She kept on banging her head up and down in front of the mirror, as if was being controlled totally by something she did not understand. Her head hurt, her neck hurt, and the pain in her head grew just as fast as her feelings of pleasure did. Her left hand kept on pulling outward as far as it would go; she was sure she was bruised and bleeding by now. The first of several screams were allowed to escape her lips, all due to pleasure. The pain was less now, less than what she felt between her legs.

Over and over her right hand shot her fingers inside her. At times, there seemed to be so much force that she seemed to raise her body upward on her tiptoes and then back flat on her feet. Each time that happened, her head would be made to raise and lower with a smile on her face. More pain in her head caused her eyes again to close. When they did, she saw images of death, of pain. Betty opened them each time in an attempt to regain control, but each time a pain more powerful than the last forced her to close her eyes once again.

Dead men, women, and children captured in various poses and acts flashed through her mind. At the same time, as she closed and opened her eyes to death and reality, she was being fucked. She was still coming; she felt herself scream and moan in pleasure as her right hand showed no signs of letting up. The left hand now was cupped again over her breasts, moving from left to right at will, but not her will, someone else's will.

Betty saw a woman smile at her and then walk out across the street and be hit by a fast-moving bus. The bus took her several feet before screeching to a halt. Her body had been dragged against the asphalt, and there were exposed bone and blood on what was left of her body. This image disappeared in an instant and was replaced by more pelvic thrusting, pleasure, pain, and then another image flew into her head behind her closed eyes.

A pale white face with expressions of pain came into view. Betty didn't wait for what was going to happen next; she didn't care to see it, so she immediately opened her eyes and watched as her head moved up and down faster. She was getting dizzy; she felt as if she was going to die. She closed her eyes due to weakness and fatigue, and there was that face again. The pale white face of death cried out in silent pain. It communicated only with facial expressions of horror, agony, and pain; no words escaped its deathly gaze.

She kept her eyes closed and watched as it continued to speak to her with images. It made eye contact a few times but mostly looked upward or off to the side as it cried out in pain with its silent lips. The face started to change; it grew hair slowly, and as the process continued, it grew female features. The face became smaller, thinner, the cheekbones less pronounced. Where there was once a bald, white featureless head, there was now hair.

She continued to watch with her eyes closed as the face behind her dark eyes looked more and more like hers, with the exception of short red hair. She opened her eyes and looked in the mirror one final time. Betty gasped and drew in several long breaths as she came. The smiles and wide facial expressions that were allowed to escape her face were that of a woman who had been brought close to orgasm several times before without being allowed to release. They were soft, sensual, and happy expressions, and as the last of several small explosions radiated outward from her vagina, she leaned forward and threw up in the sink.

Through all the pain she had been forced to endure, she was allowed some pleasure. When she was being allowed to enjoy herself, she was again brought back to pain. More images of death invaded her mind as she continued to throw up. Her left hand held the edge of the sink, while her right hand turned on the cold water and then took hold of her hair. Betty could not control anything at this point; her thoughts, her limbs, her voice all were controlled by another. Her face was pushed into the sink that was quickly filling up with water and vomit.

Several times she was shoved into the sink and held there. The duration lasted from only a few seconds to a minute at times before she was to be raised up where she gasped for air. Betty never knew how much time she had to breathe in before she would be shoved back into the sink. A few times she would hit the bottom of the sink with her head, and she would be held there until it was time to raise her up again. Again Betty felt sharp pains in her head. Her whole body ached; actually, even her vagina felt roughed over.

She was getting tired of this and growing angrier by the minute. There wasn't much more that needed to be done; it was either going to be or it was not.

"Give up, bitch. I grow tired of this. You will either grant me control or you will perish. I'll string your body up on the front of this building, ass naked, and leave this community in ruin if you do not placate me. Understand that by doing this, you will forfeit your life and the lives of those around you," she heard herself say.

"So what is your decision, whore? Give in and live to fight another day, or hold strong to your beliefs, defy me, and by taking a stand for what you believe in, you assign death to yourself and those around you?" she said again.

Betty's head was pulled up again where she was allowed to stare at herself in the mirror. She gasped for air with the first of several very short, shallow breaths. She saw herself regain control, and her breathing became steady and stable. She solemnly looked forward and then turned her head slowly to the left and then more slowly to the right; it was gone. Whatever was doing this to her had left; it had been beaten.

Betty took a deep breath and thought about raising her left hand to scratch her ear. Her left hand went up slowly, shaking as it did, but it made it to her ear where she proceeded to scratch her itch. She smiled and took in a very deep breath. Relief flushed through her body, starting from her head to her toes. She became light-headed, and as soon as it happened, it was gone. Relief, she felt relief.

Smiling at the mirror one last time, she turned to walk to the front door, but she never made it. She grabbed her head and slammed it into the mirror. A thousand cracks left from the impact site and moved outward to the edges. Betty saw her lips curl into an evil, crooked smile with the one eye that was facing the mirror. Her reflection was one of horror as she saw cuts open up and start to bleed. It was made worse by her dragging her face over the broken glass and more so due to the evil smile and facial expressions that she had when she did so. She had sliced herself up pretty good, and with each pass over the mirror, she bled more.

Betty watched on as she repeatedly smashed her head into the mirror with as much strength as she still had in her. Betty's face belied her inner grief; she looked like she was happy doing it and that she was enjoying herself, but she was in pain. She lost track counting the times that she hit the mirror, so she started over. After counting to twelve, she lost it; Betty tried to cry and scream out for help, but she was once again unable to speak, and slammed again face-first into the mirror.

"I told you, one way or the other, this would end with me being in charge, didn't I?" she saw herself say.

In an accent that she wasn't familiar with, she heard, "You know, it would be an awful shame if a plate glass window was to accidentally fall on Larry, Martha, and Tom," and with a crooked smile that seemed to extend from one ear to the other, she slammed her head into the mirror one final time, and all went dark.

She saw her lifeless body slowly fall to the floor, hitting her head on the side of the sink as she went. The lady looked bruised and beaten up, not to mention the fact that she was totally naked, but she was still breathing.

"I'll catch you later," she said to her as she exited the cupcake store.

CHAPTER TEN

Jogging Will Kill You

Robbie tossed and turned for hours but could not get comfortable. Tonight was unusually hot, and that coupled with the today's events at school had left him unable to fall asleep. Each time he thought he was going to make it, he found himself turning to his left side and staring at his alarm. It usually registered one hour later than the last time he checked, and within minutes, he would start the entire process again. The third time this happened was slightly different, and within a few minutes from his last check, he had fallen asleep. He had counted upward from one until he just knocked off.

Robbie's chest rose and fell very slowly to the beat of a distant drum. She could hear it very clearly, and once introduced to a person, she would always hear it. There was some of her kind that killed because the drumbeat drove them to madness and others just for the pure enjoyment. She didn't know what category she fit into. There had to be others; it just could not be this black and white. Looking down upon him, she sent the first of several bad thoughts his direction. Robbie's eyes moved erratically; his eye brows danced and followed the direction of his pupils. The first of his bad dreams had begun, and as she continued to watch, she saw him squeeze his eyelids so tightly that you would think they were located at the bottom, immediately above his cheeks.

His hands were clenched into fists so that he could hold on to the bedsheet for protection, but he was oblivious to that. The sheets were pulled up as far as they could go, which was right up to his bottom lip. Robbie displayed white knuckles from the death grip that he held upon those sheets, making it hard to determine where the sheets ended and his hands began. She flooded his mind with bad thoughts, images, and sounds of all manner of evil. Robbie's nightmare had grown into a full-length feature film, with him being the next to go in a seemingly unending string of deaths. Her job here was done; it was time for her to attend to more pressing matters. She left as quickly as she had come, and after almost an hour, his nightmare showed no signs of letting up. Robbie would not wake up to check the time for the rest of the night. It was not because his sleep was restful; it was because he could not escape his nightmare.

Robbie was called down for breakfast with his mom's calm and comforting voice. He sat up in bed having been startled out of a deep sleep. Robbie did not feel rested, not at all, he thought, as he let out a long yawn. He lay back down, and within seconds, he again was told to get up and have breakfast. He quickly dressed and hit the stairs. Robbie was moving quickly down them when he missed the third step, hitting the fourth. His socks made him pay for not wearing any shoes; his left foot landed off center, and the forward momentum sent him spiraling down the staircase, head over heel.

Robbie saw the floor rapidly approaching and braced for impact. Placing his heels together, he slightly bent his knees and held his breath. The impact of his feet landing in unison, timed with an exhale, made for an interesting scene. Susan watched him smile and throw his arms out to his sides, raise them, and then turn to face the crowd. Robbie broke out in laughter before he could finish his bows to the audience.

"A perfect ten!" Susan yelled as she continued to applaud.

Robbie was still laughing when his mom said, "Nadia would be so proud."

"Not funny. Not funny at all," he said as he pulled up a chair for breakfast.

Susan was finishing up the last of this morning's feast when, out of the blue, she yelled out the last of the breakfast cattle calls.

"Hurry up, hon, your breakfast is getting cold. You don't want to be late for work now, do you?" She said that with a smile and turned to Robbie, pouring him a glass of milk.

Matthew came out from the bathroom totally cleaned up and smiled at Robbie as he sat down beside him. Robbie looked at his dad with the last of his milk dribbling down his chin. He smiled as he wiped off the excess milk and began to tell his dad about his crazy dream.

Matthew drank his coffee as he listened to Robbie excitedly speak about his trip to California and everything that it entailed. Robbie mentioned a plane ride, the crash, making their way to their house, going to school, and his dad mining. He also talked about a girl named Ruthie and her mom, Chloe, and some kids that he met in school.

"That's some story, son. Did you come up with all of that since you went to bed last night?" Matthew asked.

"Yeah! It kind of just came to me all at once," Robbie said excitedly.

Susan shook her head and smiled as she continued to listen to them both. The bacon was almost ready, and she focused on it, although she still listened on some level to what Robbie was saying. She plated the meat and sat down beside them for breakfast.

Robbie's eyes grew wide when he saw the mound of bacon piled up between him and his dad. He absolutely loved it; there was nothing that didn't taste better when accompanied by bacon, he thought. They continued to make small talk until the bacon was all gone. Matthew stood up and smiled.

"Thanks for breakfast. I gotta run now, almost late for work. Now, Robbie, take care on those stairs and get some shoes on, will yah?" he said.

Robbie nodded as he finished his last piece of bacon and pointed at his shoes. Matthew stood still by the door until Robbie wiped off his hands and ran his way for a hug. Smiling as he rose in the air, Robbie held on for dear life as his dad swung him around a few times before placing him back on the floor.

"Later," he told him as Matthew hit the door.

He was half out of it before Susan quietly told him to have a good day. Robbie had turned away from the front door and was walking toward the basement as the front door slammed shut. Susan turned around and started clearing the table. Robbie grabbed his book bag and then he went to the table to finish his cereal.

"Where was I?" she asked.

Between mouthfuls of milk, Robbie told her he didn't know. Robbie didn't know, not for sure. He got the feeling that she was dead in his dream, but he dared not mention that to his mom.

Robbie finished his cereal as his mom started the dishes; all the while he waited for her to ask him again. She always asked in threes, but sometimes, she did stray from her conversation.

"So not present at all? I wasn't in your dream at all then?" she asked.

Robbie didn't know what to say, so he just shrugged his shoulders. Susan smiled back and told him that it was all right.

"No worries, Robbie. The mind does strange things at times, and your imagination is very wild, son," she said, smiling.

He smiled back at her and started to get all of his things ready for school when he turned to her, looking serious.

"Mom, it was so real, in that dream I detailed over two weeks, at least. How could I make it all up?" he asked.

Again she smiled at him as she turned away to open the morning paper and began reading the local news.

"California was great, in case you were wondering," Robbie said with a smile.

Susan lowered her newspaper and looked at Robbie, returning it.

"Just saying," he said as he walked away, smiling.

"Yes, Robbie, I know it's going to be great. We've planned a vacation there in two weeks, remember?" she said.

Robbie nodded as he motioned for her to take him to school. Susan felt a few sharp pains in her chest that seemed to radiate outward from her elbow to her wrist. A sudden feeling of nausea overtook her, and she leaned to the side of her chair ever slightly.

"Looks like you are taking today off from school, Robbie. All of a sudden I don't feel so well. I think it's not safe for me to drive," Susan said with pain in her voice.

"I can't miss, Mom, I just can't," Robbie said as he ran down the hallway.

"Wait. Don't. Stop," she managed to get out, but the words were mumbled, at best, and nearly inaudible.

She could barely talk now; her headache hurt that bad. Susan never suffered from migraine headaches, and never before had she felt pain like she experienced now in her arm and her chest. Looking down, she viewed the last two pieces of bacon on her plate with malice. She couldn't let them go to waste, she thought as she reached down, grabbing them both with her left hand. Susan slowly finished them, enjoying each crunchy mouthful of bacon. With one large breath, she exhaled and gathered her strength. Standing up, she took a few steps to the living room and collapsed deep inside their large brown recliner.

Robbie was halfway to school when he realized that he had left his book bag on the corner of the kitchen table. He made a U-turn and started running back to home. It would have done no good showing up on time without his homework assignments; he would rather be late and turn them in for grading on time instead of the next day.

Susan looked through the windows that faced the street and saw people getting on with their lives. Some were exercising, some carrying cloth shopping bags as they walked to and from the local farmer's market. A woman in her jogging suit had just passed by dragging an older dog behind her. Susan looked on as the large brown dog barked several times and bolted free, almost knocking the slender woman over.

The woman who didn't need to be jogging in the first place looked down at her hand as if injured and then looked up a few seconds later, yelling for her dog.

"Abby! Abby! Get back over here!" she said, yelling loud enough to be heard by Susan through her windows.

Susan watched the woman who was breathing heavily yell a few more times and then turn her head a few random directions. It was if she had lost her dog for good but had heard him barking around a not-so-distant corner.

"Stand still, he's not coming back," she heard a woman's voice say.

Susan watched on as the woman turned around and looked again for her dog. The jogger shook it off and then turned around to leave in Abby's direction, and then she heard the woman again.

"Walk to me, yes. Hurry, I desire you," the jogger heard from behind.

Susan shook her head as once again the woman swung around backward and looked left and right. She kept watching the jogger turn her head a few more times and then stop, facing her direction. She smiled at her and walked toward her door. This puzzled Susan, and she blinked her eyes a few times, wondering if she had seen what she thought she had seen, and then the woman was gone.

Susan looked at the door as the latch moved downward and it pushed open. She was speechless when the woman stepped inside and closed the door, locking it before turning to face her.

"Hi. I'm Marge. I saw you from the street, caught you looking at me, actually," she told the lady who was sitting in the chair, holding her head.

Susan laughed and informed the woman that she was watching people as she started to feel sick, and she didn't feel like getting up to turn on the television.

"I feel the need to apologize," Susan said.

"No need, actually. I've been jogging through here for weeks and I've never seen you outside. It's nice to meet you?" Marge paused, placing her leash on the small table by the door.

"Susan. My name is Susan," she said with delay.

Susan kept her right hand placed squarely on her forehead. She found that the pressure from her trying to separate her head from her neck was enough to keep the pain at bay.

"My head hurts badly. I think something's wrong," Susan said to Marge.

"Here, let's get you to bed then," she said as she reached for Susan.

Susan's eyes grew large, and before she could tell her no, she was being pulled to her feet and slowly led toward a few closed doors.

"Don't worry, it's not what you are thinking. I promise I'll leave just as soon as you fall asleep. My house is just down the street, and I can come back to check on you if you desire," Marge said, smiling.

Susan took one laborious step after another and managed to point to the left door with her head. The pain was growing now, and her entire left side hurt. Sometimes her eyes felt the need to close; her head hurt so bad. Marge propped Susan up by the left side of the door and opened it.

"Yup, it's a bedroom. You should be able to rest here—it's plenty dark," Marge said as she maneuvered Susan through first.

Susan felt herself slipping; she was weaker now and very, very tired. The pain would not lessen, and no matter how sleepy she felt, she still felt the pain. It was unbearable now, and even closing her eyes didn't help. Susan felt herself being moved around the bed and blankets pulled up and over her, but she didn't see it; her eyes remained closed. Susan managed a "thank you" before Marge left the room.

"I'll be back to check on you later," Susan heard Marge say as her front door closed with a thud.

Marge had an evil look when she walked across the street and knocked on the closest door three times. Holding a leash without a dog would be a good conversation starter, if she needed that. The door opened, and Marge asked if the man standing in front of her had a few hours to spare. The man looked at her for some time before asking her what was wrong. A long kiss told him all he needed to know. He placed his arms around her and lifted her up, walking backward into his house. Her lips never lost contact with his, and over and over, she made her intentions clear. When she was inside enough, she kicked the door closed and let out a giggle and a loud sigh.

Robbie had just opened the front door and quietly snuck inside to get his book bag when he was startled by the slamming door across the street. He wasn't sure if he had made a noise or loudly exhaled when it had happened. Robbie stood motionless until he thought it was safe to proceed. He tiptoed over to his mom's door and placed an ear firmly against the cold wood and listened. He heard several moans and a loud gasp for air, and then all was silent. She was really sick, he thought, as he softly walked over to the kitchen table and grabbed his book bag.

Susan looked up to the ceiling after being startled out what she hoped had been a deep sleep. It took her a minute to realize that she was in bed, covered up, and resting. She was not sure what had awoken her, but her breathing was once again normal, and she settled back down and closed her eyes. Slowly the blanket began to move; from the foot of the bed, it began pressing down upon her body. Susan's eyes widened as she pointed her nose toward her feet to get a better look. She observed the blanket being tucked in against her legs, both sides of her legs.

Immediately she tried to move them, but her legs would not budge. She went to scream, but the portion of the blanket resting against her chest said otherwise. It would not allow her to take in enough air to scream. It barely allowed her to breathe at all, and if it had anything to do with it, she would never catch her breath again. Hands pressed down one leg and up the other, pushing the blanket neatly underneath the parts of Susan's body that their lifeless fingers could touch.

Susan continued to watch what she was allowed to; it seemed that her head was the only part of her that had any free will. She closed her eyes and opened them again to the feeling of cloth against her face. The right corner of her bedsheet was inching its way toward her mouth. She closed it in protest and shook her head against it, but it came closer nonetheless. Again she tried to cry out, to scream, but she managed only short whimpers. Even though small noises were allowed to escape, they were of no count. They were barely heard at the foot of the bed where she stood watching; there simply wasn't enough volume.

"Now you keep quiet, will you? This is more for me than it is for you. You would consider yourself lucky if you knew what the big picture was, I assure you. Shut up!" the voice yelled, but she was the only one who could hear it.

Robbie walked toward the door and thought he heard something, as if his mom was dreaming.

"Weird," he said as he left as quietly as he had arrived.

A short gasp of horror left Susan as she felt herself open her mouth, allowing the sheet to enter. At this point, Susan could not move her head or speak; all she could do was to blink her eyes in rapid succession to express her protest. She was no longer able to even make small noises, as they would have been easily muffled by the wad of cotton that was exploring her mouth. Susan felt weaker and weaker; and to add insult to injury, she was almost totally exhausted from struggling against the blanket that held her fast to the bed.

"This is for your own good. Relax. My goals will be achieved soon enough, and this will end," she heard a woman's voice say.

Across the street

Jack opened his eyes where there was a pause with the kissing and stared back at the woman who was staring at him.

"Yes?" he asked.

She cracked a smile and took his hand, leading him to the couch. She pointed at it a few times and motioned for him to sit.

"I'm going to rummage through your fridge. Do you have any beer?" she asked.

"There's plenty, take what you want," he replied.

She returned with a few beers and held them up in front of him.

"Be a dear, won't you, and open these up for us," she said.

He twisted off their caps and held one for her as she sat down. Smiling at him, she accepted the beer and drank it down with him. She reached past him and placed the empty on the end table, allowing her body to linger ever so slightly before returning to her own side. His mind was sent racing when she leaned back over and kissed him again. Her hands ran the length of his chest, trailing up and down from his zipper to his neck. She stood up and said she was going to use the restroom and paused for him to tell her where it was.

"First door on the left," he said.

"Nice. Can you grab a few more beers for each of us?" she asked softly as she closed the door behind her.

The man stood up and had barely taken a step toward the kitchen when he heard her tell him to select the ones on the left; the ones on the right side were not as cold.

"Yes, dear," he said, laughing inside as he walked in to get the colder beer.

He saw his reflection in the stainless steel fridge and remarked that he looked awesome. Jack sported a nice, friendly smile that sometimes confused the women that he dated. His arms and chest said, "You shall never escape. Now come closer and kiss me," but his smile said, "I can't, I'm sorry, I just can't."

In front of the mirror stood Marge, motionless; except for her blinking eyes, no movement was seen at all. She examined her flat stomach and small ass as she turned her body counterclockwise in the mirror. She stopped spinning and checked herself out again. She had short blond hair; she was athletic, probably a runner, and sported a thin body with an almost gaunt face, all tucked neatly inside a sky-blue North Carolina University jogging suit. She stared at the woman looking back at her, and everything was acceptable, all except the face.

Marge turned her head from side to side, but no facial features were visible; she was not allowed to view them. If asked about this unnatural handicap, she would simply say that there was a process that she had to follow, and that's all she would speak of. And if you *did* have that conversation with her, you probably wouldn't be alive long enough to make much use of that information. Looking at the face, she saw blurring, as if one might be protected from recognition on a television crime show.

"Baby steps, my young one" was what she was told.

"All in good time, why, you're barely nineteen . . ." she heard him say again.

And it was for that same reason that she could not control or possess men; only women were susceptible to her power. She was tasked with learning how to kill, possess, control, and seduce women. She was to do this without the use of all of her senses and powers, hence the blocking of the facial features. Her handicap was charisma, vanity if you will. You might also consider it an inherent weakness. Who, you might ask, would strive to place so much detail and emphasis into eliminating charisma from the decision-making process? Why, him himself, the Fallen One. So at present, she was to learn all of her limitations and any weaknesses that could be found, using up as many women along the way as she could. *Nineteen,* she thought, *times one hundred . . .*

She had learned to recognize the scent of an individual and the sounds that they made as they progressed throughout their lives. She felt annoyed by the constantly beating drumbeats of their hearts. Each person's heartbeat had a slightly different rhythm, and each one she meets was ingrained into her being. She's then charged with extinguishing said noise, as she would say. *Get control of yourself,* she thought. *It's time to focus on him.*

She flushed the toilet and turned around to face the door. Marge concentrated on the gentleman on the couch. She didn't even know his name; it probably wasn't necessary anyway, *but you never know,* she thought as she tried to control him. She sent the first of no less than ten suggestions and images to him, but from what she could tell, none of them were perceived. She listened closely and heard no signs of horror, terror, screaming, or running for the door. Damn.

She attempted to overpower his thought capacity, to illicit a response, and this time, she sent him images of his mom in sexual positions with two young teenagers. Another consisted of a child being hit by a train and dragged for a mile. His perspective was standing in front and slightly elevated as the train kept moving past him. Last was an old lady who tried to cross the street who found out that a large tractor trailer thought differently; none of them had any effect.

Back at Susan's

Several minutes passed, and now a good section of the bedsheet had slid over her lips and loosely sat on her moist tongue. She was unable to blink now, and with her head still facing her toes, her neck began to hurt. She had no choice but to watch as the hands that she had felt earlier moved their way up and down her legs left marks and indentations in her skin; they actually appeared to move. The hands traveled from ankle to groin at a snail's pace until they reached a knee. Then both hands grasped her skin firmly, slightly separating her thighs, and then dug in their thumbs, sliding them upward with purpose. They reached her upper inner thigh and then released their grip, only to start over again.

The stroking of her legs occurred over and over now and seemed somewhat sexual in nature. The upward movement of the invisible thumbs that stopped just shy of her pubic area had a certain sensual arousal that made her tense up. On each upward stroke, she didn't know if they would go all the way up or if they would fail her, stopping short of the destination Susan now hoped they would reach. She wanted to be pleasured—this was foreplay; she was being seduced!

Susan became more aware of the sheet in her mouth as she went along, and it was obvious to her that it too had a sexual purpose. It was getting heavier in her mouth now and resembled a wad of cloth with the mass just short of a baseball. It was moist and soggy, and it weighed more now than when it had entered her mouth; that much was for sure. The baseball that was gagging her rolled around her mouth at will. Apparently moving randomly, it would go left or right or forward or back at will. At times, Susan found it necessary to breathe through her nose as her sports-loving enthusiast demanded it.

She stared down upon Susan and tried to ignore the thoughts in her head, choosing to focus instead on the woman without a face. The woman had a nice build with lovely breasts and short, dark hair. Her will was strong. This one would offer up an incredible challenge; it had to start with her . . .

It continued to move around her mouth slowly, and often with a jerk, it slammed against the inside of her cheek. Susan was very conscious of her baseball; she paid attention to nothing else while it was rolling. She soon noticed that when it rolled in a direction, her head quickly followed. It was playing a game with her; was she being seduced by a twelve-year-old who liked baseball? Susan laughed. It had to be her mind playing tricks on her; she had to be hallucinating. Possibly a high fever. Did she need to go and cool off in the tub? Was that it? Was that what she needed?

"No, you are not dreaming. No, you don't have a fever. You are, however, very hot. I love your body, and so do others—I've seen them looking at you. They desire you. I desire you. Prepare yourself, Susan, for the fucking time of your life," a woman's soft voice said.

She watched Susan continue to struggle free from the blanket, but she made no progress. She watched her head move left and right in response to her controlling the sheet in her mouth. This amused her. She also giggled with anticipation when she thought about who was coming to visit them.

"They are almost here, hon. Soon you will know what all this leads up to and what you have lost," the voice said menacingly.

Susan tried to speak, but the baseball moved from front to back very quickly, and she began reliving her teenager headbanger days. Her hair flew over her head and back over her neck as she tried to lash out at her attacker with head butts and lacerations from her short hair.

Robbie was halfway down the street when he glanced over his shoulder and saw a woman with an empty leash walking hand in hand with his neighbor, Mr. Riole. He had never seen him so happy before. Now that he thought about it, Robbie had never seen him outside of his house; all he did was play games on his PS4. Why, if you talked to him for any duration of time, he would quickly find an opportunity to talk about his latest conquests in Fallout 4, whether you wanted him to. Robbie made eye contact with the woman whom he had never seen before and smiled as he turned his head and started to run faster. Marge smiled back at the child in front of her, never missing a step as she continued to lead the man toward where she was told to. Had Robbie looked at the couple only a few seconds longer, he would have seen them approach his front door and walk inside . . .

Susan closed her eyes and wished she was dead. She didn't understand any of this, and if what she was experiencing *was* hell, she wanted no part of it. At least if she died, she would escape this insanity and run toward the pearly gates that she hoped existed. The baseball rested against the front of her mouth, slowly moving from left to right over her tongue. It pressed down just enough to remind her that it was still present and still in charge.

"You don't need to understand!" said a woman's voice, echoing in her head.

The woman looked at Susan and began caressing her breasts. The scene looked straight out of an exorcist movie with invisible hands groping an attractive woman all wrapped up in bed sheet and blankets. Susan looked forward because she was being directed to do so and again found herself unable to blink. Her eyes stared at the door, and as the handle turned, she began opening and closing her mouth, licking wildly at the air whenever the baseball allowed her to.

Susan opened her mouth wide and let out a soft moan as the baseball slowly rolled out and fell onto the bed, landing slightly to the left of her breasts. A large cruel smile curled her lips into something no sane man would stick his member into, at least if he ever wanted to see it again. Susan was no longer in control of anything. She was being told what to do, when to do it, and how to feel.

Staring at the bedroom door without a single thought of her own, she saw a man and a woman walk in and approach. They moved to the left side of the bed, taking care not to get too close. She smiled at them, opening and closing her mouth at random. Licking wildly in their direction, she made moaning noises and blew kisses, first, to the woman and then the man. Susan's eyes were open as wide as they could be without them accidentally popping out.

She looked on and assessed the situation in front of her in great detail. Not a thought from a woman escaped her; if it was said in one's head or if it was merely being formed, she intercepted it. The only one she could not directly control was the man. That would be done through Marge's actions and her conversation with him. So she *did* control him indirectly; was that the test? Was that what she was supposed to learn? She didn't know if she would ever get the chance to possess men, but to control through another's action . . . a goal achieved is a goal achieved.

Susan was told to lie back and relax. Shortly afterward, the blanket and sheets slid off the bed and fell onto the floor over Marge's feet. Marge smiled and took his hand, motioning him over to the foot of the bed. Kiss after kiss came from Marge, assaulting his lips as she rubbed her hands over his chest. His body was moved around the foot of the bed as she saw fit.

Command after command entered Marge's head, and she obeyed them all.

"Turn him to the side. Unbutton his shirt. Kiss him harder." She said these things and more to Marge.

Susan heard her woman's voice say, "Scoot over to your left, hon," and although barely more than a whisper, she heard it as clear as day. *More voices, seriously,* she thought.

"Relax. You're going to enjoy this. You'll have no choice in the matter actually," the woman told her.

Susan closed her eyes and took in a deep breath, which she slowly exhaled before opening her eyes again. She saw Mr. Riole on top of her new friend Marge, whom she had met only today, and, man, was he giving it to her good. She didn't have a comment on the matter and continued to watch as he pulled out and positioned his body above her agape mouth. Marge smiled at him and begged him to finish in her mouth. Her smile was inviting, and he obliged her wishes by lowering himself in her direction.

Marge was told to rise up and meet him and to take control of the situation.

"Get up there and take him into your mouth. Make him smile. Give him as much head as he needs to come, but stop just short. Lead him over here, tell him to finish inside her first, and then you'll be his," the woman told Marge.

Marge smiled as she tightened her lips around him and began oral sex. The man smiled and reached a hand downward and took a handful of her hair. He held on for balance and moved her head to the side occasionally to give him a better feeling.

Moving her head to the side, she placed a hand on his cock and asked him to tell her when he was close.

"Don't make me waste it. Let me know when you're close. I want it all," she said, smiling as she squeezed him harder.

He closed his eyes and started to move forward at times without being conscious of it. He was really hard and wanted so badly to come inside her right here, right now.

"I'm close. Please don't stop," he said between sucks.

"Come with me. She's ready for you. Climb on, push inside her. She's smiling for you," Marge told him as she took hold of his penis on a downward stroke and pulled him closer.

His eyes immediately opened, and he saw his current woman leading him over to Susan. He knew who she was; she lived across the street. There wasn't a day that had gone by that he didn't see her through her windows or walking back and forth to the market. She was very attractive, and for some reason, today she wanted him really badly. Why she would wait years before expressing sexual interest was beyond him, but her facial expressions and her writhing body spoke volumes on why she wanted him now.

He placed his hands on the bed as Marge pulled him closer.

"I got this, all right? I know what to put where, and I'm on my way," he said, laughing.

Marge released his penis and left the room. He glanced over his left shoulder and watched her exit to the left, leaving the door open. He heard doors opening and closing and what sounded like kitchen chairs being pushed across a tiled floor, but he had no idea what was going on. Susan watched as she was being directed to grab her breasts and pull on them, stretching them in the man's direction and letting go, only to repeat this several more times for him. She made eye contact with him, and his face grew longer, wider. His chin, which was now at least four inches lower, started sprouting hair!

Susan watched the train wreck in front of her unfold into what could only be described as a living nightmare. He grew cheekbones, wide and tall, with chiseled edges that stretched upward to the corners of his eyes. His skin grew tight over the bones during the transformation and looked as if it would tear open. His eyes changed to a darker brown; his eyebrows grew thicker. His mouth seemed to grow wider, and his lips would make any supermodel envious due to their increasing size; they were at least three times as thick as before.

Closing her eyes, Susan felt the pain in her head return, followed by white blinding light. The shooting sensations erupted from behind her eyes and traveled backward. Every once in a while, maybe on the third or fourth sensation, she felt her shoulders jerk uncontrollably. The pain was intense and worse than before, at least before she could move and react to it in an attempt to soften the blow or even for a distraction, but the pain was more intense. She was forced to open her eyes again and witness the thing before her.

Jack looked upon her with insatiable desire, and placing his hands on her ever-shifting waist, he pulled himself toward her. She watched on as the man turned loose of Susan's waist and leaned forward, placing his hands and mouth on her breasts. Susan felt pain. Susan felt pleasure. She turned her head left and right now; she did not know why. She felt the man kneading her breasts, and then a nipple would disappear into his warm, wet mouth. It was to be assaulted by his tongue, and the suction that he applied almost hurt. All she did in response was to turn her head faster from left to right and moan quietly.

"It's OK, Susan, let out your feelings," she heard him say.

"Marge, do you have it? Did you find it?" the woman asked her.

"No, I have not found it yet, but I'm still looking," Marge said out loud.

She didn't know why she was speaking and to whom or what she was replying to, but she felt compelled to do it.

"Try the purse or briefcase. Get creative. Go and check nearby rooms. She has to have one," she said in a scathing voice.

Marge began opening everything closed and closing everything open, looking for what she was told to procure. She had no sooner laid eyes upon it than she was told to bring it to her.

"Bring it here quickly, it's almost time," the voice said excitedly.

Marge returned to the room and stopped in the doorway, staring with fascination.

"How can *that* happen?" she asked as she looked at the man holding woman in an upright position while he rested on his knees.

Susan was standing on the bed and smiling at Marge with a crazed look in her eyes. She made no effort to hide her feelings; she wanted everyone here, right now, and in the worst of ways. Susan was turned on, and as Jack directed her to place one hand in the ten o'clock position and the other on the two, she was only happy to comply. She licked her lips over and over and blew kisses toward Marge that were exaggerated to the point that Marge actually felt them when they landed on her lips.

"Film this. Start recording now. Get all of this good action. I want you to talk to her, ask her questions on how she feels, how long she has secretly loved Jack, and what her plans for the future were. When you are done finding the answers to my questions, you can join us," the voice in her head told her.

Marge pointed the tablet toward the couple and pressed record. Jack crawled on the bed and moved behind her, cupping her breasts and pulling her backward to his chest. Susan cried out for more, begging to be allowed to touch him, to touch herself. Jack would not allow her to do such things, and even if he did, Susan knew that it was only if she was allowed to do those things that she could do those things. More pain shot through her brain, her neck, her shoulders. White light followed and made it difficult for her to keep her eyes open. She wanted to cry out in pain, but all she managed to do was to keep turning her head from side to side and moan.

"Take me, Jack. Throw me down on the bed and fuck me," Susan heard herself say.

Jack slid his left hand over her soft white skin and placed it on her shoulder. With his right hand, he squeezed her breast and held it as he pushed her onto the bed. He followed her forward, and when he was pressing down on top of her, he took both hands and began rubbing her back. Susan didn't know what to think of this; real human hands were massaging her now, not the fake ones from before. Fingers ran over her spine from top to bottom and then back up again. She looked forward and breathed through her nose several times before his palms joined Jack's attempt to pleasure her.

Marge continued taping this lovemaking session. She grew more and more envious by the minute. Looking at the small screen, she would zoom in for a close up when she thought it was a good time to do so. She moved around the bed for a better angle as needed, paying attention to keep her subjects in the center of the screen. Moving around the foot of the bed from left to right, she changed her recording angles as she prepared for her commentary.

"How do you feel, Susan?" Marge asked.

Susan responded with cries of pain as Jack pushed up inside her. Jack was more forceful now, and he had moved one hand to the back of her head, keeping it pressed down into the pillow while the other pushed on the small of her back. This he did as he continued to slide into her asshole. He had never done that before, and with such a willing woman under his body right now, there was no better time than the present, he thought.

"How long have you known that you were in love with Jack?" Marge asked her.

More cries offered themselves up in response to Marge's latest question. Susan threw her hands backward and grabbed her ass, separating her thong tanned backside as wide as she could. She did this because she was told to. Numerous thoughts and instructions invaded her head, and she followed each one of them because she had to.

"More, harder, deeper. Make me hurt, Jack. I never hurt, I need. I need to. I need to hurt," she said between his thrusting.

Jack closed his left hand and gathered up what hair he could before he pulled her toward him. Susan's body was arched backward, and the pain that soon followed rivaled the pain that was still flowing through her head. More white light preceded longer, deeper shooting pains. Her arms now hurt, and even the top portion of her back hurt from the pain that originated from behind her eyes. It wasn't so much that she was being held down by him sitting on the small of her back, having her head pulled back to his chest; it was the pain from her head.

Susan looked passionately at Jack and smiled as he continued to pound her up the ass. He marveled at how hard he was. It seemed only minutes ago he had been ready to come, close to releasing his load into the lovely mouth of a wandering stranger, and look at him now. Jack felt more of a man now than he had ever been before. He was handling Susan as a lover and taking what he wanted from her, without regret. Susan felt every inch of Jack, and as she relaxed against his thrusting, she started to enjoy him.

Jack moved her forward again and leaned back down on top of her, pressing her back into the pillow and leaving her searching for air. Susan tried to speak, but her attempted words came out muffled. It was so hard for her to breathe. She looked on as Jack held Susan's face into the pillow and continued to fuck her. Marge could take no more of this; she wanted in. Actually, she wanted him in, inside of her and not that Susan bitch. She placed the tablet down at an angle, ensuring that it would record them all and walked over to the head of the bed.

She watched as Marge approached Susan and motioned for Jack to let her go. Jack smiled and nodded, letting go of Susan's hair. Susan gasped for air, raising her head just enough to turn it sideways before it was grabbed by Marge. She took hold of Susan's cheeks and reached down to kiss her. This she did several times, and when Susan's initial shock subsided and she returned her kisses, Marge slid herself between the wall and Susan's mouth and lowered it to her pussy.

"Now eat me out, now, or I'll let Jack attempt to break your neck again, bitch," Marge said angrily.

Susan felt shocked, angry thoughts filling her head. Her feelings went from betrayal to pain in a matter of seconds as she was reminded once again that she was still being fucked from behind. The white behind her eyes was so bright now that even closing them would offer nothing toward its reduction. Her hands gripped the fitted bedsheet and held on tightly, which did nothing except keep her still so Jack could fuck her harder.

Susan felt her lips moving up and down, opening and closing again, with wild, erratic and sometimes bizarre tongue movements, all the while staring directly into Marge's little fuzzy bunny. Marge reached her hands down to help Susan do what she needed to, giving her guidance as necessary. Susan was not allowed to blink anymore and stared openly into the woman's groin. Marge moved her body in a rhythm that Susan had never experienced firsthand, and as she pressed her mouth deeper and deeper into the woman's body, she finally felt where she needed to be. Marge felt Susan's tongue enter and lick her repeatedly. She would do it three times and then suck hard on whatever she could take into her mouth.

"Now this is getting good, Susan. Keep it up," Marge told her.

Susan had not a free thought or action available to her. She would keep it up; she would do as instructed until she was allowed to do something else. Jack announced that he was coming, and taking both hands, he placed them on Susan's waist, pulling her backward and away from Marge. He turned her over and slid up higher, placing his penis in front of Susan's crazed face. Jack slapped it on her lips two times before she opened wide enough to take him. Marge looked on as Susan formed a tight seal around his penis and began to suck him dry.

Jack smiled wide as he began to finish inside Susan's mouth. *No need to make a baby at this point*, he laughed in his head. *I want a mother for my child, not a porn star.* If she could have heard that, she would have loved it. She could only imagine what went on inside a man's mind; only time would tell if she would ever understand men. Marge stood up and placed both feet on the floor as Jack smiled on, making eye contact. Marge mouthed the words "you belong to me" as she walked seductively out of the room. Jack turned to watch her again disappear to the left and then he heard her bound up the stairs. He was distracted by Susan's beast-like noises that she would make each time she ran her mouth over the length of his penis.

Jack began to explode into her mouth, and with each pulse, he marveled in what a true orgasm felt like. He had never been this crazy with a woman before, and if this was how things were to be around here from now on, he might even grow to truly love—Jack could not finish that last thought. He looked down and saw the working end of a very large butcher knife slice through his left side, just below the ribs. The skin separated and then fell back together, seemingly resealing what had just been opened. He felt no pain; the only thing he did feel was the last of him being taken by his soon-to-be wife.

Looking away from Susan's smiling mouth, he examined the left side of his body for damage. Marge stood off to the side of him now, holding the bloody knife. He looked away and back down to Susan where she had just released his penis and was licking the bottom of it while she sucked on his balls. She looked at the trio and sent thoughts to all of them in turn. Marge was told to take a step back and guard the door with her knife. Susan, now Susan was told to suck both balls into her mouth and hold him steady, using as many teeth as she needed to prove her point. Jack was told nothing, or nothing that she thought made it in. She tried to tell him to tell Marge that it was going to be OK and that she should run for her life, just in case, but Jack said nothing.

Jack watched his surroundings more closely now and was taken with horror as his balls disappeared into the smiling mouth of the woman he had just finished fucking. She was humming. She was humming, he thought. His balls vibrated, and that made the pain seem almost bearable, almost.

"What the fuck are you doing? Let them go!" he shouted as he kept one eye on Marge, who was still brandishing her knife like an assassin.

Looking down again, he saw the blood start to move slowly from the inside of his wound. Upon closer inspection, the skin was sliced open in a very long and apparently deep wound. The blood was very dark and flowed more quickly now than before. He had seen this when he cut his finger one day, something about a very sharp knife and the way it cut through the skin. It took several seconds before the pain registered, and the bleeding began to clean the wound.

Susan was still humming as Jack began to bleed. She let go of his balls and took his hold of his penis. Looking away from his wound, she told him to look at her and concentrate, to look at her eyes.

"It's OK, Jack. Look at me. Jack, look at me," Susan said with compassion as he turned his gaze back to his bloody side.

Jack turned to look at Susan again and felt noticeably weaker. The pain that he was feeling in his side hurt badly, and anything he did, even the slightest of movements, caused excruciating pain along with additional blood flow. Marge looked at him with a cruel gaze, moving her eyes down to the cut and up again to his face. Smiling, she mouthed the words "I told you," swinging her knife a few times in front of her to ward off any retribution.

He never saw those words; he looked away and sat down on the bed, continuing to bleed. Jack knew he would receive no medical attention here, nor would he be taken to the hospital; he was dying.

"Fuck all of you," he said as he began crying.

"What kind of fucked-up game is this anyway?" he managed to get out between sobs.

Susan was allowed to comfort him but only briefly before Marge jumped on the bed and stabbed him a second time. The knife plunged deeply into his left side, slightly higher than the last time and became lodged between two ribs. Marge tried once to pull it out and then let go of it before Jack backhanded her and sent her flying toward the door. Marge landed on her left cheek of her ass and then fell over on her side. Susan backed away and stood up, moving to the opposite wall.

She told Marge to go to the nearby bathroom and sit on the toilet. Susan looked at Jack as he continued to bleed out, knowing soon he would be dead. She closed her eyes, sat down on the floor against the wall, and began to cry. *Susan was in control, fuck,* she thought, *she was in control.* She kept her mind clear as possible and slowly stood, crying incessantly. She took a few steps to the foot of the bed and placed a hand on it for balance. Susan tried not to look at Jack's body, which was off to the side motionless and no longer bleeding. The area around it was bloody, sure, but it no longer was being pumped out onto the surrounding area; he was cold dead.

A few deep breaths came and went as Susan tried to regain her composure. She took the next few baby steps to reach the bedroom door when she started wondering where Marge was. Susan had heard her leave this bedroom countless times now, and each time she would return, each time except this one. What direction should she pick? Which way might Marge have gone? Was she still present, or had she left as mysteriously as she had introduced herself to her this morning? Her breaths were normal now, and all that she found herself doing was listening for any noise that would betray Marge's position.

Marge smiled at the mirror and only wondered what her face really looked like. She hoped it was as beautiful, as perfect as the rest of her; she knew one day she would find out.

"Ready, hon?" Marge said loudly enough for Susan to hear.

The left, she was to the left, Susan thought as she bolted out of the right side of the bedroom and headed to the front door. Susan cried the entire time she ran, and as her hand reached out for the door handle, her vision blurred. White pain shot throughout her mind, her head, her shoulders; it was crippling, and in an effort to shelter herself from the pain, she closed her eyes. It was more of a reflex, an involuntary reaction to a shock, to sharp pain.

The front door disappeared from Susan, and it was not to return. She watched as Susan doubled over in pain and held her head parallel to the floor. A few seconds more, she would see her fall over to her side, initially landing on her ass before crawling into a small ball and turning over to her right. Susan wanted to escape, to crawl away, but she was not allowed to. Crippling pain kept her right where she was, and although she could tell that

Marge walked slow circles around her, she could not focus on anything that wasn't pain related. On Marge's third revolution, she smiled and walked off to the bedroom.

"Come to me, Susan. Walk this way, hon," Marge said.

Marge was totally hers now. She no longer put up a fight; she had never really done so. Raising her hands slowly, she rubbed them over her face, pressing down on her cheeks and sliding her hands upward. Taking her fingers, she ran them through her hair. All this was done because she asked, not because Marge wanted her to. There was no conflict, only a series of simple instructions being followed without question. This was one of the things she enjoyed the most—possession.

Looking on, she saw Susan start to go to one knee and then stand. Susan took one laborious step after another and mechanically walked into the bedroom, although she was still riddled with pain. It showed on the woman as a whole; it was evident with every slow, unbalanced footfall. Now if she was having her smile or walk quicker, those things would go unnoticed; she would pay more attention to this later. It was one thing to control an individual, but another to possess one completely. No one can walk around like that and not attract attention, unless you're in a zombie movie, she thought.

Marge stood in the doorway as Susan passed her by without a glance. She walked to the front of the bed, neatly stepping around Jack's body, and got comfy. Marge smiled at her and took the bedsheet from the floor and slid it upward to Susan's knees.

"Don't want you getting cold now, do we?" she asked her.

Susan smiled and started rubbing her flat stomach from top to bottom. She was told to go as high as her breasts and as low as her knees, just above the sheet.

"Smile for me when you caress your body. I like it when you are happy," Marge said.

Susan smiled and continued to caress, as directed, paying particular attention to her breasts. Marge sat on the foot of the bed and crawled on top of her. Susan found it harder to follow her instructions. It pained her when she could not reach her knees. Marge waited for her response, and there it was.

"Can you move a little to the side? I can't reach my knee." Susan asked.

She watched on and concentrated on learning the full extent of her power. One thing she had never tried before, in all the time she had been doing this was to illicit raw emotion, to insert feelings. She wasn't sure she knew how to do that. Looking at Marge, she told her to scratch her left arm; it's itching. Marge followed that simple instruction.

She knew she could get her to react to an implanted image, such as a mosquito buzzing around her face and landing on her arm. Marge squashed it, sending imaginary blood through the air and leaving a briefly visible handprint. *Nice,* she thought. Now she decided to concentrate on Marge's other arm and thought about it being on fire. She saw a small flame appear just above her wrist and spread upward to her elbow. The flames were blue at first before turning bright orange. Marge burst into expletives and ran out of the room in a panic. She heard the water come on as Marge attempted to put out her arm, all the while screaming.

She quickly made her feel happy and implanted several images of her and Susan on the bed, and all was right with the world. Marge walked in and took up the same position, at the foot of the bed. Again she directed Marge to move upward toward the head of bed, but this time she had her cuddle into the left side of Susan. She watched on as Marge separated Susan's legs by rubbing them with her hands. She pushed them apart gently until there was room for her head to fit comfortably inside.

Susan didn't mind, not at all. In fact, she smiled more when she was being rubbed than when she wasn't. *Weird,* she thought, *can't explain that one.* This was all new to her; she wasn't sure exactly what the results would be from her stimuli, but she recorded them as best she could. Her goal after all was to learn her powers and weaknesses, and that she had done today with flying colors. Marge slid on top of Susan and positioned herself in the middle between her legs. She used her thumbs to part her lips, and spreading them wide, she pressed inward with her chin. Susan felt pressure and, at first, unwanted attention. It seemed to frustrate her because she no longer reached her knees the way she had done so before.

Marge made several upward movements, each one more forceful than the last, before she lowered her head to place her lips on hers. Susan followed new instructions now, her body moved slightly from left to right, and she placed her hands on her head and played with her hair. She watched on as Marge went to town on Susan as she played with her hair and giggled. She looked over at the tablet, and it was still recording the action in the bedroom, just as she wanted.

"More tongue, longer and deeper. You want this woman to love you, don't you, Marge?" Marge heard as she used her head to push further into Susan's groin.

"Your breasts, Susan, play with your breasts. Show Marge what she's missing. Make her look at you. Let her hear your acceptance," Susan heard the woman say.

She watched as Susan ran her hands down to her breasts, squeezing them larger, and asked Marge to play with them. Marge looked up and began to trail kisses upward to honor Susan's request. When she arrived at Susan's left breast, she gave her tongue a new mission and began kissing her all over. Two fingers felt for Susan's thigh and trailed down to where she had been only minutes ago. Susan felt her new friend making small circles and occasionally tease with "just the tip"; it was driving her mad.

Marge slid further up and began kissing Susan passionately. She moved her hands to Susan's breasts and even used her knee to provide pressure and some physical contact down below. She looked at the two women on the bed and decided that everything was heating up very nicely; it was time for Jack to pay a visit. Susan's mind was full of thoughts of desire, lust, and pleasure. Gone were the images of death and despair. The white lights and the shooting pains that filled her head were no longer present. They had been replaced with simple commands to move the body in response to her lover and for her to smile and giggle. All she concentrated on were the kisses and the attention from Marge. Susan felt herself close to coming now; and as much as she wanted something inside her, she was being fulfilled without that penis thing that most men say they have.

Susan felt Marge moving closer yet to her face. She was now straddling her head with her thighs and pushing herself toward Susan's mouth. Susan was told to put up a fight and not to kiss or return Marge's attention. She looked at the women and awaited the squabble that was surely to ensue. Marge was furious over the fact that Susan would not return her affection, so much so that she sat on her chest and held her arms at her side.

"What the fuck is wrong with you? All I do is give, and you offer nothing in return," Marge said as she took hold of Susan.

Susan was allowed to be Susan now, and she immediately took advantage of the situation and began to fight to free herself. She remembered Jack being killed by this woman; she remembered all the blood and that his body was still lying on the ground. She had to escape this madness. Time was running out for her, she was sure of it.

Marge slid further up Susan's body and tightened her knees around her head. Susan had begun bucking and used her legs to further aid in throwing that woman off of her. Marge leaned in with all of her weight and gathered Susan's hands, placing them above her head. She then held them in place as she used her free hand to slap Susan. Marge slapped her no less than thirteen times, alternating between the front and back of her hand—Susan counted each one; they all hurt equally.

Just as Susan began making progress, just when hope showed her a way out, it was taken from her. White lights and the accompanying pain took over, forcing her to close her eyes so hard that they hurt. There was nothing to distract her from the pain, not now, and she experienced the all-too-familiar discomfort in her neck, her shoulders, and her back. Marge had taken to pulling her hair and shaking her head, all while yelling insults that Susan really could not hear. Susan knew the drill; soon she would be unable to move again and the pain would be pushed out of her head with images of this or that. Then she would find herself in another sexual situation, all coming short of her, well, coming. It was almost enough to make her laugh, if she was allowed to.

"No, what I have in store for you is not the usual. I'm afraid this is much worse. I've found a way for Jack to come and visit you, and this time you will experience all of him," the voice said in a sadistic tone, and just like that, her pain was gone.

Marge was told to stop slapping her but to keep the pressure on her head.

"Stay on the head," the voice said to her.

Marge kept hold of Susan's hands and from time to time shook her, but she no longer caused her any physical harm. Susan opened her eyes and looked Marge in the face. She dare not anger her further, not at least until she's regained a bit of her strength. Susan tried to look away, and just as she thought, she wasn't allowed to move or speak. In fact, the only thing she could do was blink her eyes. When told to, she raised her head up and slightly to the left so she could see the floor. Looking down at Jack's body, she was reminded that this evil thing on her had killed him. She was probably next and she didn't want to be next. Susan still did not understand why at times she could not control herself or why at that time she never cared.

Marge smiled as she bounced on Susan's chest a few times and then let go of her hands. She pushed herself backward and was now sitting on her stomach when she turned her attention to Susan's breasts. Susan still could not move, but she continued to watch Jack's body because she was told to. Marge bounced a few times more, and although all the air did not leave her lungs, she did feel pain. Susan also had trouble breathing in as much oxygen as she wanted to; her lungs would never fill up all the way. It was as if she was held by a large snake that was squeezing her harder and harder.

Susan stared on as Jack's body began to move. She was not allowed to express emotion; she didn't allow it. Susan knew what she was feeling when a pain in her gut hit her so hard that she screamed only inside. Susan could not express her feelings of horror as Jack's body rose and smiled at her. He had a solemn look on his face and never looked away from her eyes. Susan was not allowed to turn away or recoil. She stayed put with her head raised and slightly angled to the left and continued to stare at him.

Jack took his left hand and placed it on his waist just above his cut. His right went lower and then pinched the skin around his fingers with both hands, separating his wound. Jack's insides looked the part of a steak, very pink and with the marbling one might expect to see in fine meat. Jack's marbling, however, was exposed cartilage and bone. Susan felt nausea overtaking her, but she couldn't do anything about it if it occurred. Jack smiled and let go of his wound and turned to climb up on the bed. Marge continued playing with her breasts and was totally unaware that he had stood up, let alone that he had just exposed his wound to Susan. She did feel the bed move, but Marge was told only to focus on Susan's breasts and not to cause her any injury in the process.

Susan was stuck in her current position, stuck there until she was told to do otherwise. She could no longer blink. It appeared that she was allowed to breathe, although somewhat restricted, but she could breathe. If she had control of any part of her facial expressions, she would have blinked a few times in shock as a pair of deathly cold hands placed themselves inside her thighs at knee level and spread her wide. Jack kept his hands there, letting his cold permeate Susan to her core. Susan wanted to escape. In her thoughts, she saw herself sliding off the bed and running out the front door, seeking help from anyone she could find.

This was not to happen, and as she thought about what her options were, her mind again filled with images of hate, of horror. She saw herself from up above, hovering slightly to the left of the head of the bed about four feet above them. Jack was there, and he looked as dead as ever, and boy was he giving it to her. She heard herself announce that she was coming and that she loved him. She shouted his name a few times as her hands grabbed as much bedsheet as they could. Susan saw herself coming, and her looks of joy and passion filled her with hope, with envy, with love.

Jack was slowing down now and reached up to caress her body, telling her how beautiful she was as he rubbed her thigh. Right at that moment, Marge ran over to him and knifed him, slicing him deeply along his back side. She then set her sights on Susan, and as she turned to her right to escape, she too was slashed from behind; a stinging and burning sensation struck her from her shoulder to her ass. Marge stood over Susan as she fell onto the floor, screaming.

That image was immediately followed by a large parking lot full of cars. A woman in uniform was trying to break into a car that was left in the sweltering sun. A small crowd had gathered, and try as she might, the glass would not break. She drew her weapon and fired a single shot into the front seat driver side window, shattering it into a million pieces of safety glass. The crowd cheered as she turned to face them and smiled. There was a man who was standing to her left who hit her in the face and grabbed her gun when she fell over from the blow. Everyone dispersed as the shooter began firing at those closest to him. He then turned to the woman in the front seat, who was Susan, and then blew his head clean off. Blood and pieces of skull came at her, coating every inch of hair and face with cerebral material.

Image after image flooded her mind. Her eyes were forced to stay open as cold hands were now working their way upward to her breasts. Jack made his intentions known as he slid up as close as he could and started to probe her with his penis. It wasn't' long before another image shot into her mind's eye, followed by the penetration from a large cold dead penis. Marge moved off of the bed as instructed, so Susan could see Jack as clearly as she was allowed to. Marge thought it odd that Susan still remained leaning over to one side, her head slightly raised as Jack was making love to her, but who was she to judge?

She watched her canvas mature as if painted from demons themselves. Unnatural expressions of lust were demonstrated in sound and by action, and whether forced to or not, everyone was having a good time. She released Susan to her faculties as she saw fit. She could now feel emotion, think for herself, feel pain, horror, everything, but she could still not move her body. The only part of her body Susan had control of was her head. This allowed for the canvas to portray fear, regret, pain, and hate like no one has ever done before. Susan tried to close her eyes, and they worked! She closed them, and since there was nothing she could do with the corpse that was fucking her like there was no tomorrow, she chose to think happy thoughts.

It was only a few seconds later that Susan had once again opened her eyes to address her rapist. He was calling her name. Every few seconds he called her by her baptized name, her Christian name.

"How the—" she spoke, Susan thought.

"How the fuck do you know that?" Susan finished.

"Susan Margaret Tackert!" Jack said in a very soft and eerie way as he continued to thrill and excite his neighbor.

Each time he entered her, he spoke one of those three names, in order. He never left eye contact as he fucked her with his dead man's penis at a dead man's pace.

Marge was masturbating before she knew it, and since she wasn't told to do that, she made sure Marge knew that there were other things that needed to be done, more important things. Marge grabbed a hold of her left lip and stretched it painfully out to one side and then the other a few times before letting go.

"OK, all right, I get it. What do you want now?" she asked.

Marge stood up and sat on the bed beside Susan, who was still looking to the floor at the same angle as she had been earlier. She placed her hands under Susan's shoulders and raised her up enough for her to slide underneath. Leaning forward, Marge placed Susan in a headlock with Susan's chin in her elbow. She took one hand and grabbed the other, applying great pressure to the sides of Susan's neck. Marge dug her chin into the back of Susan's neck and held it there as she continued to separate Susan's head from her body.

It was now Jack's turn to lean forward. He placed his hands on her hips, giving her all he had. He slammed himself into her much faster now, and although he called her name very slowly, he fucked with passion. Susan felt him deeper now; she didn't' care to know why she knew this, but he was larger than her husband, whom she had given up on ever seeing again. This was it, Susan thought, this was the end. Whatever was happening here, which she wasn't exactly sure what *that* was, was wrong; it was just wrong. She did not understand; she just wished it would end.

"It will end, hon, everything will end—everything you care about, that is. You'll be thinking of this day for the rest of your life, you know. Will we ever meet? Probably not," she heard the all-too-familiar voice say to her.

Marge continued to hold on to Susan with her death grip while she was being fucked harder than she had ever been before. To make that scene even scarier, it was being done with a dead man's penis. Throughout the entire time, she could not move her body; she experienced narrative commentary from someone or something she had never met before. And this was done all in the comfort of her house. Susan prepared to ask Marge to let her go when she started coming. Susan expressed her frustration, her lust, her pain and joy, all with one long inarticulate word: holyshitfuckjesusfuckshit.

Susan became light-headed, and her eyes started to close. Jack was continuing to fuck her as he still needed to come. She watched on with amusement as she threw the last images into Susan's head. Susan looked through fading eyes into darkness. In the distance, a white object approached. *So this is death–this is it,* she thought. The white object came closer still and started to resemble a disembodied face. It was pale, long, and gaunt, and it displayed expressions of eternal damnation. Its face contorted every way imaginable, and although it never spoke, Susan felt its pain. The face hovered in front of her suspended in utter blackness for another second and then it was gone.

Susan had lost consciousness, but her body never went limp; she was still in the exact position she had been for the last hour and a half. Marge let go of Susan and slid out from beneath her. Smiling, she looked at Jack, who was still pumping away at his comatose partner.

"Run, hon, you need to run—now. He wishes to repay a favor," Marge heard in her head.

Marge looked over at Jack and cautiously walked toward the bedroom door, making sure to stay just out of his reach. He continued to make eye contact with her until he lost interest in Susan and suddenly had an urge for Marge. With a very large and crooked smile, Jack slowly turned to her and started after her. Marge broke into a frantic run and hit the front door several times in frustration when it would not open. She turned the dead bolt back and forth and tried again after she knew it was unlocked, but it would not budge. Jack was walking slowly toward her; his every step shook the skin around his wound. This made an audible suction noise every time the skin moved back into its original position, but it no longer produced any blood.

Marge screamed. She bolted for the nearest window, and when she arrived, she grabbed a nearby picture frame. She reared back to gather enough force to strike the window and then she felt his icy-cold hands press around her stomach and hold her tight. The picture fell to the floor as Jack began squeezing the life out of her. He had raised her about a foot off the floor, and try as she may, Marge could no longer scream. She attempted to kick the man holding her, and when she didn't make contact, she began shaking as violently as she could so he would drop her. She even tried to use the back of her head to hit him, to have her chance at freedom, but his grip was that of death. He didn't feel fatigue; he wasn't tired, he just was.

She watched the two in the living room as Jack took several slow steps back toward the bedroom, taking Marge with him. She was hoisted even higher and presented to the one he could not see as an offering or a trophy of sorts. He lowered her enough to get her inside the bedroom and raised her again as they stepped inside. Jack looked on the bed at the woman who was not moving; she was exactly as he had left her. He examined her breasts, her hips, the slight arch of her back; all of her was perfect. Looking down to where he had recently been, Susan displayed the fruits of her orgasm.

Marge looked at the man holding her and smiled.

"One last time, huh, for old time's sake? You'll find me more interesting than her, I assure you," she said with laughter.

"Put me down now and then sit on the head of the bed next to Susan," she said with a stern voice.

Jack looked confused. He had not been given instructions like this before, not verbally. They had always been as thoughts inside his head. She watched Jack place Marge on the floor and then walk to the head of the bed to take his place beside his partner.

"Nice. Now stroke her forehead and play with her hair. Pull it, gently, and let it go," she said to him.

Jack obeyed and slid a little further down on the bed to grab the ends of Susan's hair. He gently pulled her hair and curled it between his fingers several times before letting go and sliding his hand again over her face. Marge let out a sigh of relief and took a backward step to the door. Jack lunged at her and managed to close his right hand around her ankle. He pulled his arm back to his chest, sending Marge falling headfirst in the direction of a small table that hugged the right side of the bedroom door.

She threw out her hands, but she still hit the edge of the table, softening the blow that would have surely killed her. Two of the three thin wooden legs broke in half in response to her fall, sending the contents of the wooden table down on top of her. In slow motion, she saw a glass of water, an ash tray, and the

knife that Marge had used earlier coming her way. She landed
on her right side, which resulted in a pain that shot through her
left ankle. Although she did a stellar job of reducing the damage
she could have taken from the fall, Marge could not protect her
head from following through and introducing itself to the floor.

The impact dazed Marge enough to leave her moaning on
the floor for several minutes before she regained her senses.
Her vision was the first to respond and about four feet away
gazing back at her was Jack. He held his eternal stare of death in
her direction as if peering into her very soul. Marge felt sickened
and tried to turn away from him, but she lingered to take in his
death. His death, she thought. He's been dead this entire time,
lying there in the same position that he was in when she had
sliced him with that knife.

Moving her head closer to the floor, she squinted and then
looked down the length of her body again at Jack. She wasn't
herself when that happened; she was in a jealous rage, or that's
what she thought at the time anyway. Looking around, she saw
the left side of Susan's body angled toward them, with her head
still tilted so she could observe her dead lover. She wondered if
Susan knew that she would be looking at them both as they lie
dead on the floor.

Marge crunched her eyebrows in a puzzling gesture as her
eyes moved left and right, thinking about that last thought. She
wasn't sure that it was hers, and if it was, why would she think
"as they both lie dead on the floor"? She had regained the use
of her limbs, and her head no longer worried her. It hurt, sure,
but the pain was not that intense. She drew in another breath
before sitting up. Marge turned her body to the left to place her
back flat on the floor so she could pull her feet in and stand up.

Searing pain ripped through the Marge's left calf, causing
her to scream out in agony. At least she was allowed to scream,
she thought as she tried to understand her pain. Looking at her
leg, she saw that when she had moved it to her, she pressed her
left calf against the sharp edge of the blade.

Marge was left with the knife sticking in her leg as if it had been placed there during a downward movement. The pain confused her. She was bleeding heavily now, and when she looked at her leg to decide what to do, she marveled that the knife looked as if it had been buried into her calf. In all actuality, it had sliced through her muscle and the skin had closed around it, giving the illusion that it had been a stabbing instead of a slicing wound.

She saw Marge begin to crawl away from Jack. The knife was not picked up or removed; she just pulled her leg away from it.

"Fuck, that hurts, you whore. Whoever you are, fuck you!" Marge said loudly.

"Stop bitching and stand up—you are fine," she told her.

Marge angrily looked around the room and prepared her next sentence in her head, choosing very carefully the best of the colorful expletives that she could throw together and still get her point across. Looking down at her leg one more time, it looked normal. The pain in her leg was gone, her head felt wonderful, and her ass that had initially taken the blunt of the falling damage felt fine. The floor held no blood, and even Jack's body was missing from the doorway.

She scanned the bedroom for Susan, and there she was, lying on the bed on her back. She was covered up to her chin with a warm blanket. Susan's chest slowly rose and fell as she soundly slept. Turning around to finish the last of her 360-degree turn, Marge saw Jack standing in the doorway, smiling back at her as usual. Marge let out a bloodcurdling scream and jumped back a step.

"Well, are we going to do this thing or not? I'm can't stand here forever," Jack said.

"No, I can't believe this. You were dead—I killed you," Marge said excitedly.

"I'm not sure that you could kill me, I'm pretty strong you know," he said to her.

Marge was alert now and she trusted no one. She believed nothing she saw and she barely put faith in anything she thought or said. Jack smiled at her and threw up his hands in a "let's get going" gesture, tilting his head to the right and waited for a response.

"Why are you still hear? I told you I was fine. There's really no need to check up on me any further. I'm going to be fine," Susan told her as she fought with her blanket.

Marge thought herself crazy, and at this point, she was willing to give up. Maybe she just needed some sleep. She still didn't understand how she was capable of taking a human life anyway. Susan smiled at her and turned on her left side, pulling the covers to her chin and off of her feet. Marge looked down at the bed as she turned around to take Jack back home. Pulling up the covers had exposed Susan's bruised ankles. It took a second or two for that to register, and when Marge finally thought about it, she knew she was still in her nightmare.

Jack took a handful of her Marge's hair and pulled her toward him. Marge had no choice but to follow. She had no leverage, and her head was going to be pulled clean off if she didn't move closer, so she obliged him. He stepped to her and placed his cold dead hand below her neck and pressed her against the wall on the right side of the door. Marge was looking down when he told her to look at him.

"Look at me," he said calmly.

Marge did nothing to show fear, she didn't have to. Her breathing was irregular, short, and shallow, which only made her more attractive to him. Her breasts went out of their way to call attention to her body.

"Look at me!" he yelled as he pressed harder on her chest.

She threw him an upward glance, and there he was, the man of her dreams. Jack looked even younger than he had before; his chin was tighter, his cheekbones were higher, and he was thinner overall. He wore an eternal smile, as always, Marge thought, the way he did when he was alive or dead. Alive or dead struck a chord with her—was she still dreaming?

Jack moved against her and placed his feet between hers. Smiling, he positioned her hands above her head and held them in his left fist. Marge felt her spine extend as the weight of her body stretched her out. Her wrists felt as if they were separating from her arms, mainly from his grip and the weight of her suspended body. His right hand caressed her head, her neck, and moved down to her breasts. Those he kneaded for a good several minutes while he kissed her hard. Taking what he wanted was never Jack's way, but he was kind of enjoying the step-by-step instructions provided today. Spreading his feet outward, he spread her legs and then pressed in further until he was once again searching for a temporary home for his penis.

Marge found herself trying to escape his hold and remove her body from the wall. Only her stomach and thighs were allowed to respond to her request; the rest was held in place by Jack. She participated as much as she could, and before long, she had forgotten entirely about her nightmare. This was different, she thought, this was love. Closing her eyes, she returned each one of his kisses. Marge timed her escape to maximize the attempts by Jack to hammer his penis through her into the wall. He wasn't hurting her; he just demanded all of her, right here and now.

Jack kissed her softly and took an ear into his mouth. He sucked it a few times and then lowered her hands as he held his teeth on her lobe. He bit down, and taking her hands lower, he placed them behind her back. He placed both of his hands there, keeping hers pinned against the small of her back as he pushed her toward him. That was an incredible angle for her, and it was all that was necessary for Marge to attempt to drown his penis in cum.

A large exhalation of air preceded several grunts from his woman, telling Jack he was treating her right. More kisses came her way, and if she didn't know better, she thought he was trying to stop her from breathing. His mouth never left hers, muffling her moans of pleasure. He was breathing heavy in her direction, which she had no choice but to inhale what oxygen she could, used or not. Marge could not turn her head enough to replace what she had earlier grunted away, so, yes, he was trying to kill her.

Her eyes opened and gazed upon Jack's lifeless body. Her body grew colder, and with him still pressing her onto the wall, she once again found herself unable to escape his grasp. It wasn't hard for her to understand her current situation was dire. She was coming, his penis was still pounding away, her head was pressed hard against the wall, and she was having trouble breathing. Marge felt her second orgasm coming, or was it that the first never stopped? She wasn't sure of that question, but several more grunts exhaled the remaining oxygen from her lungs.

Marge's eyes widened as his mouth expanded vertically. Jack's mouth now encompassed her nose and mouth, totally stopping her from receiving any air at all. Jack squeezed her harder now and maintained eye contact as best he could.

"How could this be?" she asked one word at a time between Jack's attempts to extinguish her life.

His hands tightened around her wrists yet again, pushing them against her ass in an attempt to further control his pray. She was still coming when her lungs decided that they have had enough and she started to jerk and spasm. This was an unusual pairing of sensations consisting of a complexity that she could not fully comprehend. She was basically physically held in place by the brute strength of a man as he fucked her, all the while depriving her of oxygen. She was experiencing something that had never happened before, an extended orgasm. All this was second to the fact that she was dying. Marge found herself thinking that she would do so before her orgasm completed, thus being robbed of its full effects.

Jack removed his mouth from hers and slid his face to her right side, keeping her pressed up against the wall. Marge took the first of several very deep breaths as her body welcomed the air it so desperately needed. He moved his face back over hers and pressed into her again. Jack pushed upward aggressively with more force than before, so much so that Marge felt her feet leave the carpeted floor. Her chest hurt very badly. Although she was sucking in oxygen in an attempt to breathe normally, she screamed out in pain and reflexively closed her eyes against it.

Jack stuck the knife into her stomach with the sharp end pointing upward just to the right of her pierced belly button, raising her higher off the floor. The knife was sharp and made quick work of separating her muscle and fat from her ribs. Jack let gravity do all the work. The mere weight of her body was enough to push down over the knife as he held it stationary, and her body slid down the wall. Marge could not stand the pain; it was as if her entire body was on fire. Soon she would pass out and then what? Jack's hand released her wrists; gone was the icy death grip that had almost cost her the circulation in her hands.

A million pinpricks presently occupied every inch of her hands, followed by numbing and tingling sensations. She threw her fists toward his face, landing several punches into those black pools of hell. Jack was not amused by any of this, so he took the opportunity to head-butt her. He hit the front of her hairline with his forehead, and the back of her head smashed into the wall. This effectively dazed her, leaving her slightly wobbling and with a blank look on her face. She took a step to the right, exposing the red indentation that she had recently left behind.

Punch after punch hit Marge in her midsection, raising her up for a millisecond before letting her back onto the floor. She wasn't sure what hurt more, the filleted section on her side or each impact from landing back on her feet. Three more came her way, and she found that she grew now numb to the pain. Each blow that landed devastated her psychologically, but she knew she was going to die, and for this evil thing to postpone it was, well, what it did. It was hate. It was evil. It cared nothing for her.

Marge turned to her right, gathered her strength, and sent a single fist flying to Jack's nose, effectively breaking it. It moved to the left side of his face, which now resembled the letter *L*. She continued turning to her right and shot her right elbow into his lower chest. Jack made a grumbling noise and slightly bent forward. The air that left him really wasn't important to him anymore, so it did nothing to stop him from his next move. Jack slapped Marge across the left of her face with an open hand. Her head rolled to the right and recoiled back as she stumbled against the wall.

This was a classic battle of good versus evil, the quick speed of a lightweight versus the brute strength of a heavyweight, the classic role-playing character with a focus of dexterity versus strength; one would get hit multiple times with less impactful blows, and the other would receive a mind-numbing blow. Marge was still bleeding from her side; the proof of that was all over the walls, the floor, and even part of the foot of the bed. She leaned against the wall with her left hand that was balled into a fist. Her right was holding her side together, trying to slow her blood loss.

Marge waited for him to get closer, hanging her head and breathing as heavily as she could to fake exhaustion. She wasn't too far from displaying an accurate portrayal; she was really badly beat up and bleeding to death, she knew that. Marge stood an arm's length from an undead monster of a man. On the foot of the bed was the knife that Jack had placed there when he had earlier pushed away from her and sliced her open. Jack stepped to Marge with his never-ending smile and a gleam in his eye.

"One more time, for old time's sake then?" he said coldly.

"No thanks, I'm holding out for someone special," she said as she slid down the wall with the help from her blood.

Leaning forward, she reached out and pulled his legs out from under him, and down fell Jack. He hit with a thud, landing squarely on his back. Marge reached her right hand to the foot of the bed and took the knife and stabbed him over and over and over and over. Marge's tears filled her eyes, making the scene she witnessed surreal. Her arm grew tired from the downward strokes that drove the knife deep into his body. Her side ached, and she saw the blood flow more quickly now due to her exertion. Jack raised his hands up to protect his chest and his face, receiving numerous cuts to his forearms in the process.

Marge slammed the knife into his chest, and using the handle, she started to pull herself up on top of him. It took all of her energy to pull the knife out of Jack this time, and leaning forward, she raised her hands high and sunk the bloody knife into his chest as deep as it would go. This time it pierced his collarbone and slid inward toward his neck. After climbing up further to get a better angle, she sat on his stomach and pulled on the knife one more time. Jack was not putting up a fight any longer, and Marge would not wait to experience anything different. She continued to pull the knife out from Jack and slam it down into his upper chest two more times before getting it stuck once again in a bone.

This time the knife would not come free. She jerked back on it a second time and then a third. Jack's body moved slightly from the strength used to pull out the knife, but it was still stuck in his chest plate. Marge twisted the knife back and forth, and placing both hands on the handle, she yanked upward to the ceiling. With the knife raised above her head, held in two hands with white knuckles, she leaned forward and fell lifeless onto Jack's chest.

She watched as Marge slumped off to the right side of Jack's body, dropping the knife between them. She moved around the room and took in the entire picture. A major battle had occurred here; good had triumphed over evil, only to perish in the end. With as easy as it was to bring more evil into this cruel world, she considered this a victory and looked back as Susan one more time before leaving the room.

"I told you there would be loss, Susan—there is always loss," she said, smiling as the door closed behind her.

Chapter Eleven

The Man in Black

Robbie entered the store and stepped inside, enjoying the fresh cool air. He looked around at the unusually high shelves. They must have stood seven feet tall, and every inch of space was used. *Surely I'll find some here,* he thought. A man was walking toward the door with a paper bag and a shovel, whistling as he went. Robbie greeted him by nodding in his direction and continued walking. The man stopped by the door and placed his shovel and bag to the side.

"Son, come here," the man called out.

Robbie looked at the man more closely now and wondered why a cowboy was in a candle shop.

"Yes, sir?" Robbie said.

"Why, don't you know that Lucky Lathaniel is in here somewhere?" the man asked him.

"Who? No. Who?" Robbie said, answering a question with a question.

"He's a killer, son. He's a cattle-rustling, cold-blooded killer," he told Robbie as he locked the door from the top and bottom.

"Stay put, hear?" he said to Robbie.

Robbie saw him remove a pistol from his holster and crouch. He had not really taken a good look at that man, but he did pay attention to his face, just like his dad had taught him. When he took in the entire situation and the way that the man dressed and talked, Robbie stepped back a few feet and watched as the man moved forward.

"Listen here, Lucky Lathaniel!" the man yelled while continuing to move forward.

Robbie saw him turn to the right and disappear behind some shelving. When that happened, Robbie backed up even further to the closest corner and listened for any movement.

"I'm not coming out without a fight!" the other man said loudly.

Trying to see anything he could, Robbie slowly moved to the middle, and stopping just short of the end of the shelf, he crouched just like the first guy had done before he disappeared and listened. Robbie heard no movement, nor could he see anything at all. Robbie wanted to escape this shop. He wanted to be free of this store and out of the danger that he felt was all too real.

Slowly, Robbie stood and backed up to the door. Reaching down, he listened for anyone close by, and when he heard nothing, he felt for the lock at the bottom and turned it. The click that he made was the loudest noise ever, and he knew someone would come for him soon if he didn't get out of here. Robbie didn't wait to see if anyone was coming or if they were close by; he wanted out. He pushed on the door, and it failed to open. This he did a few times more before he looked down at the door. It was unlocked, it moved when he pushed it, but something was still wrong.

He crouched and listened more, and when he yet again heard nothing, he stood up and looked at the door one more time. Robbie pushed on it again and noticed that the top did not move. He had to unlock the top too; he had forgotten that part. Robbie was out of luck; he would have to stack boxes to reach that high. They would surely see him attempt that and then they would come for him. Looking for a safe place to hide, Robbie started to move left very slowly when out of the corner of his eye he saw movement.

Rounding the corner to his right was the man in black. The two made eye contact, and when it looked as if the boy was about to speak, the man pulled his pistol from his holster and placed the tip against his lips. The gesture to be quiet did not go unnoticed as Robbie crouched even lower and didn't make a peep. The man in black was crouched very low as he took small, quiet baby steps toward the door. When he arrived at it, he looked around but did not move or speak. He looked at Robbie again as he slowly stood up. When he reached the top, he unlocked it and slid back down to the floor.

Robbie could hear the first man yelling out for the man in black, but he could not see him. He wanted to tell him where he was, but he knew that he would be shot if he did. He tried not to cry, but a few times, he found emotion getting the better of him. Robbie might have trembled a few times just thinking about it, he wasn't sure. Lucky Lathaniel crouched back down and waited for something to happen, but it never did. He tipped his hat to the boy and slowly stood up to the side of the door. Lucky didn't move; all he did was listen. He was receiving the same results that Robbie got when he did that—utter silence.

He smiled at Robbie, opened the door, and stepped out. Robbie watched that door close behind him with the sound of metal hitting metal. Robbie said the word "wow" under his breath and turned his body so he too could exit this building. The first man was yelling very loudly now as he ran to the door and exited immediately behind Robbie. Letting out a small scream, Robbie moved to the side to allow the man to pass and then froze in place. Robbie didn't mind helping to hold up the building; he thought it represented his civic duty to do so.

The two men squared off on the street, each one throwing insults at the other while brandishing their pistols. Robbie took this time to sneak back into the building and close the door behind him. He would be safe here behind the window, he thought, as he ducked for cover. Both men could be heard from behind the glass of the candle shop, and as Robbie stuck his head up to see how heated it was getting, he saw the good guy shoot first.

Bluish-gray smoke left his pistol as he slowly walked to the man in black. Robbie looked on as Lucky returned fire. Both men moved forward in an attempt to increase their odds of killing the other. Shot after shot rang out as each man fired and moved slightly to the side, advancing on their foe. Robbie lost track of the amount of times that the first man shot Lucky, but he saw the last one take him down. Lucky Lathaniel's body twisted violently a turn and a half before ending up on his back.

Robbie felt fear as he watched the man shot multiple times fall over violently and die. It was always cool when playing guns to shoot the other and to run through the house as fast as his kid legs would carry him, but this was real. He didn't know it, but he was crouching again now and barely visible as he watched everything unfold. So much so that the man who was looking for him gave up and just walked to the front door, calling for him to come out.

"Wasn't so lucky, was he?" the man said as he approached the door.

All Robbie could do was to walk backward and to the right. He wasn't quite there yet and he froze as the man came through the front door before he was hidden in the corner.

"It's OK, son. It's all over," the man said as the door continued to close.

From outside, a single shot rang out, and blood began to soak through man's shirt and onto his stomach.

"They don't call me Lucky for nothing!" Lucky yelled as the good man took one step and fell over, landing against Robbie's shoes and continued bleeding.

"Run, son, *run!*" the main said as he poured blood over the tips of Robbie's shoes.

Robbie took off through the shop, looking for another exit. The back door was visible, but it was so far away. Robbie looked over his shoulder and saw the man in black point his pistol at the one on the floor and fire. An empty click was heard, and without missing a beat, he raised it to reload. Robbie froze as the man inserted six more rounds into it and spun the cylinder, just as he did when he played at home. He watched in slow motion as Lucky Lathaniel lowered his pistol and shot the man three times in quick succession. There was so much smoke that he was barely visible on the floor. Lucky kicked at the smoke and shot him one more time before yelling out.

"You! Boy! Don't make this harder than it needs to be. Stop running, Robbie," Lucky finished in a slow, mean voice.

His efforts to reach the back door were hindered by fear. Robbie had frozen in place when Lucky called his name; he had no idea how he knew it. The mountain lion did not scare him. The noises outside his bedroom window, which were probably from the same, did not scare him. This man who was coming for him now scared him to his core. He took the fight right out of him, and Robbie could not move. Robbie told himself to snap out of it and thought on a way to get to the back door.

He listened for Lucky to see how close he was, which was easy; he was knocking things off the shelves as he searched for him. Robbie had less than a minute to find a way out before Lucky caught up to him, he thought. He looked again at the back door and took a step before he saw something to hide behind. Lucky was close now and he had to take a chance. He had just got into position when he heard him yell.

"There you are!" Lucky said as he sent smoke Robbie's direction.

Two more times he fired at him, filling the back area of the shop with smoke. He had chosen a hiding place behind two large sacks of sugar, but Lucky still found him. He continued walking closer as Robbie looked around for a way out. He was scared, and though the door he was trying to reach wasn't far away, his legs would not move.

Lucky Lathaniel stepped in front of Robbie and placed a boot on either side of him to keep him in place. He lowered his pistol and fired as Robbie shut his eyes. Horror was placed on hold as Robbie heard a click; the pistol had not fired, and

Lucky was once again reloading. His eyes opened and Robbie dug deep for the courage to take off running. He went straight through Lucky's legs and continued to the front of the store. The door in front was his only hope, but Robbie could not stop worrying about the lock on the top. The bottom one he could get, but if Lucky had locked the top one, he was yet again stuck.

He finished reloading his pistol and yelled at the kid he was chasing.

"Stay put, Robbie. I'm almost there. Don't go outside, son. It's not a good place for you!" Lucky shouted.

Robbie panicked and ran faster to reach the front door and escape this mad man. When he turned past the last shelf, he saw his dad standing just to his left beside the same shelf that he had taken refuge only minutes ago. Matthew grabbed his son up and held him tightly. To Matthew, it was a make-believe gunfight, one that he had paid for two weeks ago for Robbie's birthday. The panic and horror in Robbie's eyes defined today's events differently.

"I'm sorry, Robbie, this is all make-believe. I wanted you to be part of an Old West gunfight," he said to Robbie.

Robbie shook and held on for life as he began to cry. Matthew comforted Robbie as best as he could; he really felt bad about all of this. Robbie presented himself around the home and at school as someone who had it together. He was someone in control, an adult, but as much as he saw his son growing up, Matthew knew he was still a kid.

"It was just a reenactment, son. The good guy at your feet and the bad one back there are both friends. They do this for a living, and they are still alive, son," Matthew reassured him.

Robbie looked down at the man by his feet that was still bleeding on the floor and searched for signs of life. He was unwilling to reach down or to touch him, so he just looked at his chest. Robbie saw slow and steady breathing as the man's chest rose and fell. He began to calm himself and asked his dad to let him go.

"I'm OK, Dad. I would like to stand now," he said, smiling.

Matthew let go of him, and Robbie gathered himself. He sniffed a few times, but he no longer shook. Lucky called out again for Robbie and he was very close, probably just beyond their shelf. Robbie took a step back to the side of his dad and watched as the man in black came into view. His gun was held low, pointing at the ground as he continued walking to them.

"That's right, son, it's just for fun. I'm sorry that I chased you to the back of the store. I should have just told you then," Lucky said, pushing his hat up with the barrel of his pistol.

Robbie looked at his dad and back at Lucky before lowering his head to check out the bleeding man on the floor.

"Oh, go on and get up, Herbert," Lucky said, laughing.

When Herbert didn't get up, Lucky looked over at Robbie, whom he could tell was still upset about everything.

"Maybe things did get out of hand, but the bullets were not there. We used blanks that made noise and smoke, see?" he said as he lowered his pistol and shot Herbert in the back.

More smoke filled the air, and with Lucky being so close to them, the noise was incredibly loud. He smiled as he raised the pistol to Matthew and pulled the trigger a second time. Another deafening explosion followed by more smoke erupted around Robbie.

Robbie saw his dad lifted about a foot off the ground in slow motion, his arms going to his sides and then up into the air. Matthew was traveling backward, and Robbie saw his feet rising upward and his chest coming down first. It reminded him of some action scenes in movies that he had watched with his dad. Matthew hit the middle shelf hard and slid to the ground, facing Robbie. A slow red stain grew on his chest, soaking his shirt pocket. Matthew sat there, propped up against the shelf as blood continued to soak his shirt below.

The last thing Robbie remembered before sitting up in his bed was Lucky Lathaniel standing over his dad, firing repeatedly at point-blank range into his chest. Robbie was covered with perspiration from head to toe. The bed he slept on was wet with it, that and urine probably. It was obvious to him that he had peed himself out of fear. He felt beads of sweat form on his face and then roll downward, taking the path of least resistance.

He looked around his room to gather his thoughts. Robbie didn't know where he was at first. As soon as he realized he was safe in bed, he erupted into tears. Shortly afterward came the cries for help and some shouting, which was all done between sobbing. Robbie was shaking very badly when he called out loudly for his dad.

"Dad, help now. Dad! *Dad!*" Robbie yelled.

Immediately after yelling for him, Robbie became quiet and listened as best he could. He still shook, but as long as he could hear his dad coming for him, he knew all would be well. Robbie heard his dad's feet hit the floor before he heard his voice.

"Robbie, stay right there, I'm coming. What's wrong?" he yelled as he opened his door into the hallway.

Upon hearing his dad, Robbie picked up where he had left off before and cried even louder. He was shaking uncontrollably by the time his dad threw open the door to his room and walked inside. Matthew stood there wearing only his pajamas with bare feet. The smell of urine hit him in the face as he looked around the room. Robbie sat on his bed with red eyes and a frantic expression on his face. He was crying, shaking, and breathing excitedly when he slid off the bed and ran to grab hold of his dad.

"It will be OK, Robbie," he said, holding him tightly.

Robbie felt his shorts press up against his dad and stick to his leg. It was cold and wet, unfortunately from Robbie's urine, but his grip was comforting. Matthew held on to Robbie and told him again he was sorry for their trip into town.

"I didn't think it would be that scary, Robbie," he told him.

Holding on to his dad's waist, Robbie grew calmer by the minute. His breathing became normal and Robbie no longer shook. A few sniffles were all that remained from last night's nightmare. Robbie dug his head into his dad's chest and moved his head left and right to wipe away his tears. Matthew rubbed his son's shoulders and his back, telling him that it would be OK.

"Hang in there, little guy," Matthew told Robbie in a calming voice.

Robbie took in a deep breath, which further soothed him, but when he went to let it out, he felt his dad squeeze him harder. Matthew's left hand was wrapped around his waist, while his right continued to rub his shoulders.

"I'm OK, Dad, you can let go of me now," Robbie said.

Matthew squeezed even harder now, effectively immobilizing Robbie. He slid his right hand upward and took a head full of hair and pulled Robbie upward while still holding him with his left. Robbie struggled now and began to cry because he knew something was wrong.

Matthew released his left hand, keeping Robbie suspended by his hair with his right. He extended his arm as Robbie began screaming to be let go. Robbie kicked and flailed his body every way possible, but each time he did, he felt excruciating pain. It was as if every one of his hairs cried out, preparing themselves for eviction. It was apparent to Robbie that his dad was intent on pulling out each hair on his head. What had he done wrong? Why was he being punished?

"Dad, I'm sorry. I won't do it again. Please tell me what's wrong so I can correct it," Robbie pleaded.

Robbie looked at his dad. He had an outstretched arm in which he was holding him suspended about two feet above the floor by his hair. His arm was fully extended, and even if Robbie tried, he could not reach him were he to kick. Between trying to shake himself free and making efforts to talk to him, Robbie looked at his dad's face. He wasn't angry, nor did he display a smile; he just was.

Robbie watched for any signs of affection or acknowledgement in what he had just said to his dad, but he just looked right through him. Matthew shook Robbie very violently, causing him to scream out in pain. Robbie almost hoped his hair would all come out so he could run away, but they held fast. Looking at his dad again with eyes full of tears, he called out his name several times between sobs.

"Come on, Dad, let me go. Let's talk about this," Robbie barely said between his sobs as his dad tried once more to remove his head.

Again Robbie was shook hard by his dad; the pain lessened somewhat now by numbness. He wasn't immune to the pain; it just felt unimportant at the time due to his dad's eyes slowly turning black as he watched them. He looked away but was shook violently as soon as he did. It seemed to be a warning of sorts, so Robbie turned his head back and again looked at his dad's face. A small smile crossed his dad's lips, and Robbie again avoided eye contact, looking down at his chest.

Matthew began bleeding from his chest at about the area where he had been shot earlier on their recent trip into Murphys, Robbie noticed. Redness poured from his chest quickly, soaking a large circle of dark crimson on his baby-blue pajama top. Robbie thought it was his fault that his dad had been shot and began crying. He no longer cared about the pain and fear that he was experiencing—he wanted his dad safe; he wanted him to get better.

"Let me go so I can get help. You're bleeding again. Let me go!" Robbie shouted.

Robbie was thrown into the corner furthest from the door and landed on his backside. His head hit the wall upon impact and smarted very badly, but it still wasn't hurting as much as the top of his head was. Robbie wasn't sure he still had all of his hair, but that didn't matter now; he had to go and get help. Matthew stood blocking the exit and continued to bleed as Robbie closed his eyes a few times to clear his head.

Matthew looked confused and sad as he stared at his son, who was sitting against the wall. He wanted to talk to him, but nothing came out. Robbie saw his dad's expression and stood up; he was trying to make a run for it, and he thought that now was the right time. Slowly he moved forward and off to the right of his dad. He was hoping that he could squeeze through on that side before his dad could grab hold of him. Robbie wasn't sure that he would make it, but he had to get out of this room.

Slowly Robbie progressed until he almost hugged that right wall, sliding closer and closer to the doorway. Matthew never budged or said anything; he just watched. Robbie was one step away from being able to run past him when his dad lowered his arms. He took this as a sign of winning, and Robbie took his last step, which placed him just inside the doorway, adjacent to his dad. Robbie walked through the bedroom door and never looked back. He was headed for the front door when Matthew drew a pistol and shot him.

Robbie felt the first of three rounds enter from behind. Shortly after the pain registered, he smelled and saw the smoke. The noises were deafening as again the shots came toward him. They were very close, and Robbie's ears rang. Sounds became muffled, and when his body was lifted off the ground and thrown forward into the wall beside the front door, he did not hear himself hit. He felt it, though, once his head hit the wall. Blood poured from Robbie's back onto the wall and down to the floor quick enough for him to feel his life draining away.

Robbie was light-headed now, but for all he knew, it could have been from the impact of the wall and not from blood loss. *What should a kid know about blood loss after all?* Robbie thought. He was not concentrating on anything at the moment. Robbie didn't even remember he had been shot. He did remember being held up by his head, though, and he paid close attention to his dad walking his way from his bedroom.

Matthew held the gun on Robbie as he walked closer. Robbie watched him quickly approach and then lower the gun once again to his chest. Robbie was making eye contact with his dad when he pulled the trigger and shot him one final time. Robbie turned on his side and started crawling for the door. He knew he would not make it, but he had to try, he just had to. Darkness overtook Robbie as his dad shot him two more times in the back. Robbie never experienced the effect from those last two shots or the kick that his dad gave him before he walked to his bedroom and closed the door.

CHAPTER TWELVE

Not Alone in the Dark

Matthew spent the next six hours mapping all of the areas he knew about, focusing on moving toward the original mine. He was sure that they were interconnected; it made perfect sense for them to be. Matthew saw separate mine entrances as a distraction meant to confuse would-be claim jumpers. If they chose the first one, which was easier to find than this one, they would be wasting their time and resources in a barren hole.

The time he spent detailing distance between rooms and occasionally calculating how far he was from the old mine would have driven most people mad, but not him. Matthew understood the importance of this, and after taking a look at his most recent numbers, he had found his answer.

"You sneaky son of a bitch!" he yelled out.

They were connected after all, he thought, as he stood in front of a cave-in. Normally, one would think it unsafe, but when he examined the ceiling and its surrounding walls, several places showed signs of picking and hammering. There were no other logical explanations; the old man had caused it himself on purpose.

He stood there several minutes longer studying the room and adding applicable details to his notebook and then his map. *Time for lunch,* he thought as he packed up his papers and headed out. On his way back, Matthew stopped to check his map and noticed an area to his right, the maps left, that he had not explored yet. He promptly took out his notebook and placed the following entry inside:

New area, totally overlooked, weird, area #69.

Matthew closed the book and continued walking on.

Rounding the next corner, he stepped into water, making some ripples that disappeared in front of him, never to return. Water filled this corridor and beyond as it sloped deeper the further he went in. Matthew was unwilling to explore the new area at this time. He didn't have the right equipment, and to boot, his feet were now cold and wet. Matthew made it back to the main corridor and stopped to add a capital *W* to that location on his map.

He would take a break for now and map this out another day; Matthew would have to come back here later to learn more about this water area. This morning, Matthew would stop early and try to make it home just in time for breakfast and spend some time with Robbie, he thought, as he closed up shop early and headed home.

Robbie awoke to the smell of bacon and eggs hovering directly above his nose.

"What a wonderful way to start one's day!" he yelled out for his dad to hear.

When no response came, Robbie crawled out of bed, put his shorts on, and grabbed his shirt. He walked into the kitchen and called out for his dad, putting his shirt on when there was no response. Looking around, he saw he wasn't in the house, but there was a plate with his breakfast on the table. A lovely plate of two eggs and no less than five pieces of bacon awaited him. Robbie poured a small glass of milk and sat down at the table to enjoy his meal.

Next to Robbie's plate was his dad's empty one; he had eaten already, but he was still close by. Dad never left dishes lying around when he left the house; it was not his way. He took a piece of bacon and placed it into his smiling mouth. Still warm, it was still warm, Robbie thought as he ate another piece before he even thought about eating any eggs. *Dad had to be outside,* he thought as he dove into his eggs.

Matthew was working on the old truck when Robbie came over and assaulted him with questions. He smiled back at Robbie, answering most of them with a yes, a few with no, and the last one with "ten minutes, probably."

"Yay, we are finally going to town!" Robbie yelled as he jumped inside the open passenger side door and closed it with a noticeable thud.

Matthew closed the hood and jumped in beside him, asking him if he was ready. Looking over at Robbie, he told him that today would be a long day and that they were probably going to have dinner out somewhere.

"Just as long as I get to shop in town, I'm good," Robbie replied.

"Not *town*, Robbie, *towns*, as in more than one. We are going to Murphys first and then Arnold after that," Matthew stated.

Robbie's smile was a large one, and to say that it stretched from ear to ear was not too far from the truth. He tightened his seat belt and looked forward with eyes wide open in preparation for his journey.

"All right, Dad, I guess we can go to both today, if we have to. I hope you have enough time to finish all your chores, or there will be no mining for you until you *do* finish them!" Robbie said seriously at first but busted out laughing after pausing.

"The key to saying statements such as those, Robbie, is not laughing until the message has been delivered," he stated.

Robbie looked over at him as Matthew turned to pay attention to the road. Now it was Matthew's turn to break out in laughter.

"Just think how many marbles you can find searching through two towns!" he told Robbie excitedly.

He remembered, Robbie thought. *What a great dad!*

The road to Murphys was rough and slow, the many holes and bumps in the road saw to that. From a distance, one watching someone drive down that section of road would think them drunk, unless they knew that the driver was changing lanes numerous times to avoid man-swallowing potholes. It was comical to watch, for sure. Matthew was conscious of changing lanes and often looked in his rearview mirror to ensure no one would speed up and attempt to pass him on the right.

A visit to Murphys from his town took longer because he had to take the local roads, but it was a lovely scenic trip. The countryside was wonderful and offered views that he just didn't have back home. Matthew never spoke of back home, their old house, Robbie's younger brother, or his mom. Robbie knew it to be too painful for him, he understood that. He also knew that his dad missed them both very much, but it was time to move on, as he would put it.

"Finally, Dad, what's our plan again?" Robbie asked as they pulled into town.

"Well, we need fuel, groceries, mining supplies, and marbles," he replied.

Robbie's eyes grew even wider with anticipation as he wondered how much time he would actually have to search.

"How about I promise to meet you here in three hours and I'll go and explore the shops?" Robbie queried.

Matthew thought about all that he had to do and where he had to go. He didn't want to drag his son along for the ride and have him bored out of his mind. Matthew didn't want to be *that* guy.

"Sure, sounds good to me. Three hours then and we'll meet back here," he heard himself say.

"It's more than enough time for me to check out these shops. If I find what I need, do we still have to go to Arnold?" he asked Matthew.

Smiling at Robbie, he put the truck in reverse to parallel park between two nicer cars. Matthew knew that if their owners were watching, they would be terrified; his truck looked *that* rough.

"We'll see, son," he said, smiling.

Matthew headed for the general store, while Robbie ran to the nearest store on the right side of Main Street. Robbie entered the first store he came across with his intent to check every store on this side of the street before changing to the other, all in the pursuit of marbles.

Meanwhile, in Murphys . . .

Another store was coming up on the right, opposite of the large hotel he had previously visited. Opening the door wide, Robbie walked in, letting it close behind him with a click. Cool air comforted him. The smells of fresh bread, garlic, and olives were wonderful; it reminded him of when his mom cooked Italian. Although Robbie had a late breakfast, the incredible smells sent his taste buds into action. He welcomed a chance to walk around slowly and look in the shop for his marbles; if he found a piece of bread or two, that would be a bonus.

"Welcome to my shop. Take a look around," the woman said.

"Thanks. Nice place here," Robbie replied as he hunted for a piece of bread.

The woman smiled back and walked to the back of the store and then moved behind the counter.

Large brown stone squares adorned the floor that welcomed those who visited the olive oil tasting bar. They found the atmosphere inviting, and the transition from floor to ceiling was spectacular, consisting of at least thirty shades of colors ranging from tan to brown. It was a major attraction for Murphys with customers coming in from around the world to taste their blends.

The company specialized in oils and vinegars, and their take on preparation and extraction was second to none. The scents that wafted around the room and out the front door were incredible. One could simply close their eyes and follow them into the store, mesmerized by their goodness. Why, passersby and those lucky enough to get a room in the historic Murphys

Hotel were drawn to the place upon taking one step in front of their building.

Along one wall at chest height stood the decanters with small tasting cups and various pieces of crackers and breads. The oils and vinegars were nestled inside wooden shelves with products such as olives up high and the dispensers toward the bottom. You just had to select your passion, dispense a small amount into the cup, and then dip into the olive oil or vinegar mixture with your cracker or bread to taste its goodness. It was as much an assault on one's senses as could be offered. The store was visibly appealing; it was air conditioned, and it was full of pleasant tastes and scents.

Scattered about were a few small tables with assorted popular flavors in bottles for tasting, additional crackers, breads, and few stacks of small tasting cups. The opposite end from the front door stood two glass door coolers with assorted fruit, cheese, and fine meats. A single woman walked around the store gracefully with a very large smile, assisting in her customers' needs. There was a nearby bottling station and a small counter where one could pay for their wares and sign up for the company's newsletter, if they felt so inclined.

A locked beige door stood between two rows of decanters and, for the most part, was never used during normal business hours. Regular customers never saw the door open, nor were they able to peek inside. Whatever was behind that door might as well have been Fort Knox. On the back wall by the coolers stood a second door that was used by management and staff only. Inside of it were a computer, a small safe, and the most meager of desks that was used to conduct their daily business. That door was opened on certain days of the week while a manager was on duty, keeping true to their open-door policy.

After a few pieces of delicious bread dipped in a red pepper–flavored olive oil disappeared; he prepared to ask the dreaded question to the woman.

"Might you know where I could obtain some marbles?" Robbie asked with a lingering smile.

"No, I'm afraid not." The woman smiled back.

"Well, you have a very nice store anyway. Thanks for the bread," Robbie said as he left to go meet his dad.

Robbie could not count on his two hands how many times he had entered stores and asked about marbles, to no success. Matthew did, however, locate a few items of importance and managed to order everything else. He was probably looking at a week or two before everything came in. Mining was tough all around, especially the wallet. Matthew did find savings online at Black Cat Mining's website, although he would have preferred to have driven there directly. He's never been closer to their store in Oregon as he was now, but it was still a good distance from Murphys, and time was of the essence. They both agreed that today they would not visit Arnold because they were just too tired from shopping.

Another week begins

Robbie walked to school today the same way he had done all week long, stopping at Ruthie's to pick her up along the way. During their trip, they talked about their weekend, past homework, and today's assignments. It wasn't long before they saw each other as friends. Sometimes after a hectic day of school, they would stop by a small grove of trees and take a break.

Ruthie would talk about her mom, the weather, how easy school was, and sometimes flowers. Robbie would speak about learning the trails around their land, hiking, and how bored he was at school. Sometimes he would mention mining with his dad. Neither of them talked about the mountain lion that had recently laid waste to their school, killing several teachers. It still wasn't normal, but until the principal interviewed other candidates, she was their only substitute teacher.

Robbie talked less and less about marbles with Ruthie, as he knew she didn't care much for them. In contrast to her, Robbie dreamed of marbles, often practicing at home with the few that he did have. Robbie could not wait for the weekend to arrive. He was going to get a big bag of marbles with his allowance.

It was midafternoon, and Matthew continued to make his way outside from down below. The air was fresh, and as he took his first step outside, a warm breeze flooded the mine entrance; he absolutely loved the fresh air. Sitting down on a nearby rock, he grabbed his lunch from the backpack and proceeded to eat his sandwich. He smelled a storm brewing. The wind was strong and it came at him from the east, which was bad for his area.

Matthew quickly finished his lunch and enjoyed his short-lived break. His feet were hurting now having walked for over four hours. He doubted that he would make good time if he chose to go home now. Looking back into the mine, he decided to spend some time safely below the elements and see if it would blow over. With the time that it had taken him to eat his lunch and relax, Matthew had planned his entire day.

Robbie read on as the first of three heroes fell to the ground in agony before the man with the bejeweled glove. Over the last three pages, he had seen them beaten one at a time and then held suspended in the air. When the man grew bored of the lack of challenge that they presented, he dropped them to the ground. Slowly he walked over to the girl on the left and placed his jeweled hand upon her shoulder. The woman who wore the red cape glowed bright blue for a second and then vanished without a trace.

Robbie turned the page and read the text boxes on both sides before checking out the detailed drawings. An evil laugh escaped the purple-cloaked villain as he picked up the man in green tights by his neck and raised him above his head. Totally relaxed now, Robbie turned the page to see what happened to the last hero, but he never made it; he had fallen asleep. Over the next few hours, his mind would see new heroes rise up to fight the good fight. Robbie had a large smile as he watched them doing battle in his imagination until he fell into a deep, restful sleep.

Another busy day lay ahead of Matthew as he swung his pick with madness. He wasn't accurate now, not as he had been when he first started this morning. He didn't sleep well last night and thus began his day half empty. Since he did not have his own team, Matthew had to perform all the jobs of the hard-rock mining process by himself. He would pick through an area for about four hours or so before taking a break. Several minutes later, he would classify the rocks by size and then he would sweep the area's remaining debris into a corner. Last of all, he would classify down and pan out his material.

For six days, he followed his process to the point of exhaustion. Matthew was filling up an adjacent room with extra muck because the room that he was mining in was almost full. There was so much clutter that he decided to take a break and get some rest before proceeding.

Matthew spent the next few evenings listening to Robbie talk about school and marbles while he reviewed his maps. He circled a couple of areas of interest, areas that he needed Robbie's help with, so he could talk to him about them later. One was a tight fit through natural rock, a crevasse that Matthew wanted to know more about. He wanted to know if it was worthwhile to expand in that direction or if it leads to a dead end. The other section was a hole that led deeper into the earth. This section was a natural occurrence, not man-made. The second one was very exciting, as it went off in a totally different direction, which Matthew hoped that it led into mine three.

Mine three would be the largest area thus far and probably was the least mined of them all. Rumor had it that the old miner who worked these mines found something wrong with mine three, closing it immediately. The very next day, he headed off in a different direction and started the fourth mine. He would ask Robbie sometime tomorrow if he wanted to help with his mapping of those two areas. Matthew was tired and said good night to Robbie, telling him not to stay up too late. Robbie was also tired and he followed Matthew to bed only a few minutes later.

Today's classes were almost done for the day, Robbie thought, at least the hard ones anyway. The homework assignments handed out for tonight were easy; they would take no time at all to complete. Robbie's decision was obvious—he would leave early today, possibly during lunch, and try to make it to town so he could search for marbles. He could not tell Ruthie of his plan to leave; she wouldn't understand. Robbie walked down the hallway and turned left instead of right. It was better that she did not know, he thought as he quietly closed the door.

Moments later, Robbie experienced freedom. He walked through the trees and past the hills that kept this land beautiful. Robbie had to walk three more miles at a minimum to reach the outskirt of Arnold. During Robbie's entire trip to town, he saw only one car on the roads. Robbie was reminded of the simple life that he and his dad were living now and how it was relaxed, or what some would call country.

Robbie risked life and limb traveling to Arnold. It was a bit further away than Murphys; he was walking through the wilds and he knew he was going to be late for dinner. Even at a very fast walk, with a little running, he would still arrive home past 6:00 p.m., if he was lucky. He didn't even know if they would have any marbles anyway. Halfway on his journey, Robbie's common sense kicked in and he knew he would have to wait for his dad; Robbie turned around and headed back home.

Another day at the mine

The cave-in looked daunting. Matthew looked at his map from time to time and then stared at the hole. *There might be another way in,* he thought as he once again peered at his map. It could very much be a load-bearing wall now. Who knows— maybe it was the only thing keeping all of these tunnels safe.

Soon it would be time to go outside for some fresh air and to await the arrival of his son and his lunch. He had eaten and drank all of his supplies; next time he reminded himself to bring more! A few more moments of rest and then he thought, he would try to make the holes lightly larger so his son could easily crawl through. He hoped he could talk him into going through with a lantern and a shovel to look around. Who knows—maybe he could find another way in.

Matthew really wanted to examine that room; looking into it with his head sticking inside the hole, swinging his lantern from left to right, really didn't help him much. The room was large enough for the exterior walls to remain hidden given the small amount of light provided from his lamp. His head was also restricted; he could only see forward for a few feet. He thought on this a few more moments before he grabbed his pick and struggled with the opening. He swung it with the strength of the largest lumberjack he had ever met. Very little progress resulted as glancing blows minimized his results.

It wasn't long before he heard his son's voice.

"Dad? I'm lost," Robbie's voice softly echoed.

"Son! Stay put, I can hear you. I can come and get you," Matthew said loudly.

"I have lunch, I didn't forget it," Robbie said.

"Stay put, Robbie. I'll find you," he replied.

Matthew looked around slowly, listening as he turned his head.

"Whistle, Robbie, and keep doing it so I can find you," Matthew said just short of yelling.

Robbie began whistling the "Happy Birthday Song." Over and over again, he whistled it, and each time his dad waited a few seconds for him to start again as he continued walking in his direction. He started walking back out of the section of tunnel that he had just been mining, and Robbie's whistling grew fainter with each forward step. Matthew stopped and, turning his head back to the hole, he listened. He walked back to the large hole he was trying to make through the wall and stuck his head back in, asking Robbie to talk a little bit about how his day was at school.

"Anything will do, Robbie, just talk to me. Can you hear me?" Matthew said frantically.

"Well, school was boring, I am tired of doing all of that homework and I can't wait to have lunch with my dad!" he said quickly.

Matthew was sure that Robbie was inside the hole; he was on the other side of this wall! Carefully removing his head, he took the lantern from the small table and placed it into the hole. The light the lantern did produce was necessary for Matthew; as he moved the lantern to the other side of the wall, his world became dark. What was once lit, albeit barely so, slowly disappeared into darkness as the light was funneled to the other side.

Matthew talked into the hole and told Robbie to walk to the light.

"Dad! That never works out in the movies!" Robbie said, laughing as he looked for it.

"Walk slowly and mind the ground—there are obstacles everywhere," Matthew said.

Robbie didn't see any light; it was very dark, and although he walked slowly, he still hit the sides of the walls and occasionally an object on the ground.

"Dad, I'm scared. I brought lunch, you know. I'm sorry that I was late, I tried to be on time," Robbie said.

Matthew didn't talk; he continued listening to Robbie and tried to discern his location. Matthew told him to stop walking and to keep talking where he was. Robbie began talking about Ruthie and their classes together. Right in the middle of wanting to mention that he liked her a lot, he switched his topic to marbles.

"Yeah, those boys think they are so smart and that I don't notice that they give each other their marbles back after they win them, keeping mine. I'll show them!" he said loudly.

Although Robbie became excited when he was discussing his marbles, he wasn't loud enough to be heard by Matthew. Matthew could not hear Robbie anymore. He had asked Robbie to stop moving and to keep talking, but he doesn't know how much Robbie heard and if he was still moving or just stopped around some wall, waiting for him. He was probably scared out of his mind, and the more Matthew thought about it, he felt horrible that Robbie was in this predicament.

"Robbie, whistle again for me!" he yelled, walking back down the corridor.

He heard no responses, not anymore; Matthew grew frustrated as he turned once more and started heading out of the mine. He wasn't sure if he would run into him or not. Maybe he would turn a corner and see Robbie sitting down and eating his part of their lunch. Matthew smiled as he moved forward with the lantern in his left and the pickaxe in his right.

Although in darkness now, Robbie had only taken a few turns from the beaten path; he knew where the light would be. He headed that way after waiting a few minutes for his dad to talk. He didn't know why they could not hear each other anymore, but he knew that eventually his dad would have to leave the mine. A few minutes later, Robbie arrived at the mine entrance and looked around for his dad. After seeing no sign of him, he called out for him one more time. After hearing no response, Robbie sat down against a small boulder to grab a little snack. He looked around at the walls as he ate his bag of chips; shortly after that, he attacked the sandwich that he had made for himself.

Robbie knew that his dad would be hungry, so he saved half of his sandwich for later. They would probably eat outside, in the shadow of the boulders that blocked the entrance. No doubt his dad would say that someone would see them and know where the mine was.

"Gotta protect the mine," Robbie said, imitating his dad.

Robbie waited for his dad to come out; it had been over a half an hour or so since he last heard him. To put his concerns lightly, he was bored as hell. Robbie would, however, have to apologize to him for eating all of the chips! Not only did he eat his small bag, but also he ate the one for his dad.

Robbie opened the bag again, pulling out a soda, and twisted the cap open. It was hot outside, even in the shade of the boulders. It tasted so good, and although it wasn't really cold, it still hit the spot. He would choose slightly cool soda over warm water any day, he thought. Robbie sat counting the minutes until the weekend was officially here. He wanted to go into town so badly to get those marbles. He knew it wouldn't take much gold to buy some marbles; they were cheap. He knew his dad would find enough gold to buy enough marbles for the rest of the year; that would be easy for him.

It was getting dark outside now, and his dad had not come for him. It was time to go on in; he had to find his dad. Robbie gathered up all his things and walked into the mine. He walked slowly, calling out for his dad as he went along. As Robbie entered the mine, wind blew past him, freshening the air around him. He continued calling out for his dad as he made his left and right turns. Before long, he sat down to take a break. The lights from the opening of the mine had long since left him. Robbie relied now on the first of his three light sources his dad always made him bring, just in case. It was something he called redundancy.

Robbie walked on, concentrating more on his turns—left, right, right, right—but something was different. He remembered much more lefts; they just weren't there. Robbie stopped and examined the walls, the floor, and the ceiling. It all looked different to him; he had never been here before—Robbie was lost.

Matthew kept walking, and when he finally stopped to listen again for Robbie, he was at the intersection where the water was, the lower tunnels. Looking at the water, he could tell it was disturbed. Someone had recently been through there, he thought. Matthew called for Robbie again, and as he stood motionless, he listened and waited for his response. He received the usual response returned from today's searching—total silence.

Matthew took in a deep breath from the air around him; it smelled stale. It smelled the way he imagined it would if he had been the first to move a large boulder that had blocked this entrance for thousands of years. He really needed to get those fans running down here, he thought. Matthew could not wait for his trip to the general store this weekend; he needed supplies badly. None of that would matter if he didn't find Robbie alive down here. It would crush him and break his heart to no end.

Looking around, he called for Robbie one more time, and when he received no response, he took in a deep breath and held it. Matthew walked as quickly as he could, entering the recently disturbed muddy pool. He couldn't walk too fast; occasionally a rock would find itself either in front of his next step or under foot and cause him grief. Slowly he trudged through the water, looking left and right as he went. It was easy enough to spot; there it was—a footprint. It was small, but it was a footprint. Holding on to his breath, Matthew took a few seconds to examine the size and guessed about whether it was Robbie's.

Matthew checked to determine whether he was walking or running when he made it. Reaching down, he stuck his first two fingers through the water and into the footprint. He knew that there were too many variables, such as walking or running, empty-handed or carrying things, a backpack, perhaps, way too many, but one thing was for sure: it was a kid's footprint.

Matthew exhaled and took in another breath, but not as much as he did before. The air was unusually foul here, and as soon as he tried to breathe some in, he knew it was too dangerous to continue taking deep breaths. He continued deeper down the corridor, not knowing where he was going. One thing was for certain: the water was getting deeper. At its deepest point thus far, the water merely reached the height of his ankles. With rocks that covered most of the ground that he stepped on, it was hard to judge how deep it truly was. There were some open areas that contained only mud, although he avoided those as best he could.

He heard echoes of a child laughing, but Matthew could not determine the distance or direction; it was faint, though, and didn't last long enough for him to discern anything else. He covered more distance down the flooded corridor, calling for Robbie as he went. Each time he did that, he was forced to breathe in more foul air. The water now seemed to be deeper, and even though it looked as if it wasn't rising, it now covered his boot. The first of the cold muddy water raced down to greet his toes, chilling everything it ran over on the way.

Matthew traveled a few feet more and found himself forced to take another breath of bad air. As it entered Matthew's lungs, he suddenly felt the need to cough. He held it in, only making a few restricted noises. Those were followed by a minimal amount of air loss each time the loud cough was held back. He moved over to the right side of the corridor to stay close to the edge, even though it offered very little comfort; it too was covered with water, offering no protection from what lie beneath and from what floated in the air.

Matthew walked slower now with every step being more deliberate and measured. He was not sure how big this area was, if the water got deeper, or if it would level off. The ground he covered now had less and less rock and debris; it was muddier here. Occasionally he would find a flat rock with his feet that would press down into the mud when his weight stood on it. These would turn slightly to the left or right or front or back, depending on where he stepped, making it slightly uneven and very slippery.

"Robbie! Are you out there, Robbie? Answer me!" he yelled out, expelling the last of his valuable air.

He took another breath and moved forward with his left foot, sliding it onto and off of a flat muddy rock. Matthew felt disorientated; he found himself stumbling forward and to the right, off balance. He needed more steps to try to catch his himself, but he was quickly moving headfirst into the wall. He tried to move to his left and use his hands to break his fall, but he overcompensated and spun his body to the right, launching his lower body into the air. He came down on his butt and promptly sank waist deep into the cold muddy water.

Matthew tried to shake off what had just happened. He almost found it amusing, almost. If he wasn't half buried in mud, he would have laughed. The weight of his body pushed him down about a foot, and cold water covered his feet to just above his ankles and his hands past their wrists. His jeans were soaked from his thighs to just below his chest. Matthew sat in the crab pose, with his butt, hands, and legs in the cold water.

Taking a short breath, he composed himself and drew a small smile on his face before yelling out a dozen expletives. He figured it didn't matter at the moment; Robbie could not hear him anyway. Sitting in the muddy water was something he didn't care too much for, but as he looked around in total darkness, he wasn't sure which way to go. His lantern had obviously broken or had fallen into the mud, or both. The air still smelled bad; he was dizzy, wet, and in the dark, and he was getting colder by the minute.

Matthew tried to pull his left leg out of the mud, but it would not budge. An attempt to remove the right one only frustrated him further. Even his hands, which were back somewhat behind him at an unusual angle, were glued to the cavern floor, stuck in the mud. Matthew realized very quickly how dangerous this place actually was. He was always careful when he planned his endeavors, but he didn't have enough planning in place for this area, not yet anyway. His fans were the first thing on his mind. Matthew had placed an order for several pieces of large equipment that he needed. Two generators, six fans, an acetylene torch, and pieces of an old stamp mill, but none of them had arrived. He was hoping to check on his order this weekend, if he and Robbie were still alive.

His mind wandered back to Robbie and how he was coming here to spend a little time with his dad. "Just bring lunch and we'll spend the day together," he remembered telling him. Matthew shut his eyes and squeezed them hard. Leaning his body backward, he then pulled his shoulders upward, trying to free his hands once more. His left hand was moving upward; he was making progress! It was as his left hand came out of the mud that he was grabbed from behind.

Matthew felt a pair of helping hands take hold of his sides and firmly start tugging at him. He smiled and looked over his shoulder, but it was still very dark. The palms of the hands pushed into him harder now, and they slid to the front. He prepared himself to be pulled up and out of this mud, but by whom he did not know. Wait, Matthew thought, he was not being pulled out of the mud; the hands moved downward now, and in one quick movement, they went from holding his chest to pressing down on his thighs.

The hands jockeyed for position, moving independently they pressed down on him against his jeans. Fingers assaulted his thighs in an attempt to tear holes in them to get to his flesh. Matthew could not see anyone at this time, and thinking he was hallucinating, he smiled again. He would have been right except that the hands continued to make their way to his— groin? It was now that Matthew began to frantically struggle against whatever was happening to him. He took turns trying his right leg, his left arm, continuing to remove them from the mud's death grip. Making little progress, he moved his body left and right as best he could, but he was still buried in the mud, hindering his progress.

Fingers moved in unison, clawing at his jeans with the power of a man. This was a man's grip; Matthew felt the large, powerful hands pressing down on his thighs, and what worried him the most was that now they were close enough to let the fingers touch his penis! Pressing downward even further, he found himself unable to raise his body out of the mud. Matthew could not leverage himself enough to wiggle out of the mud's hold and continued struggling only seemed to make matters worse. Matthew wasn't being saved; he was being pushed deeper into the mud by something unseen.

Matthew felt the air around him growing colder. As impossible as he thought that it could be, he now saw the room grow darker. He screamed out for help; it was a cry of desperation, which was full of excitement and pain. He wasn't sure if anyone would ever hear him down here; it was more for his sanity than anything else.

"Robbie! Robbie, can you hear me!" he yelled.

His response was what he thought to be a slap, possibly a backhand to the face. With Matthew being stuck in the ground and somewhat immobile, the impact was strong enough to daze him.

Crickets could be heard from time to time down here; that was nothing new to him. What *was* new was how loud they were at present. He couldn't see them, but they were there and they seemed to get louder by the minute. He wondered if that was to be his fate to be beaten up and left for the carrion to eat him. Matthew's repeated attempts to draw attention to himself for Robbie or anyone else to hear failed. They were increasingly silenced by the crickets that were crawling on the ceiling and the walls.

Earlier, Matthew had felt one of the hands leave his groin before he was struck. It quickly went back to his thigh now that it had made its point and was once again groping him. Matthew tried to yell out for Robbie again, but he was drowned out by the cavern's denizens. He knew this was not normal; he had to escape whatever *this* was. Pushing forward with all of his strength, he tried to dislodge his backside. Matthew was met with slap after slap. They increased in damage, and he knew that he was in trouble when the first of three blows landed against his chest. He made backward progress mentally, but physically, he was in the same spot as before.

Matthew felt beaten, literally and figuratively, and he was sure he had the bruises to prove it. Just as he was sliding down that slippery slope of regret, he felt both hands remove themselves from his body. The crickets became more normal sounding, and he no longer feared that they would eat him. Sighing deeply, he redoubled his efforts to escape the mud. Matthew felt himself weaker now; it became clear to him now that he was being softened up. Every time he struggled, he was beaten harder than the last until there remained no fight of any credible resistance.

No sooner than he finished that thought than the hands were felt again on his chest. They pressed gently against his shirt, rubbing small circles over it, pressing harder as they went along. Lower and lower they traveled; Matthew could do nothing more than lie there at this point and offered no struggle. They converged over his groin, and as he looked down in horror to their purpose, it was immediately understood: they were unbuttoning his jeans. It didn't matter that he could not see in the darkness; he heard and felt them open and slowly unzip.

Roughly the hands cupped his balls and rubbed his penis, pressing and pulling them in every direction imaginable. Matthew found this in no way arousing and he began struggling against it. He felt one hand was stroking his penis really firmly, and the other one had left to pay him another kind of visit. The first of three slaps tried to break his cheekbones, caring not if the head came off in the process. Matthew felt the life leaving him between the dizziness from breathing the foul air and being beaten.

Matthew focused on his son; he had to stay alive for his son. He didn't know how much longer he had in him as he slumped forward, relaxing his shoulders. One hand pushed against his lower chest, and the other continued to stroke his manhood. Over and over it pulled up on it, stretching it as far as it could go. The hand pressing against his chest definitely exerted more force and was enough to keep him in place without any help from the other.

Another series of three blows struck him with each one having more force than the last. Matthew felt himself becoming hard, but he didn't understand why it was happening along with the beating that he was receiving. Stroke after stroke lifted the head of his not-so-little soldier to just shy of being painful. He closed his eyes and moved his head backward, enjoying what he thought would be his sensations if he had been handcuffed. But who was he with? Surely it would not be Susan, and there had been no one since he left. It would be Mary Sue Elberts from Tacoma. Yeah, that's as good a name as any, he laughed.

The upward strokes became less forceful, focusing on pleasure, and were no more painful than his first time was. He pictured a woman's hands closed around his penis, moving quickly up and down. The fingers were smaller now, he thought, and the grip not so firm. Yes, he liked this, for a few moments longer anyway, as he recognized the beginning of his ejaculation. It was an incredibly ferocious orgasm, with several waves of semen being forced to leave in what his mind imagined as an angled stream with epic proportions.

The only problem was that it all happened in slow motion, and his penis was in the muddy water. His body began to tighten, and although he was half in the mud, he still tried to stretch out his feet. It began very slowly, growing with force until he could not stand it. He likened it to being tickled where one's almost paralyzed with laughter. As dumb as it sounded to him when he thought about his overall experience, it hurt.

Matthew let out two long garbled acknowledgements of his attacker's endeavors. The stroking of his penis that was being done by an invisible attacker intensified, stretching his penis again to the max and squeezing hard enough to remove any last drops of his reward. The hand pressing down on his chest moved lower and started massaging his inner thighs. It went from left to right and back again, each time pressing the fingers in deep and allowing the palm to slide over his balls.

This drove him mad, and he instantly felt ready for more. A few minutes longer and the hand left his thighs and forcefully rubbed its way north. It rested just beneath his neck and appeared to be waiting for some cue. Matthew was ashamed and embarrassed that he liked the sensation. It had been some time since he last had sex with his wife, and even longer with another woman. It was never if the sensations had been produced from something male, but there wasn't really any way of knowing what happened here; he just knew it felt wrong.

Repeated attempts to sit up were met with pressure on his upper chest. It was just a guardian; it appeared to stay put and only threaten when he attempted movement. The second hand was not felt anywhere on Matthew's body. Thinking about where it could be started to mess with his head. He still didn't understand it, but when he thought about it, things like this had been happening since before the plane trip. He wondered how

Robbie was, but he wasn't going to call for him with this thing around him.

Struggling again, he soon felt the hand on his chest warn him to be still. Matthew couldn't just stay here forever. He had almost forgotten about the cold temperature of the water that he sat in. To an extent, the mud did insulate him from it, but he had to respect it. In most places, where weather was involved in one way or another, cold kills. Who knows how long he has been in this place trying to escape? Who knows how long he's been in the mud?

Matthew took a shallow breath and held it as he tried to look around and listen for anything around him. The hand on his chest slowly started to move lower, and from what he could tell, it was again headed straight for his groin. He was still in pain from his last attack, and since he didn't want to take in any more foul air than he had to, he waited to see how it would play out. Soon he would make another attempt to free himself, especially since there was only one hand present.

He saw his opportunity and Matthew took it. Pushing with his left side, he pressed down on his arm and leg and tried to tilt his body to break the suction. The hand immediately hit the thigh and then grabbed as much skin as it could through the wet jeans and started to push him down. It wasn't long before the other hand took hold, but this time was different. It pressed against his thigh, but it went down through the mud. It was going to attack him—that much was sure; he just didn't understand the logic.

The hand on top pressed him down into the mud, while the one below had just grabbed his ass and was pulling him deeper. Matthew again screamed for anyone close by to come and help him. He wasn't sure how much was heard immediately down this corridor, let alone if it would be heard down at the entrance. Maybe Robbie would hear him and come and distract this thing. Maybe it would give him time to escape the mud; he didn't know, but it was worth a try.

The hands changed positions, but they kept a hold of him. When they moved, they hugged his body, never letting go of him. They were not the hands of a lover, not by a long shot. The only time that he had felt otherwise was when they tricked his body into doing what they wanted. He presently felt both of them on his inner thighs, where they both took handfuls of him and began pushing again.

Matthew began rocking to the best of his ability left and right. He tried these movements in his head; he thought they would work, Matthew knew they had to. For anyone witnessing the scene, though, nobody would have guessed it would have worked. If it were not for the facial expressions and occasional grunts and cries for help, no one would have known he was struggling at all. He was lower than a crab now and sunk into the mud pretty good. The water covered him from ankle to midchest with only his knee caps above the waterline. Matthew didn't see how bad the situation was; he was still in total darkness. He felt the height of the water, though, and that was his barometer on how bad his dilemma actually was.

He was sure that he was bruised all over, having been pinched, poked, and prodded; at least he was alive. He was also beaten around the neck and face, as well as several blows to the chest. Worst of all, he was made to breath in the foul air. He thought that was the purpose of this endeavor; whatever that thing can do to keep him here, it would do. Matthew was meant to absorb the gasses of this flooded tunnel, and he was to die.

It appeared to him that what he just thought of was the plan, but plans change, they always do. What was happening now was that he was sinking lower, or truer to the fact being submerged or pushed down into the mud. Wasn't much longer now, he thought, before his face would be beneath the water. The hands maneuvered for this change in plans, and they used their fingers to walk up his chest. They reached into his flesh and once again grabbed what skin they could find and began pushing him down. By focusing on the chest, the neck and head would follow; it was only a matter of time, really.

The water was brushing up against his chin now; the beast that held him tightly was taking him to China, and there was nothing he could do about it. Matthew began thinking about his sons and his wife. He had lost his wife and younger son forever; nothing he could do about that. It didn't stop him from thinking about them from time to time. Robbie was his angel, his golden nugget, his sole purpose for being, and he couldn't bear the thought of leaving him, let alone leaving him down here.

Matthew had to buy himself some time, so against his better judgment, he took in as much air as he could and held his breath as the water crept over his mouth and started pouring down his nose. Damn, he had forgotten to breathe out of his nose, or at least try to stop the water from entering by not reflexively breathing through it. He kept his eyes open to the last, and as the water covered his eyes, he closed them to keep out the mud.

He didn't know what was worse—the noxious smell of the air that he had just taken or the mud that was slowly entering his nose, his eyes, and his ears. Matthew could not effectively free himself from the mud, and he was being taken deeper. Struggling only burned more oxygen at this point; he hoped for someone to have heard his last screams for help. Matthew was aware of his knees now being colder, and wet; it was continuing to take him into the mud, all of him. He was now totally submerged and unable to move. His oxygen was running low, and his lungs demanded an exchange, an exchange he could not willingly offer.

Matthew held on for as long as he could, but he was harboring a cough. He was also aware of an itching inside of his left ear; something obviously was crawling into its new home. Equally disturbing was the fact that he could not keep the mud out of his nose; it was slowly creeping in. Sometimes he made an involuntary cough that allowed a small amount of liquid to seep in through his nose. The coughs became harder to control now, and as he felt himself getting more and more light-headed, he had no choice but to let one go.

The cough was the last thing that he wanted to do, but it was inevitable. He had to breathe, his body demanded it, and when it occurred, the surrounding mud entered his mouth. There was immediate shock and horror as he tasted it, and although it was only for a split second, he knew that unless he was pulled out soon, there would be more.

The hands were moving again, pressing firmly against his body as they went. This time was different, though; more changes to their plans, he thought. Each time a hand moved, it grabbed flesh and propelled itself that way, instead of being moved against or pressed over him. More painful, sure, but their trips were longer because they traveled much slower now. Matthew thought that to be better than just running quickly over his body, as the pain informed him, that he was still alive and that there was still hope.

Turning his head to the left was what he concentrated on doing now, but it was surrounded by mud, and the only movement occurring at this time was him being pushed deeper into the mud by forces unseen. The hands moved inches at a time, bruising him as they traveled to their new destination. They had started from his lower back, now they had bruised their way to his lower stomach. His stomach hurt the most; the skin was the softest, and the surrounding area offered little muscle and bone to hinder their progress. Not to mention that it held in some seemingly soon to be unnecessary internal organs.

Matthew focused on the direction of the hands; he could not tell if they were staying put to hurt him or if they were going somewhere else. The answer came as another cough left his body; they were moving just between his stomach and chest. They were almost there, and all he could think about was that the hands were going to work together to push all of the air from his body. Matthew felt the hands pressing down repeatedly on the upper part of his stomach, just under the rib cage. Together the hands pushed in unison; they held nothing back.

He felt the first of several exhales push the remaining oxygen from his lungs. That occurred only a few seconds earlier than it was going to, as he would have coughed it out anyway. He didn't even know why they would do that; he was already a goner, unless . . . Matthew knew that someone was coming! He was sure of it. He smiled inside and grew happy with excitement; all of this happened as the mud that had just entered his mouth was being swallowed.

Mud flowed down his throat, gagging him. He didn't have to fight the reflex to throw up; it was already happening. Although Matthew had not eaten since early morning, the liquid in his stomach was being told to leave him; his body knew impurities were present and he was being made to throw them up. The process was vicious, and there was no way to stop it unfortunately, shy of being pulled from the mud. He was throwing up due to the mud being swallowed, and swallowing is what caused him to throw up in the first place.

Horror had taken hold of him unlike anything he had ever experienced before. Being beaten to an almost unconscious state, sexually abused, and sequestered in mud before being pulled down into it to drown will do that to a man. Even in the face of death, he maintained his pleasant demeanor and wit, but none of that helped to keep him alive. He wondered if Robbie would have a full life, but he knew later on he would find him in heaven. As Matthew was forced to breathe in more mud, he struggled with decisions that he had made in his life. He regretted none of them, smiling to the very end.

Robbie saw light coming from the end of his corridor. It looked like it came from a lantern because the area around it was illuminated evenly as opposed to only one direction. He couldn't tell how large the room was, but he knew it extended beyond the end of the corridor. Robbie continued walking as he called out to his dad. Doing this a few times as he walked closer, he hugged the right wall, stopping to listen just shy of the room.

It was very large in size and upon closer inspection looked to be man-made. Robbie wasn't sure if his dad had made this room or if it was one he had found. The lantern that was on the ground was his; that much Robbie was sure of. Looking around, he slowly walked in the direction of the light, watching the ground as he moved forward. There were a few tables present, against one of the walls, and right above the lantern was a hole in the wall. Robbie looked back at the tables and back at the hole and chose to stick his head into the hole and yell out for his dad.

"Dad, I've made it to the lantern over here by the tables. Where are you?" he said in a very loud squeaky voice.

Robbie laughed at that last attempt to reach out to his dad; he didn't think he was that nervous or scared, but maybe he was scared, he thought. He pushed his head further inside the other room and looked around, but it was too dark. Robbie turned around and used the lantern to light up that room. Seeing nothing of interest in what light it provided, he turned back around to examine the room he was in. He walked around the edges and looked closely at the two tables.

One table had a barrel and a small wooden crate resting against the wall behind it. He walked over to check them out and raised the lantern above the barrel. Looking inside, he found an assortment of mining tools in various conditions of repair. Among these were pickaxes, knives, a few metal spikes, a hammer, and an old piece of rope. *Cool,* he thought as he swung the lantern over the wooden crate. Something brown and furry jumped straight into the air before taking off the way Robbie had entered the room. He let out an "ah" in a very squeaky scream, and as soon as it happened, Robbie understood it was probably a rat and nothing to be afraid of.

The ceiling was high enough for Robbie to hold up his lantern and barely see it. From what he could tell, there were no bats or creatures hiding, but it would be better if his dad was here to hold the lantern closer, just in case. He thought about him, and looking around here, he saw only the lantern to prove his dad had been here. Robbie now moved over to the other table, and when he got close enough for the light to display what was on top, he froze. He barely breathed as he watched a very large rat gnawing on what might be a loaf of bread. It had eaten through the plastic bag and half of its head was inside the wrapper. Robbie was sure it was eating and he slowly backed up to the barrel to grab a weapon.

There were some rocks piled up on the wall past the rat, Robbie noted as he reached into the barrel to grab a knife. Pulling out the biggest one he saw, he turned around, and the rat was gone. Looking around the room a second time didn't offer anything to the vision that he had not seen before. Robbie sighed and took a breath before moving toward those rocks. Robbie moved at a more comfortable pace now that he knew the rats were afraid of him. He held the lantern out in front of him to see as much as he could. Rocks were piled up into three groups by size, he guessed. With the light that the lantern threw on them, the rocks looked normal. They were nothing like what his dad told him gold looked like.

Robbie walked over to the last of the walls and held the lantern high. This is what his dad had spoken about before— white crystals in the walls. *Quarts,* he thought, *no, quartz, with a z.* Where you found quartz, you can find gold, Robbie remembered. He can't wait to tell his dad about this, he thought, as he moved the lantern from the left side of the wall to the right.

"Wow, there's so much of it. There's gotta be gold here," he said excitedly for only the rats to hear.

His last comment reminded Robbie to get out of this room and continue searching for his dad. *This can wait,* he thought. Robbie turned and took off toward the corridor, keeping the lantern in front of him as he navigated the rocks and debris on the cave floor. He looked to the right at the hole one more time as he went to find his dad. A few more steps and he was just to the right of the corridor entrance. He was maybe ten feet or so away from it when he hit a rock with his foot and stumbled forward. He caught himself on the wall, thanks to his shoulder hitting it first.

"Man, that hurt," Robbie said as he looked back at what he had tripped on.

He moved back over what he had kicked loose and saw it was a dirty white rock. There were different-colored rocks inside of it, and being the size of a baseball, it caught his interest, so he reached down to pick it up. Most of it was in the ground, leaving only a small side exposed; that was probably why it was missed in the first place. He turned it in his hand and examined the rock and then placed it in his pocket. He took another step and he eyed the hole that the rock had come from; there was something inside.

Robbie took a knee and reached his hand inside, pulling out a small white stick. He held it in front of the lantern and examined it. Halfway down it had a knot, as one might find on a tree. *Weird,* he thought. He went over to the wall and picked up one of the larger rocks from the pile on the left and placed it inside the hole, marking it for later and ensuring that no one would break an ankle by hitting it. He placed the stick in his pocket with the rock and headed out again in search for his dad.

Not one step had been taken before Robbie caught something out of the right corner of his eye. It was something white and it was sticking out of the wall at just his eye level. He walked straight over to the wall, noticing a small section of quartz immediately below the hammer. There was a hammer that had been stuck in the wall, and attached to it were the bones of a human hand.

Robbie stared at it from different angles as he moved closer to the wall. The bottom of the hand had part of the forearm bone still attached. It was a skinless dead piece of bone that still held on to its hammer. Robbie didn't know the name of that bone; they had not covered that in class yet, but he knew enough to recognize a hand when he saw one. It fascinated him, and for one who was afraid of rats, he held no fear when he gazed upon the hand. Robbie had to remind himself that he was distracted once again from finding his dad; he had to leave and make his way back to the main entrance.

Had Robbie paid extra attention to the hand on the hammer, he would have seen that it had a missing finger. He already had that finger in his pocket, along with a piece of quartz that he intended to show his dad later, if he ever found him. Robbie placed the lantern on the ground, marking his direction, and took off running toward the entrance. He knew the way by heart now, and as long as he didn't get distracted . . .

Moving quickly through turns in the first two corridors, he promptly took a left, another left, a right, and then Robbie lost track of the lefts. As he began stopping to backtrack, his feet splashed through cold water that was up to his ankles within seconds. Looking down, he saw something in the mud, but there was no time to react; his left foot was already moving forward and hit the object mid stride. Robbie saw himself falling forward in slow motion and recognized his dad's old brown shirt right before he slammed face-first into his dad's chest.

CHAPTER THIRTEEN

Robbie's Monsters

Matthew didn't feel like cooking. Matthew didn't feel like eating. Matthew didn't feel like doing anything at all, but he had to keep up a strong façade for Robbie. Cooking Robbie macaroni and cheese, bacon, bacon, more bacon, and for the main dish—bacon was just what he loved to do. Although Matthew had cooked that feast for Robbie, which had the added benefit of leftovers for the next three days, he still found it hard to talk about what he had experienced.

He had thanked Robbie over and over for saving him. Even though he did that, he still mentioned that it was a very dangerous place and that he should never go there alone. Dinner passed with very little details about Matthew's day; Robbie was to know only what he did up to the point of finding him, and nothing more.

"Dad, I know this is a quiet dinner and all, but I just wanted to say I'm glad you're alive," Robbie said with a serious face.

He thought about how he had found him sitting on his butt, waving his hands crazily in the air. It had taken Robbie several minutes of pulling on the back of his shirt to get his butt out of the mud and onto the dry rocks. Several minutes after that he convinced him to crawl out to the clean air with him and look at an interesting rock he had found earlier. Well, the rest was history; a few deep breaths of clean air and he was himself again. Robbie had never showed his dad that rock; it was used only to lure him outside into the fresh air. He made a mental note to show him that rock another day.

Matthew looked on speechless, letting his eyes wander from the table to Robbie a few times before he knew what he would say.

"Yeah, whatever!" he barely got out before Robbie broke out in laughter.

Shortly after that, the two placed their dishes in the sink and went to relax a bit to a movie. They sat on separate sides of the living room and watched a man in black wrestle a rodent of unusual size to save a princess.

"I love this movie," Robbie said as he got comfortable on the couch.

"Yes, it's a classic, son," Matthew replied as he closed his eyes to take a nap.

Robbie slept well that night; no bad dreams came his way. He awoke at 7:00 a.m. per usual with his alarm clock telling him it was time to get up. He silenced the alarm by slapping it off onto the floor, stretched, and then threw his feet off the side of the bed and onto the floor. It was colder than normal, he remarked, as he took one step forward only to fall flat on his face. He was in the mine! His head smarted enough to cause him to close his eyes against it.

Robbie opened them; he was staring at the dark ground and a nearby rock that was large enough to have killed him had he hit it. The ground was dirty—dirty and wet? Robbie reached down and stuck two fingers into the mud. It was red clay, from what he could tell. He was bleeding pretty hard at the moment. He thought it was his nose, but he could breathe just fine; nothing felt broken. Maybe it was his lip, maybe he had bitten it when he fell forward, he didn't know.

He called out for his dad, but he never answered. Robbie looked around; it was dark everywhere he turned. He felt a breeze coming from behind him, but still he saw no light. He heard nobody at all as he stared at the wall and concentrated. Robbie called out for his dad again as he slowly started to crawl toward the breeze.

Matthew stretched and yawned, throwing his hands out above his head, and pointed his toes to the wall. He moved them left and right, pretending to be his metal detector. He moved them until he was centered over where the gold was and started laughing as he sat down to dig. Smiling to himself, he turned his head and listened; he thought he heard something. Matthew was very quiet, and as he turned his head to the right, he heard it again: claws over stone or rock. Something was coming his way; he listened again and reached to his left to grab his pickaxe.

Not coming his way—no, it was moving away from him, he was sure of it. Matthew was determined to continue following the noises. They were always around the next corner, but he had memorized this part of the mine, and soon they would be at a dead end. He was following something that was trying to get out, or away from him; if that was the case, why move toward a dead end?

Matthew had been unable to sleep last night, so he made a cup of coffee and two portions of oatmeal and headed off to the mine. Today he would make an early start and dig down a corridor opposite of the water. He thought it ironic that upon traveling to it, he became tired, and when he arrived at the mine, he settled in for a little nap.

Robbie heard things now too, creepy crawly things. *Monsters,* he thought. He was sure they were monsters; he heard claws, scratching, and clicking noises in the dark. He heard them all around him, especially in the corner to his left. Robbie stopped breathing just to be sure. He told himself that if he heard them one more time, he would scream as loudly as he could and make for the breeze at full speed. Claws, it was right in front of him in the darkness, just out of sight. It was the mountain lion, he was sure of it. Robbie heard its breath and once again the claws.

Bloodcurdling screams echoed from left to right one tunnel ahead. Matthew panned the flashlight in front of him as he ran toward them. He turned left and hit the corridor with his hand on the left edge of the wall, keeping his balance. He took

another step and he knew where he was. Water rose above his
boots and flooded his toes. The screams were much louder now;
they were his son's, and he was heading right for him.

Turning the corner, Robbie hit the water running. At times,
he thought his feet didn't hit the water at all. He splashed
ferociously as he ran toward what Robbie thought was the
entrance. He heard his dad yell for him between his screams.
Robbie screamed less now and even tried to yell his dad's name
as he continued to splash through the water.

Matthew noticed his son running toward him and called
out to him as he started moving through the watery tunnel. He
finally saw Robbie screaming, running his direction with wide-
open crazed eyes. He grabbed his son, holding him tightly as he
kept flailing. Robbie continued screaming a few seconds longer
as his dad continued to console him. A few seconds after that
and his dad held him calmly against his chest.

He told his son how much he loved him, as tears filled his
eyes; looking down at Robbie, he scolded him in the same
breath.

"What were you doing here? You could have drowned!"
Matthew said sternly.

Robbie started crying again as Matthew continued holding
him tight. He took one knee and hugged Robbie even tighter,
trying to console him. A smile came over his face that Robbie
could not see as Matthew turned Robbie over and placed him
over his knee.

"Be still now, Robbie," Matthew said.

Robbie awaited his discipline, but it never came; instead, he
was slid off the knee and placed into the water. Seconds later,
Matthew pressed his head down into the water, making sure to
keep it above the mud. Robbie felt the water hit his cheeks and
bury his mouth and nose, but it fell short of his ears.

"Tocha slafês sliumo, triuua uuerit kraftlicho," Matthew sang
as he listened to Robbie blowing bubbles.

The bubbles came loud and fast at first but slowed the longer
he held his head under the water. Gradually they slowed down

even further as Robbie became short of breath. He raised him up, and as Robbie gasped for air, he slammed his face down into the mud. Robbie's ears felt the cold water fill them; the coldness reached his brain. The water in his ears made everything he heard sound hollow, distant, and unclear. His breathing attempts were as loud as a passing train.

Robbie's hands reached backward as he tried to free himself. A knee was pressed down against his back, down on the back of his head. That caused more bubbles to escape, although Robbie tried to hold his breath. The knee was lifted from his back, and again he was raised out of the water and allowed to breathe. He was weakening; his lungs held less and less, and each time he tried to breathe, he found it more difficult.

Robbie didn't understand any of this. He didn't know how he had gotten in here or how this all transpired. Repeatedly he threw his hands backward and to the sides in an attempt to dislodge his dad to regain his freedom. Robbie found it harder and harder to breathe, and struggle as he might, he could not get free.

"Get up, son," his dad said to him as he pushed harder.

Robbie was sure his neck would break from the force. He felt his dad's fingers close around his neck as he slid his other hand down to his shoulders. At this point, his ears were now above water and his chin was being pushed lower into the mud. Robbie could open his eyes now and looked at the distant wall opposite of where he was. He saw something shiny reflecting light back at him.

"Get up, son. It's time for school," his dad said.

Robbie awoke on the floor of his bedroom, half beneath his bed. It was quite comical, his dad thought, as he saw only his son's ankles hanging out.

"Come on, Robbie, let's get moving," Matthew said, and grabbing him by his exposed ankles, he pulled him out.

Robbie's eyes were wide open and he breathed heavily as his dad tugged on him. Robbie recoiled at first when his dad reached to help him up.

"It's OK, son, you were dreaming. You woke me up with your screams. You are safe, son. Why, you haven't had a bad dream for several days now," he said.

Robbie had recently caught his breath when he hugged his dad hard around his knees.

"I don't remember anything, Dad. Honestly, I don't," Robbie told him.

"Well, you must have fallen pretty hard—you cut your lip. Here, let me check it out for you. It's all stopped now. I'll clean the floor up later. Let's get you ready for school," he told Robbie.

Robbie's walk to Ruthie's house was uneventful. The hills and trees were as beautiful as they always were, and as soon as he passed one, another one in the distance offered up its beauty. Robbie and Ruthie walked to school and began their day as usual; the only thing different was the course assignments and the clothes that they wore. The day was almost over when Robbie realized that it was soon to be the weekend! Although he didn't have major plans, he did plan on going into town with his dad; it was always a good time to search for marbles, he thought.

Ruthie continued walking with Robbie, enjoying all the trees and hills along the way. Robbie didn't talk too much; he was enjoying his time with Ruthie and the great outdoors as well.

"There's something I have to tell you, Robbie," Ruthie said.

Robbie looked over at her as they walked forward to a small group of trees.

"Let's stop over there for a few, OK?" Ruthie asked.

"Sure, sounds good to me," Robbie said as he looked for rocks to sit on.

"No good way to say it, so here it is. Dad's taking me to Sacramento for at least a week, if not more," Ruthie said matter-of-factly.

Robbie looked away and continued to listen.

"I'm not leaving for good—it's just to meet his wife-to-be. He's been looking now for years, and he's finally found one he wants me to meet," Ruthie said, laughing.

"Oh, well, that's important, I guess," he replied.

"She's never going to be my mom. I just want to see my dad and say hi—it's been a long time," Ruthie said.

"Well, I'll miss our walks and the fun we have talking about school. I'm sure I can wait for you," he said.

Ruthie looked to her left and then turned back to him before laughing about what he said.

"OK . . ." she said as she took off running to her house.

It took Robbie a few minutes to realize why he could not catch her; he was carrying both of their book bags!

"Hey, wait up or I'm dropping your bag!" he yelled out.

"You better not! I'll tell my mom!" she yelled back as she slowed down so he could catch up.

The rest of the walk was as it ever was, fun and relaxing. They stopped by her mailbox, and Robbie turned around to ask her a question. Ruthie leaned in, closed her eyes, and gave him a single kiss. Robbie was surprised and shocked as he finished his kiss with his eyes open; he was almost afraid to move.

"Good-bye, Robbie," Ruthie said as she grabbed her book bag and closed the door behind her.

Robbie stared at her door a few seconds more and then started the last of his trip home. He came home to an empty house; his dad was mining most of the day and into the night now. Some days Robbie came and left without seeing him, but there was always a note telling that he loved him and giving him any important information that his dad thought he would need.

Robbie thought about dinner and his homework. It would not take long for either, he thought, as he searched for the remote for the TV. Turning it on, he switched channels until he saw nothing that he liked, so he put on a local news channel and listened to it while he cooked his bacon on the stove. Tonight was to be a peanut butter, banana, and bacon sandwich, with a small bag of chips. The bacon wouldn't take that long to cook, and while it was cooling, he would slice the banana lengthwise and coat the bread with enough peanut butter to kill a mule.

The news was boring as usual and lacking of anything remotely discernable as *local* to his area. Animal attacks, gas prices, and an occasional rumor usually made it. There wasn't much in the way of murder and criminal cases around these parts, Robbie noticed. He thought back about the one that slowly walked the halls of his school and it made him shiver. *Now that was a story for headlines,* he thought. Robbie enjoyed his dinner in front of the TV alone and thinking of his dad.

Robbie cleaned up the kitchen and washed his dish before cracking his books for tonight's homework. He was sure that Ruthie had already finished hers, and she probably had time to check it three times over for correctness too. He gave it a best effort approach and only checked it once; that usually meant the difference between her A or A+ and his B or B-, but, oh well. Finishing early tonight, like expected, he turned off the TV, locked the doors, and went to bed to reread a good comic adventure. He was asleep before he finished it, but he knew how it ended. Robbie had read that one numerous times and he loved it more and more each time he finished it.

Matthew was mining into the early morning hours of the night to make progress against that damnable wall. He just knew something was behind it and he had to make the hole larger for Robbie to crawl into. Even after all his work over the last two days, he still had an entrance large enough for Robbie but too small for him to pass through it. Matthew was able to use his flashlight to explore the hole. He moved it left to right and took notes on what he was able to discern about that hidden room. There was a wall immediately behind the hole, roughly cut out, but it did not go back far at all. This crushed Matthew; he didn't understand it.

Frustration took over as he sat down to make entries into his notebook. He would still need Robbie to come and check it out. Matthew had to be sure that it didn't reach out in another direction and open up. Looking at his notebook map, he thought it had potential, but Robbie would have to prove that theory for him. Matthew hoped that Robbie would think it fun. He wondered if the information that he gave Robbie would be helpful or if he should just continue to make the hole wider for him to go through.

Another lovely day, Robbie thought as he stepped out of bed and began his morning ritual. Stepping out of the shower feeling refreshed and alive, he began drying off and getting dressed for today's endeavors. This was to be a quick day at school; he thought about cutting and running to town to see if they had any marbles. Robbie was always looking for them, and what better way to spend the end of one's school day than to search for them while possibly drinking a handmade strawberry shake.

Robbie walked into the kitchen and opened the fridge to remove some bacon and eggs for this morning's feast. He would use the gas range this morning and cook them as quick as possible. Speed was a good perk, but the taste was actually better when his breakfast was cooked in that cast iron skillet. Robbie quickly set the table and opened today's homework to double-check his work. He did that while waiting for the pan to heat up, which was paramount to his success; the pan had to be hot before cooking could begin.

It wasn't long before the eggs needed to be turned, and by this time, he had already closed his book and placed it back inside his bag. The smell of bacon filled the house; it was present everywhere he wanted to it to be. In particular, it hung heavy over the kitchen area. When he turned off the burner and removed the pan from the grate, he breathed in two lungfuls before he left to sit at the table.

Taking his homework assignment and placing it into his book bag, he looked back over his shoulder to ensure the kitchen and table were picked up before leaving. Robbie didn't know if his dad would be home so sleep soon or if he would be spending all of his time in the mine. Either way, he wanted the house to be clean and ready for the next family interaction, no matter when it would occur.

The school day went on as usual, boring and uneventful. He did not play marbles with the guys and spent the day conversing

with Ruthie before, during, and after classes. He changed his
mind on going to find marbles; he would just wait for his dad
to take him to a few places to search for them. It wasn't because
skipping school wasn't cool, which is what he was told by his
teachers. It was because he was actually having fun with Ruthie.
Between classes, he was harassed by Thomas and Luke about his
inability to play marbles; that too was normal, but it bothered
him less nowadays. Robbie really loved spending time with
Ruthie, so Thomas and Luke didn't bother him.

Finally, Robbie thought, the end of the day was near. Tonight's
homework didn't look bad, not at all. Taking a look out the
window, the weather looked like it would be accommodating,
with not a cloud in the sky.

"Almost ready for our walk, Ruthie?" Robbie asked.

"I was meaning to talk to you about all of those, Robbie,"
Ruthie replied.

Robbie looked at her with serious eyes and then turned to
look outside before looking back at her.

"Yes?" he asked.

"Maybe we should take a break, just for a little while," Ruthie
said without her usual smile.

"Seriously, why?" Robbie said with a squeaky voice.

Ruthie looked around the room and peered over at the
clock; it was almost 3:00 p.m.

"Because you look frail and I don't want you to hurt yourself,"
she said loudly as she bolted for the door.

Her timing was right on, and when she hit the door, the bell
rang and she took off running.

"Catch up, you slow and frail son of a miner." Ruthie laughed,
disappearing out of sight.

"No fair!" Robbie yelled as he quickly followed her out the
doors and into the parking lot.

The two spent another lovely afternoon walking home
through nature and enjoying each other's company. After
leaving her at her mailbox, per usual, he smiled and walked to
his house. He was unusually tired today and looked forward to

taking a nap before dinner and homework. This he could do if his dad wasn't home. Robbie wasn't sure if he would come home or not; it's only been a few days since he saw him last. The record was four days without seeing a living and breathing dad at the dinner table; today would be three.

Robbie's walk up to the house saw no signs of Dad thus far. He might come in before dinner; Robbie would check around for a note and see what the plan for the day was. He opened the door and walked inside, locking it behind him. Looking around, he saw nothing to indicate his dad had been home and left; there wasn't even a note. No worries; with as little homework as he had, he would start off today by watching a movie before dinner. Digging through the movie rack, he pulled out a personal favorite, *Reservoir Dogs*.

Running up to the kitchen, he dug through the pantry and pulled out a bag of walnut halves and poured some in a bowl for a healthy alternative to popcorn. Robbie had just jumped onto the couch when the movie started. *Great timing,* he thought. He remembered movie quotes and trivia from all of his favorite movies; this one was no different. For example, he would often say to people, "Did you know that they say the f-bomb in this movie 269 times?"

His dad wasn't proud that his son knew that fact, but his son never acted out or did things that he wasn't supposed to; well, not that he knew of anyway. Matthew always spent time helping to grow his son's mind and morals, and he didn't believe in restricting or sequestering one's loved ones to "protect them." It was all about exposure and education, Matthew always said. He would introduce his son to things he wanted him to learn about and then explain why it was or was not a good idea to go down that road.

Robbie enjoyed his movie, and when it was finished, he let the credits roll, like he always did. He would use that time to start dinner; multitasking is what it was called. He would make a bag of sweet peppers, two heads of broccoli, and two chicken breasts. That should provide enough leftovers in case

Dad doesn't make it home in time for dinner. He cut up all the peppers and placed them with the chicken in the oven at 375 degrees for forty-five minutes and then set the stove timer for a few minutes to allow the broccoli time to steam in the microwave.

He walked over to the couch and started the movie over to watch as much as he could before he had to get the dinner out of the oven. Robbie made it through most of the movie before he had to place it on hold to take care of the oven. Tonight he would eat by himself and in front of the TV as he finished the movie for the second time today. After the dishes were cleaned up, the table and TV trays wiped off, he grabbed his book bag to peruse his homework for the day.

Robbie found his procrastination more formidable than he had thought, and as he ran into writer's block, he decided to watch a new movie for motivation. It was about seven thirty before he paused the movie and again hit the books hard. Making good progress but not completing it, he decided to truly take a nap and get back up to finish his work later. Minutes after laying his head down on the pillows, Robbie became more comfortable and relaxed, and then he fell off to sleep.

Robbie awoke to the sounds of breaking glass and gunfire. From underneath his door, he saw shadows walk from left to right and then disappear out of sight. He jumped off his bed and grabbed his slingshot and a few metal balls for ammo. He crouched by the side of the bed, waiting for his door to be opened. He was sweating heavily now, his heart raced; all he could do was listen as he stared at the shadows that came and went beneath his bedroom door.

Robbie listened closely and tried to determine how many people were robbing him when he heard one man say, "I think whatever doesn't kill you makes you, stranger." Robbie let out a "fuuuuck," as he knew that voice to be from the Joker . . . He stood up, placed his weapon on his bed, and opened his door. Peering inside, he saw no one moving around the living room. Next, he looked at the front door, which was closed and appeared to be locked. Looking around as he walked slowly in the room, he found no broken glass. When he approached the TV, his movie was still playing. He walked over to the DVD player and pressed the off button and shook his head, laughing as he went back to bed.

CHAPTER FOURTEEN

SWYFTP . . .

Robbie woke up today at a normal time, but he already felt rushed. He quickly dressed, and instead of having breakfast, he had lunch to deal with. Going to the kitchen, he started making the first of three beef, turkey, bacon, and cheese sandwiches. Robbie decided to make one more, as he would probably eat one along the way to the mine. Walking back into the bedroom, he emptied out his book bag and carried it into the kitchen. He would use it to carry everything for his trip to the mine. In the bottom, he placed cold drinks and, on top of them, the sandwiches. Last but not least, he placed a few bags of chips on top and then closed it.

Today was Saturday; the weekend had begun and not a minute too soon. He took a few steps toward the door before he remembered to grab a small notebook and pen; Robbie wanted to make some sketches of the mine himself. He also thought it would be cool if he and his dad both took notes while they looked around at the mine; his dad would think that very funny. Robbie opened his front door and took one step outside, and the sky turned black. The storm was moving in quickly, and with it were high winds and a sudden drop in temperature.

A single bolt of lightning came down and struck a distant tree followed a few seconds later by a deafening clap of thunder. It became darker, and the wind picked up even more as Robbie took the first steps in the direction of the mine. Everything became wild around him as bushes, trees, and everything not nailed down moved around in the air. The bushes shook as if they held monsters that were trying to escape. Trees were bent over from left to right in an eternal bow to the storm's power.

Robbie turned around and sought shelter underneath their porch and sat on the swing. He watched the storm move closer with the comfort of a slow front-to-back movement. Large fluffy clouds rolled in very quickly only to be immediately replaced by new ones as they dropped their rain. At times, the rain fell straight down in buckets, and others it was almost sideways. The trees bowed over and over again as the rain continued to pour from the heavens.

He pulled out a sandwich and a bag of chips and ate his snack while the winds ripped through the area. Bite after bite of Robbie's sandwich went down as the wind took its bite out of the area. When Robbie had finished his sandwich, he started on his chips, and within a few seconds of doing that, the winds became calm and the rain subsided. The last to clear up was the sky, which he saw turning bluer by the second. The clouds kept moving as if still being pushed by the wind. Those on the ground no longer heard or felt it; the storm was gone.

Robbie started once again walking to the mine, this time without the storm over head. His shoes and socks became wet as he walked through the tall grass. The rest of the trip would be a soggy one, which resulted in him being wet from head to toe by the time it was done. He wished he had put dry clothes in with his book bag when he saw the storm come through. *It would have been helpful,* he thought. Robbie took a break standing against a large tree to squeeze out his socks and drain the water from his shoes.

He wasn't too far away now, probably half the distance to the mine when he decided to turn back and get cleaned up. This was a surprise lunch for his dad, and if it never happened, he would be none-the-wiser. Robbie made a sigh as he turned around and started squishing his way home. His shoes spurted water from the sides every time he took a step. They would not be dry when Dad came home; he would help them out and place them in the dryer, he thought as he continued past the last hill on the way to his house.

For weeks now, Matthew had thought about finding someone to help out around the house, a babysitter or a home helper. He wanted to break it to Robbie before he just saw some old lady breaking into the house one day after school. Matthew had no idea of what to do or where to go, but he was sure that he would thoroughly interview the woman. Maybe she would work out. He hoped she would have common interests with him and his son and that she had enough time to clean up and cook for them. He made a point to tell him one night soon so he could get his reaction.

Matthew had conquered several obstacles since he and Robbie decided to travel to California. Their family had taken a financial hit that could possibly take over a year to recover from. Matthew couldn't wait that long, so he cashed in his 401K to pay for his fresh start. He gambled that a hobby and his recently obtained knowledge would provide enough for his family. Mining was the way to do it, and when he saw a property for sale with a local history, he could not pass it up. The only thing he didn't think about when he planned his adventure was a woman.

Women were not in the picture for Matthew, not after what had happened back East; it was too soon. He had only seen a few of them in town and only one neighbor since the plane crash landed in his front yard. With all of the time that he worked and explored the land around him, there wasn't much left for his son, let alone a woman. That didn't mean that he didn't think about them, and often. So it was with this in mind that he wanted to run into Chloe in town or on the road and ask her and Ruthie over for dinner. Matthew wrote a reminder in his notebook to ask Robbie about this tonight to see if he was all right with it.

The next few days, Matthew spent mining from early morning into the early evening and then he would come home to have dinner with Robbie. He cooked most of the meals throughout the week, but one of those nights, Robbie would get to cook whatever he wanted for them. Tonight was Robbie's night, but if Matthew had his way, he would be cooking for four. All that Matthew had to do was just to run into Chloe.

Matthew closed the shop early today with plans on making that happen. It would take him approximately three quarters of an hour to walk home, another thirty minutes or so to get cleaned up, and then depending on traffic . . . *Hell with that,* he thought as he headed off in her direction at a good pace. He could make it there in half the time, and if luck was with him, he would catch her there and put her on the spot, right in front of her daughter.

'I've no shame," he said as he walked on.

"What's that, Ruthie, you wouldn't mind coming over for shrimp macaroni and cheese?" He laughed.

Climbing the last hill offered a view of Chloe's house and driveway. As luck would have it, she was not home, or at least the truck wasn't. It's not that Ruthie had it; she's too young to drive, he thought, laughing. Matthew took a few more steps and then turned around; he would need his truck after all. He would continue his conquest in town, checking every store on Main Street to find her. It was with good planning that one was successful, and great planning one could really stand out. Matthew saw himself going down the path of greatness, all because he had allowed plenty of time to find her before dinner would have to be rescheduled.

Matthew planned his next moves, wondering all the time how all of this would work out. He saw the need for a person to help around the house during the day and sometimes at night. While walking, he thought about something between a babysitter, a nanny, and a substitute teacher, and how that person would fit in. Down the road, he did want a mother figure for Robbie and a wife for him. He also didn't rule out an interim girlfriend until everything else worked out. Matthew was almost home now and he debated whether he would shower first. Making his decision, he jumped in the truck and quickly headed out.

The trip to town was laborious but beautiful. It offered a variety of rocks and trees to distract the nature lover in any driver. Matthew made numerous turns in the winding road as he continued to think on the girlfriend angle. Maybe he could find a woman who was a good fit for their chaotic life—possibly someone who can help out around the house and who is old enough for him to consider dating? Rounding the last bend, he yielded to invisible oncoming traffic and began looking for her truck. It was nowhere to be found, so he parked midway down the street and got out to canvas the area. Somebody probably saw her, he thought; it was worth a shot.

Walking down the street, he kept an eye open for Chloe and her truck as he moved from store to store. Matthew was running out of time to search for her in town. Soon he would have to make a decision on whether to go back and check her house on the way home. He would hit the general store and just ask about her before he left. Opening the door, Matthew saw several men and women walking around, but not Chloe. He walked past a few women who were looking at the garden center and smiled widely as he approached the owner.

"Hey, I'm looking for Chloe," Matthew said, not knowing her last name.

"I'm sorry. I don't know who you mean," the store owner replied, puzzled.

"She's Ruthie's mom. They live back past the school," he stated.

"Ah. Nope. Not seen her in a week," he said as he prepared to ring up a customer.

"I'll try back later. Thanks for your help," Matthew told the man.

Matthew walked toward the front door and grabbed the handle. He wanted a backup; he needed to see what local help was available, if at all, and here was a good place to start. He turned and faced the man again and asked him if he had a bulletin board of want ads.

"Whatcha looking for, son?" he asked Matthew.

"I need someone to help around the house, general chores and possibly some babysitting," he said, smiling.

"There by the door, on your left," Mr. Wilson said, pointing to Matthew's right.

Matthew nodded and turned to the board that if it were a snake, it would have bitten him and looked at all the business cards and flyers.

One small yellow paper caught his eye: SWYFTP seeking household with young family—references available upon request.

Toward the bottom of the paper was her phone number. It was different from the rest because if didn't offer individual vertical tabs with her number; hers was listed solely on the bottom. He smiled as he took it down and walked out the door.

Matthew would never find Chloe that night in time to make dinner, but he did stop by afterward. He brought Robbie along for the ride so he could keep Ruthie occupied. Chloe and Matthew made small talk in the kitchen over a few cups of coffee for hours. They seemed to hit it off, exchanging cell phone numbers and talking late into the evening. Before they knew it, both kids were asleep in front of the television.

"I thought they would never turn off," Matthew said, smiling.

"It's called sugar, they crave it!" Chloe said, laughing.

He knew it was time to go when he started picturing her naked. Long gone were those days when he just met someone and had sex; he was more responsible and older now.

"It's late. I really ought to get him home," he said to her.

"Oh. Yeah, right. Sorry to keep you out this late," Chloe said.

They both stood up and walked into the living room to wake the kids up. After a few minutes, Matthew and Robbie were ready to go. Robbie said good-bye to Ruthie, and Matthew smiled and shook Chloe's hand. She shook his hand and told him that they should have dinner some night soon. They said their good-byes, and Matthew drove the short distance home.

Over the next week, Matthew mined throughout the day and sometimes into the night. Robbie and Matthew saw Chloe and Ruthie a couple of times in passing. Both couples were too busy for normal life, so dinner never happened. One night, while Robbie was doing homework at the kitchen table, Matthew remembered the yellow piece of paper. He went over to his kitchen counter and sorted through several inches of papers before finding it. Matthew took it to the couch and sat down to dial the number.

Robbie knew what Dad was doing; he was calling that girl. He saw him take the yellow paper from the pile on the counter and go into the living room. Earlier, he found that paper and hid it in the middle of a stack of junk mail so his dad would forget about it. Robbie didn't want a babysitter; he was doing just fine as it was. He also did an excellent job of cleaning the house; he didn't want to see is allowance money cut because someone else was doing the vacuuming. Listening closer, he stopped writing so he could concentrate on his dad's conversation.

Matthew left a message for the woman, leaving his name, number, address, and times that he was available for an interview. He gave her the option of coming over to the house or doing it over the phone. Robbie heard him end with "I look forward to your phone call" and then sat the phone on the armrest. He took this time to walk up to his dad and stand in front of him, effectively blocking him from standing up. Matthew looked up at him and laughed.

"I know what you are here for, Robbie." He smiled.

"You have no idea how hard I work around here, Dad," Robbie said.

Matthew looked on and continued listening to his son.

"Dishes, laundry, some cooking, and the garbage—these are all things taken care of by me. I do them well so I can get my allowance," Robbie said seriously.

He nodded and paused from speaking to give his son the attention that he needed.

"You can't take that away from me, you just can't," he said excitedly.

Matthew had already thought about this and he was prepared as much as he could be when he told Robbie that he understood.

"I know you need your allowance, Robbie. You'll get it no matter what. I will make sure she does a good job and I'll also check that she's really bad at video games so when you guys play, you can beat her really badly!" he said to him.

Robbie looked at him and waited for the "but, Dad"; there was always a "but," he thought. Matthew had paused enough before finishing his argument.

"She's not going to boss you around, son—that's my job! There's also no way that I would ever allow anyone to replace Mom. You know I wouldn't do that, Robbie. No matter if I meet anyone or not, she won't be Mom," Matthew said seriously, stretching out his hands.

Matthew gave Robbie a big hug and then sent him into the bathroom to get cleaned up before bed. Robbie's smile was enough to let him know that all was well, and if he had any doubts, Matthew knew for sure when the bathroom door closed to a very loud "yeah!"

"Did you hear all of that, Gwen?" Matthew asked after picking up the phone again.

"Sure did. I know everything will work out just fine. Four o'clock then?" she asked.

"Sounds good to me, Gwen. Bring your appetite, and we'll watch a movie with Robbie afterward and then I'll make my decision," he informed her.

"Nice talking to you, Mr.?" Gwen asked.

"Matthew, you can call me Matthew. Good-bye, Gwen," he said and ended the call.

Matthew smiled and turned on the TV to relax a bit before settling in for sleep.

Robbie took his shower like a man with a purpose and cleaned every nook and cranny with military procedure. He ran the washrag over his face and chest before moving it to his pits. He was covered in soap from head to toe before he stepped forward to rinse off. The water was nice and warm against his clean body. He had to hurry up and ask Dad a few more questions before he went to sleep in front of the TV like he always did.

Matthew was already asleep when Robbie stepped out of the bathroom and began drying off. He walked over to the chair and took a blanket over to his dad, covering him from his feet to midchest, and then went to bed. Robbie could wait to ask his dad about weekend time with Ruthie; he wanted to know if he could stay the night over at her house. He had not mentioned this to Ruthie yet, but he thought it would be fun.

This night was a rare one for Matthew and his son because they had both slept through the night without a care in the world. Neither of them tossed and turned or had bad dreams. They both woke up fully rested, and at their normal times and places; Matthew on the couch around 3:00 a.m. and Robbie in his bed at exactly 7:00 a.m.

Matthew had gotten up and raided the fridge for some lunch meat, cheese, and bread. He gathered his mining bag and ensured he had three flashlights and his basic gear, grabbed his lunch, and closed the door quietly behind him. He needed a head start today if he was to make it back by 4:00 p.m. for his interview.

Robbie dragged his butt out of bed because the alarm had told him to. Since he had showered last night, he didn't have to worry about that today. He quickly searched his closet for something to wear. Robbie had forgotten to set his clothes out last night and he didn't want to miss his chance to make bacon for breakfast. If it came to being late for school and eating bacon or not eating bacon and being on time, the bacon would have to wait.

By the time Robbie decided that he was going to be late if he cooked the bacon, Matthew had already been hard-rock mining for several hours. He had also had time for his first break where he devoured the first of two salt cured ham sandwiches next to a four-foot-square pile of muck.

"Yummy! You can hardly taste the dust!" he said, laughing.

Matthew wasn't used to eating underground among rocks, let alone not seeing daylight for most, if not all, of his day. Within two minutes, he had finished the ham, and several minutes after that, he was sorting his rock pile into four categories. After that was completed, he swept up the remaining debris into a corner for him to go over it later. It was then that he found it—his first true nugget. It was much larger than what he had found before, but it wasn't about how big it was; it was the promise of hope that it carried. He wondered if there would be more, if he was close to a vein, and if he was going in the right direction with his new tunnel. He thought about this for about half an hour as he consulted his map while sitting on a flat rock in the corner of the room.

Every few minutes, Matthew would look up, examine the direction the tunnel was going in, and then lower his head to consult the map again. He was once again trying to calculate distance between the two mines when his first light source failed. The white notebook pages went pale and then disappeared into the darkness around him. Matthew didn't panic; he just reached in his pocket and took out a small flashlight. He used that light to find his way to his tool bag and pulled out a large one-foot-long flashlight.

Placing the small one into his pocket, he used the larger flashlight to examine the map. Staring at it for a few moments before glancing back up at the tunnel, he stood up and walked over to his second lantern and cranked the igniter. A soft glow of yellow light lit the immediate area around Matthew until he turned the knob that increased the flame. The room now was as bright as he imagined the outside would be. It took a few minutes for him to get used to the light, and when he did, he picked it up and walked around the edges of his newly expanded room.

It was as restrictive as it was beautiful; the room had been expanded about forty-five feet in length and about three feet in width, but it was more than half full of debris. Matthew did not have his rock crusher and therefore could not easily remove the gold from his muck. The only gold that he could quickly obtain was in the smaller pieces and the fine debris that he kept sweeping into the corner. He would go through that first, then the smaller rocks, and finally whatever he could break with his sledgehammers until he received that equipment.

Robbie's day was normal in every way, affording him no surprises as he slowly went through it. Ruthie was waiting for him by her mailbox, and they walked to school, talking about their week ahead. The guys were playing Black Snake when Robbie and Ruthie arrived, and he still could not play with them, not until he had more marbles. Homework assignments came and went with the usual grades for both of them: An A for Ruthie and a B for Robbie. Even lunch came and went with them sharing half of their food, just as always.

Ruthie talked to Robbie about their parents meeting for dinner one night soon. She expressed concerns that her mom has been different recently.

"She's just not been happy lately and she seems to worry about everything," Ruthie said.

Robbie continued to listen as he finished his bacon and bacon sandwich, nodding his head from time to time when he could not reply. He had to enjoy his bacon, and sometimes it was in his mouth too long as he crunched up every tiny morsel.

"It's just not work either. She worries about the yard, the food, the wild animals, and even the deer in the nearby woods," Ruthie said sadly.

Robbie purposefully delayed taking another bite so he could respond.

"I'm sure it will be fine. They talk to each other a lot when we are around, and they seem to have fun. Who knows if they will like each other enough to spend more time together, but I do like any time that I have with you, Ruthie," Robbie said, smiling.

Ruthie loved the time she spent with Robbie too; she just didn't want to let him know that.

"I guess," Ruthie said with a smile.

A few hours more and the two would be on their way home, climbing over the hills that blocked the view from the school to their houses. It was a lovely walk, as always with the two side by side.

Matthew had already finished his lunch and began working hard to increase the length of the tunnel. He had progressed forward about five more feet before he knew he had to stop. There wasn't much more time left for him to get back to the house. He had a little cleaning and prep work to do, he was sure of that. Looking around one final time, he turned off the lighting and made his way to the entrance. Like Robbie, his day was uneventful too as he moved the dead brush and tree over the entrance to hide it. Climbing out, Matthew looked around before making a beeline home.

Robbie stopped on the top of one of the last hills before reaching Ruthie's house and waited. Ruthie looked at him and back the way he was facing with no idea of what was going on.

"What do you see?" she asked.

Robbie looked from left to right and then focused on a small group of trees about a mile away.

"There, by those trees. Not the ones close to us, the ones further away. There's someone moving away from them. I think it's Dad, and that's where the mine is," Robbie said, smiling.

Ruthie looked on and watched a small shape moving slowly in the direction that they were going. She could not tell who it was, but it had the shape of a person.

"Nice. We'll have to go there one day, just you and I," Ruthie said.

"You bet. I want to draw a map of that place. Dad would be so proud to look at it, and hopefully it would match his. He makes awesome maps," Robbie said with an excited tone.

They continued to Ruthie's house, and Robbie smiled and gave her a hug. Ruthie loved hugs and held on a bit longer this time than the last hug, which did not go unnoticed by Robbie.

"I'll see you later then. As soon as one of us finds out about dinner, we need to tell the other, OK?" Robbie said.

Ruthie nodded yes and walked to her door.

"Good-bye Robbie," she said as she waved at him before closing her front door.

Robbie smiled and then took off running home; his only goal was to make it there before him.

Matthew walked slowly while keeping an eye out for predators in the area. He was sure that there was another mountain lion present, there just had to be.

Within minutes, Robbie was home, and Matthew was still nowhere to be found. He quickly put his stuff away, changed his clothes, and sat down in front of the TV to await his dad. Robbie made no effort to pick up the house, although he knew tonight was the dinner for the potential babysitter. He wanted to see how Dad felt about tonight's interview. Was he thinking it was a date? Would he clean up and spray the living room with a nice-smelling floral scent, or would he organize the kitchen and living room to look prepared when she arrived?

Robbie finished watching a special on the local educational channel about climate change and got up to grab a soda from the fridge. Closing the fridge, he searched for a clean glass and put a few ice cubes in it before opening his bottle. He was always good on cleaning as he went, so when the glass was full, he placed the empty bottle in the recycling bin to the left of the trash can. It was another of his chores that could possibly be taken from him, but as long as he still received his allowance, he was OK with it. Losing a few chores would free up some time for him to practice marbles and explore the mine, if he could get away from his dad to do it.

The front door opened, and in came a tired and sweaty Matthew. Robbie stood in the kitchen, sipping his cold soda and smiling at him as he closed the door. Matthew raised his hand and waited for his drink.

"Can't a man get a cold drink after a long day's work?" he asked.

Robbie laughed and got him one from the fridge and walked it over to him. He smiled and nodded his head, raising the drink to him in approval.

"Thanks, son!" he said, laughing.

Robbie walked back to the kitchen table and sat down to look at tonight's homework. It didn't look too bad, he thought; Robbie guessed he would be done before dinner. Matthew took off his shoes and walked to the bathroom to shower. This would have been a wonderful way of life, Robbie thought. If both of them arrived around the same time and could spend more of their days together; that would be nice indeed. He missed that part from his old home—the way it used to be with mom and his little brother.

Matthew climbed out of the hot shower and was drying off when he heard the toilet flush.

"Seriously?" Matthew questioned.

"When you gotta go . . ." Robbie said as he washed his hands and left the room before his dad stepped closer.

Matthew saw the door close and smiled as Robbie took two steps and broke out in laughter.

"Yeah, funny. You'll get yours later!" he yelled to Robbie through the bathroom door.

When Matthew came into the living room dressed for tonight's interview/date, Robbie still could not tell how things were going to go. The two worked together to get dinner ready. Robbie prepared the macaroni and cheese, and Matthew cleaned and rinsed the shrimp. It would take them all of ten minutes to get everything ready to cook. Robbie started setting the kitchen table, and Matthew went and checked the living room and bathroom, ensuring that they were presentable for company.

Still, Robbie could not tell. He watched his dad as he set the table. It took him longer than normal to finish, mainly because he watched his dad more than he worked on the table. Matthew watched Robbie as he moved around the living room and then ducked into the bathroom when he went to get more dishes. Robbie was looking for him when out he came with the floral spray and walked through the living room, leaving a trail of mist behind him. It was official—it was a date. He would have to work hard with Ruthie's help to get their parents together before this babysitter found her way into his family.

Robbie and Matthew sat down in the living room to watch TV; Matthew in the love seat, and Robbie in the couch. Mindless TV was just what the doctor ordered, Matthew thought, as he relaxed and let Robbie change the channels. He was pleased when he stopped at a nature show and put the remote down on the end table. He would have really been proud if he had known that it was the same show that Robbie had watched earlier. It was almost 4:00 p.m., which meant that the candidate would be arriving soon, and shortly after that, they would have dinner. Robbie did not know that she would be staying for a movie and that it would be part of the hiring process.

They were both watching as a nature kill was shown in great detail. The mother bear was fighting off some coyotes when one off to the side latched on to one of her cubs and dragged it off into the bush. It was all the brown bear could do to protect her closest cub and herself from the four that were attacking them directly. When she saw her cub being taken away, she raged and raked two of the closest coyotes and bit a third as she lunged forward.

The coyotes managed to scatter and run away, except for the one that she held tightly in her mouth. She shook it violently and raised her head high before slamming the coyote on the ground. Robbie swore he had heard the coyote's neck break as he watched it become lifeless and limp. The momma bear let out a loud growl and waited for another attack, but it never came.

"Nature has a way of balancing out situations that occur in daily life. A life for a life is not uncommon here in the bush. Tune in next week when we discuss the Western deer population and trophy hunters. I'm Lou Markens, until then," the announcer said as the show ended.

Matthew and Robbie looked at each other and laughed at the same time. That bonding moment was disturbed by a knock on the door. They looked at each other, and Robbie went into the bedroom as Matthew walked to open the door. Standing in front of Matthew was a five-foot-five-inch woman of medium complexion with long blond hair. She smiled from ear to ear, showing her whitened teeth, and extended a hand for him to shake.

"Hello. My name is Gwen. We spoke on the phone the other day. I'm here for the interview," she said politely.

"I'm Matthew. Please come in," he said, smiling at the woman.

Matthew shook her hand and invited her inside. Gwen walked in and took a few steps, turning to await her interviewer. Matthew watched her walk past him and into the room and closed the door as soon as she passed.

"The kitchen table has been set for our dinner, so we'll have to sit in the living room if you don't mind," he said to her.

"That will be just fine," she said as she walked to the living room.

He caught up to her and pointed to the couch and the love seat, giving her a choice for venue, if you will.

She threw him a small smile and sat on the love seat and opened her small folder for him and a notebook for her.

"Love seat it is then," he said, smiling.

At that instant, he wished he would have chosen different words. *Love seat, how funny,* he thought. Gwen blushed and looked away as she silently laughed. Matthew accepted her resume and read through it for a few minutes before placing it aside and beginning his questioning. He asked her the usual questions about her employment history, why she's the best candidate for the job, and how she would react in certain situations. She took notes as they went along, and before they knew it, an hour had passed.

Robbie walked out of his bedroom, and Matthew introduced his son to Gwen. He told her hello and asked his dad if he could start dinner while they wrapped things up. Matthew laughed and told him sure before turning around to continue with Gwen.

"Any questions for me then?" he asked her.

Robbie continued listening to their conversation; he just did it now from the kitchen instead of his bedroom.

"Well, what company do you work for? What are your hours? And when can I start?" she asked him.

Robbie turned on the burner and started boiling the water necessary for dinner. He pulled out the shrimp from the fridge and made their salads, complete with tomatoes and onion slices while all the while pointing one ear in their direction.

"It's almost time for dinner, if you wouldn't mind staying for it. Afterward, there might be a movie. I'll have to see if Robbie's up to it first, but I'll extend that offer for you to consider," Matthew said cautiously.

He knew that both sides had heard his offer. *How fun,* Matthew thought as he let the others do the work for him. He understood that Robbie knew he invited her for the movie, and Gwen knew that Robbie had heard this.

"We'll see how dinner goes then. I would love to watch movies afterward, if it works out," Gwen said loud enough for Robbie to hear.

Gwen was hoping Robbie thought that it would be cool for her to stay for a movie, and that Matthew thought that she had other things planned for her to say "movies" instead of "movie." When she heard no grumbles or comments against her plans, she knew she had just pleased two men at one time, which was something that she had not done in years.

Gwen closed her notebook and sat with perfect posture, smiling at Matthew. He extended an arm and helped her up so they could both walk to the table for dinner. Robbie had just finished placing the salads on the table when they sat down.

"I hope all will be to your liking, Gwen," Robbie said as he sat down in his seat.

Matthew thought it was funny; Robbie appeared to be on his best behavior, but he wasn't sure why. Gwen smiled back, nodding, and looked to Matthew.

"Oh. We don't usually say grace here, not anymore, but if you would like to?" he asked.

"Grace? She passed away thirty years ago," she said with a serious face.

Robbie looked sad and confused, but Matthew laughed; he got it.

"It's OK, Robbie, it's from a movie. I think you've only seen it once. We'll have to get it so we can watch it for the holidays, it's a Christmas movie."

"Dinner tasted great, Robbie. You did an excellent job with the salad, and the shrimp were not over cooked. My kudos to the chef!" Matthew said, raising his glass.

"Yes, remarkable indeed! I loved it all. Thank you," Gwen added.

Robbie smiled as he finished the last of his macaroni and looked at Gwen. Matthew knew things were wrapping up, so he spoke up and asked everyone into the living room.

"Well, Gwen. We don't usually have informal conversation at the dinner table, and since I can tell Robbie has a million questions for you, let's go into the living room and get the movie ready," he said.

It took Robbie all of two seconds to stand up, slide his chair back in place, and make his way into the living room. Matthew looked at Gwen, and they both laughed as they did the same, just only slower.

Robbie asked Gwen to sit on the love seat and he took the spot next to her, leaving his dad all by himself. He would have to choose the couch or the recliner, but for now he wasn't sharing her at all; Robbie had several questions for her and he wanted her to focus. Matthew laughed as he walked over to the recliner and sat down.

"Pick out our movie, Robbie. Make sure you go easy on her—she's our guest after all," he said, laughing.

Robbie turned to face her and asked Gwen what kinds of movies she liked.

"Action or cartoons?" he said, staring into her eyes.

"Cartoons," Gwen replied.

"Funny, adult, serious, or make-believe?" he asked her next.

"Funny or adult—really, they are all acceptable," she said.

"Oh, just get the movie and start it, why don't you?" Matthew said as he knew Robbie would pick *Frozen*.

Robbie smiled politely and went to pick his movie. After looking at the handful of movies that he saved when they left their old home, he grabbed *The King of New York*–he just loved Christopher Walken—and pressed the play button.

They watched the entire movie with no talking, just as one might do in a movie theater, and when the credits rolled, Matthew looked over at Gwen and then to her left where Robbie was. She smiled and mouthed the words "I should be going." Matthew got up and walked to the love seat and picked Robbie up.

"Let's get you to bed, big guy," he said, picking Robbie up.

Robbie was sleepy but understood that the movie was over and it was time for bed.

"Good night, lady," Robbie said with his eyes closed.

"Night, Robbie," Gwen replied.

Matthew whisked him away and tucked him into bed, closing his door as he walked out. He noticed that Gwen was sitting on the other side of the love seat, she had gotten comfortable, and she had changed the movie.

"Time for *Frozen*," she said, smiling.

Matthew smiled back and walked to her with the intent of sitting beside her.

"Do you mind if I?" he asked, motioning to the space beside her.

Gwen smiled back and rubbed a few small circles with her hand over the seat cushion, offering up another inviting smile. Matthew sat next to her and tried to respect her side of the couch as much as he could. The movie progressed, and just after the ice scene with the dog, Gwen asked for a pillow.

"The one over there would be great, if you don't mind," she said, pointing at the couch.

Matthew smiled back and went to grab a few of them and turned to walk back. Gwen was standing in front of him and reached up on her tiptoes to plant a kiss. She placed her arms just under his chest and pushed him away when she was done.

"You had your part of the interview process. Now you'll have to humor me and fulfill mine," Gwen said as she walked him back to the love seat.

Matthew responded with "Yes, ma'am" and sat down beside her.

He slid toward the middle and, placing his hands on her waist, turned her body slightly to her side.

"Try to watch the movie as best you can. There will be a test afterward," he told Gwen as he began undressing her.

Gwen turned her head to the side and watched the movie as Matthew entered her from behind. He moved in very slowly, taking great care not to hurt her. Matthew started getting hard from the moment she stole a kiss; he was more than willing to do his part with her interview. He had undressed her enough for his liking; her pants were off, her panties to her ankles, and he had undone her bra.

Matthew cupped her breasts while leaning in and pressed his face against her shoulder blades. He held on tightly and pushed her against him as much as he could. Gwen did all the right things; she sounded interested, she participated by matching his movements, and her overall level of comfort with her body was enough to drive him mad. Pulling back on Gwen, he turned her yet again and faced her toward the TV. Matthew remarked on what perfect posture she had as he brought her to orgasm.

Gwen came to life when the penis that had pleasured her to this point exited and inserted itself into her anus. Again she was held in place, sitting on his thighs as erect as he was, watching *Frozen*. The timing could not have been better as she began to sing along with the movie as she came a second time.

"Let it go. Let it go!" Gwen sung.

What Matthew actually heard was her saying those words with pauses between them: Let . . . it . . . go. Let . . . it . . . goooo; she said those words between Matthew's thrusting. It was this distraction that brought him to his climax. He slid his neck toward hers and whispered into her ear.

"You are incredible, Gwen. I've waited so long for this. It's been a long time for me. You . . . are . . . wonderful," he said as he forced out the last few words, continuing to come.

Gwen responded by tightening herself around his penis as she placed an evil smile on her face.

Gwen continued to slide against Matthew while she talked to him in a seductive voice.

"Come on, baby. Yes. There, right there. Oh. Yeah. Come for me, baby," Gwen said softly.

"Yes. More, please more. Push harder. Yeah. Pull. Pull my hair. I'm coming again! Fuuuck," Gwen said a bit louder than before.

Matthew was finishing now and kept her pressed tightly against his body. Knowing that he was spent, Matthew did his best to hold on for a few minutes longer. He felt Gwen tightening and releasing his penis multiple times, which helped to keep him where he needed to be. A few moments later, he gathered her up and carried her over to the couch where they stretched out and covered up under a warm blanket.

"I think it's better if we spend the night out here for the first time, unless you have to leave?" Matthew asked.

"No worries here, Matthew," Gwen said as she searched through the blanket for his penis.

Matthew smiled and gave her a kiss as Gwen stroked him in an effort to get him hard again. Gwen wrapped her legs around his and smiled as she repositioned her backside against him.

"There's nothing better than a little forkin' when you're spoonin'," she said as she pushed him inside her to continue his work.

Matthew felt alive as he held her firmly once again and listened to her lovely voice.

Matthew and Gwen would be gone when Robbie's alarm clock woke him up. He grabbed his clothes and walked out half asleep into the living room, looking for his dad. Robbie made his way to his dad's bedroom to check there, but he already knew the answer: he was off to the mine.

Peeking inside the doorway, he saw his dad's bed fully made and he was nowhere to be found. Robbie yawned and made his way to the bathroom to clean up for school. He chose again not to make bacon but to instead grab a quick bowl of cereal and then head on out to Ruthie's. It bothered him more to be late for Ruthie than it did for school. *Weird,* Robbie thought as he closed the door.

CHAPTER FIFTEEN

Gwen's Contact

Chloe had been working on her newest project now for over two weeks. She thought she was organized and she had been making good progress. She had met and even exceeded several goals, but over the last two days, something was off. It took her several minutes of thinking about this before she came to the conclusion that she had not heard from Matthew since the last time he had visited her, which was several days ago. Chloe had not thought about visiting him at home or catching him in town when he shopped for supplies; she had not thought about him at all.

Being a single mom was hard, especially in these parts. She laughed as she said that, but Chloe guessed it didn't matter that much; he was single with a boy and he still found time to pay us a visit. "Us," she said, "he came to pay 'us' a visit"; he was a nice man indeed. Chloe took a break and went to sit on her front porch. *Most houses around these parts*—another laugh—*had porches,* she thought. It was relaxing, and before she knew it, she had been there for over an hour. It was time to get back to work, so without another thought, she stood up and went back inside to her computer.

Slightly after midnight, Chloe awoke to Ruthie's screams coming from the bathroom. Jumping into action, she took the Mossberg from behind her bedroom door and ran into the living room, looking for trouble. Ruthie continued screaming;

she was franticly calling for her mom. Chloe opened the door and saw Ruthie sitting on the toilet, smiling at her, covered in blood. She put the safety on the shotgun and placed it against the wall behind the door. Looking at Ruthie, her eyes were bloodshot and tears were running down her cheeks.

Chloe told her it would be all right as she moved closer and grabbed Ruthie up. She held her tightly and carried her over to the sink to rinse off her face. Ruthie was dead weight; she was limp and didn't seem to care what Chloe did for her. She stopped up the sink and turned on the warm water. Searching for a washrag, she noticed Ruthie still smiling, looking into the mirror. Chloe took great care in wiping off Ruthie's face, spending as much time cleaning her off as she did trying to determine what was wrong.

Ruthie stared back at the woman whom she saw in the mirror. She looked much older and had long blond hair, which she didn't mind that much, but it didn't seem like her. Her cheekbones were higher, she wore too much makeup, and her eyes were—brown? She felt her mom rubbing her face with a warm cloth very roughly. It was the last thing she remembered before passing out and falling into her mother's arms.

Chloe held on to Ruthie and stopped her from hitting her head on the mirror. She gathered her up and took her into her bedroom, turning her body to the left and right as she navigated the doorways. Placing her at the foot of the bed, she arranged the sheets around the pillows to snuggle against her body. Chloe turned to face the foot of the bed and reached for Ruthie's hands. She moved Ruthie toward the pillows and then pulled the covers up and over her body. This would be enough to keep her warm, she thought as she tucked the blankets underneath her sides.

She reached down to give Ruthie a kiss on her cheek and walked out of the bedroom, leaving the door slightly ajar so she could easily hear Ruthie if she called out. No sooner had Chloe taken one step than she heard Ruthie call her name.

"Mommy, Mommy, are you there?" Ruthie asked.

"Coming," she said and she turned around to the bedroom door.

Ruthie was standing in the doorway, smiling and shaking as she looked at her mom. Chloe looked at her without taking another step for over a minute before she moved forward. Blood was dripping from her nose, and her smile never faded; it was as if she was crazy, Chloe thought. She had never acted this way before; she didn't what to think about it as she took Ruthie by her hand and walked her back into her bedroom.

Taking the same hand cloth she had used earlier, she wiped her nose and cleaned up her face.

"No more work for me tonight, hon. I'm going to sleep next to you and take care of you," Chloe told Ruthie.

"Thanks, Mom. I really don't feel well. I don't know what it is," Ruthie stated.

"Well, don't you worry your pretty little head. I'll make us both safe tonight. I'll be here right next to you," she said as they both got under the covers and cuddled.

Ruthie's head was pretty, that much was for sure, but it wasn't hers, she thought as she fell asleep.

Chloe didn't sleep at all that night as she lay beside Ruthie, watching her toss and turn. She wasn't sure that Ruthie could or should go to school today. Chloe just wanted her to be safe and for her to get better. She would ask Ruthie how she felt when she woke up and make her decision then. Chloe tried to stay awake, but when the alarm went off, Ruthie awoke to her mom sleeping next to her. She vaguely remembered her coming in and keeping her comfortable last night, but she didn't remember why.

Ruthie turned off the alarm and slipped out the bed a refreshed young girl. She moved around her bedroom with the grace of a ballerina as she tiptoed around the room, grabbing her clothes and her book bag. She dressed outside in the kitchen and had a quick bowl of cereal as she stared at the bathroom door. For some reason, it made her feel uneasy, and she didn't want to go in there alone.

She ran some water in her empty cereal bowl and left it in the sink with her spoon. Ruthie took her book bag and quietly closed her front door as she walked to the mailbox to await Robbie's arrival. *School would be a good escape today,* she thought as she tried to remember more about last night. Try as she might, she could not remember what happened in the bathroom to make her fear it. She would eventually have to use it to shower and to relieve herself. Ruthie knew she could not avoid that room forever; she just wanted to know more details about last night.

Ruthie saw Robbie come over the hill and immediately grew happier. Robbie noticed the smile on her face that remained the entire time it took him to reach her.

"Happy to see me, I see," Robbie said to her as he turned left toward school.

"Better than a bear or a mountain lion, I suppose," Ruthie said, laughing as she took off behind him.

They both laughed as they made their way to school, talking about their usual things. Robbie didn't mention the new babysitter, and Ruthie didn't discuss her bad dreams; as far as they each knew, everything was normal.

Robbie would spend the next few days with the babysitter during the afternoon and into the evening. Gwen would help pick up and do the dishes and the laundry and cook dinner, while Robbie worked on his homework and cleaned up his room. Toward the end of their evening, they would have dinner together and watch a movie; Gwen would tease him and call him her date. They took turns selecting the night's movie, and at the end of it, Gwen would ask him what he would like for tomorrow's dinner.

This went on for three nights; for three nights, Matthew went to work early and came home late, missing breakfast with his son, and dinner with them both. He obviously felt comfortable enough to leave Robbie with Gwen, and from the perspective of most people, he would have been found guilty of taking advantage of Gwen in her new role. It was Friday now, and Gwen had plans this weekend, plans that didn't involve her new family. She was hoping that Matthew would come home earlier than his new normal so they could talk.

The last three days, Matthew made phenomenal progress in every area of his prospecting except gold recovery. He had extended his tunnel, widened his initial recovery room, and sorted all of his muck into five category sizes now. He had experienced unbelievable earth-shattering sex, and he actually saw his family coming together. Matthew could not wait to tell the others about his recent mining activities. Looking at his watch, he determined that he had just enough time to get home and get cleaned up before Robbie and Gwen arrived.

Matthew left the mine following the same protocols that he always did. He left quietly, carrying no extra gear that would make noise when moving. He wore nothing that would reflect light during the day or the evening. Matthew looked around and covered the mine entrance with some brush before slowly setting off for home. These steps took several minutes to perform, and each was an integral part of keeping his mine a secret. Matthew would be home in time to do everything he needed for his little surprise; he was so excited.

He would arrive to no car in the front yard; he had beaten her. It was now time to peek inside of the house to ensure that Robbie was still at school. *Success number two,* Matthew thought as he walked to the front door and unlocked it. Stepping inside, he quickly locked it and went to take a shower. Matthew liked to take his time showering; Robbie had known him to run them out of hot water before, especially with the limited supply in this place. Although the water heater was full of wonderfully hot water, Matthew showered for enjoyment, not to get clean, so it would always run out.

Walking out of the shower, he quickly ran to his bedroom to change. Looking one more time for Robbie and Gwen, he was unaware that he left a trail of water droplets behind him. Smiling as he entered his bedroom, he grabbed a T-shirt and jean shorts and dressed comfy. Matthew rummaged through the fridge and searched for ideas for tonight's dinner.

He found steak, shrimp, chicken, and lunch meats for the main courses. Steak and shrimp sounded awesome to him, and when he searched a bit longer, he found radishes, cucumbers, lettuce, and cheese. All he needed now was some sort of power vegetable and possibly some bread. Taking out everything he chose and placing it on the counter, he searched around for potatoes. He was all set now, and as he grabbed a knife to make french fries, the door opened, and Robbie and Gwen came in.

Gwen saw Matthew and smiled at him as she closed the door.

"Surprise!" he yelled.

Robbie's eyes lit up when he saw Dad home, let alone early. Gwen turned back to him and blew him a silent kiss. Within seconds, Robbie had closed the distance between himself and Matthew. He threw his arms around Matthew's waist and gave him a very big hug.

"I'm giving you both a break from your regular evenings. I'm going to cook and pick up for you both," Matthew told them.

"Awesome!" Robbie said.

Gwen walked to the kitchen table and placed her purse and her keys on it. She watched as Matthew returned Robbie's hug and told him he was happy to see him.

"Now go and get cleaned up, Robbie, and then hit your homework in your bedroom, please. Gwen and I need to talk," he told him.

Robbie happily left for the bathroom as Gwen walked into the living room and sat down on the love seat. It took Robbie a few minutes to come out of the bathroom spiffy clean and run into his bedroom for homework.

"Take your time, son, you have about an hour. Please stay there until I call for you," Matthew told him.

Robbie smiled and closed his bedroom door to do his homework. He had taken the phone in there with him so he could call Ruthie in his downtime.

Gwen walked over to Matthew in the kitchen and gave him a kiss.

"I wanted to surprise you both tonight and give you some time off from the stress of your busy workweek," Matthew said, returning her kiss.

"It's a wonderful surprise, it really is," Gwen said, kissing him softly as she cupped his balls.

"I really have to finish preparing the meat," he told her, laughing between her kisses.

"I'm doing that for you right now," Gwen said.

Matthew picked her up and carried her to the counter. He sat Gwen on it, and they continued to kiss as he slid down his shorts and underpants. Picking her up again, he placed her on the floor in front of him, kissing her passionately. Matthew placed a hand on her shoulder and lowered her to his penis. He went back to preparing dinner as Gwen gave him head. Gwen would sometimes hit the back of her head against the cabinet door when she slid her mouth off his penis, preparing to slide her lips back over it; Matthew found that amusing.

She was devouring him whole each time she slid back onto his penis; it was driving him crazy. Matthew had been this hard before, but Gwen seemed to get him that way quickly any time she tried. He was close to coming now and he didn't know what he was thinking when he thought he could do both, dinner and Gwen. He took hold of her hair, and holding her head tightly against him, he took a step backward.

Gwen walked on her knees as directed to, never missing a stroke. Matthew placed one hand on her right shoulder and kept the other holding her hair and began fucking her mouth. Gwen stopped making her long movements up and down his penis and tightened her lips. He was doing all the work now; Gwen only applied pressure and moved her tongue around him. A couple of times he pushed her face all the way against his groin, but mostly he went forward, as far as tickling her nose with his pubic hair.

Gwen made quick work of her man. When she felt him begin to come, she dug both hands into the meat of his ass and pulled him forward. She increased her speed, sucking harder now; she applied more pressure with her lips. Sometimes she took him down to his tip, but she mainly worked him from the base to the middle of his cock before moving back to his groin to do it all over again. She moved as fast as she could and repeatedly squeezed his ass, randomly distracting him. Gwen continued until Matthew had stopped flooding her mouth with his cum and he became softer. Leaning against the counter now, he let go of her head.

"You . . . are . . . incredible," he said, pushing out each word separately as he continued leaning forward.

Keeping her mouth on his penis, Matthew continued to talk to her.

"So how was your day?" he asked.

"Oh, it was fine, thank you," she replied.

"Nice. Busy, were you then?" he asked her.

"No, not unusually so, why?" she said.

"Tonight we'll watch a movie and I'll return a favor, but you are drinking with me," he told her as he pushed her against the cabinet.

"Sounds good to me," Gwen hummed.

Sucking him harder, she ran her tongue against the bottom of his penis. Matthew was hard all over again, backing up slightly from the counter to allow her room to work. He had a conversation with himself about his new friend.

She obviously did it for him; here he was being pleased while he haphazardly used a butcher's knife to make dinner, he thought.

If she didn't like him, she wouldn't treat him in such a way, Matthew continued.

Matthew loved the attention that he received, and he was starting to want to reciprocate; he wanted to please her too. Gwen continued to work him over as he decided that she was more than a girlfriend, more than a babysitter; she was a live-in girlfriend. At least she was in his mind; he considered asking her to move in, for everyone's mutual convenience, of course. Matthew felt her hands gliding over his chest; they tried to grab handfuls of flesh, but with all his muscle, her hands chose to hold on instead.

Gwen felt him releasing for a second time, but this time would be different. She held him in place by sucking him hard and using her teeth. She moved them up and down his cock in a threatening manner. It would be a show of trust, of faith, Matthew guessed as he held on to the counter for dear life. The excitement was there, and fear had come along for the ride. As Gwen swallowed several times, she moved faster over him.

Matthew's breathing increased, his orgasm intensified, he felt more pressure from her, he truly didn't know what to expect next, but he was her hostage. He meant that literally as Gwen sucked him harder using her teeth and removed the last of the juices from his penis. Matthew was totally drained now; he stood against the counter devoid of bodily fluids and mental capacity. He felt himself growing soft as Gwen changed back to all lips and gentle sucking, with no teeth involved.

"Holy fuck," he said quietly as to not attract Robbie's attention.

It was the first thing that he had said in over twenty minutes, and to be honest, Matthew didn't know how loud he spoke those words. Gwen released his penis from her lips and moved her hands down to caress him. Matthew took her by her arms and raised Gwen to him, pressing her firmly against his sweaty chest. He hugged her so hard that Gwen thought she might break. She buried her face into his neck and said she felt the same way and continued to gently move his disappearing penis between her hands.

"So what's for dinner?" Gwen asked.

"You are," Matthew said as he pushed his butcher's knife into her stomach and moved it to her left side.

Gwen looked into his eyes as she felt the pain in her stomach radiate through her body. She tried to move away, to recoil, but he held on to her with strong force. She was wedged between him and the countertop. By now, she was bleeding heavily on his waist; she had to be, she thought. Her arms were held close to her sides and could not be moved. She watched as Matthew's smile widened. Shortly afterward, she felt the knife move again, this time in an upward direction. He pressed harder against her and then removed his knife, throwing it across the room. He took his hands and roughly massaged her flat stomach. Gwen's pain was crippling now to the point of becoming light-headed and passing out.

"There, there. It's not that bad," he said as he raised a bloody hand to her face and rubbed it violently across her cheeks.

He smeared her with her own blood, and with another pass, he pressed his palm against her lips, her chin, and then back up to her eyebrows, sliding directly over her eye as he did. Gwen saw her vision cloud from the liquid and the pressure from his hand. Matthew watched as Gwen lost facial expression and half blinked her eyes. He slapped her face and then pushed his hand against her throat.

The pressure was enough to cut off her air supply, and it physically hurt, but it did not match the pain she was feeling below. She could feel him sticking his fingers inside of her wound, and it made her vomit. Gwen gave all the warning signs that she was going to throw up, giving Matthew time to remove his hand and turn her head to the side. To help her, he kneed her in the groin and pushed upward on her stomach with both hands. Gwen felt the vomit ebb and flow, and as she fought to breathe, her body fought to expel the contents of her stomach onto the floor.

Matthew released his hold and turned her around to face the counter. After positioning her the way he wanted, he again pressed his body onto hers. She felt squished as she was pushed forward onto the counter; the coldness against her breasts chilled her to her core. Her blood poured onto the surface at an alarming rate, washing forward and to the sides of her flattened breasts. Gwen continued to vomit on top of it and watched as the rest of her partially digested chicken sandwich mixed with her blood. Gwen felt another rush of nausea course through her body, making her light-headed; she struggled to keep her eyes open.

Gwen could not talk from throwing up and being pressed even harder against the granite countertop. Matthew now took her hands and held them behind her back, slightly elevated. He placed both of her small hands inside his left and pushed her forward with his right hand that he placed on her neck. She was dry heaving now; only water and stomach acid were left to mix with her blood. Matthew raised her hands even higher and then pushed into her from behind. Gwen's eyes lost all life, her facial expression lost in emptiness as she felt him begin to fuck her in the ass. She felt him pumping slowly away to the beat of her heart; he was matching her heartbeat, which aided in evacuating the rest of her blood onto the granite.

The blood was spreading out in a large circle around her breasts and in front of her face; some had found its way to the floor after dripping down the cabinets. Matthew looked down and noticed that he stood in a pool of Gwen's blood, wondering if she would ever stop bleeding.

"You are cleaning all of this up later," he angrily told her as he emphasized his words by pressing her against the granite.

On each forward thrust, he spoke each one of those words, in order, one at a time.

Her vision blurred; Gwen became weaker and more light-headed. She doubted whether she would be able to stand if given the chance. The last thing Gwen thought about before she closed her eyes for the final time was the orgasm that shot through her groin and moved upward to her breasts. Contracting and expanding her muscles in response to her orgasm caused her great pain. It forced the last of her blood from her body in a dramatic spray that shot across the room and painted the fridge door.

The mixture of pleasure and pain flooded her mind with a myriad of sensations that caused her to breathe excitedly.

Excruciating pain replaced the wonderful feelings of her orgasm that had been there only seconds earlier. Matthew witnessed Gwen's body tense up from her orgasm and then relax, ceasing to struggle against him. He pulled out and left her leaning over the granite countertop. He replaced his underpants and shorts and walked to the bathroom, closing the door.

Gwen floated above her body and looked around the room, turning herself slowly to the left. She was looking back at herself, facing the kitchen when she heard Matthew open the door and go into his bedroom. The water could still be heard running as he walked out naked, holding a shotgun. He approached her body, raised the shotgun, and shot her several times. Gwen watched as her body flew into the air and made its way to the fridge. Matthew smiled as he emptied slug after slug into her body. He knew why she didn't bleed anymore, he thought as he admired his handiwork on the granite counter and the tiled floor. Gwen could not bear to watch anything else on the scene of her death. She started moving to the door when she heard him call out.

"What are you doing?" he said, walking closer.

She could not move; she didn't have the ability to float forward or to pass through the wall—she was immobilized! Gwen didn't ever wonder if a ghost felt fear, she had never thought about it before; she now knew that answer now. What if she could never leave this house? What if she was to spend the rest of her days haunting this place? What if she would relive her murder every day? Her mind raced as she saw Matthew walk past and turn to face her. He placed his arms on hers! He was no longer carrying his shotgun, but she still feared him.

Gwen felt his touch and saw his gaze. He didn't look through her; he looked *at* her. His smile grew as he shook her hard. Gwen could not escape; she could not flee. Gwen could not close her eyes. He grew angrier, his face now contorted as he continued violently shaking her.

"What are you doing!" he yelled at her.

"What are you doing! What are you doing!" he repeated loudly.

"What are you doing, Gwen?" she heard Matthew say to her.

Gwen awoke in a pool of sweat; she had soaked her blanket and pillow. It took her a few seconds to realize that Matthew was waking her up from a bad dream. Matthew smiled at her and asked her if she was OK.

"Hey, you were tossing and turning. I figured you were having a bad dream, so I woke you," he said softly.

"Thanks for that—it was horrible!" Gwen said, short of breath.

She could not remember everything, but bits and pieces came back to her; it was an intense experience for her.

"No problem," Matthew said, smiling as he plunged the bloody butcher knife into her chest, burying the tip of the blade inside her body.

Matthew's smile changed into that of a cruelly parted, gaping mouth; he laughed as he stabbed her repeatedly in her chest. He never went deep enough to hit bone; it was obvious to her that his intention was to remove her breasts. She laughed inside as she thought about her implants popping out onto the floor; it was all she could do to keep her sanity as he continued slicing. The pain was unbearable, but she had experienced worse . . .

Gwen closed her eyes and prayed for death. Matthew removed the knife from her left breast and plunged it into her left side, above her stomach and slightly below her ribs. He moved it to her right side, opening a deep cut that spanned from one side of her waist to the other. Matthew's smile never left his face; it was present when Gwen opened her eyes in her response to that immediate pain. She screamed out as he twisted the knife before removing it only long enough to place it right back into her chest. She cried uncontrollable at this point, sobbing loudly as he stabbed her over and over. Her body shook from both his stabbing and her crying, allowing her blood to leave her stomach in spurts.

Gwen felt his weight on top of her now. She opened her eyes again in time to witness Matthew pulling himself on top of her. He took her hands one at a time and stretched them upward above her head. With his free hand, he pushed down on her bloody chest, moving it around and kneading her breasts as he smeared her own blood over them. He took hold of them one at a time, stretching them and letting them come back down. Matthew pinched a nipple between his thumb and forefinger, twisting it before pulling it up into the air. The pain was there for Gwen, but it was not as intense as what she was experiencing in her stomach.

When Matthew had enough blood on his hand, he smeared it on his smiling face, all the while making eye contact with her. His crazy eyes were so wide, she thought, and distracting as he inserted his fingers into some wounds on her breasts. Gwen jumped in the air as Matthew's finger and thumb pushed inside her right breast. He closed his hand into a fist, holding on to her breast with his fingers still inserted. Pulling it up and to the left, he caused Gwen the most amount of pain she had felt in her entire life. Screaming out loudly, she jumped and flailed and screamed some more, but he held on and moved her around easily by her breast.

Letting go, Gwen hit the love seat and drew in several deep breaths as she attempted to manage her pain. He still pressed down on her, pushing her a few inches deep in the cushions and rendering her unable to move unless he allowed her to. His free hand slid over her bloody stomach and pushed down before he slid it back up to her neck. The blood washed over her lower stomach and onto the cushions, disappearing into the material against her waist. The pain sent her flailing as she screamed once again for him to let her go.

She turned her body left and right, attempting to roll him off onto the floor, but he would not budge; he was too strong. He had leverage on his side now, and he proved that by pulling her up by her wrists, just to show her he could do it. Each time he raised her into the air, he would slap her face with his right hand. It landed on her left cheek with enough force to temporarily stun her. The pain numbed her body, giving Gwen a sensation of movement with a delayed sensation of pain. Several seconds after he slapped or punched her, the pain would register. Sometimes she would be recovering from a prior slap to the face or punch to the chest before she would feel the impact from another blow.

Matthew now moved his hand roughly over her face, pulling her cheek or nose as he saw fit. A little lower now and then he closed upon her throat, effectively cutting off her oxygen. Gwen's eyes were almost as wide as Matthew's now as she pleaded for him to stop. Gwen lay there on the love seat on her back, naked and bleeding from multiple stab wounds in her stomach and breasts. She was unable to breathe as Matthew continued choking her with one hand while he held on to her hands with his other. He pressed down hard enough to bend her neck further into the cushions than her head was, and looking into her eyes, he held her that way until she stopped struggling.

She was wrong about her death; Matthew had kept her alive long enough for her to experience the lack of oxygen to its fullest. She would have told you that it was best described as an unquenchable urge to breathe with no fruitful result from your labors—if you had asked her that before she had died, that was. Matthew let go of her neck and stood up above her lifeless body and looked around the room. He turned back to her and looked at her bloodshot eyes. She had red streaks in the whites of her eyes that were easily noticeable, although her eyes were swollen. Gwen's cheeks were bruised; she had a black eye and a few cuts above her right eyebrow. Her neck displayed purplish bruising that resembled part of a hand. Her chest no longer raised or allowed blood to spill out over the side; she was dead.

Matthew again looked around the room and thought about Robbie.

"Robbie. Come out here, son," Matthew said as he walked to the front door to lock it.

Hearing no response, he walked into the kitchen and took hold of a chair, dragging it across the floor. Robbie heard the scratching sound of wood over wood but didn't know what was happening; he did notice that Gwen was once again quiet. Matthew positioned the chair to the right edge of the love seat and pointed it to the front door. He sat down and leveled his shotgun toward the doorway.

"Get up. I know you are faking. You are not dead," Matthew said slowly.

"I said get up. Make a run for it. You might make it, and you might not," he said coldly.

"To be fair, I'll load both barrels independently. Starting right—" Matthew said without finishing his last word.

Gwen jumped forward, hitting the floor, running. She had almost reached the front door when both barrels went off, taking her feet off the floor and sending her into the air straight for the door. Gwen hit the door about a foot off the ground chest first and then followed her face. She managed to turn her head slightly to the right before forward momentum smacked her head against the door. She slowly slid to the floor on her stomach, with her face limply leaning against the right side of the door.

"Almost made it," he said.

Matthew reloaded his shotgun while he slowly walked to Gwen. Taking her right ankle, he pulled her backward, away from the front door. Using his foot, he lifted Gwen to her right side and then kicked her over onto her back. Blood splashed around her as her body settled on the floor. Matthew stepped on her bloody stomach to hold her in place. More blood spilled out of the long cut in her stomach, rolling off her body and making small puddles around her butt. He lowered his shotgun to her chest and pulled the trigger. Two more slugs went into her body at close range, throwing blood up into the air and onto the wall to the height of three feet.

Gwen would never feel those gunshots; they were more for Matthew's enjoyment than hers. He didn't understand why she was so difficult to kill; God knows he had tried several times today. He knew she was a bad person who was confused about most things in her life, but there were many things about her he did not know. No matter, it was his duty to stop her, to give her time to reflect on how she was choosing to spend her life, in hell. Matthew reloaded his shotgun and went to sit on the kitchen chair that faced her body; he wasn't so sure that she was dead. After all, she had been beaten, stabbed, and choked and she still refused to die. Only after several 12-gauge slugs went to discuss things with her did she appear to listen.

Matthew thought he saw something and slowly stood up. He didn't move, but he kept his shotgun facing the front door. He listened intently, but he no longer heard what he thought he had heard; the crying sound was gone. He turned to see Robbie peeking from his bedroom; his body was barely visible, with only half an eyeball showing.

"Robbie, I wanted to know you were OK. Go back in your room and lock the door. Don't open it unless I say our secret word. Go!" he yelled and watched as Robbie gasped and shut the door.

Matthew turned around and saw Gwen swing a kitchen chair at him with lightning speed. She swung it from above her head at an angle, when it came down it hit Matthew in several places. The first of three chair legs slammed into his left shoulder, breaking upon impact. Some wooden support pieces broke against his head, and two more chair legs smashed against his head and other shoulder.

Gwen fought for her life against the man who had tried to kill her. She twisted the chair and sent him to the floor; it was his turn to be disoriented. She kicked him in the face as he went down and then ran for the kitchen. She returned with another chair and raised it as high as she could before she broke it over his head. Matthew was on his knees when the second chair leveled him, breaking in two. Gwen dropped an elbow on Matthew's neck, sending him to la-la land. She looked around and grabbed a broken chair leg and then placed it down when she spotted the shotgun standing up in the corner.

Gwen turned to the side and blood spilled out onto the floor in front of her. Doubling over in pain only caused more blood to be forced out. It wasn't long before she would be dead. Although he was unconscious with Gwen finally in control of the situation, she was still going to lose; she would die here today in this house. If she made it over to the shotgun, she wasn't sure that she could get close enough to shoot him. Gwen didn't know if it was loaded or even how to push that safe lock thing. She didn't know guns, so she stuck with what she did know—wood.

Reaching over for the table leg, she slowly turned her body as a whole, holding her stomach with her left hand to apply pressure over her wound. When Gwen touched the flat of her palm against her stomach, she heard nausea tell her to give up. She removed her left hand and placed it on the floor to aid in her balance. She breathed in a few times and then placed the hand back over her open wound and pressed inward to keep it closed as best she could. Gwen finished turning and reached for the table leg and found it gone; they were both gone.

Looking for him, she saw the front door had been opened halfway, but he was still nowhere to be found. It couldn't be that easy to escape, not after all she had gone through. He had done everything possible to keep her sequestered in this house; he was close, he had to be. More crippling pain struck, and she bowed her head forward, once again throwing her hand down to the floor to keep her from falling.

Gwen felt weaker than before; she felt horribly drained, and when she threw her head back and stood up, she felt light-headed and passed out. Gwen fell toward the love seat and landed with her face between the seat cushions. Matthew put his hands on either side of his eyes and pushed against the glass, hoping to reduce the reflection, and peered inside. It was quite comical to watch her struggle for her sanity only to be undone by the simple act of standing to escape.

Matthew walked over to the couch and scooped her up into his arms. Raising her head to him, he stole a kiss as he walked her into his bedroom. He tucked her into bed between four pillows and two blankets, looking around the room one final time before leaving. Turning around to check on her, Gwen looked comfortable and very, very tired. Smiling at her, he blew a kiss and quietly closed the door. He was hungry from today's activities, and wasting no time, he set the oven for 350 degrees with a timer of fifteen minutes and let it preheat.

Robbie was in his room doing his homework, Gwen was sleeping in his bed, and Matthew was almost ready for dinner. He had decided to bake a chicken with potatoes and carrots around it. That coupled with biscuits and chocolate chip cookies for dessert would have to do. Matthew set the table and brewed some ice tea, taking away some of Robbie's part of the dinner process. He had cooked everything and even cleaned as he went; that was Gwen's part for tonight. All they would have to do would be to come and sit at the table and afterward pick out their movie for tonight.

It would be half an hour or so before dinner would be ready, so Matthew sat on the couch and put the TV on to relax. A few minutes later, Robbie came out and placed his butt on the love seat. He searched for the remote so he could put on something he liked; looking around the room, he found it next to his sleeping dad. He quietly got up and took small baby steps, creeping up to him, and took the remote back to his couch.

Gwen heard the TV in the living room changing channels and she sat straight up. She felt wonderful, rested. Looking around, she had never been in this room before—it was Matthew's bedroom; it was cold, dark, and comfortable. She raised the sheets and looked under them for blood, but everything was clean. She looked at her stomach and it was as flat and sexy as it ever was. There was no bloody wound; she was not injured at all. Smiling Gwen took a deep breath and slid off the bed, looking for her clothes. A small chair in the corner of the room held her clothes, just where she left them.

Gwen got dressed and opened the door, and the smell of roasted chicken hit her right in the face. Looking around, Robbie was changing channels and Matthew was sleeping; he looked exhausted sitting there in his T-shirt and blue jean shorts. *How cute,* she thought.

"Robbie, are you hungry?" Gwen quietly asked.

Robbie nodded positively and pointed to the kitchen. Gwen shook her head and told him to go and get ready. She was hesitant to wake Matthew up with the dream that she had just recently experienced still fresh in her head. It was so real to her that she was actually shaking as she approached him.

"Clear your head, woman. Shit. It was just a dream," she said to herself as she grabbed his arm and called his name.

"Matt, Matt, time to get up, sleepyhead," she said.

Matthew started out of his sleep, which in turn startled her. He saw her expression of horror and told her it was OK.

"Sorry to scare you, Gwen. I was sleeping hard. Earlier I cooked dinner and even set the table, though," he said apologetically.

"I saw," she said as she reached down, hugging him around his neck.

Matthew got up and held Gwen around her waist, mainly because she never let go of his neck. Gwen hung on to his neck and kissed him several times.

"I missed you today, you know. I'm sorry that I took a nap, and in your bed. It seemed like the place to go when I was exhausted," she said.

He didn't mind that she had taken a nap; she had been more than helpful over the last several days. He wasn't about to tell her that she could do no wrong, that her companionship alone warranted a raise, and along with that a possible relationship title change. He liked the idea of her sleeping in his bed; he wondered, though, if she knew that he had carried her in there. Matthew had found her on the couch tossing and turning, as if she was an active participant in a nightmare. He loved making her feel safe and doing his part to take care of her. He thought again about asking her to move in.

Matthew and Gwen walked into the kitchen for dinner to full plates and filled glasses. Robbie had placed the food on the table and filled their glasses with water while he waited for them to come over.

"Don't thank me, I was just hungry," Robbie said, laughing.

Matthew got the chair for Gwen and then sat down himself to have dinner.

"Everything looks wonderful. Thank you, Matthew," Gwen said as she looked from him to Robbie.

She found her dream unnerving; it was so real to her, so much so that it was difficult to look him in the eyes. Dinner was eaten quickly on movie night as everyone wanted to get in front of the TV sooner than later. During the dinner, Robbie talked briefly about school, mentioning that he had finished his homework in preparation for movie night. Gwen talked about a crazy day of interviews at the local school. Matthew talked about his son and his girlfriend.

"I'm just not sure about that school. I don't know if it's a right fit for me," Gwen said.

"Robbie likes it there. Ruthie too," Matthew told her.

Robbie watched them both talk about his school as if they knew about it. He went there several days a week; he's definitely the expert in this group.

"I think it's a nice place overall and the building could stand for an upgrade or two and the staff definitely needs training and I don't think they are up to speed on some of the sciences, if you ask me," Robbie said as he grabbed another piece of chicken.

"Well, now, you don't say, Robbie. That's what we English teachers call poor grammar. It's an excellent example of a run-on sentence, offering many opportunities for you to improve," Gwen stated with a serious face.

Robbie looked at Matthew. Matthew looked at Gwen. Robbie looked at Gwen, and after a few seconds of staring, they smiled at each other and started laughing.

All through dinner, Gwen thought about Matthew and his busy schedule. He entertained unusual hours, apparently burning the candle at both ends. She felt that his family could benefit from him having more normal hours and spending more time with his son. It wasn't her place to speak of such things, but she did see it as an issue. She had learned how to look for troubled kids and issues with their families that might affect their grades and personal development; Robbie had many red flags.

Dinner wrapped up with none of them talking about their nightmares or unusual "happenings" that they had recently experienced. Robbie didn't mention his dreams about the mine, nor had the fact that he thought the mountain lion had stalked him before attacking the school; it never came up. Matthew didn't speak about the history of the mines or the sounds that he heard when he mined by himself. Gwen didn't tell Matthew about her nightmares; she was still looking to learn more about him and trying to fit in.

"All right, everyone, let's all go to the lobby. Let's all go into the lobby. Let's all go into the lobby to get ourselves a treat!" Matthew sang.

Robbie looked at Gwen and shook his head as he passed Matthew, who was dancing as he sang that old song a second time.

"Did that just actually happen?" Gwen said out loud.

"Yeah, sorry about that. He kind of gets carried away with nostalgia," Robbie said, laughing.

Matthew lost his playful mood and sat down on the love seat and thought about his wife. She used to say that about him all the time; that's where Robbie heard it. Deep down inside, he missed her, but it was time to move on. It was ironic that only this week he had found out that it was official.

Gwen came over and sat beside Matthew, somewhat cuddling in before she asked about the movie. Matthew told her that it was up to her to choose the movie because Robbie chose last.

"You pick, Gwen. You can choose tonight's movie. I'm not sure I could watch *Frozen* again," Matthew said.

"Oh, I could," Gwen said as she slid a hand over his package.

Robbie said he didn't care and that he wanted to see what kind of movie Gwen would pick.

"Go on, choose your movie," Robbie said curiously.

"Twelve, the answer's twelve," she said as she stood up and began counting from left to right.

"You mean you are just going to count to the twelfth movie and put it in?" Matthew asked.

"Cool!" Robbie said as he stretched out on the couch and got comfy.

Gwen smiled and bent over to grab the movie and placed it into the player.

"It is done," she said as she turned around and threw her hands up into the air.

Chapter Sixteen

Chloe's Bags of Flour

Chloe placed her hand on the door, pushing it forward and then walked inside. An old brass bell announced her arrival as the heavy glass door closed so quickly behind her that it almost caught her right heel. Hot air followed her inside and was instantly greeted by air that was hotter than it was, if that was even possible. She remarked how warm it was and wondered if she should even stay in this store. The general store carried all manner of odds and ends necessary for daily life in a small town. You wouldn't find a big box store here; it was all small business, and most of those were family owned. This one probably wasn't doing so well if they could not afford decent air conditioning, she thought.

She looked around at the numerous shelving full of this and that and then she peered down at her shopping list. There were half a dozen things on the "needs" side and about ten on the "extras"; as she looked around again, she knew she would leave here wanting. Taking a few more steps forward, she heard a woman's voice giggling. Turning the end cap, she turned right and saw a woman leaning over the counter, kissing someone behind it. He was probably the storekeeper, and the woman was probably bartering for services. Chloe laughed at that thought and took another step toward them.

"I'm sorry to interrupt, but are you guys open?" she said as she looked past the woman.

At first glance, the proprietor looked to be a middle-aged man with thinning hair, but she could not see his entire body from the counter. She also had not heard the man speak, so she could not truly tell his age, but from the looks of what she could see, the man did have his own business . . . The woman who was still kissing his ear when Chloe spoke looked at her and then back to her man, kissing him one more time before standing. Suze smiled at the woman as she removed her hand from her pants and buttoned them back up.

"It's time for me to leave anyway. Don't mind me, I'll get the door," the redhead said as she pinched his cheek and walked away.

Chloe made eye contact with the woman, and the shopkeeper noticed the two women smile at each other as his new friend left. The sweat on the woman's face beaded and slowly ran down her thin neck, disappearing into her cleavage. Chloe turned her back on the woman when she walked past her and then approached the counter. He had as much sweat on his face as she did on hers; it really was hot in here, she thought.

The man looked at her and said that he was sorry about that and asked her if he could help her find something. Chloe handed him the list and went to a nearby shelf to grab some bleach and a ten-pound bag of flour. She only saw five pound bags, so she only took the bleach to the counter.

"Most of this I ain't got, lady. I'll do my best," he told her.

"Flour—the ones on the shelves are five pound bags, and there's only one remaining. Do you have any more?" Chloe asked.

"The flour is in the back. I'll bring up a few bags for you. Be right back," he muttered as he turned and walked into the back room.

The old wooden door swung easily to and fro, and it took a few times swinging half open and closed before it settled and remained closed. Chloe heard the old brass bell ring again and then close with a thud. What she didn't know was that Suze entered the store again, locked the door, and flipped the Open sign to Closed.

Mr. Wilson came out carrying two ten-pound bags of flour, wearing a simple smile.

"I saw that the flour on your list said two ten-pound bags, so I brought them both. It's all I have, but you're welcome to 'em," he said in a kind voice.

"Thank you very much, sir. That was the main thing on my list. I can do without the rest today if I have to," she replied.

He smiled at her again and looked down to total up all her things. He looked her up and down a few times more and told her the total.

"Fourteen dollars and fifty-six cents, please," he said with a distracted smile.

Chloe was aware of another person walking up behind, so she turned around to greet the individual. She saw that it was the same woman that was here earlier, shot her a quick glance, and then turned back to dig in her purse. She couldn't easily find her credit card, so she glanced up, smiling, and then back down to her purse. All the time she was searching through her purse, she was conscious of the shopkeeper staring at her breasts. Chloe looked up smiling, produced a credit card, and extended it to the man. Mr. Wilson looked at the credit card and back to the woman.

"I'm sorry, but today's not a good day for the Internet 'round these parts. It will have to be cash," he said as he smiled at the other woman.

"Let me grab a twenty," she said as she opened her small wallet.

Suze placed a bottle of aspirins, a few bandages, and some rubbing alcohol on the counter to the side of Chloe and told her that she forgot those items. Chloe handed the shop owner the twenty and looked down at the counter.

"I'm sorry, those aren't mine, I don't need those," she said as she raised her head up to the shop owner.

"Take her, she's yours. She's yours first and then mine. Later we'll both share, and after that, you are all mine, so don't get used to her," Suze said seductively.

Chloe asked herself if she just heard what she thought she heard and turned to face the woman behind her. Mr. Wilson took this time to reach for the knife he had for security under the counter and waited for her to turn around.

"Your change then?" he asked.

"Oh, yes. Yes, thank you," she said as she reached for the money on the counter.

Chloe looked into his eyes and remarked how red they were; it was if the man had not slept in days. *Owning your own shop had its drawbacks,* she thought. Suze laughed as she saw the man looking at her with a confused expression on his face. Suze moved her eyes in Chloe's direction, and he took his knife and pressed it down against Chloe, taking hold of her hand when she didn't move it away.

"Now you just stay put, little missy. Let's not be rash," he said as he pressed the knife down against her arm.

Chloe panicked and stood motionless, wondering what she should do next.

"Place your other hand on the counter beside this one. Do it now!" he yelled at her.

Chloe recoiled as little as she could when the shop owner yelled at her, but she did not pull away; instead, she placed her other hand on the counter, pushing it close to the first.

Suze watched on as the man took both of her hands and cuffed them together. Chloe felt desperation and fear start to take hold of her. She knew that she was in for an interesting day when Suze told the shop owner to pull her forward onto the counter. She felt sick, and if this room had been of a normal temperature, she would be sweating from fear instead of the room being hot. Chloe closed her eyes as the man began pulling her on the counter; she wanted to vomit.

Chloe felt the woman press against her legs and part them, moving herself in between. Her hands pushed against Chloe's

body and slid forward to her ass. Mr. Wilson pulled down on
her hands now, bending her arms at the elbow and keeping her
upper body in place. This action flattened out her breasts that
were now resting on the counter, hanging over the sides of her
thin body. It was as sexy a look that the shop owner had ever
seen and one that Suze watched with contempt.

"Pull down on her harder, pull harder," Suze told him.

Mr. Wilson pulled down so hard that Chloe thought her wrists
would pull off; she began crying and tried to look away. Suze
left her ass and moved her hands underneath of her flattened
breasts, cupping them as hard as she could. She jerked back
and pulled against her wrists that the man was securing. She
pinched and squeezed the woman's breasts, paying particular
attention to their nipples. Each hand was tasked to deliver pain,
and each one had found their mark.

"Stop crying, for Christ's sakes. You should love this attention.
It's been a while, hasn't it?"

Chloe heard those words, but she wasn't sure that it was
spoken out loud or in her head. Suze let loose of the nipples
so she could get the woman's blouse undone, but not before
twisting them one more time for good measure. Chloe would
have jumped clean off the counter had she not had her arms
nearly pulled to the floor. Mr. Wilson watched as his new friend
fondled and undressed his newer friend, all the while putting
all of his weight toward the task at hand.

It had been months since this town had anything interesting
happen to it. People would come and go, and fortunes would be
made and then lost. No new houses went up around Murphys
nowadays; not a lot of land was exchanged or traded off here.
Those who had land kept it and those who were looking kept
looking, for the most part. Now he was in an interesting situation
with two complete strangers; he didn't knew where all this was
heading, but it was a pleasant distraction for him.

Suze continued undressing Chloe as the man held her
stationary on the counter. Chloe tried to breathe normally, but
she was having trouble. *Of all the times to have an anxiety attack,*

this was a good one, she thought as she fought for her breath. No matter how hard she tried, Chloe could only breathe short and shallow breaths, and she really didn't get any extra oxygen from those failed attempts. She felt embarrassed and violated as the woman undid her bra, leaving her wearing only her panties. She opened her eyes and saw the man smiling at her, his eyes wide with excitement.

"Please. Please stop this. Don't do this," Chloe said softly, making as much eye contact with the shop owner as she could.

She saw that no progress could be made talking to this man; he had it too good. Chloe closed her eyes and squeezed them as hard as she could, but none of that changed the fact that the woman behind her was now massaging her ass.

"It will be fine. I can tell you've done this before. This time will be a little different from your last experience, but you'll find it more intense. That's what you really want, isn't it?" Suze asked her.

Chloe struggled more against the unwanted attention that she was receiving, but each time she did that, the woman behind her dug her nails into her backside and the man pulled down on her wrists even harder. There wasn't really any chance that she would escape this situation; the man used all of his weight to pull her arms down, which gave Suze ample time to respond to anything she could do. Again she struggled against the man, shaking her body violently left and right, but his grip on her handcuffed wrists was strong; he would not be budged. Chloe let out a string of cuss words that was not to be believed; her daughter would have dropped what she was holding and lowered her jaw as she took in the horror.

"Put me down, fuck wad. Let go of my ass, you whore. The police will be here shortly dumb asses. My daughter just took off running for them," Chloe said, laughing.

It wasn't much of a bluff, and to be honest, she had never said words like that before, but who knows—maybe they would believe her. The man loosened his grip and actually stood up to try to get a better view of the window. He had to move to his side about a foot and then rose up on the balls of his feet to check.

Suze took this chance to show Chloe how much she believed her by climbing up on her back and placing her knees to the left and right of her body, keeping her in place. Chloe continued squirming, but the weight of the woman on her back flattened her like a turtle on a log. Mr. Wilson listened to a few barked orders from Suze and again pulled down on Chloe's arms, causing her to wince in pain.

"Hold her down, stupid. She's just making that up," Suze said as she reached for his knife.

The man looked on and watched as the woman he was holding stopped moving.

"There. Nice. Now be still. We don't want you hurting yourself now, do we?" Suze said as she placed the knife against Chloe's neck.

Chloe's response to failure and defeat up to this point had been to close her eyes and cry. She did so again, trying not to shake too much as not to move the knife. Mr. Wilson did not fail to notice Chloe's breasts flatten even more, and the closest one almost showed a nipple. Suze had Chloe raise her head and pucker up, telling her to kiss him.

"Go on. Pucker up, bitch, and give your man a kiss," she said menacingly.

When Chloe didn't raise her head, Suze added more pressure to the knife, and, voila, up came her head. Chloe's eyes were wide with fear; she didn't know if she was bleeding or not, but she had definitely felt the pressure of the blade against her skin. She opened her eyes and stared into his. The shop owner's breath smelled of alcohol. His teeth were imperfect with a few that were missing; those were her takeaways.

Suze was effectively straddling the woman whose head she held at an elevated level at knifepoint. The man smiled and went in close for a kiss. Chloe saw what to be an inevitable situation; he was coming in fast with an open mouth. The shop owner was drunk, and she was being made to show him affection; this was going to happen—he was going to rape her. Suze told her to open her eyes and look at him.

"You are after all his date. Why shouldn't you kiss him?" Suze asked her.

With yet another raise of her hand, Chloe obeyed and open her eyes. He was much closer now, and when he smiled, she remembered again why she had given up men. Chloe had to remind herself that he was not a good example of a man; he was a bad person. Bad people infect others, often leaving them damaged and beaten. In her case, that phrase was literal; she was hurting physically and emotionally.

Mr. Wilson was smiling the entire time that he kissed her. His open eyes took in the lovely woman in front of him as if he could not believe she was real. Chloe closed her eyes several times to lessen the damage from this man, but each time she did, the knife told her to open them. Every time she did that, Chloe saw the man's Cyclops eye, and try as she might, it would not mask the fact that his lips were mashing against hers, and occasionally he would suck one into his mouth.

Suze watched Chloe struggle to keep her head in place while the man kissed her repeatedly, and she held the knife against her. She found it amusing when she asked him if he was ready, and he answered between kisses that he's been ready for quite some time now. Chloe could not stop herself from crying as it was, but when she heard his reply, she lost it. The man became quickly frustrated when his kisses were not returned as affectionately as before. It didn't help that his lips were covered in her tears, and she shook uncontrollably as he held her hands down.

Chloe's entire body trembled; she yearned to be free. It was the reason that she closed her eyes; she thought that she would wake up out of this dream and it would all just go away.

"I told you before, Chloe, this is not a dream!" she heard an angry voice tell her.

Suze moved the knife away from her throat and took a handful of hair. Raising her head up higher, she told the man to kiss her one last time. The man moved closer and moved his lips over hers, throwing in a tongue for good measure. Chloe was not expecting that, not at all. The tongue darted around like crazy, and although she tried to recoil and back away from it, she found herself wanting it. She caught it with her lips and sucked it a few times before letting it go.

It was the man's turn to be shocked; that was the first participation he had experienced with her, and he loved it! Chloe moaned and kissed him hard while she searched for his tongue with hers. Suze let them kiss a few more times before slamming her head onto the counter. Chloe saw stars and bright white light for a brief moment and then began softly moaning. Suze slid off of her and positioned herself on the counter by her side. Chloe moaned as she slowly moved her body in pain while the man stared at her body.

Suze cuddled in to Chloe, pulling her toward her until she was on her side. She then hopped off the counter to finish turning her on her back.

"Let go of her hands and get up there," Suze said to him.

The man looked at her to ensure he had heard her correctly and nodded, letting go of her hands. Chloe didn't recognize this as a chance to escape; she was still wondering why the room was spinning, and it hurt to open her eyes.

"Fuck her hard, she wants it. Why, just listen to her—she's moaning for your big boy," Suze said.

Chloe heard bits and pieces of words due to being dazed and her vision was still cloudy. She had a headache so awful that even if she could clear her head, she could still not be able to describe it. Chloe's head lulled to the left and she found it difficult to think. Random words like "ice cream," "shopping," "potato," "tattoo," "fire," and "monkey" popped in her head; they were no more than random words, unassociated with any thoughts.

All of this was happening as Suze watched the man undue his belt buckle and drop his pants to his ankles. Shaking his left foot first and then his right, he stepped out of his khakis and onto a nearby wooden box.

"Done this before, have you?" Suze asked, smiling.

Mr. Wilson smiled as he placed both hands on Chloe's thighs and climbed up. He slid his hands up to her breasts and swung a leg over her, straddling her waist. Removing his penis from his underpants, he felt for an opening. When he found one, he leaned forward and once again found her breasts.

"The room was hot. Friday. My back hurts. I'm having trouble with my eyes. Flower. Where are my glasses? Potato;" these were all things that she said to herself, broken thoughts and words that were confusing at best.

The man continued to squeeze her breasts as he thrust himself into his new girlfriend. *Why is the ground shaking? Puppies. I can't move my legs;* she thought about those while the man continued to fuck her.

Suze noted that he was sloppy and angry, and he often slammed his lower body into hers as he went. Equally amusing was the fact that he reached under the counter for a pint of whiskey on one of his thrusts.

He rose up and placed one hand on her stomach, while the other held the bottle to her mouth. Mr. Wilson poured some over Chloe's trembling lips, giving her a taste. Not much went in at first, but it didn't matter to him; she was going to taste it anyway. Taking a few sips himself, he gave Chloe more. This time he pushed the bottle inside and held it up for her to finish. Reflexively, she swallowed a good portion of the liquor until the bottle was emptied. Mr. Wilson remarked that she was having two men inside her today, Mr. Beam and Mr. Wilson.

"Look at me, Chloe," Suze said as she played with her hair.

Chloe looked at upward for the voice that was speaking to her, but she could not find it. There was a man who smiled back at her from time to time, but he wasn't talking to her. Suze pulled her hair again and shook her head around pretty good before letting it go. Chloe's head hit the counter for a second time, sending more pain her way. She still could not move her legs, but she was having a nice wet dream. She felt her body warm with affection; Chloe desired to play with herself, but her hands would not cooperate. They hung lifeless above her head and were stuck together. She didn't understand any of this, but she liked the way she felt.

It wasn't long before she was rhythmically moving her body in response to the man on top of her. She still didn't put two and two together, but the man intensified his efforts and again reached forward to pay attention to her breasts. Suze watched on as the man began counting his thrusts. On every thrust, he pinched a breast, and when he reached the third one, he slammed his body forward and then started over. It was the funniest thing she had seen in years, Suze thought, as she continued to follow the train wreck.

Chloe was regaining her senses at just about the time Mr. Wilson's alcohol was kicking in. That, coupled with how her vagina felt, brought back old college memories. She was on her back feeling a buzz as a man held her down and gave it to her good; back then there was nothing more important. She was still dazed, and although the random words and thoughts from earlier were lessening, she still could not remember fine details. For example, she didn't recognize her surroundings and didn't remember the name of her boyfriend.

Suze rubbed the man's ass, massaged his lower back, and gave him words of encouragement, asking him to go quicker.

"Faster. Lean forward and kiss her more. Place your hands on her sides and hold her down and thrust your body through hers," Suze requested.

Chloe heard those words too, but she didn't see the woman who spoke them or recognized her name. Mr. Wilson leaned forward and began passionately kissing her as he continued counting. Chloe returned the kisses and moved her body in unison to get the most out his cock. This made him harder, and with Suze rubbing his back, he felt unstoppable.

Chloe was sliding forward as Mr. Wilson became harder still and more forceful. Suze took that as a sign that she was needed

and moved to the end by Chloe's head. She slid her body against
hers and positioned herself to aid in centering Chloe's mouth
over her pussy. Her head was hanging off the counter now,
making it nearly impossible for him to kiss her. He refocused
his energies on her breasts, mashing them down and taking as
much as he could in his hand every time he hit three.

Mr. Wilson announced that he was coming and yelled out
for her to keep going.

"Don't stop. Right there, bitch," he said as he slapped her
across her chest with a flat hand.

Chloe knew something was wrong; her boyfriend would
never hit her, she would never stand for that, but she wasn't
standing and she was being held down. Everything was coming
back to her now, but she still had her buzz on. Suze saw her
begin to struggle and pushed into her harder, keeping her head
at a downward angle and still wedged between her legs.

Chloe found it difficult to breathe as the shop owner
continued pressing down on her, taking his new girlfriend. He
was grunting passionately now, and his thrusting was irregular.
She no longer helped him by responding to his thrusts; she
just lay there. More voices in Chloe's head told her to enjoy the
woman in front of her and to eat her out for old time's sake.

"Taste her. Pleasure her with your tongue. Breathe your life's
breath into her pussy. You know you love her," the woman's voice
said.

Chloe sucked the woman into her mouth and bit down on
her clitoris. Her lips roughly rubbed against Suze's with such
anger that Suze looked down at the woman whom she thought
she had been in control of. The pain caused her to lean forward,
placing two hands on Chloe's chest for balance. Sensation after
sensation shot upward from Suze's toes to her head. She grabbed
the sides of Chloe's breasts, making her message clear: do that
again and I'll cause you more pain.

Mr. Wilson was finishing when he felt his girlfriend's legs
wrap around his body. That gave him all the leverage that he
needed to reach his full orgasm, but it was a selfish endeavor.

Chloe thought about doing that a few seconds after she started to come. She did that so she could get the last of him before he became soft. She had spent her time trying to push the man off of her when she realized what was happening was wrong, but now she spent her time in getting as much strange as she possibly could.

He rammed his penis into her with all the strength a raging alcoholic could muster. More grunts and moans escaped his lips, but this time he did not hit her; he enjoyed her participation. The smile on his face was as large as it had been in years, and though it was not initially consensual, it sure felt that way now.

Suze held on to Chloe's breasts, which allowed her to control the speed and intensity of her orgasm. Mr. Wilson was finishing due to his girlfriend's powerful legs. Chloe held a death grip on the man's ass, helping him to thrust deeper inside her. All was right with the world, she thought as she moved around the room, visiting each person in turn. Her work here was done; there were bigger fish to fry. She left the way she had come, passing right through the front glass window, and just like that, everything stopped.

Mr. Wilson looked down at the woman underneath him and reached backward to free himself. Chloe found that she could concentrate now and moved her head to the side, effectively releasing Suze's clitoris. He tapped Chloe on her hip twice and slid off to stand on the floor and began searching for his pants. Suze looked forward and wondered why Chloe was naked on the counter and why she had just removed her mouth from between her legs.

A few casual glances and fake smiles were exchanged as they rummaged through a pile of clothing. It took them a several minutes to find their clothes and get dressed; no one spoke during that process. It was an awkward silence with the equivalence of tomorrow morning's walk of shame, except it was happening today.

"OK, I have to ask. What just happened?" the shop owner asked.

Chloe looked at Suze and then to the man before turning away to face the front of the shop. The man watched on as Suze spoke first.

"I saw myself directing you to have sex with her. You were really into it, and within a few minutes time, I witnessed you change into a porn star—a porn star that I wouldn't mind meeting myself one day soon . . ." Suze said with affection.

Chloe turned back to them with tears in her eyes and looked down as she spoke.

"Suze, I've never seen you act that way before—you were not yourself. I don't know where all that passion came from. I've never seen you care much about anything," Chloe said coldly.

"I'm the one with attitude? I'm the bad person? You bit me, you bitch!" Suze yelled out.

"OK. Let's all calm down. None of us understand this. Just think back to when this all started. What is the last thing that you all remember?" he asked them.

The three looked at each other, but no one spoke. The fact is no one remembered anything. Mr. Wilson did not remember either woman coming into his shop. Hell, he didn't even remember opening his shop today. Chloe didn't remember driving here, and as she thought about Ruthie, she didn't know if she came with her today or not. Suze did not remember she was on her way to apply for a substitute teacher position when she received a suggestion to go to the general store.

"All right then, our silence says it all. We can't explain this away. The only thing that I know for sure was that your penis filled me with a plethora of emotions ranging from anger to lust," Chloe said.

The man blushed and turned away. Suze laughed at that statement; she didn't doubt it was full of emotion, but she knew that Chloe was confused. She had not had dick in years, not that she knew of anyway.

"Yeah, let's talk about penises, shall we? It wasn't that long ago since you gave them up. You only knew pussy, hon. I'm surprised that your she-box still functioned in that capacity," Suze said with a smile.

The shop owner saw the two women arguing back and forth and recognized a certain level of sexual tension. He was still trying to understand what had happened and didn't have time for this.

"OK. Listen up, the both of you. I understand you have a history together, I get it. Can we focus on all of this and not make it personal? I really need help understanding which one of you wants to be my new girlfriend," he said with a serious face.

Chloe and Suze looked at each other and back to him and then broke out in laughter. He smiled back and told them that since things were now civil; he would go in the back room and put on a pot of coffee.

"I'll be right back," he told them as he walked through the back room door.

CHAPTER SEVENTEEN

The Chocolatier

Ruthie walked up the left side of the street, looking at all the shop windows. This place sold jewelry; the next displayed puppy treats and dog collars. She kept walking, and as she approached the next window, she read the words "fine chocolates"! She just loved candy. Ruthie pulled on the door, but it would not budge. Closed, the sign read; she would have to come back in a few minutes and check again. Ruthie brought about seventeen dollars with her today to spend in town. Her mom had let her bring her piggy bank today to spend as she saw fit. This chocolate shop was definitely on her list, she thought, as she continued onward.

About four shops down on the right was the general store. Ruthie would visit that place last because her mom told her to meet her there when she was ready to leave. She was to look for her outside the shop before entering. Looking at the store, her mom wasn't outside, so she had more time. On to the next store, she thought while she skipped across the sidewalk. Food! The next store had a food theme.

Opening the door and stepping inside set off the electronic bell, announcing her presence to the entire store. Looking around, she saw books on cooking, plastic food art, jars of peanut butter, assorted nuts, and chocolates for baking. The name of this store was called All Things Baked, and it would be tied for first place until she could gain access to the Fine

Chocolates Store. It would take Ruthie several minutes before she came to the realization that this store had nothing for kids; it was an adult baking store. She soon grew bored and exited the store without saying a single word.

Ruthie stepped onto the walkway and saw a woman across the street standing inside a store behind a large glass door. She smiled at Ruthie and turned to her left, walking out of sight, disappearing behind a tall display. Suze walked back over to Chloe, who was still sitting in the exact spot where she had left her. She didn't address Suze; all she did was to raise her hands and await the arrival of the shop owner so he could remove the handcuffs.

Ruthie headed off to where she had started so she could check out the chocolate shop. The streets were devoid of traffic, and the lack of cars meant that few people were walking around or visiting the shops. That must be why most businesses on Main Street in Murphys opened as early as noon, and generally they closed earlier than their signs said they did.

Ruthie had eyed the Fine Chocolates Shop with anticipation from down the street. She could not see the sign from where she was, so she left and took that chance. Walking at a fast pace was something she did regularly, but she also ran. When in town, though, she was always on her best behavior. When she reached the door, she became excited; the closed sign had been turned to open and there was a gentleman inside with an apron sorting his goods.

The door opened easily, and Ruthie slipped inside with the highest of expectations for her chocolate lover's addiction. Her mom always told her that chocolate is a want, not a need; and that when she gets older, she'll understand more. *Forget that,* she thought, *I'm having some now!* The man behind the counter looked at the little girl and then around the shop.

"My mom's over at the general store for the moment. I'd like some chocolate, please," Ruthie said, answering his questions before he asked them.

"I have your chocolate in the back. It's not all ready yet, but I think I know what you will enjoy. One moment, please," he said as he walked into the back room.

Ruthie looked around the shop and walked from one end of the glass display to the other. She couldn't choose if she had to, she thought. The man came back with a small tray of round chocolates covered with white powder.

"Try one of these chocolate-covered cherries. If you like them, you can buy four for the price of one. Let me know what you think, they are brand new," he asked.

She smiled and took one chocolate and bit it in half. If quickly started leaking and she stuck in the second piece so it would not leak out.

"They are very messy," she said as she noticed the strong cherry flavor.

"I love it! Yes, I'll take four more please," she said excitedly.

The man smiled as he walked over to the front door to lock it; he knew it would only take one. The chocolatier reached his hand for the knob, and a woman pushed her way inside.

"You're not closing early, are you?" Suze asked.

"Yes. Well, no. In a few minutes, actually," he said, smiling as he looked at her and turned the dead bolt.

He watched as the woman walked straight over to Ruthie. Suze remembered the little girl from across the street earlier and asked if she was OK.

"All right? Are you all right, little girl?" she asked the child.

The man awaited a response as he turned the sign over to read Closed.

"Me? Oh, yes, I'm quite well. I've just paid for these chocolates and I'm on my way out," Ruthie answered.

The man walked back to the front counter, passing the woman who was looking for a chair to sit in.

"Are you OK, ma'am?" he asked as she sat down and held her head with her right hand, rubbing it slowly.

Ruthie smiled and told the man she had left him exact change as she headed for the door. Unlocking it, she took a step outside and turned to thank him again. The man walked over to the door to attempt to grab the little girl, but she was already walking down the street. He looked back at the woman who was now using both hands to rub her head and again locked the door.

Ruthie took a left out of the shop and walked back to the one that she had recently been to. Looking in the window, she smiled and then entered the pet store. She walked around and looked at this and that before going to a wall full of leashes. Selecting a large one that was retractable, she chose a matching adjustable collar. She placed them both in her bag with the chocolates she had recently been given and ate another one. Noticing an unusual taste that she did not recognize first and then the cherry that overpowered everything, she shook her head as she exited the shop to search for her mom.

Chloe looked around and saw the naked ankles of an approaching man. She begged him to set her free. He never spoke as he took her calves and raised her body into the air. Her hands were still handcuffed together, and a heavy table leg provided the anchor to keep the woman in place. He positioned her against his groin and slowly entered her from behind. Chloe let out a scream of pain as he continued his forward progress. His door opened up, and a little girl walked in.

"Be a dear and lock the door, please. I'll be right with you," he told the girl as he started fucking Chloe.

"Mom, is that you? Are you there?" Ruthie asked as she locked the door.

Tears welled up in Chloe's eyes as she looked out to her daughter. The image of Ruthie on the security camera was blurry at best, and she seemed to jump and bounce as the man made love to his newest girlfriend.

"Take a seat, girl, where you can. I'm going to be a few minutes here," he told her as he started giving it to his new girlfriend harder.

Several broken words came out as complete sentences in Chloe's mind but were fragmented all to hell due to the alcohol that she had consumed.

"Ruthie . . . is . . . that . . ." she said with a long pause followed by a sigh of pain and a "you?"

She loved the controlling aspect of her tasks; the ones that fought back were the challenges. This one here didn't seem to put up much of a fight at all, and it was almost boring to watch it all unfold. As more and more alcohol took effect, she had to look for another.

Concentrating on what Chloe felt, she was amazed that the man was still hard after all they had been through. It was more like hard again, she thought, instead of still hard. The pain was almost unbearable, and when Chloe was allowed to feel, she wished that she couldn't. With another cry for mercy, the man dropped her and exited her anus. Chloe heard herself ask him to do that; she had just asked the man to exit and reenter her all at once, finishing with the phrase "Thanks, baby."

Who was he to judge? This woman loved every position imaginable and had earlier told him that unless she says "pretty please," to ignore whatever she might say. That followed with a "make me hurt, you man of men" was enough to do it; he became immediately hard and spent the next few minutes following her initial instructions.

Ruthie suddenly felt drowsy and tired; she experienced fatigue and weakness flow through her body. She had felt this way before, but it was only after becoming nauseous, not starting out that way. It was either the presence of another or she was drugged. What kind of sick fuck drugs a child at a candy store? She made a note of that; she would have to visit that shop again, and soon. For now she had more pressing issues at hand. She was vulnerable now and soon to be totally incapacitated. Her options were limited and not to her liking. She could stay the course, stay with Ruthie, or possess her mother.

The chocolatier looked at the woman sitting at his table holding her head and squinting her eyes.

"Are you OK?" he asked again.

The woman did not speak. She raised her hand and waved it to tell the man she was indeed OK and stood up. The man watched her take two steps and fall over face-first onto the edge of another table. That she hit with her left shoulder, which turned her slightly on her side. She continued falling and landed on her back. From his angle, the man could not tell if she had hit her head or not. Time would tell the answer to that question, he thought; if she did, there would be blood, a goose egg, or worse. The chocolatier walked around the tables to check on the woman who had just fallen. Her moans of pain were loud as he reached down to take hold of her.

"Come with me. Let's get you up. Can you stand?" he asked as he took hold of her left arm and helped her up.

Suze screamed in protest to his help but had no choice to follow as he led her to the back room. He walked her through a room with bright lights past some stainless steel tables and to a plush couch. He sat her down and told her to rest a minute and that he would be right back. He quickly went and closed his shop, turning off the lights in the front and locking the door. He had taken a few steps before he turned back to flip the sign. He laughed when he thought about closing the candy store when he was actually going to open her legs for candy. *What a lucky day,* he thought. *You gotta love tourism.*

Ruthie fell to her knees with her eyes growing increasingly tired and heavier. She found it very hard to concentrate on anything. *It wouldn't be long now,* she thought. Soon she would be passed out, cold and lifeless on the floor. Ruthie had to think quickly; she concentrated as best she could and she made her decision.

Mr. Wilson walked to and fro as if confused. Chloe saw him contemplating something; she tried not to cry, but she started sobbing again. He looked at her with an agitated expression and then walked over to her. Kneeling by her side, he smiled at her as he reached for a bottle. He took hold of her hair and raised her head to meet him, staring into her eyes as he spoke.

"You look thirsty, my friend. You had better be very thirsty, if you understand my meaning," he said as he unscrewed the cap on the bottle.

Taking care to pour slowly, he pushed the bottle against her lips until she opened wide enough for him to stick it in. He went slowly, pouring never more than she could quickly finish. Noticing her small sips, he pushed it in further and up ended the bottle.

"I said drink!" he said as he moved it around her mouth.

Chloe had been taking smaller measured sips before, but now it was all she could do to keep breathing. She had cleared her mouth four times now and she was losing this battle, as sometimes liquid found its way into her lungs as she breathed. Chloe felt the alcohol burn the entire way down. Her eyes watered, the fumes hurt her lungs, her mouth and throat burned, and her stomach felt warm from the sheer volume. She saw no way out of this situation; once again, she was fucked. Mr. Wilson pulled the bottle away and let go of her hair, allowing her head to hit the floor. The cool thing about being drunk is that she didn't necessarily care about that and she sure didn't feel the pain. She tried focusing on the room, on the lights, but every time she closed her eyes, the room began to spin.

Chloe spent the next several minutes trying to breathe normally without choking on whiskey and to keep her head from lolling over this way or that. Mr. Wilson would not witness any of those events. He slowly walked over to his counter, pulled out a shotgun, and continued to his front door. Mr. Wilson looked out of his window for what he was told would be his last time. He didn't understand it all, but he was ready for it all to be over.

Watching the traffic slowly drive down Main Street and determining who was driving was sort of a game for him. Normally he was plenty accurate, as he would say, but this time of year, he saw an increase of tourists. *Wine or gold,* he thought, *they came mainly for wine or gold.* The Huckabees drove by in their '94 Dodge minivan; it had been three days since he saw them last. He watched the van make a laborious left turn and disappear out of sight.

Looking down the street made his rounds looking at the shops and stopped at the Fine Chocolate Shop. Earlier, he saw Tom Lewis lock the door and look left and right before turning off his lights. Mr. Wilson leaned forward and rested his forehead on the glass window and raised his shotgun to his chin. He exhaled and reached for the trigger, closing his eyes for the last time. Earlier, he saw Tom looking around and heading to his back room; he knew exactly where he was going. He would make his intoxicating mixture and use it to extract his sexual needs from his victims. Mr. Wilson took a deep breath and knew what he must do.

He opened his eyes, lowered his shotgun, and left his shop at a normal gate. He had forgotten to lock his shop, but it didn't matter anymore. There was no coming home from this; he pictured what he might look like to his neighbors and tourists. Mr. Wilson looked to the right to ensure that it was safe to cross the street, and driving his direction were the Thompsons. He knew that it wasn't Sarah behind the wheel; she never drove. As they passed him, Bill beeped his horn like always. Sarah turned her head, wondering why he was naked and crossing the street with a shotgun. Bill pulled over to the curb, checking his rearview mirror, and watched him walk up to the door to use his key.

Suze started to come to; she could not see anything in the room—it was too dark. She was aware of herself lying on her back; she felt her heels touching a cold surface. In fact, her entire body was cold. Trying to move, she quickly realized that she was tied down in several places; Suze could wiggle but not much more than that. She was able to call out for help; she did not feel a gag or anything else over her mouth.

Suze yelled for help one time; that's all it took for her to understand that she had trauma to her head. The pain was so horrible that she almost pissed herself and passed out. Never had she been this bad before; she had done assorted party drugs and taken various flavors of alcohol her entire life, but this was something she had never known.

"Is there anyone there? I need help. Can you go and get help?" she asked quietly.

Closing her eyes, she fought against localized pain behind them that almost crippled her. She did not know where she was or how she got here; the only thing she knew is that she could not move.

Tom was at his stove heating up several batches of chocolate in his double boilers. Stirring constantly was the key, he always said as he continued to follow his own instructions. Dropping several pieces of raw cocoa, he stirred them around until they melted. The pieces were blended into the mixture within a few minutes, and everything was almost ready. He searched for nutmeg and some vanilla extract and measured twice before adding them. Reaching in his pocket, he took a variety of his favorite narcotics and crushed them up; it was the last ingredient he added before removing the chocolate from the burner. The mixing was enough to keep them soft and creamy. He moved the double boilers off to the side and let their hot water keep the bowls warm.

He grabbed a ladle and placed it into one bowl, and taking the contents from another, he combined them. This he took into the other room, using his foot to push open the door. As quietly as he could, he approached her and placed the chocolate bowl next to her strapped-down shoulder, admiring his handiwork. She was totally naked, blindfolded, and strapped down in several places on his favorite chocolate table. It was where he worked his masterpieces, and it was where he was going to work today. She was very beautiful and she was all his. He had never seen her before in town and figured her a tourist. Hopefully she would be a tourist that no one would ever miss, or at least come looking for her at his shop.

It was a spontaneous occurrence, he would say. Tom had never thought about capturing a woman in his store; for him, it had always been children. Candy was a lovely way to get them; that strategy had been around since the times of nursery rhymes. He wasn't sure of the proper amount of tranquilizers necessary to put her under, so he made a best guess and used three, as she was a medium-sized athletic-looking woman. When Suze heard movement in the room, she pleaded for help; she begged to be set free.

"Please, please, if you can hear me, I need you to set me free," Suze said quietly.

He never responded to her requests; he just continued to occasionally stir his chocolate and to look at her body. This went on for several minutes before he was ready to work on her.

Suze became aware of the scents around her, picking out vanilla, something Christmas-like, and another strong aroma, possibly bourbon? Again she pleaded to be set free, stating that she was experiencing a lot of pain in her head.

"I need medical attention. I need you to call an ambulance," she begged.

Mr. Wilson held his head with his left hand and massaged his temple.

"So much pain, there's so much pain," he said in a low voice.

He had just stepped inside and locked the door when it hit him. It had been bad before, but it was intolerable now. He squeezed his eyes as tightly as he could and kept them shut until it lessened and then he continued walking.

There was so much pain that he could barely think clearly. Mr. Wilson wondered if he was thinking clearly when he came to the determination that he needed to kill Tom. He had known for quite some time now that things weren't right around here, but he never had any proof; he was really never sure, until today.

Mr. Thompson watched through the window as Mr. Wilson rubbed his head roughly with one hand, holding on to his shotgun with the other. Back and forth he paced, as if contemplating something bad. Bill had to talk to him; something was wrong, something was very wrong, he thought. Bill pushed against the door, and it would not give. Looking to the side, he saw the closed sign and looked back at the door to check when they normally closed. Bill peered back inside the shop, placing his hands on the window to block the glare, and Mr. Wilson was gone. It was if he had vanished from sight. It was too far to get to the back room from when he saw him last. He looked around the shop and saw no movement, no Mr. Wilson.

Bill turned around to wave at his wife, asking for five more minutes, sticking a hand up in the air. Sarah nodded and turned back around to listen to her radio. Bill smiled, turning back to face the window. Right in front of him stood Mr. Wilson with the shotgun pointing chest high. Bill jumped backward and into the air as Mr. Wilson delivered a heart-stopping scare. Before Bill had placed his feet on the sidewalk, he was again lifted off his feet as Mr. Wilson released both barrels.

Sarah turned around in time to see her husband making his way through the air toward her. He landed in the street on his back; the impact threw his blood a foot in the air. Shortly after that, a thousand pieces of glass fell upon his body and the street, littering them like glitter.

He reached for her head and removed her blindfold. Suze's eyes adjusted to the flood of light that sent pain to the back of her head. She hurt; her skull throbbed, and the pain she experienced seemed at times quite unbearable. She looked through half-closed slivers of eyes at the salesman. He had long, thin facial features, which included a pointy chin and gaunt, raised cheekbones. *Ironic to be that thin and work in a chocolate shop,* she thought. His lips curled into an evil smile as Suze saw long thin fingers coming her way.

He massaged her face, making small circles with his fingers, saying, "There, there, now, aren't you pretty?"

Suze begged him to go and get help. She was hurt; she needed to be free. After saying those words, she wasn't sure why she had said them. She had a puzzled expression afterward, and he was equally confused.

"Must be from your concussion. You had a pretty good fall back there. I'm making you some chocolate, it's what I do—I'm a chocolatier. I'm going to give you a service, and it's important for you to enjoy it all. No time for molds," he said as he inserted a number three funnel into her mouth, interrupting her protests.

Suze could speak, sort of, but she could not be understood. Her pleas for help were not discernable, even to her. Suze watched on as the creepy thin man poured a ladle of chocolate into the funnel. It was very warm and smooth. Suze had no choice but to swallow the chocolate waterfall. The chocolatier did not speak as he ladled another service of melted chocolaty goodness into the funnel.

He then turned away and walked over to the stove and used a spatula to remove the chocolate from one bowl and add it to the other. He then brought it over to Suze and used the spatula to pour chocolate over part of her face, her breasts, her neck, and her navel. Suze was still disoriented, but she had enough sense about her to know what was going on, and that the chocolate was warm, very warm, but not scalding. She was aware of where the chocolate was and where it had traveled as it started to cool against her body.

The chocolatier used the large silicon spatula to thoroughly scrape the remaining chocolate from the bowl and onto her body. When he had finished that process, he sat the bowl down beside her and brought the spatula down quickly against Suze's chocolate-free breast. The noise was worse than the pain was, but it scared the hell out of Suze and caught her attention at the same time. It reminded her of just how much danger she was presently in, of the possibility of shock and the pain that lingered. It was also a reminder that things could always be worse and that they would probably be worse sooner than later.

With most of the chocolate gone now, all that was left was an aftertaste. It had notes of coconut, almond, vanilla, nutmeg, and possibly bourbon. Her tongue was heavy with the chocolate, even though she tried to get rid of it by swallowing it and sucking it down. She swallowed repeatedly and rubbed her tongue over her teeth, but some still remained. The pain in her head lessened, probably due to the drugs and alcohol; for all she knew, she was dying.

He reached for the empty bowl, and they both heard an explosion from somewhere up front. It was loud enough for him to turn his head in response. The noise was so loud that he thought a car had crashed through his front plate glass window, so he walked to the front of his shop to see what had happened. Suze tried to watch him go out the door and see what he saw, but turning her head sent shocks of pain from her wrist to her thigh. Tears flooded her eyes, and she shut them immediately against its force.

Mrs. Thompson had a front row seat; she saw thousands of small pieces of safety glass follow Mr. Thompson on his journey toward the street. He appeared to fly backward in slow motion as the glass pieces around him kept pace. Landing on his butt, his back and arms kept moving backward until they too rested on the street. The glass seemed to sprinkle everything within a four-foot diameter with broken glass, which reflected the light from today's midday sun in every angle imaginable. Mr. Wilson looked on with sadness, but he could not have anyone intervening with what he must do.

Mr. Wilson turned around and walked softly toward the first of the three doors that led to the chocolate shop's back rooms. He was told that the back rooms were where he performed his magic. He thought that the chocolatier referred to chocolate candies, cookies, and other culinary baked good, but lately he wasn't so sure. He felt uneasy about something, he didn't know what. Lucky for him, he was on the town council. Mr. Wilson had access to the buildings on the street and in the downtown area in general; without it, he might have had to shoot his way inside.

As he took another step toward the door, he was greeted by a "Who's there?"

All he could do at this point was to acknowledge that someone *was* there.

"It's me—Roche. Someone's gone and done it. They accidentally drove through your front glass window. It's pretty bad, so I wanted to get you," Roche replied.

"Oh hell, is the driver all right?" Tom asked as he opened the door and stepped out.

Only one step was necessary for the chocolatier to notice that the glass was gone from the front of his store; it looked more like a break-in than a car wreck. Tom looked back at Roche and noticed the shotgun leveled at his midsection.

"Wait, no. Roche!" was all Tom was able to get out before being lifted off the ground and thrown aback against the side of the back room door.

Suze again tried to remove her neck from her head when she involuntarily jerked her head up into the air when she had heard the explosion. It sounded like a gunshot, she thought, and it was very close. Suze tried to call out, but she was disoriented, muffled, and confused; she slurred her words badly now, and after a few tries at correcting her speech, she gave up.

Roche stepped over Tom's body and walked into the back room to see what was going on there. He looked around and saw nothing out of the ordinary in his first inspection, so he stopped to reload his shotgun for the second time today. He approached the second door, which was closed like the first one, and placed an ear against it to listen. He closed his eyes to concentrate, but that hurt his head. Roche opened them and made a puzzled expression with both of his eyebrows moving down and inward and stared at the wall. Again he was confused on why he was here and what he was to do.

Ruthie stared outward through the walls that blocked her view of the chocolate shop and slid onto her side, losing consciousness. *Fuuccckkkk* was the last thing she thought before she thought no more. Her lifeless body fell limp to the floor with her mother only ten feet away in the back room.

Suze heard the door open as she stared at the ceiling, listening to the area around her. The thought of him coming back sent fear through her body, and she began crying. She was emotional as it was, and although her mind was clouded, she felt somewhat relaxed now. Suze felt drugged, maybe even drunk, she wasn't sure. She still tasted chocolate; it invaded her senses, most of which was smell. The entire area smelled chocolaty to her, and she was hungry; yup, she was indeed drunk.

Roche placed his shotgun up against the wall and tried to clear his head. Man, did his head hurt; it felt as if it were to explode. He felt different now, more relaxed, but his mind was foggy. He wasn't sure why he was in the chocolate shop one minute and where he was in general the next. Had he not smelled chocolate and taken a quick look around to notice the equipment along with bags of coca, he might not have put two and two together.

Roche looked the woman up and down a few times from head to toe. She had a lovely body and lovely breasts, one of which was half covered with chocolate. Other parts of her body were covered with chocolate as well; she looked absolutely delightful. He looked her over a second time before removing the funnel from her mouth. The man saw his chance, a chance to do something and get away with it. *Who would know?* he thought. He looked at the woman's breast again and watched it move up and down as she breathed.

Suze still had her head held straight and only saw the ceiling and what her small amount of peripheral vision allowed. Her eyes watered; her mouth and jaws were sore. He thought again about what he could get away with as he looked at the side of her face. She licked her dry lips and managed to speak.

"Thank you. I am not good. I feel drugged, and—" she paused.

"I'm finding it hard to think to focus, and my vision is blurry. I'm afraid that I am going to pass out, and—" Suze never finished her last thought, but what she did say was done quietly.

He began untying her, starting at her legs and then her hands, and finally finishing with her head straps. She was trying to stop crying and began sobbing heavily instead. Roche had just finished untying her when she reached over to hug him. He held her tightly and pulled Suze to her feet. *A second chance with his girl, how lucky,* he thought. He held her upright for a few seconds and let her go to get a better grip. Suze leaned to the side and started heading for the floor, unable to keep standing.

Roche tried to grab her, but his reflexes were slightly less than what was required; he only managed to grab hold of her hair. Suze's body fell hard and jerked her head at a slight angle when her hair straightened out. She never realized what happened and she would not be alive to find out; her neck had been broken. He looked at her and instantly knew what had happened. *What a shame,* he thought, looking down at her head. It was suspended right in front of his groin, with her chin pressing against his thigh; just where he needed her to be . . .

He wasn't sure if he had killed her or if it was an accident; he wasn't sure of much lately—he didn't feel himself. Looking around the room frantically, he panicked, not knowing what to do next. No one would ever believe him. What a crazy day. He didn't know what was made up or what was real, not anymore. What had actually happened? What had he dreamed? Roche felt really bad about what had happened, as he thought it to be, so he placed her back on the table and strapped her back down.

Roche turned to walk out of the room and saw Tom lying dead, sitting up with his back against the door. He had a large bloody spot from chest to stomach. Small darkened burn holes peppered his chest. He stopped walking and looked around the room. There was another door in front of him; he wasn't sure which one he had come through. This door was closed; the one with Tom against the side wall was open. He closed his eyes and breathed deeply a few times before stepping around the chocolatier.

He placed his hand on the wall to balance himself as he walked past him, and that's when he noticed his shotgun resting in the corner. Roche stared at it for a second before picking it up. He wondered how it got here and if it was him who had used it on Tom. If he had done all of this—why? Could it have been Tom who kidnapped the woman and tied her to the table? Was it him? Did he tie her up? Maybe Tom came to save her? Maybe Tom was trying to save her from him? It was all a blur; he only knew that he had to leave this place. Roche could not be found her, nor could he be seen leaving the building. Holding his shotgun firmly in his hand, he stepped back over Tom and to the other closed door, opened it, and then left through the back door.

Mr. Wilson walked a few feet to a small parking lot and opened the door to his Chevy S10 and tossed his shotgun on the passenger's side, closing his door. He sat staring at the back door to the chocolate shop; he had forgotten to close it. He didn't want to go back there; he wanted to leave. He looked away and started the truck. Looking up, he placed it into reverse as someone walked out of the back door. He recognized her as Mrs. Thompson.

She stood in the open doorway, looking at him. She told him to turn off the engine. Roche placed the truck back in park and killed the engine. His head hurt again, another headache and more voices . . . When would this all end? *Take your shotgun and place the barrel in your mouth,* he heard in his head. He reached for the shotgun and maneuvered it around his body. Placing the barrel into his mouth, he looked back up to Mrs. Thompson.

"Now pull the trigger. It will be all over soon," he heard her say.

"Close your eyes, lean forward, and pull the trigger," she told him.

Mrs. Thompson walked back into the store and waited for the shotgun to go off. The explosion sounded closer than she thought, and she paused a second before looking over her shoulder. Mrs. Thompson saw there was no one behind the wheel; all she had to do now was to wait.

CHAPTER EIGHTEEN

Better than Most Deserve

Months ago

The DJ bounced to the music with all the passion of a twelve-year-old holding a nearly empty half gallon of chocolate ice cream. Sharleen had the build of a twelve-year-old in height, size, and voice only; her breasts and piercings said she was a mature woman, and probably outside of your league. She controlled the lighting, the music, the mixing between midrange and bass, and everything in between. The only clothing she wore was a white string bikini bottom. The rest of her was covered in neon body paint.

Roughly from her navel down were earth tones, browns, greens, grays, and blacks. Those colors were used to make the ground of a deciduous forest in midfall. That much was always common; it was the same, and if you knew her, you would expect nothing less. Now the top portion of her body would be different every day that she worked. Today was no different; today was pecker day.

Sharleen's right breast was occupied by the bright red colors of the red-headed woodpecker. The bird stretched from her top right breast to her bottom left hip, covering both of her breasts with the bird's main colors of red, white, and blue. The tail feathers wrapped around the lower left side of her waist, and its claws held on to a tree branch that grew upward from her belly button. It was a beautiful thing to behold, and that was without recognizing that her breasts were a perfect C cup.

Sharleen queued up the next song and turned on her microphone to yell at the crowd.

"Get your asses movin', bitches!" Sharleen yelled with great emphasis on the "bitches" part.

The *Electric Slide* was wrapping up and in came the fade for *No Parking on the Dance Floor*. The crowd shifted from a throbbing mass of bodies in a forty-foot square to utter chaos as they dispersed to the lyrics "If you don't get a move on that body, I'll be forced to give you a ticket, so get with it!" She had planned the song to transition with the clock hitting twenty-five minutes after midnight. Sharleen stared at the clock until it was the proper time and then announced to everyone present that it has begun.

"Our twenty-five-cent beer for the next twenty-five minutes starts at 12:25, ladies!" Sharleen announced.

The entire length of the bar was covered with opaque plastic cups full of beer. Two assistants stood at the ready to collect the money as the masses approached. Within minutes, there wasn't a woman in sight who wasn't carrying two to four beers as she walked through the bar. It was designed sparing no expense, to offer the masses a way to meet in a safe and organized way.

Body Talk was a popular bar that locals referred to as "broken" because the building was a huge triangle. It looked like an explosion of neon in the middle of nowhere had chosen to assault the woods around it. Each point of the triangle catered to a particular crowd. They offered their own separated area with a one-way see-through mirror that stretched from floor to ceiling. There were numerous dancing areas and sections where tables were so close that those who "teach" can hang out. There was only one bar area, and it was centrally located one level lower.

Triangles were used as a theme in every way imaginable, with circles and squares used only to confuse the unwary. The geometry of the building itself was triangular, not just the main walls that were protecting the people from the forest. The building seemed to expand and contract as if it was breathing, making some drunk people a bit uneasy if they happened to notice it.

There were four giant segmented triangles inside Body Talk's main floor. Only the raciest of men and women, dressed in sexy attire or nothing at all, were asked inside the center triangle. Anyone in the center could not look through into the glass into the other areas, but they were all able to be viewed. Rumor had it that the men and women inside were given free apps and drinks as a thank-you for dancing and making out for all to see. There were no additional costs for voyeurism; it was included in the cover charge.

First-time visitors would follow simple signs to their entrance and approach two, sometimes three, bouncers standing in front of red velvet ropes that blocked off all entry. As the club reached capacity, they turned away the gentlemen and only allowed women inside; there was always room for more women. Soon they would fall in love with their area, with their desires changing toward the center. Once in the center, it wouldn't be too much longer than a month of weekend visits before they asked about the basement . . . If rumor mentioned the fun times in the center triangle with its free appetizers and drinks, they said nothing about the basement. No one really knew what happened down there; most employees had no access to that area, and even fewer knew where the door was.

Walking inside displayed more of the same: red velvet ropes segmenting the entrance from the bar access, surrounded by two or more bouncers. A neon sign to the left read: "Charity Kisses—one dollar," and the fine print underneath it said "One free drink per hour with wristband."

Over to the right was small sign that said "Invitation ONLY" with only one bouncer in front of that roped-off area. No one ever saw anyone push through that area, let alone cause a scene in front of it. It was just sort of off limits, and everyone respected that.

Somewhere walking around inside an area was a key master. That was the most important person in your section, as once you paid your six-dollar cover charge, unless you received your token, you could not gain access. So if someone did something stupid and caused a scene and they were, how do you say, "ordinary," they would forfeit their money and be out the door. That person would leave on their own accord or they would be escorted out.

This club was a very nicely designed public place where one could act out within reason inside a controlled environment and feel that someone had your back. It was a great place to let off steam on any night of the week because they never actually closed. *Technically*, they were closed from 4:00 a.m. to 6:00 a.m., where they did not sell food or drink and they locked the doors. When it hit 6:00 a.m., they would actually unlock the doors and it would be business as usual; this was referred by the locals as "slippage." It was defined as "being too lazy to leave the bar because you are having a bitchin' time."

Going back to one's initial impression of this bar, upon approaching your area, there would be a greeter. This person actually screened you as you approached and helped you to find your own area. A woman stood outside the women's only area, a man for the men's, and a couple for the rest. It was more to screen out troublemakers than it was to aid the patron, but it was done so professionally that no one ever questioned it. Everything about this club exuded courtesy, professionalism and pride. That message flooded through the local communities and surrounding areas including Bigelow Hollow, keeping them busy with almost as many locals as they had out-of-towners.

"This club's a little far," Lucy told Mercedes.

"It'll be fine, you'll see. Everyone's coming here. It's new, it's popular, and it's remote!" Mercedes replied.

Lucy was looking out her window and laughed when she read one of their advertising slogans: "It's worth the ride. Come inside, and enjoy you, for hours." Mercedes laughed at her and kept scanning the road for vermin.

"Put that away and have one with me before we get there," she told Lucy, handing her a large green plastic cup.

The roads wound themselves around fewer and fewer houses, until at last the nearby forest announced that they were close.

"A few minutes more," Lucy said as she turned another curve, and there it was, in all its illuminated goodness!

Mercedes was so excited when the club finally came into view.

"We are going to dance our asses off tonight," Lucy said with a very wide smile.

"I might not even look at a man, or a woman. I might just dance all evening long!" Mercedes shouted.

Lucy slid her car into a spot in the fourth row, and both women checked their faces in their compact mirrors.

"Better than most deserve," Mercedes said, laughing.

Lucy just made some "mmm" noises and closed her mirror. Making their way to the club, Mercedes told her she had forgotten to lock her car and that she would be right back.

"Go ahead, I'll catch up," she told Lucy.

"Sure, sure, I'll see you inside," Lucy said as she blinked her eyes against the bright lights.

Lucy walked on and queued herself up for entry for the woman's only section behind two young twenty-somethings and waited her turn. She saw a woman pick up a bracelet and pay a brunette named Charity a buck, and then watched closely as she leaned in for a kiss. Lucy read the sign on the table and knew what was going on.

"I'll take a few, please. I'm feeling charitable tonight," Lucy said and leaned close to the woman.

In the parking lot

Mercedes pressed the lock button on her key fob, but nothing happened. She heard no sounds or saw the flashing lights to acknowledge that her alarm had been set and the doors locked. She stopped walking and pointed her arm out in the direction of her Mercedes and tried again; when she heard nothing for the second time, she continued walking to her car to check it out.

Inside the bar

"Feeling generous, are we now? Come closer then," the brunette said.

Lucy leaned in even further over the table and puckered up. The brunette cupped Lucy's breasts, kissing her twice before she gave her two bracelets and let her go.

"Meet me in the center later on, I'll catch you later," she said, smiling to Lucy.

Lucy tightened the bands around her wrist and danced her way past the bouncer and onto the dimly lit dance floor. Soft well-placed neon lights lit up armbands all over the dance floor, making small illuminated circles in all colors appear to float through the air from various directions.

This place is incredible, Lucy thought as she headed for the stairs.

A few more drinks would put her in the mood, and Lucy looked for a place to get them. She stood shoulders above the rest of the women around her. If she was to abruptly stop while walking, her hair would cover the woman's face that walked too closely behind her. Lucy raised her arm higher than the rest and mouthed the words "long island ice tea," followed by two fingers, displaying both wristbands.

The bartender smiled and nodded, turning around to reach extra lemon slices from the bottom shelf. In doing so, she displayed her yellow panties to everyone who was facing her direction. Rising back up to smile and finish her drinks, she looked around the crowd and noticed that tonight was unusually busy. Lucy smiled back at the bartender and thought that she still had it; that woman was definitely into her. The only problem was that others close to her had it too, and they had it for others . . . Lucy tipped her and waited for her drinks with a ten-dollar bill that included her name, her phone number, and her schedule. She took her drinks and walked off to a nearby table to await Mercedes.

In the parking lot

After mashing the button on her remote a third and fourth time, she stopped again to look for her car. She found it right behind a large SUV and immediately started walking over to it. She reached her vehicle and saw the interior dome light on. Looking around, she noticed that her passenger door was open, and that's probably the reason why the alarm would not trigger. She started walking back to the club and pressed the lock button on her keys one more time to the same effect. She turned around and looked at the car and pressed the key fob another time before walking to her driver side door.

Mercedes took a step back in shock as a man stood up and demanded her cell phone and purse at knifepoint. The man moved forward as quickly as she had already stepped backward. Taking hold of her arm, he pressed the knife against her stomach, leading her away. Several rows behind her car, they stopped in front of an old gray minivan. The side door opened, and a pair of arms reached out to help Mercedes inside.

"Shut up and you'll live through this. Make noise and I'll have to steal another vehicle due to the mess. Understand me?" the man asked.

Mercedes found herself unable to struggle, unable to speak, so she just nodded her head in agreement, as her eyes began to tear up. She was quickly silenced by duct tape and then twisted around the inside of the van. Again she was told to keep quiet as the first man got inside and closed the door behind him. Mercedes made squeaky noises through her taped mouth and watched the men through her salty tears.

This was the first time that she actually looked at the two men. They had Bluetooth devices in their ears. They dressed in mainly black colors and had dark, short cropped hair. The man who had captured her reached out and grabbed her legs. He twisted her around on her back and pulled her toward him.

"What a beautiful body, and that ass, perfect," he said, producing handcuffs.

The man secured her feet to the middle row seat and tugged on them to ensure that she would not escape.

"You'll be safe here. Keep quiet, and we'll be right back to set you free," the first man said.

"We promise" came from the back from the second man.

Mercedes continued crying tears onto the floor of the minivan as the two men exited the vehicle and closed the door. She wasn't sure about the situation she currently found herself in. Mercedes surely wasn't going to sit by and wait for them to return. She tried to escape and struggled against her handcuffs with such passion that Houdini himself would have been jealous.

She was just as much a part of this van as the tires were, and try as she may, she could do nothing about the handcuffs. She focused on breathing normally and tried to control her emotions. Her crying had just stopped when footsteps were heard beyond the door. A few seconds later, the door opened enough to allow a man to slide inside. He quickly closed the door as Mercedes turned her head and saw man number one rest his back against it. He was breathing heavy and smiled at her briefly, as he too tried to control his emotion.

Approximately two minutes or so later, the man nodded at Mercedes and slid toward her on his knees. At the exact moment that he reached her, gunfire erupted around them. What sounded like very large cannons came from the left and right sides of their van. A brief pause and then the sounds of semiautomatic gunfire were heard. The cannon fire was less now and more distant to them, but occasionally broken glass was heard nearby. Mercedes counted no less than twelve shots from very large caliber weapons from the hand cannons that she had mentioned earlier.

Where's your partner in crime? she thought, staring at the man's body that hovered over her.

Mercedes still could not talk from her taped mouth, but she tried to get his attention as the first of several shouts were muffled silent. The man patted her on her shoulder a few times and then announced his intentions by moving her hair out of the way and unzipping her blouse. Mercedes had corrected her breathing and was working on calming down when he started to undress her. It wouldn't take too long for him to finish getting her naked; she was scantily clothed as it was. She had made her intentions clear to those who saw her tonight just by what she chose to wear, by how her makeup made her eyes pop, and by how she smelled; heavy jasmine scents permeated her pores, well, now mingled with sweat and fear.

The man stared at the woman who was handcuffed to the seat wearing only tape over her mouth and told her that she was too beautiful to pass up. He pushed his pants down to his ankles and turned the woman over. Placing his hand under her stomach, he raised her to her knees and entered her from behind. He wasn't hard yet, so he focused on rubbing her hanging breasts with both of his hands. She felt him harden inside her as her nipples complained about the unwanted attention they were receiving. Moving his hands up her sides and placing them on her shoulders, he kept her tightly against his as he tried to come as quickly as he could.

She was different, not like the others, he thought as he repeatedly pushed inside her. This one was perfect in every way; she was a petite, dark-complexioned, long-haired beauty. He thought all those things as he fucked her. *That is what the magazines said,* he thought as he continued thrusting. *That is what the commercials on TV said,* he thought as he pressed against her ass. Those things didn't matter to him; he was attracted to a woman's personality, he thought as he pulled all the way out and entered her asshole.

Mercedes breathed heavily through her nose, wincing in pain upon his initial thrusts. The man felt her tense up; he saw her lean forward and lower her head slightly. This he corrected by pulling back on her shoulders.

"Raise your head," he said softly.

She raised her head, and he released her shoulders, sliding his hands to her waist. As pleasurable as this experience had been at first, it was equally painful at the present. Mercedes was being forced to have sex, and it was more extreme than she was used to. He raised her up by her waist just enough to place his pants legs underneath her knees and placed her back down. She turned her head to the side and threw her hair over her shoulder, making as much eye contact as she could. She wasn't sure if she was acknowledging his kindness, pleading for help, or trying to say she liked it harder.

He nodded to her between thrusts and pulled her hair enough to put her view back forward, facing the window. He turned his head left and right as he continued to explore his new girlfriend. He pulled out and turned her on her back, sliding his body toward her breasts. He removed her tape and lowered himself to her. She finished him off as she mouthed over him very roughly. He paid attention to her intent as he finished inside her smiling mouth. Pulling away, he held her close, thanking her with a few small kisses before reapplying her tape and turning her back on her stomach. He sat on the small of her back and rubbed her shoulders firmly, telling her she was his new girlfriend and that he would be taking her home soon.

Marvin kept his head low and looked around the vehicle as he pulled his pants back up. Someone outside the minivan hit the side of the vehicle two times.

"Hurry up, it's done. We have to go. Leave the bitch," he heard Ralph say.

"All right, one sec," Marvin said, leaning forward to her ears.

"I'm undoing your hands and feet. Wait ten minutes before you open the door. I'm sorry, Mercedes. I'll catch you later," he said with a serious face.

Mercedes counted herself lucky that his partner didn't take a crack at her. He was an angry man, a dirty cop. Marv had been documenting events for over six months now, reporting directly to Internal Affairs. She had never met him before, and Marv only came to her apartment when Ralph was with his family. Two separate lives, he called it; home and work, and he did his upmost to never let them meet.

He would definitely have to make it up to her—this was over the top, she thought, even for him.

"Gonna pay big time," she said as she removed her tape and checked her face out in the mirror.

Closing her compact, she slid into the front seat and opened the passenger side door. A single cannon shot was heard close to the front of the van. It was very loud, it was very close, and it was fired in her direction, she was sure of it. She looked forward and saw Ralph in the distance with his gun drawn. He sidestepped something on the ground and disappeared behind another row of vehicles.

Mercedes looked forward, making sure that it was safe to exit the van. She froze when Ralph stepped back out and pointed to her.

"Don't run or scream. Get out and come to me or I'll kill you," she heard in her head, but he had only mouthed the words to her general direction.

She opened the door all the way and got out, walking slowly in his direction. He leveled the pistol at her and took a step forward, placing it firmly against her stomach. Tears filled her eyes as she looked down at Marv.

"Get down on your knees," he told her.

"Fuck, Ralph! Here? Seriously? Just come over tonight, I'm exhausted," she told him.

Ralph didn't know who was working over whom, but he always loved the outcome.

Just make it quick. I've plans tonight," she told him.

How this happened, she'll never understand. She actually started to fall in love with Marv, but always Ralph was present. He was the one who introduced her to Marv in the first place; it was only done to keep tabs on Marv, Ralph told her. Shortly afterward, she fell in love with Marv and she found it very difficult to manage both men. Remembering their schedules, keeping dates, finding interests in their individual lives, all these were different for each man. She held all these facts and details in what she called her mental rolodex.

Mercedes continued to cry tears on Ralph's cock as she worked hard to make him come. Ralph kept eyes on Marvin the whole time. He could not relax; he could not think of anything else. It was her job to relax him; she always did that for him, no matter how bad of a day he was having. He took a handful of hair and slowed her down ever so slightly. It was more for the feeling of control than for the need to slow her down. He began coming and then he motioned for her to speed up.

"Yeah, faster, I'm coming. Fuck, that's awesome, Mercedes," he said to her.

She didn't like him mentioning her by name, especially now after he had killed her lover. She finished him and kept going placing her warm hands on his thighs. He liked it that way; he liked stopping her, controlling her. A few more minutes went by before he moved her off his penis.

"Later tonight I'll introduce you to another friend. What time's good for you?" he asked.

"Can we do it tomorrow, hon? I'm seriously wiped," she asked.

"Sure, that works for me," he replied, lowering a hand to help her up.

Mercedes stretched her hands out to her sides and rose up to kiss him on the lips. He held on to her and kissed and groped his informant.

"Tomorrow then?" he said as he pulled his pants up.

"Tomorrow," Mercedes said, smiling.

Ralph said good-bye again as he took a step forward, turned, and shot Mercedes dead center in her back. Marvin's cannon fired loud and true, dropping her like she was not even there. Ralph took hold of her hair, dragging her closer to Marvin, and tossed his weapon between them. He had Marvin follow him here on a lead to meet some drug dealers. In reality, he had hired those guys to kill Marvin. Marvin and Ralph dispatched them easily enough, and when they checked them out, he told Marvin to go back and call it in. He was planning on killing Marvin tonight if his hired thugs hadn't done the job. When he went looking for him, he saw him fucking his girl. Ralph saw red and knew then and there that he had to kill them both tonight. Ralph called in the officer down and waited for backup to arrive.

In the bar

Lucy finally found a small table with two chairs and sat down to enjoy her drink. It was a very nicely mixed long island iced tea. Another sip through her neon straw, and her opinion had not changed. She sipped away and people-watched, waiting for Mercedes to arrive. Everywhere she looked, people were drinking and dancing. Some were paired together, and some were in groups of three of four.

Many times she returned smiles to dancing women, but she always pictured Mercedes's face behind that smile. It didn't matter much now; when her straw started making noises, she looked down and noticed that her drink was gone. It was time to switch to Mercedes's drink now.

"Too bad, hon. If you snooze, you lose," she told a woman who had just walked past her as she placed her straw into the other glass and sucked on them both.

She sipped slowly on the second of what she hoped would be many teas. When she had finished her drink, Charity walked over and asked her if she was ready.

"Come on, let's go," Charity said seductively.

"I'm waiting for a friend," Lucy told her.

"Oh, don't worry about Mercedes, she's already there," Charity said.

"Well then, what are we waiting for?" Lucy said, laughing as she stood up and found herself a bit wobbly.

It was as if both of her legs had filled up with her long island iced teas. Charity helped her to the velvet ropes and laughed as she called her a lightweight.

"Party animal, right?" Charity said to her.

Lucy found herself being led to a small corner table with a reserved card on it. The bass down here was sick; it made her breasts move against her chest when she wasn't even moving. It gave her a second heartbeat, and at times it even seemed to interfere with her breathing. It was a little cool down here, necessary to keep all of the dancing people comfortable, she thought.

"Sit here. I'll get some drinks and look for your friend. She's already been approved to join this private party," Charity told her.

Lucy scanned the crowd for Mercedes, but she wasn't found. Smiling, skinny, sexy bodies bounced to the beat that the DJ provided. It was time for a break, so the DJs changed. Now it was DJ Mahbel; Lucy had heard of her before. Mahbel had come to this area straight from Vegas on the premise of expanding her career. Others would say that she was just offered more money; either way, she was happy. Her music was seamless; the beats never ended—it was a win for everybody. Every now and then, someone would stand out; an attractive Latino, a dark-skinned brunette, a pale redhead, even a very light-skinned African American, but for the most part, five-foot-six, light-complexioned blonde was the norm.

Looking back to the left, she was startled as Charity was standing there holding their two drinks, smiling as always. She could not have been any closer to Lucy, and as she smiled, Charity moved but an inch forward to plant a sloppy kiss across her lips. Another smile from Charity, and Lucy found herself returning it twofold. A blue neon straw sticking out from her drink approached and stopped inches from her mouth.

"Thanks," Lucy said as she turned to scan the crowd yet again.

"First one to finish their drink makes the other drink theirs next, *go!*" she heard her say.

This didn't make much sense to Lucy, as she was already drinking her teas at an alarming rate, but what the hell.

"No fair, you have already started," Lucy said as she turned around to face Charity, but she was no longer present.

"Finally, bitch! Where the hell have you been?" Lucy asked her.

"Don't ask. That parking lot will kill you!" Mercedes replied between sips.

"Hurry up, you're losing!" Mercedes said again to Lucy, who had so much tea inside her mouth that she could not talk.

"Catch up, bitch," Lucy managed between breaths.

As the two women finished their drinks, Lucy was reminded about how much fun she was. She was glad that she found her tonight instead of her running off like she usually did. Smiling back at her, Lucy raised her empty glass and then slammed it down on the table.

"Suck it, bitch!" Lucy shouted above the music.

Mercedes finished hers, and then another kiss came at Lucy. She felt her bottom lip sucked on, and Mercedes even bit it once before letting it go; Lucy was glad she found her. The music changed to another song, switching to a slightly faster beat, which was only noticeable by breasts, which bounced a little higher.

"Keys, I want your keys," Lucy said to Mercedes, sticking her ass out to her.

"Oh, *it's like that?*" Mercedes asked her.

"Yes, *and that's the way it is,*" Lucy said, smiling back.

It was good times all over again, Lucy thought. Mercedes slapped a twenty on the small table and told her to get four more.

"After that, we dance!" Mercedes said, waving an empty glass.

Lucy danced her way back over to the bar, paying more attention to the setup this time, a triangle-shaped bar with a staircase in the center. It was a central location where all could obtain their ill. On one side of the triangle men were lined up from arm to arm dressed in various types of clothing. They ranged from sleeveless T-shirts to white long-sleeve dress shirts, with and without ties. Another end had men and women, either in pairs or solo, but definitely straight couples over there. On her side women were barely dressed at all, and they too ranged from high school to graduate school attire. Lucy laughed as the breasts on her side were much more beautiful than the others.

Lucy approached the only empty spot on her side of the bar and danced her way into the slot. To her left, a few women talked loudly about getting a room in town between kissing each other. On her right, a short blonde responded to the DJ's request to "back that ass up" and ground it over Lucy's thigh. Turning around to see whom she had assaulted, the lady smiled at her and turned back around to get her drink. Lucy cracked up and laughed as she waited for her turn to get drinks. She placed her hands on the woman's hips and picked her up to turn her around. She called the woman closer to her, and as she approached to hear what Lucy had to say, Lucy stuck her tongue down her throat. The blonde's hands held on to Lucy's waist as they continued to suck face. Pulling away, Lucy licked the woman's cheek from right above her lip to just beneath her eye and asked her for her car keys.

"Later on, meet me in the parking lot. I'll be the hot bitch standing next to your car," Lucy told her.

The blonde smiled back with a drunken expression and walked out to the dance floor.

"Later then, I wanna dance!" she told Lucy over her shoulder.

Lucy tracked down the bartender and ordered four more teas.

"Two sets of keys in one night, I'm so getting laid tonight!" Lucy yelled out.

"I would hope so, hon," the bartender said to Lucy.

"Four teas *coming* right up," she continued, with the emphasis on "coming."

Lucy smiled back and handed her the twenty. She shook her head at Lucy and touched a tea to the bracelets on her wrist.

"Double links means your money's no good here. Enjoy your complimentary drinks. Have a good time," she told Lucy.

Lucy smiled at her, grabbed her teas, and turned to the left as she juggled them back to her table.

"Later, precious," the bartender said.

Lucy turned her head to the right and thanked her before going back to her table. The blonde from earlier had come back to talk to her, and to get her attention, she cupped Lucy's breasts and leaned into her ear. Taking it in her mouth, she sucked on it and bit it before letting it go.

"I just love preoccupied women," she said as her hand slid inside Lucy's pants.

Lucy stood motionless as two fingers entered her panties and darted around like crazy. Her lips parted, and the blonde moved to kiss her. A few passionate kisses later, the fingers pushed up deep inside and then she removed her hand.

"It's Louisa," she told Lucy.

"Yes. Louisa. Well, thanks for that. I have your keys. I'll find you later, hon," Lucy said.

"I'll run into you tonight," Louisa said to her strangely.

Lucy smiled and walked off to her table, swinging her ass like a pendulum from left to right as she went. *Stay focused,* Lucy told herself. *Mercedes is the prize.* Once again, the DJ yelled out for women to "back that ass up"; Lucy obeyed and turned around and continued dancing to her table, ass first. Bumping into her table, Lucy turned around to begin speaking to Mercedes, and she was nowhere to be seen.

Lucy sat their drinks down and looked around for her. She looked back at the bar; she scanned the nearby tables and she then checked the dance floor, but still no Mercedes. Looking again to her left, she saw her dancing with an average blonde. *How sad,* she thought as she started walking to them with two drinks.

"Your friend is over there dancing. She dances with more women than I do, I'm sorry," a nearby woman told Lucy.

Charity raised her glass to Lucy, and the women drank together. Lucy stopped walking and stood beside this woman, continuing to watch Mercedes dance.

"Do you think I'm attractive?" Lucy asked the blonde.

"Yes," the average blonde replied, finishing her drink.

"Earlier today when I arrived, I received keys from another woman who also thought me attractive. Let's take her car and go get a room in town?" Lucy proposed.

Charity finished her drink, placed it on the table, and handed Lucy her second one.

"Bottoms up now and then bottoms up later," Charity said as she finished the second tea.

Lucy placed her empty glass on the table beside the three others and walked out of the club with car keys to an unknown car in her left and a gorgeous blonde in her right, smiling ear to ear. She threw the bartender a smile and mouthed "good-bye." The bartender mouthed "good job," as she saw Lucy disappear beyond the stairs.

"I'll catch you later," the bartender said under her breath.

Stepping outside, they noticed the lights and commotion of several cop cars in the back of the parking lot. Lucy used the key fob, and lights flashed to their left about three rows back. The couple headed that way, and when they were closer, Lucy hit it again. The lights of a bright-colored canary yellow Ford Mustang flashed, showing them the way.

"That's what I'm talking about," Charity said.

"Shall we?" Lucy said as she unlocked the doors.

The two women got inside, closed the doors, and buckled up before telling the Mustang to come to life. The car's horses screamed "me first, me first" as Lucy revved the engine.

"Too bad it's an automatic," Lucy said as she drove off.

The windows were down, and summer insects buzzed around, looking for their mates. The night was dark and devoid of a moon. Charity closed her eyes and enjoyed the peace and quiet of the night; it was calming. The alcohol helped with that, and to add to her enjoyment was a beautiful woman beside her. Lucy told her to open her eyes.

"Don't fall asleep on me, silly," Lucy said.

"I'm much too excited to sleep, I promise you," Charity said.

A few minutes more of winding roads brought up a large expressway sign.

"Almost there, hon," Lucy said as she saw her exit come and go.

Lucy was confused; she didn't know why she kept driving.

"Here looks good. Pull over here," Charity said.

She pulled over as instructed and looked over at Charity.

"Nice. Now turn the engine off," she heard Charity say, but she didn't see her lips move.

"Put your seat back, recline it, and please close your eyes," Charity said.

Lucy felt nauseous, confused; she closed her eyes and felt Charity's warm body slide over hers. "I enjoy your pain, precious. I smell your addiction, I drink you in," Charity told her.

Lucy tried to escape, subtly struggling against her, but she only managed to fall deeper into the chair.

"For months I've followed you, altering your path, influencing your friends. I dispatch when I desire to. To manipulate others is what I strive for. Alas, you bore me. I tire of your lack of esteem. I detest your feelings for Mercedes. She's above you, you know." Charity paused as she removed Lucy's shirt.

"What lovely breasts you have there, Lucy. I plan to know them well over the next several days," Charity said as she continued palming them.

Lucy noticed her heart rate increasing; she felt warm and flushed. The hairs on her arms stood up; her nipples were erect. Charity paused again for full effect and continued caressing.

"Pleasure, I'll provide it. Pain, I'll deliver it. Death, well, I'll provide that too. You will have to choose, so think hard. What do you want tonight, Lucy?" Charity asked.

There was no response from Lucy, but Charity already knew what Lucy's response was.

"Even now I read your thoughts. I'll oblige you. Undo my blouse, take my breasts and nipples into your mouth, enjoy my body," Charity said to her.

"Your inability to flee, to run away, that's me. It's not just the weight of my naked body upon yours. It's not that you find me attractive. *Open your eyes* and kiss my cheek," Charity commanded.

Lucy leaned her head forward, placed her lips on Charity's cheeks, and closed her eyes, kissing Charity softly.

"More to the point is that I have thrown down all of my will against you. You are beaten, Lucy, and I haven't laid a finger against you," Charity boasted.

"The tickle in the back of your throat, the itch inside your shoulder or your leg that you cannot scratch, the orgasm that occurs too early or again after you have already had one—that is us. We allow it to happen, we make it so. We've thrust ourselves into your being because it is our duty, because we can," Charity said boldly.

Lucy kept her eyes closed, listening as best she could. She was frightened, truly frightened. It would have been different had she not believed in good and evil, in spirits, but she did. Lucy thought herself a nonpracticing Christian; she never allocated time for organized religion, but it didn't mean that she didn't believe.

"Pleasure yourself, precious. Use your left hand and be quick about it. You've not much time left, I'm afraid," Charity demanded.

Lucy used two fingers to make small circles over her clitoris. This she did faster, as she was commanded to.

"Do you feel that, hon? I'm massaging your breasts, but I'm not physically touching you. Open your eyes. Open your eyes!" Charity yelled.

Lucy felt her breasts pushed flat against her body, moved left and right, with what she thought were thumbs pressing her nipples inward.

"Faster, fuck yourself. Use 'em to fuck yourself. Let me hear you. Moan for me, Lucy," Charity said.

Lucy began thrusting her fingers inside her repeatedly now, following her orders as expected, although she actually thought that the circles felt better.

"Who cares? It's not about you," Charity said, scolding her.

Lucy wondered if she would read her thoughts too. Lucy opened her eyes as the fondling of her breasts became painful.

"Have your attention now, don't I?" Charity asked.

Lucy felt it hard to breathe, as if her lungs were only able to expand half as much as they normally could.

"Yes. I'm massaging your lungs now, well, holding them, actually. I'm afraid they can't open as much as they need to. You're dying. Soon your body won't have enough oxygen to supply what your body needs and you'll hurt all over. Keep your fingers moving, hon, faster. Go back to circles now. Faster, please, Lucy," Charity demanded.

Lucy found herself close to orgasm, and her breathing quickened. She breathed harder, faster, but still she didn't receive enough oxygen.

"Look at me. Look into my eyes. That tingling in your thighs is due to me. Let's play a game, precious. Do you feel me, hon? I'm sliding in slowly. You should feel your pussy lips slowly parting, widening. We'll call this one just the tip," Charity said, laughing.

Lucy felt her breasts mashed between invisible hands; her nipples were being squeezed now too. It was forceful and meant for the spirit's pleasure, not hers. Charity placed her hands on Lucy's face and gently squeezed.

"You should feel me inside of you now. I'm only in a few inches but probably more of a man that you've had in a long time," Charity said softly.

Lucy felt what she thought was a penis entering her and leaving, entering and leaving, while she made circles over her clitoris.

"Faster, precious. We're close now," Charity directed as she continued to hold on to Lucy's face.

She slid her arm to her neck and squeezed both sides. Lucy felt panic overtaking her now. She tried to stop pleasuring herself, but her hand would not listen. Her breasts hurt more now, and her nipples were raw. She still found it hard to breathe, and now she was being fucked by an evil spirit.

"There. Nice. Do you feel it?" she heard Charity say in her head.

"Do you feel it? I'm traveling up your ass now. Struggle for me, fight me, move your body away from me. Move it!" Charity yelled.

Every time Lucy rose, she was pushed back down onto the car seat. The invisible cock traveled deeper into her anus when seated and less when she tried to escape. *Simple physics,* she thought as she continued to struggle.

"There. Fuck me. Continue what you are doing, precious. Moving upward removes me, giving you what you want, and when I push you back down, I get what I want," she said to Lucy.

"That tingling you feel is my handiwork. I know you are coming. Double penetrations are very erotic, I always loved them myself," Charity told her.

Lucy saw the expression of hate on Charity's face, her curled, thin lips, a dimple that was only visible when she displayed it. Charity was killing her; Lucy didn't want to die this way. She thought about Mercedes as she came on the seat. The spirit switched to pleasure now, and Lucy felt her hands slide downward from her neck to her breasts. No longer were they assaulted by invisible hands; they were being massaged by Charity's physical ones. Lucy saw her own face in the rearview mirror now smiling as Charity rubbed her hands gently over her breasts. Lucy's fucking subsided, the penis in her ass was removed, and the one in her vagina slid in passionately, not roughly, like before. Lucy breathed in full breaths now as she continued to moan through her orgasm.

"Still coming, seriously?" Charity asked as she slid her hands back up to her face.

"What was it the boys called you when you were younger, hon—Train?" Charity said with hate.

Lucy looked up at Charity, making eye contact. She didn't have a memory of that anymore, not until now. She had blocked out those painful memories, she thought as she continued to moan. Charity continued squeezing Lucy's neck on both sides again. Lucy breathed faster now, too fast. She moaned as she continued to rub small circles; her hand was tired. Lucy kept moving her fingers faster, harder, against her clitoris; and all of a sudden, there it was.

"Woo woo wooooo," Lucy moaned as her orgasm continued.

"Yes, like a train. Come for me, baby, come for me," Charity said as the cock in Lucy's ass again made its presence known.

Uncontrollably, Lucy's moans became louder; her breathing grew shallow.

"Woo WOO WOOOOOO" escaped her lips again, even though she fought against it.

Her asshole tightened, her vagina latched on to her invisible man, and her nails dug into the seat cushions as she climaxed ferociously a second time. Lucy's breasts rose higher and higher as her train noise became louder.

"Now is when the bad things happened, wasn't it, precious? Three more boys came out of a nearby closet, totally naked. One slid underneath you, pressing his pathetic pecker between your spread ass cheeks. Another prepared himself for his turn, as little Timmy slid off of you. The third masturbated over your face, all the while with you continuing to make train noises," Charity said as if scolding her.

Lucy's eyes widened as the cocks in her vagina and pussy became larger. They penetrated her further now, forcing their will against all parts of her body's cavities. Her breasts again felt pain as the spirit pinched her nipples and stretched them upward before letting them go. Charity's hands were squeezing her neck again, having just left her breasts, who rose higher still as more air entered Lucy's lungs. And just as she felt herself close to orgasm, yet again, it all stopped. Her hand was allowed to relax, and reflexively, she reached for the steering wheel. Her eyes welled up with tears, and they began finding paths down around her thin cheekbones. Lucy blinked her eyes, and a flood of tears ran down her cheeks. Opening her teary eyes, she looked straight ahead through the windshield.

Lucy laughed. Mercedes would say "forward'"; she always replaced the word *straight* with *forward*, saying that "gay people can't go straight, they go forward." Lucy looked down and saw herself dressed, sitting in her seat upright, with her seat belt on. Looking over to Charity, she saw her smiling softly back.

"Is everything all right? You said you had to pull over, that there was something in your eye," Charity asked her.

Lucy breathed a sigh of relief as she smiled back.

"I'm fine, wow," Lucy said as she reached for the gear shift to place the canary yellow Mustang into drive.

"You looked freaked out. We'll get something to drink when we get to our room. Hurry up and get us there," Charity said, laughing.

"No problem, let's do this," Lucy said confidently as she raced the Mustang's engine before squealing tires.

Charity put the radio on and picked a good station. Dancing in her seat, they sang out loud together. Within minutes, they saw the hotel and casino come into view. Its size was immense, and it was bright enough to light up the sky to be seen for miles were it not for the surrounding hills and forest. They would have seen it a lot sooner had it not been hidden in those hills, Lucy thought as she looked over at Charity.

"Wow," Charity said with surprise in her voice.

"Yup, we're stopping here," Lucy said as the Mustang found an empty parking spot close to the front entrance.

Lucy shut off the engine, removed the keys, and smiled at Charity.

"Relax, put your chair back. Place your arms by your sides, please," Charity said as she began undressing.

Lucy obeyed and peed herself as the lady slid on top of her.

"Take your clothes off, precious, shirt first, please. Nice. Now rise up so we can get those wet pants off of you," Charity said as she started to remove Lucy's clothing.

Lucy began crying as the woman kissed her breasts and fingered her pussy.

"I'm sorry, hon, I couldn't wait. You look so beautiful. I'm sure you are remembering our previous conversation, our lovemaking—Train, are you not?" Charity asked.

"Well, no need. I'll cover everything again for you. Does that feel good, hon?" she asked out of the corner of her mouth while sucking on her nipple.

Lucy continued to cry as Charity licked her cheeks, her neck, and her breasts.

"I love your body. I'm thinking I like it more than this one actually. Kiss me hard, Lucy. Kiss me hard," Charity said.

Lucy kissed her mouth firmly as a penis entered her pussy.

"Yes. Enjoy me, Train," Charity said with a smile as another cock slowly slid between her ass cheeks.

Charity watched as a look of horror swept over Lucy's face. A third cock entered her mouth as Charity smiled with as much eye contact as Lucy would allow. It pushed Lucy's head back against the seat's headrest several times as it made love to her mouth. Her head hurt from the force that slammed against her over and over as it entered her mouth. Lucy felt it touch the back of her throat, and at times it held her there as it roamed against the inside of her cheeks. Lucy imagined balls hitting her in the face, landing on her chin, slapping her in the throat.

"Suck me," Charity said.

Lucy was going mad, she had to be insane; there was no other explanation for it.

"Suck hard. Suck harder, Train, suck," Charity said before she inserted a hand into her chest.

Lucy felt pain going up her left arm, and her face was tingly and almost numb. Her chest hurt badly; it wasn't her breasts, it was her chest. Charity massaged Lucy's heart as she continued to pound away in every opening that Lucy had. She felt her life leaving her as thrust after thrust assaulted her vagina, her anus, and her mouth. Her neck ached from it; it was as if she was slapped over and over by a man's body as he threw himself into her.

She found it difficult to control her breathing; each time she tried to take a breath, she would be slammed backward against the seat, against the headrest. This along with how her chest felt was reason enough to give up, to quit; Lucy wanted to die.

She began to follow instructions as best she could and started giving her invisible man head. It was damn near impossible to do, and for the most part, all she was able to do was to pucker or pout her lips to offer some resistance. Lucy could not move her head up and around, or along, well, the invisible penis that was beating up the inside of her mouth. Lucy swore that a few times it exited all the way and slapped her around her face before entering her again.

"Keep those eyes open, Train. A few more minutes and it won't matter, hon," Charity said as she inserted several fingers inside herself.

Lucy felt her anus muscles tighten as her man grew larger. The one in her pussy followed suit, and what might have been misconstrued as pleasure quickly turned into pain.

"Slut. Whore. You're a whore, Train," Charity said as she continued fingering herself.

The cock exited Lucy's mouth, which allowed her to beg for mercy. She found it difficult to speak at first; her words were quick and broken. Lucy didn't know if the penis would charge back inside or if she would be punished if she spoke them.

"Please stop. I don't want to die," Lucy said between loud coughs.

"There, there, Train. All you have to do for that is to orgasm before I do," Charity said, smiling and making her fuck face.

"Woo woo. Hurry up, Train, I'm close" came out softly from Charity as she made a fuck face, mocking Lucy.

Lucy moved against the seat as best she could. When she tried to move forward, she was pushed back down deep inside the seat. This aided in her fucking, and as painful as it was, she tried to increase her experience by trying different angles.

"I want to hear you, if you know what I mean. Telling me that you are coming will not cut it," Charity said as she intensified her efforts.

Lucy lowered her head against Charity's breasts as Charity pressed against her. She bounced against Lucy's thighs a few times before Lucy slid her knees under her. It was Lucy's turn to bounce, and as she struggled to leave the seat, the penis that fucked her in the ass didn't reach inside as far as it would have had she been sitting on the cushion. Lucy had a reason to bounce; it was less painful when the cock rammed into her ass.

"Me first, me first," Lucy said playfully.

The penis in Lucy's ass became more tolerable, and she began experiencing pleasure once again. Charity took hold of Lucy's breast and closed her hand around it, causing Lucy a fair amount of pain. That would take the edge off of her orgasm, she thought as she tugged on it harder. Lucy leaned up and kissed Charity firmly, trying to forget about the pain in her chest and her breast. Charity let go and placed her hand on Lucy's waist as she explored Lucy's mouth with her tongue. Charity pulled away and kissed her neck as the penis again slammed into Lucy's mouth.

Charity sat back against the steering wheel and watched as Lucy was slammed backward into the seat headfirst, multiple times. One might think she was having a seizure with as much force and animation that was being exhibited. It was almost unfair, Lucy thought. She found herself kissing Charity. She wasn't told to; she just did it. Her hands palmed Charity's breasts; she called out her name a few times and even pulled her hair. Charity felt wonderful; she tingled all over.

"Looks like you're losing, hon. Try harder. You know what to do, Train," Charity said, smiling as Lucy half interrupted her again with her tongue. Hell, she was French kissing her now, Lucy thought. Lucy found herself making love to Charity, and Charity just took it all in. Lucy felt nothing save the desire to make love to her new friend. She wasn't being kissed, groped, fucked, or raped.

"Fuck me, make love to me," Lucy said between kissing Charity harder.

She sucked her tongue and French kissed her a few more times before she was allowed to speak again.

"I want you inside me. Fuck me," Lucy managed to get out before her face was again slammed against the headrest.

Lucy sucked in a nipple, and then her hands began to feel for Charity's pussy.

"What did you say?" Charity asked, pushing Lucy's mouth from one breast to the other.

Lucy was almost unable to reply, unable to breathe as Charity's breast seemed to close over her nose and mouth.

"I want you inside of me," Lucy said between breaths.

"I'm coming, precious, but why not?" Charity said.

Cocks again became larger, longer, and no amount of bouncing or twisting would take away from their exploration. They were harder now too. It was pretty painful, and Lucy once again found herself wanting to be dead. Over and over they rammed their messages home, balls deep.

"You will not live, you will not exist, and you will not be without me," she heard in her head.

Lucy struggled further against this, but she could not make progress in any direction. She was being slammed from front to back in her pussy, from bottom to top in her anus, and from front to back inside her mouth. Lucy's mind raced; it filled with pain, with anger. She struggled harder against this; she looked for inner courage, inner strength, and when she thought she had enough, she pushed upward toward the steering wheel. Charity felt her raise up and slammed Lucy's head into the window. The glass did not break, but Lucy saw stars. She threw her hands in the air and felt for Charity's neck, twisting it sharply to the left. Charity's lifeless body fell backward against the passenger seat, and her head slid forward. Blood slowly dripped from her nose. Charity no longer talked or moved; she was dead.

Lucy wanted out; she panicked over what had just happened. She was crying so badly that she shook the entire car. Her breathing was erratic, sharp, and many short breaths failed to do what a normal one could. Lucy opened the door and stepped outside, falling flat on her face. She had trouble walking, she was weak, and she was fatigued. Lucy smelled of sex, of urine, and lying on the ground totally naked for longer than she liked, she struggled to sit up.

Lucy rested her back against the back of the Mustang and closed the door. In the side mirror, she saw her face; her eyes were black raccoon circles, the likes of which any Goth queen would be envious of. They were bloodshot red and irritated, with small streaks of injured capillaries toward the lower center of both eyes. Her hair was wet, sweaty, and disheveled, but her main takeaway was that she was naked, and she looked and felt like shit.

Anger controlled her, driving her to move forward, to endure; it was displayed on her face like a badge of courage. Lucy stood up and started to walk to the hotel for help. Her limp was the second thing that people noticed as she walked closer to the door. Some people thought she had been in a car wreck, but to her, it was as if she had been fucked really well. She did not speak to those she passed; she concentrated on taking short, deliberate steps toward the entrance.

As she approached the automatic door at the entrance to the casino, she noticed two valets. They stood there at attention, smiling at her with their jaws dropped and their eyes wide open. Lucy changed her course to the closest one and continued walking. When she was close enough to reach out and touch him, she asked for his coat.

"I'm sorry. I appear to have been almost killed and I need your coat. Can I borrow that, please?" Lucy asked painfully as she pointed to his chest.

The taller valet continued examining her breasts as he removed his jacket and handed it to her.

"Thank you," Lucy said, walking inside the main lobby wearing only her bruises and her new jacket.

Chapter Nineteen

Susan's Box

Lucy walked through slowly and still limped pretty badly. People turned to look at her when they walked past her, but they turned their head less now that she was wearing the jacket. A couple of guys stared at her as they walked past, and a woman wearing not much more than her smiled at her when she walked by. Making her way further inside, Lucy was confused; she was tired and probably in shock. A large neon sign to the left said "Antique Show" and flashed an arrow that led down a hallway to her left. *Why not?* she thought as she headed for the door at the end of the hallway.

She was thirsty, she was hungry, and these urges were followed closely by the need for sleep. Lucy reviewed tonight's events over and over in her mind. She was fatigued, tired, and at the same time excited; she smiled as she saw a few women giving their partners shit for checking her out. Lucy looked around for a restaurant or any place to get a meal. The large conference room held about ten large tables where experts in their fields sat to examine treasures that people brought in, organized by category.

The lines to see them stretched to the other end of the building, for some experts. Lucy watched some people leave from their meeting pleased, but most were unhappy; she guessed that this was due to the estimated value of their antique. Some old things were more valuable than others, she laughed as she continued walking around. A few tables sparked her interest as she moved past people to check them out.

There she was by the table, all queued up, waiting to be seen by all. Oh, and she was seen, Lucy thought. Dark on the top, a golden center, and a lovely red bottom; she was very slender, not too old, but aged, experienced. She was being held close by another. Lucy thought of ways to get closer, to place herself into the situation, or a conversation even. Lucy had to go in for a closer look. She walked past the table and took one step forward when she turned and addressed her.

"May I?" Lucy asked.

"Sure," said the lady who was holding the jewelry box steady against her chest.

Lucy opened the drawers one at a time, very carefully examining the craftsmanship.

"It's lovely. Good luck," Lucy told her.

"Thank you," replied the woman.

She probably could get enough money to buy it outright, but if the woman chooses to put it up for auction, Lucy might be out of luck. She had to have it! Lucy stared at the object and thought hard about her next course of action. She turned her head to the left and blinked her eyes. She had an idea. Lucy turned to face the woman again and she was pushed aside, bumped if you will, by another woman who was also interested in the box.

"Oh, I'm sorry, didn't see you standing there," she said to Lucy.

Lucy smiled and walked away. She stopped at a few tables down and turned back to watch. There was the man beside the woman who had bumped her. They were a couple, and probably married. Lucy thought she would make the old lady an offer after she had her box examined, but she soon lost all hope of that when the young blonde gave the old woman what appeared to be a check. Lucy watched her box change hands, and she grew very angry. She followed the couple for several minutes from a distance, being careful not to be seen. She watched them sit at a nearby table and check out their newest member of their family. Lucy walked forward to the table and pulled up a chair. She sat down between them, slightly to the left of the man. She let her valet's jacket slightly open and addressed the couple on their box.

"It's a very nice piece," Lucy said to the woman.

"Lucy, my name's Lucy," she said to them.

"Yes, thank you. I'm trying to decorate my living room," she replied.

The man smiled at her briefly as he looked into her open coat. He was a bit sad when he noticed that all the good parts were covered up. Lucy turned slowly to her left so she could check out the doors on the box, exposing the right side of her left breast. She smiled further as she heard the man say, "All right!"

"Can you show me the insides, please?" Lucy asked as her right hand slid over the man's knees.

He parted his legs as she slid her fingers down and over his groin. Several firm downward motions caught him off guard, and when she latched on and held him tightly, he asked her if she liked the drawers.

"Oh, very much so, can I make you an offer?" Lucy asked.

The lady looked up at her husband, but his eye contact didn't really matter to her.

"I'm sorry, it's not for sale," she told Lucy.

Lucy's grip tightened on the man and she began stroking him. He really could not believe this was happening.

"OK then. I'll catch you later then," she said as she smiled to the man and removed her hand.

As Lucy stood up, turned, and walked away, he couldn't help to notice that she wore no underpants.

"Honey, we didn't even listen to her offer," he said.

She looked at him but didn't speak.

"If we make double or triple our money back, we can purchase more. I'll be right back," he said as he took off after the woman.

She called the man's name one time and watched as he caught up to the lady very quickly. Matthew took hold of her arm and asked her to wait.

"Wait. What do you offer?" he asked as he waited for the woman to turn around.

His eyes focused only on a two-inch gap of flesh visible between the edges of her jacket. It ran the entire length and promised excitement.

Lucy smiled at him and said, "Forty dollars and a fuck," placing a hand on her hip; she exposed a nipple to him and the fact that she was a natural blonde.

Matthew moved his hair to the side with his hand and turned to his wife, being careful to hide the woman's body from her view. He held up ten fingers and waited for a response. Susan shook her head no.

Turning back to the woman, he said, "Well, you'll have to fuck us both, and we'll need two hundred, hon."

He delivered that message with a very large smile and awaited her decision.

"Deal. Give me your room key. You can use hers," Lucy said.

Matthew turned to face Susan and walked away. Lucy stood still, defiant, and positive that her offer was acceptable. She smiled at Susan and blew her a kiss.

Matthew reached for Susan and told her, "She's game. Two hundred dollars and she'll do us both for the box."

"She wants my room key, are you sure?" he asked Susan.

"She's beautiful, why not?" Susan said as she walked over to the woman.

"Eight o'clock then?" Susan asked Lucy.

"Yes. Works for me, hon. I'll catch you later," Lucy replied.

Lucy wanted something new to wear tonight; she just didn't know exactly what. She walked over to a nearby corner and entered the casino's bar. The sign read Lucky's, and somehow she thought that wasn't true for some poor man. Sitting down at the bar, she ordered four beers and four shots of whiskey.

"I hear boilermakers are making a comeback," she told the waitress.

Mary smiled and told her she would be right back. Before Mary left, she grabbed her arm.

"Can you find me someone to pay for those? Be a dear and hurry up," Lucy told her as she watched her walk away.

Mary walked past a table of four guys and told them that a woman was looking for someone to get her drinks.

"A soon-to-be totally drunk blonde bitch wants you to buy her drinks, anyone interested?" Mary asked in passing and laughed as she walked away.

They all looked at each other and began arguing on which one should do it. A gentleman at a neighboring table heard and saw everything. He walked to Lucy and placed two twenties on the table.

"Have fun tonight, enjoy yourself. Those guys are trouble," he said, smiling as he walked away.

"I intend to, sir," Lucy said, smiling back.

Lucy looked to the four and then back to the man who was quickly leaving her. *Well, there's one lucky guy, I suppose,* Lucy thought, turning her head back to the four. *Focus, woman, geez.*

She could still smell the couple that had just left; the man smelled unique, strong, and virile, full of testosterone, but educated. The woman was less motivated, angry inside, and even bitchy or stuck up. That woman was not a nice person, not nice at all, Lucy thought; this was going to be fun. All Lucy cared about was obtaining that box. It was old, it had purpose; Lucy found the whole situation interesting. Why, it would be the most fun that she would have since she left the other bar . . .

Lucy motioned toward the staring young men to come over.

"Here you go. You can each have one. Do it now. Take them. Here's my room key. I'll be with another man and a woman, and we'll be having sex. I want you to come in and beat up the man really good, make him hurt, real bad. Then stay with him as you all take turns with his girlfriend and me," Lucy said in a quiet, serious tone.

"Seriously, lady?" the tallest one said.

"Yes, and when we're all done, you can take pictures for all of your friends. I guarantee you they won't believe you unless they see them." She smiled.

They looked at each other and turned their backs comically, talking among themselves as if she could not hear them.

"Now take your drinks and commit to my offer. By drinking them, you'll be bound to fulfill your end of the deal. Now hurry and tell me you'll be there," Lucy said to them.

"What time?" another asked.

"Eight thirty, on the dot, not a minute sooner," she told him.

"Remember, I want a shot at him first. He's wronged me and must be punished. You'll need to hold on to him for a few. When I'm done, he's all yours, and so is my girlfriend," Lucy told them with a firm voice.

The quiet one smiled at her and told her that there was nothing to worry about and asked for the key.

"You'll get your shot first, and then we'll fuck your friend before you do us—deal," he said, smiling, with an extended hand.

Mary looked at the guys and laughed as Stewart stuck his hand out and was given a room key from the older blonde. *That was way too funny,* she thought, Mary doubted that he knew how to use one. She watched on as they finished their drinks, and the blonde left the bar, wondering all the while about the four young men that stayed behind.

The four continued talking about the woman they had just met and about her offer.   "She didn't even tell us her name," Timmy said.

"No harm in it. There's four of us. We can take care of whatever goes down. We just have to have each other's back," said Joe.

"Her name's Free Ass for a Night, because when we're done with her, we are taking her back to the house to do her again!" Mark cheered.

"Mary! Another round of these, please," Scott said, pointing from above at the empty glasses.

Lucy walked to the lobby very slowly as she looked for a woman who was approximately her size. Several couples mingled through, coming and going, but nothing. The valet outside was looking inside the lobby through the window at the woman who was wearing his jacket, waving. Lucy waved at the man who was wearing a wrinkled white shirt and smiled as a newlywed couple passed in between them.

The valet smiled back, thinking that Lucy had smiled to him, but he was crushed as she was still smiling when she turned her head to the right. Lucy followed them at a distance, listening as best she could. Lucy's heightened senses took them in; she was a virgin, smelling as pure as an unopened night-blooming flower. And like that flower that opened this very evening to enjoy only a single night of existence, she would be gone by morning.

When she took in the man, she knew he was older and definitely wasn't pure of heart; he was, however, nice to her. She was absolutely beautiful; the man's mind was clouded with thoughts of sex, lust, and, wait, there it was, he planned to kill her. *Can this be?* Lucy thought. Maybe she had use for this man after all.

"And here's your room key, Mr. Jones," the lady at the front desk said to him.

He smiled at her and then to the woman by his side. They both walked to the elevator, hand in hand, totally oblivious to the woman who was following them throughout the main lobby.

"I can't wait. We are going to have so much fun on this trip," she told him.

Lucy listened to them as she continued to search their thoughts. She laughed as she saw all of the ways he wanted to make love to her. Her thoughts now were something different; they were harder to read, damn near impossible to gain access to—wait. The woman looked directly as her and put a finger to her lips, telling Lucy not to tell . . . "Find your own casino," Lucy mouthed to her. "I was here first," Lucy heard her say.

Fuuuuuuck, Lucy thought; all she wanted was a nice dress . . . Lucy smiled at her as the elevator doors began to close. Lucy leaned toward the two-inch gap that was rapidly closing and spoke to the couple.

"She knows of your plans, she knows everything. Now is your time. Strike now while there are no witnesses," Lucy said as the door closed shut.

Lucy hung around the elevator doors for a few seconds more, watching the elevator floor lights above the door light from left to right. She started counting to ten, and when she had reached three, she heard his screams of horror with great clarity; they could be heard four floors away. The screams lasted for a few seconds and then became silent. The elevator light stopped on floor five, and a few seconds later, it started descending.

Lucy had started walking around again, looking for a like-sized woman, when she heard the elevator doors open. A woman in a lovely white dress stepped out and slowly walked to the main entrance. She shot Lucy an "eat shit and die" look and immediately headed for the casino door. Lucy smiled at her, mouthing the words "I told you" as the woman left through the casino door.

She spotted another couple that had turned the corner and started heading for the elevator. Lucy continued following them, noticing the strong smell of jasmine. The elevator doors closed, and again Lucy watched where they stopped. She smelled jasmine. *It would be easy enough,* she thought. Waiting where she was, Lucy watched the light stop at four; the fourth floor it was then, she thought as she hit the stairs at breakneck-speed.

All she needed now was champagne. Passing back by the bar, she looked at the bartender and told her to prepare a cheese tray with two bottles of champagne for room 410. She waited until she started gathering the request before she took the elevator up. Looking around, Lucy quickly found the service elevator and waited nearby. A muffled ding could be heard, and then a man came through the doors, pushing a cart.

"You're all done here, John. Leave the cart, please. Move along," Lucy told him and stuffed a twenty into his pocket.

John left with a "yes, ma'am" and a smile. She left the cart where it was and followed the faint smell of jasmine through the hallway. It became stronger at door four fourteen. *Not too far off,* she thought, laughing. Lucy turned around and walked back to the cart and pushed it to the couple's room. A door opened, and a woman walked out wearing a black dress and ready to party. She smiled at Lucy and walked past her with a condescending glare; Lucy would deal with her later.

Lucy stopped the cart in front of their room and knocked three times. A few seconds later, the door opened, and she was greeted with a smile.

"Oh, sorry, you have the wrong room." The woman smiled at Lucy again and started to close the door.

"No, it's complimentary. We've selected your room at random, along with two others. Enjoy," Lucy said as she started to push the cart into their room.

Lucy guessed that the man was in the bathroom; she had just heard the toilet flush. She turned to face the lady, telling her to undress where she was and then to go inside the bedroom to await her man. The woman started stripping off her clothing and stepped out her dress before walking into the bedroom completely naked. "You can thank me later, phantom shitter," Lucy said under her breath.

Lucy heard another flush from the bathroom. *Nice,* she thought, *that would make the first one a courtesy.* She smiled as she bent over to pick up the woman's dress. Lucy turned her head to the bathroom and waited for it, and, voila, he had turned on the fan. The woman smiled at Lucy from the bedroom doorway, waiting impatiently for her partners.

"Get on the bed and wait there," Lucy told her.

The woman obliged and took her place on the right side of the king-size bed. Lucy placed the dress on a nearby table and waited for the bathroom door to open. The handle turned, and the man came out, turning off the fan.

Lucy raised her hands in the air, holding up a bottle of champagne in her right hand, allowing her jacket to open, and said, "Room service."

The man stared at her, smiled, and then asked where his wife was.

"In bed awaiting us—champagne then?" she asked, moving the bottle around in the air.

"What a joker, sure," he said, taking his trousers off.

"Shall we?" Lucy said as she grabbed a glass from the cart.

"Forget the glasses, bring the bottle, please," he said and turned for the bedroom.

Lucy gave suggestions to the woman and followed the man into the bedroom. He walked in to his wife on the bed, totally naked and masturbating like there's no tomorrow. Lucy told the man that she's going to sit on the corner of the bed and watch him make love to her.

"When it's right, I'll join you," Lucy said to him.

The man crawled up and mounted his wife while she continued to help him. Lucy was watching them go at it like rabbits when she sent more suggestions her way. She told the woman that she had to pee really badly, and then she told him that he should go faster, hold her down, and give it to her real good.

Lucy told the woman that she should hold her breath as he made love to her so it would intensify her orgasm. The woman was nowhere close to coming, but she followed her instructions and held her breath. She did this for about thirty seconds until she was told to start breathing again. Her husband loved the noises his wife was making at present and redoubled his efforts.

Messing with this couple wasn't really doing anything for her; all she thought about was that antique jewelry box. Lucy told the woman that she needed to be on top and that she should ask nicely first and then apply herself.

"I want to be on top, Ralph," the woman said.

"Fine by me, roll over on your side," Ralph said.

The woman rolled over, and he crawled to the head of the bed and turned to lie on his back, allowing his wife to get on top. Lucy came over and gave them both some champagne straight from the bottle. She poured until they could not swallow fast enough, allowing some to escape down the sides of their faces. She told the woman to instruct her man to close his eyes so she could kiss him all over.

Ralph closed his eyes and relaxed as his beautiful wife made love to him. She kissed him on his cheeks, his nose, and his ear. She slid off his lips after another kiss and moved back to his ear. Taking it inside her mouth, she gently sucked on it; all this the woman did while raising and lowering herself onto his penis. She grew more passionate and vocal when she wasn't using her mouth to kiss him. When her mouth was occupied with an ear or a small nibble of his flesh, she hummed against him, licking where she could. Letting go of his ear, she moved her tongue down his neck and nibbled over his collarbone.

Lucy stood up and walked out of the bedroom, giving one more command to the woman. She turned to watch the woman grab the lamp on the nightstand and slam the base of it into the man's face three times. He was dazed and bleeding when the woman rose and slid herself over his face. She held him firmly in place as he continued to breathe what air he could get past the woman's body that pressed down upon him. Lucy saw the man release his load against the woman's back as she worked on suffocating him.

Walking out the door, Lucy mumbled, "Chaos and carnage, one. Newlywed couple, zero," as she closed the door behind her.

Lucy looked around the room; she noticed the flashing clock on the cable box displayed 12:00 and laughed. She walked over to the dining table and looked through their things, finding his wallet and cell phone—only 7:30 p.m.; she had an hour to waste. Lucy picked up the remaining bottle of champagne and walked out into the hallway, making her way to the stairs, passing a few older women who scoffed at her when they thought she could no longer hear them. She stopped on the landing and sat down to finish her champagne.

Matthew took his time as he made his way back to his room. He still had about half an hour. *Why not take the stairs?* he thought. He laughed about the thought of being $200 lighter, but he knew he could make it back up later. Damn those fours that he had double downed . . . The tables had not been good to him this evening. Matthew bounded up the stairs, taking them two at a time. He had just turned the corner passing a large number four on the wall when he ran past Lucy.

"Greetings!" she said, waving the champagne bottle in his direction.

"It's a little early, but you can come on up if you like," Matthew said as he caught his breath.

Lucy smiled and offered him a hand, and he pulled her up from the ground. They walked hand in hand until they reached his room.

"Nice dress," he said, staring at her ass.

"Cute, you do know that I can see you staring at my ass, don't you?" Lucy asked.

"Probably, but I wasn't sure. I figured in a few minutes it would not matter anyway," Matthew said with a grin.

"I most assuredly agree, sir. I have determined that my box is worth your box," she said seductively.

"And then some, Lucy," he said, referring to the $200.

Several more flights of stairs came and went; they had just passed the eighth floor when Matthew felt pressure in his head. He blinked his eyes a few times and held back pain when bright light and shooting pains ripped through his skull. This did not go unnoticed by Lucy.

"Are you all right?" she asked.

"I'm OK. I just suddenly feel nauseous," he said, squinting.

Images of aggression, hate, and fear flooded his mind. He saw his wife sitting on their bed; it was as if he was watching a movie. She was lying down naked as four men burst into the room wearing only underpants. He opened his eyes and saw Lucy standing in front of him, looking at his face.

"Are you well enough to walk?" She smiled and turned back down the hallway.

Matthew saw more violence and again closed his eyes against it. There was a tall man and a noticeably shorter man, possibly both in their twenties. He saw himself enter the room, and then they turned their attention to him. A fight ensued, and Matthew was overcome and beaten to the point of exhaustion. Two of the men held him tightly in place, while the other two went to his wife.

Matthew tried to clear his vision by blinking several times; he even reached out and placed a hand on the wall for balance. He felt his wife was in trouble and that he had to be there, right now. They picked up the pace and walked with a purpose. The two had just passed the ninth-floor marker when white light again invaded his mind, followed immediately with more images. Matthew saw another man moving to Lucy. *Lucy was there,* he thought. She was cornered by another man as his wife cowered on the bed.

The pain was almost crippling now, and was it not for Lucy holding his hand, he would have fallen over.

"You are definitely unwell. Take my shoulder and walk with me. We are close now," Lucy said to him.

Matthew and Lucy made it to the tenth floor and had taken a few steps into the hallway before he fell over. Lucy didn't understand what was going on, but she played along with him anyway. Leaving him on the floor, she walked over to the room and knocked three times. Susan came to the door, and Lucy asked her for help.

"Come quickly. Matthew fell in the hallway and he's doubled over in pain. He's not moving," Lucy said, pointing to the right.

Susan stuck her head out of the door and saw Matthew propped up against a wall, sitting on his butt. They walked over to him and helped him stand up.

"It will be all right, honey," Susan said as they walked him into their room.

"Help me get him into bed," Susan asked Lucy.

"I thought you would never ask," she replied, smiling.

The two women placed him on the right side of the bed, and Susan covered him up with a sheet to his neck. Looking down at him, Susan suddenly had the urge to drink.

"I'm getting a drink. Do you want one too, Lucy?" Susan asked.

"Sure, I'll share one with you," Lucy said.

Lucy walked out of the bedroom first, followed by Susan, who closed the door behind her to all but an inch. Lucy watched as Susan followed her instructions and began pouring a glass of gin.

"Keep pouring," Susan heard in her head.

The glass was almost full when Susan knew to stop filling it. Smiling, she raised the glass to Lucy and took a sip.

"Keep drinking," she heard again.

Susan upended the drink and finished it all with an exaggerated "whew" and teary eyes.

"Nice, good job, Susan. Let's go to bed now. Bring the bottle, will you?" Lucy asked.

Nodding, Susan strode into the bedroom, bottle in hand, followed closely by Lucy.

Lucy instructed her to undress and get on the bed beside Matthew and then to begin pleasuring herself.

"Your breasts are large and lovely mounds of flesh that I must have. Beg me to make love to you," Lucy said to her.

Susan began rubbing her hands over her breasts and in a soft seductive voice asked Lucy to finish undressing her.

"Do you mind bringing your body over here? I want your pussy," Susan politely said as she pulled off her shirt.

Lucy watched as Susan slid off her gold blouse and threw it toward a small recliner. Lucy noticed that her black bra worked very hard to keep the girls in place.

"Take your pants off, but leave your panties and bra on for me," Lucy said to her.

It was the first of several suggestions that sent Susan into a frenzy of sexual desire.

Lucy moved to the side of the bed and lowered herself to kiss Susan. Susan tried to fight the urge to ask, but it came out anyway.

"Is he going to be fine?" she managed to get out as Lucy closed her mouth with a passionate kiss.

"Oh sure, he's a strong man. He'll be fine," Lucy said between kisses.

Matthew was vaguely aware of what was going on as he fought against white light and random images of horror.

The first of several instructions came into Susan's head.

"Take off her dress, kiss her gently at first, and then hard. Pull her hair, lead her to you, and place her on her back" were the suggestions that she heard from Lucy.

She began undressing Lucy and kissing her with her tongue. Lucy returned her kisses and caressed the woman's breasts. Susan followed her instructions as if queued, completing each one before continuing on to the next, as directed. It wasn't long before Lucy found herself lying on her back, while Susan climbed on up to kiss her repeatedly.

Susan forgot about Matthew and concentrated on pleasing the woman underneath her.

"Fight it, Susan, fight. You can win this. You don't have to do this," she heard.

Matthew saw his wife climb up on Lucy out of the corner of his eye but could do nothing to neither join in nor interfere. He was held in place by forces he did not understand; he felt as if he was under attack, physically and mentally restrained.

Lucy started to slide out from Susan to move on top of her and was pleasantly surprised when Susan resisted. The women fought like animals, scratching each other, pulling hair. A few attempted kicks never made it as they grabbed and groped each other for position. Susan was able to fend off several blows that would have hurt her pretty badly had they made contact.

Susan went in for a headlock as Lucy grabbed a nipple, twisting it counterclockwise. Susan's face exploded in pain first, and then anger. When Lucy completed her combo by pulling it into the air and letting it go, Susan slapped Lucy across her face. She immediately went in for another attempt at a headlock but missed. Lucy kneed her in the stomach, and when Susan doubled over, she took her head and slammed it into her knee.

Susan's bell was rung; she looked around the room with droopy eyes, dazed and confused. Lucy grabbed her hair and dragged her half off the bed, leaving her head hanging over the side. With the two women going at it out of control, Matthew sat up in bed and tried to separate them. Again white light flooded his mind, and pain not to be believed sent him backward, holding his head.

Susan heard the voices in her head tell her to undress her husband, to take his pants off, and then climb on top. They instructed her to have anal sex with her husband and to work as hard as she could to pleasure him. They gave her three minutes to get started or there would be trouble. Susan fought this and stayed put as the voices became angry and grew louder. White light permeated her mind, and images of pain shortly followed. She wasn't used to this, but Susan knew what to expect.

She slid off the bed and on to the floor and crawled over to the foot of the bed. She made quick work of his pants and pulled them off, leaving them on the floor by Lucy's dress. Susan climbed on the bed and backed onto her husband's chest so she could get him hard.

"Rub his penis, caress it. Pull it to the left and then upward again. Lean over and kiss it, make it hard," she heard.

Lucy stood up and walked to the recliner to get comfy. She watched as Susan worked on making her man interested and then slid down over his penis. It was almost time, Lucy thought, and as if commanded by her for maximum effect, four half naked men burst into the room and pulled Matthew onto the floor. Two men grabbed Susan and pulled her further up on the bed, while the other two proceeded to hold Matthew in place. He was on his knees, and although he struggled, he could not stand with the two men holding his arms.

Susan screamed as a man climbed on the bed, slid in behind her, and held her tight. The other guy grabbed the phone and ripped it out of the wall. He approached his friends cautiously, and when he was sure that Matthew could not move, he hit him with the phone.

"Message for you, buddy—you're fucked," he said as he used the phone like a club.

Matthew felt himself losing consciousness as the young man whipped his ass with the phone. He stopped and threw the phone in a corner and kicked Matthew a few more times before turning to his wife. He took off his underpants and climbed up on the bed, moving forward to Susan. He took hold of her ankles and pulled her closer to him. Susan struggled and kicked, but he held on. The man was almost on top of her now as he put his hands on her waist. She tried to kick him, but he kept his weight on her thighs; all she could do now was to rock to the side in an attempt to dislodge her attacker. Susan screamed again, but it was quickly silenced by the man holding her from behind.

"Do that again and I'll cut you," he told her.

The man in front of her now pushed himself closer to her and slid his knees between her legs, spreading her wider. He took his time getting closer before he reached for her breast. He pulled on her bra and slid it down enough for them to fall out. Sliding forward, he placed his knees on the outside of her legs and sat on her thighs, kissing her a few times before punching her right in the face.

Lucy was shocked by this and continued watching as the man almost knocked Susan out, causing her great pain. Susan could not keep her head still; it wobbled back and forth as the man slapped her several times. The one that was holding her now let go of her and started removing his underpants, while the man on top slid her to him and began fucking her.

Matthew struggled on, held in place by two men, while the other two fucked his wife. Susan started crying as she continued to rock in place, trying to fall off the bed.

"Stop moving, bitch, or I'll kill the both of you. You don't want to die, do you?" he said as the man who had just finished undressing grabbed a handful of hair and shook her.

The man on top leaned forward and held on to her breasts as he fucked her faster. Susan felt him slam into her over and over, and it made her sick. He spent as much time hitting her as he did trying to move his little pecker around inside her. Susan would not tell him that, though; she was being beaten up pretty badly as it was, no sense making them any angrier.

Lucy watched as the men took turns fucking the woman and then came over to Matthew. They picked up the phone again and hit him a few times before they kicked him and changed positions. Matthew was now being held up by two naked men who kept him on his knees. He could barely keep his head level now and only listened to what was happening to his wife; he could not bear to watch. It was like the changing of the guard, Lucy remarked, except the only thing at attention were their penises.

The men on the bed rolled her over on her stomach and placed a few pillows under her chest. A man stood on the floor and entered her from behind, while another masturbated in front of her. Lucy stood up and walked over to Matthew and raised his head high. He was forced to look at the woman who only a few hours ago was his conquest but who now was his master. She moved in closer and then kneeled in front of him, letting his head rest on her knees.

"You never had a chance, guys like you never do," Lucy said as she slapped his face.

She grabbed his hair again and stood up to knee him again and then told the guys to finish him.

"Make him hurt real bad and then come and finish me," Lucy told them as she climbed on the bed beside Susan.

The two kicked and kneed Matthew several times before letting him drop to the floor. The tall one walked over with a hard cock and, pushing Lucy forward, entered her from behind.

"Ah, now you can do better than that," she said as she leaned a little further to kiss the man who was still masturbating in front of her.

The other man kicked Matthew as he stepped over him to reach Lucy.

"I said you could do better than that. Get out. Go over to her and take over. Get out of me now," Lucy said.

CHAPTER TWENTY

Burt and Ernie

Present time

When the police arrived, they saw Mrs. Thompson standing on the street next to her husband's car. It was running and parked at the curb about a hundred feet from the chocolate shop. He approached her and asked what she saw. Mrs. Thompson was an expert witness; she had seen it all. She articulated today's events to the sheriff with horror in her voice.

"He's still in there. He never left, from what I could see from the front door," she told them.

She watched Burt and Ernie leave for the chocolate shop, guns drawn. To anyone who didn't know their name combination, it was funny; to those who did, it was hysterical. Burt told Ernie to wait at the door while he checked things out. He continued to watch the street and keep the front door protected. Burt slowly made his way inside the room, carefully stepping over Mr. Thompson along the way.

Seeing nothing wrong or out of the ordinary, he continued slowly walking through the several doors that led to the back room. That's when he saw him; the chocolatier was lying on the floor in a large pool of blood. Looking around the room, he saw a woman on a table, totally naked. The woman had several areas of her body that were covered with what he thought was chocolate. Upon closer inspection, Burt confirmed that one of the woman's breasts was covered with chocolate; it was hard to look away from her, she was so beautiful.

Looking back at the man on the floor, nothing had changed. The chocolatier was still dead; the woman was still motionless on the table. Burt moved his eyes from the woman and back to the man. Burt looked back at the woman on the table and noticed that she seemed to breathe from time to time, but she never moved. That wasn't the worst of it, he thought as he watched a man splattered with blood carrying a shotgun step out from a door that led to the outside.

"We have a live one here Ernie, code 8, code 8," Burt said loudly.

Ernie entered the store room quickly and worked his way into the first of the two back rooms. Mrs. Thompson heard this and looked up as Ernie disappeared into the shop. She looked around confused; she thought he was dead. Mrs. Thompson grew very angry that she hadn't checked to verify he shot himself when he had used the shotgun.

"She made me do it. I didn't want to do those things," Mr. Wilson said.

"Stop right there, Roche, not a step further," Burt said as he cautioned Mr. Wilson and leveled his 10 MM pistol.

Ernie heard their conversation and kept inching closer to get a better angle.

"Put the shotgun down and we can talk. Stop moving, Roche," Burt said sternly.

"Horrible things, that man did horrible things, and mainly to children," Roche said.

"Stop, Roche. Stop. Don't do it!" Burt said.

Mrs. Thompson mumbled words quietly under her breath; "Kill him. Shoot him," she said.

"I don't want to!" Mr. Wilson said out loud.

"Roche, I'm asking you one more time," Burt said loudly.

"I can't. I won't," Mr. Wilson said, answering the voices in his head.

"Roche, look, I'm going to have to shoot you if you take one more step. I'll—" Burt never finished that sentence.

Roche swung the shotgun up to Burt's chest and fired both barrels. Ernie saw the whole thing and barely had time to move as Burt's body flew backward toward him.

"Kill him," Mrs. Thompson said again.

Ernie took aim and shot Mr. Wilson four times center mass, taking him down. The bloody old man slid backward and hit the wall beside the back door. Blood ran down the corners and cracks of that wall in slow motion as he removed his eyes from the man he had just shot. Ernie ran over to Burt and saw he was already dead. He then walked over to Mr. Wilson, kicking the shotgun away as he knelt down and checked his pulse. It was too difficult to determine what blood on this man was his or what belonged to another, so he checked his pulse. The man was dead.

Ernie stood up and looked around the room, taking in the situation. There were bodies all around him. There was blood on the floor, the walls, nearby tables, and everybody present, save him. He took a deep breath and walked over to the woman on the table. She was secured to the table with straps and splattered with chocolate. Parts of her body were untouched, while others were either partially or fully coated in chocolate.

Ernie recognized the woman as a substitute teacher, but he had trouble remembering her name. She had recently applied for some positions in the local school, and they had done a background check on her. He looked at her breasts, imagining what they would look like rising and falling with her breathing; he tried to remain calm and focused. He thought he should document the crime scene, and so he took several pictures of her body, concentrating on her breasts and her chocolate-covered nether region. A few minutes later, he strayed from her and took pictures of all the bodies, the bloody walls, the blood on the floor, and then went back to Suze for a different angle before taking his radio out and calling dispatch.

"Marge, come in, Marge. You got a copy?" Ernie asked.

"I copy, Ernie," Marge answered.

"10-71, shots fired, officer down. Marge, Burt's down," he stammered.

"Roger that, Ernie. I'll give the state police a call. Are you OK? Is everything under control?" she asked him.

"Yes, all golden here now, but this place's a mess. We're going to need an ambulance, the coroner, and get Macey over here, please," he said.

"Roger that. I'm sure he'll just love taking those pictures. Glad you're safe, Ernie. Marge, out," she said.

Ernie looked around one last time and went to go talk to Mrs. Thompson. He figured that the woman was safer secured to the table than she would be if he were to try to free her. When he approached her, he saw Mrs. Thompson peering through the storefront window. She watched him approach and then addressed him with a smile, although it was short lived.

"Everything all right?" she asked.

"There's nothing to see here, Mrs. Thompson. It's pretty bad in there. Come over here with me and I'll take your statement, if you don't mind," Ernie said.

"Oh, I'm all right," she said as she stared down at her husband by her feet.

"Come, Mrs. Thompson, let's get you away from here," he said softly as he began leading her away from the crime scene.

All she was doing was buying time; she just had to wait for one of them to regain consciousness . . .

"The girl, did you find the girl?" she asked.

"What girl, the one in here?" Ernie asked, pointing inside.

"No, there was a woman who was in the general store, Mr. Wilson's store. Her daughter was waiting for her in the chocolate shop. That's why Mr. Wilson went in there, he was looking for her," Mrs. Thompson said.

Ernie had not known about the little girl, nor had he thought about checking neighboring stores. In his defense, though, there was a lot going on here, and he really needed to secure the crime scene. The state police were coming after all, along with his department's staff.

"I should probably go and check it out," Ernie said as he crossed the street with his gun drawn.

Ernie had just approached the door to the general store when he heard the ambulance pull up, squealing tires with their sirens loudly blaring. Turning his head to face them, he motioned for them to cut their sirens and he pointed to the chocolate shop but threw up his hand, making a stop gesture. The EMTs nodded and waited for him to come back before entering the building. Ernie turned again to face the general store shop window and looked inside. It was packed with all sorts of things, as usual; he would see nothing from out here, he thought as he opened the door and walked inside and disappeared from sight.

He moved closer to the counter where Mr. Wilson rang up his customers and approached with caution. He looked into the backroom and immediately saw a human leg lying on the ground. Ernie took a small breath to steady his nerves before walking around the counter and into the back room. He saw Chloe handcuffed to a long wooden table. After several pictures from his smartphone to document the crime, he reached down to undo her restraints. He picked her up, throwing her over his shoulder, and walked through the store to the ambulance.

Onlookers and passersby were shocked at the image of a naked woman's bikini tan-lined ass bouncing up and down through the air as he crossed the street. No one noticed whose shoulders she was on; man, woman, and child all stared the same with their mouths agape.

"Unresponsive woman, late thirties!" Ernie yelled at the EMTs to get their attention. When he was close enough, he placed her on the cart, and they took a look at her. It didn't take them long to come to a diagnosis involving alcohol and/or drugs; everybody could tell that she had been drinking. They secured her on their cart for her safety as Ernie asked one of them to come with him. The other EMT addressed the

issues that Mrs. Thompson might be having and walked over to
evaluate her.

"Ma'am, are you OK?" the EMT asked her.

"What. Where, where am I?" Mrs. Thompson asked.

"Do you know your name, ma'am?" he asked her.

Ernie approached the first set of doors of the chocolate shop
that led into the first of the back rooms. He saw an old wooden
box jerk to the side, but he wasn't sure. He had noticed the
box before, but he didn't recall it moving. The EMT and Ernie
watched and listened as it moved again, but no noise came from
the box.

"This might be what we are looking for. The box is big
enough for a child, right?" Ernie asked the EMT.

"I guess so, I dunno," the EMT replied.

"Hello? Is anybody in there?" Ernie asked.

The box responded with a couple of small jerks, which
moved the box ever so slightly. The movement inside was so
weak that it made almost no audible noise at all. In fact, if they
were a few more feet away from the box, he doubted that they
would have heard anything at all.

"Open it!" Ernie shouted to the EMT.

The EMT searched the wooden box for the latch to open
it. The side facing the men had hinges on it; the back of the
box was toward them. Ernie watched as the EMT turned the
box around, exposing the latch with a large padlock on it. He
looked at Ernie, and they looked around the room, coming to
the same conclusion: check their pants.

Both men started searching the four dead men's pockets for
the key that would open it.

"Just be careful not to move their bodies, just enter the
pockets," Ernie told him.

Ernie thought about who might be the one to have it, and he
dug through the chocolatier's pockets, and there it was.

"I found it," Ernie said, giving the key to the EMT.

He again took a defensive posture and trained his pistol in
the direction of the man. He opened the chest, and they saw

the little girl inside. Her hands and feet were taped and she was gagged to keep her quiet. Their hearts broke when saw her like that. The EMT bent down and picked her up and set her on the floor beside it. Ernie put away his pistol and helped him remove her tape. This was a win, Ernie thought; the girl was found alive.

Just as soon as the tape came off her mouth, Ruthie began screaming. Her eyes were bloodshot. She looked dazed or out of it; she was probably drugged too.

"Where's my mommy?" Ruthie said through her whimpering.

"It's going to be OK. She's outside. Let's go and get her," Ernie said, nodding to the EMT.

The two men walked to the entrance with Ruthie in the EMT's arms. They passed Macey on the way out, warning him with their eyes.

"Go slow, there's a lot to do in there, Macey," Ernie said.

"Will do. Can you finish locking this place up for me? I don't want anyone else in here," he asked them.

They carried the child over to her mom, and Ernie let them finish their job; he had to get these two buildings locked down, and even a good portion of the street.

"Where's my backup?" Ernie said with frustration.

All the victims were killed within approximately four feet of each other. What a crazy day. How this would be sorted out, he had no idea, he thought as he sat down on the curb to take a break.

"Man, do I need a beer," he said.

CHAPTER TWENTY-ONE

No Girls Allowed

Several days later . . .

The entire town talked about the recent events; there wasn't a person whom you talked to that didn't have an opinion on the subject. Rumors of affairs, crazed sex friends, psychotic breaks, and serial killers flew rampant through the city streets. The state police interviewed people for days. They canvassed every local establishment and house in a six-mile area, taking notes on everything from what people remembered having for breakfast to where they were when gunshots were fired.

On the third day, they took their data with them and told the sheriff they would be in touch, thanking him for his help. Over those three days, Matthew and Robbie worried equally over Chloe and Ruthie. They had little interaction with them; and what they did have was over the phone. Although it had been days since everything happened, Ruthie only missed one day of school. Matthew had enough of not being needed or necessary; he felt missed, and he knew she needed him. On the way home today, he would run into town for some ground beef and chicken breasts. Matthew knew he had to leave early today to make it to the store on time, so he planned for that.

Robbie's day at school was uneventful, boring, and, yeah, uneventful; he didn't even play marbles with the guys before, during, or after school. His walk to and from school took him past vaguely interesting tree-covered hills that he barely noticed as he traversed them. Robbie's only goal was to get Ruthie's house in his view. He desperately needed to see her standing by the mailbox so he could talk to her and catch up. He tied to bring her homework to her, but the principal refused, stating that he had to give it to her mother.

Robbie maintained a steady pace until he reached her house, and then he slowed down. He wanted to increase his chances of seeing her, or for her to see him, and then come outside. She was not there. Slowly walking on, he looked at the windows; they were all empty, save one. He kept walking as he saw Ruthie smile and wave one time before disappearing behind the curtains. Robbie stopped walking and waited for her to open the front door, but she never did. He continued walking home, making a note to call her after dinner. Arriving at his house, he saw his dad standing outside by the truck. It was pulled around to the front of the house. The only time he ever did that was when he was going into town.

"Get in, Robbie. We're going into town for some groceries, and this afternoon, you and I are cooking. We are going to bring Chloe and Ruthie dinner," he said as he jumped in and closed his door.

Robbie ran around to the other side and barely had enough time to close the door before Matthew had started down the hill. Several bumps later, Robbie had finally buckled himself safely inside.

"Remember, always safety first, Dad, good job!" Robbie said, laughing.

Matthew gave him a stern glance and broke into laughter before turning again to face the road.

"Sorry, son. I thought you were quicker than that." He turned to him with a serious face and then looked forward to the watch the road.

Robbie stared at him until Matthew quickly looked over at him and then stuck his tongue out. Both smiled and then sat there quietly as they focused on the matter at hand.

"I can't wait to see them, Dad," Robbie said.

"Me too, son, me too," Matthew replied.

Matthew stopped the truck and waited for the red light to change. A small car pulled up behind them, and in his rearview mirror, he saw the passenger look at the driver and point her finger at them. She was obviously talking about them. *Small community,* Matthew thought as the light turned green and he sped away.

Pulling into the parking lot, Matthew told Robbie to grab several types of vegetables and then find two boxes of macaroni and cheese.

"I'll meet you up front and we'll check out. Make haste, son," Matthew said as he quickly took off down the aisle.

Robbie nodded and took off turning right as his dad went left. Several minutes would go by before Matthew had all of the meats he needed and walked back to the front of the store. He found Robbie there waiting in line to pay for his food. Matthew added the meat to the escalator belt and paid, while Robbie bagged everything up. No more than seven minutes later, they were on their way back home to cook several meals for Chloe's family.

Matthew preheated the oven and prepared a skillet as Robbie worked on his part. He was to peel and boil the potatoes, steam the broccoli, and make the macaroni and cheese. Within an hour, their entire house smelled every bit like an old Italian restaurant. The thick aroma of Italian seasonings hung heavy in the air, allowing thousands of molecules to invade one's senses. That, coupled with garlic, sage, and several other scents that Robbie didn't recognize, caused chaos in his nostrils.

Matthew and Robbie took turns showering, and when they were finished, they made the first of four trips to the truck and then drove to see Chloe. He knocked on the door several times before looking at Robbie and trying the door handle. He let himself in and asked Robbie to stay put until he came and got him.

"Take the boxes to the kitchen," Matthew said as he returned and stuck his head through the open door.

Matthew slowly walked through the house, and when he didn't see anyone, he called out their names.

"Chloe, Ruthie? Are you there?" he asked.

The door, opened and Ruthie stepped out in her Sunday best, wearing a lovely white dress with soft, flowing material with lace edging.

"It smells good out here. Thanks for the food," Ruthie said.

Robbie lit up from ear to ear and stood with twinkling eyes when he saw Ruthie smile and walk over to him.

"I was worried about you guys. Where's your mom?" Matthew asked her.

"She's in bed. I'm afraid she's not well," Ruthie said as she slowly looked away.

"Ah. I'll just check on her then," Matthew said.

Looking around the house, he thought for a minute before actually doing it; he entered her bedroom door after knocking twice and closed it on Robbie and Ruthie. Chloe was lying on the bed with about ten blankets on top of her, crying hysterically. Ruthie watched the door intently as Robbie started to tell her about school.

"Chloe, are you all right?" Matthew said with kindness.

He watched Chloe continue shaking and turning her head away from him, further burying herself inside her covers. Matthew spoke calmly to Chloe about his day and how it went for him in the mine earlier today. He started with what he ate for breakfast and what time he had left for the mine this morning. Chloe listened to him speak of his mining activity and she felt calmer. Matthew noticed Chloe was shaking less now, and the more he talked, the more she felt in control. Chloe was by no means happy, but she regained her control and gathered herself together.

Matthew continued to talk about the weather, how many hills he's walked over since he moved here, and how the local chipmunk population was on the rise. The last part of his conversation produced chuckles from Chloe, who sat up in the bed and thanked him for coming over. He smiled at her, and taking a break from speaking, he took in her beauty. She sat in front of him a broken woman. Red eyes, smeared mascara, lipstick that was all but worn off; she had not taken a shower since she came back home, he guessed.

"Let me get dinner ready, and if you want to, you can grab a shower and freshen up. Do you feel like joining us?" he asked her.

"Sure," she said, sniffling, "I'll be out in a few," she reassured him.

Matthew stood up and smiled at her as he turned to leave.

"Thanks for that," Chloe said.

Smiling over his shoulder, he nodded and then left the room.

Chloe left the shower a new woman; there weren't many things that a hot shower could not fix, she always said.

Dinner was buffet style; there wasn't a person present that had two of the same foods as another. Matthew would have rated it a success except for the fact that Chloe and Ruthie hardly talked. He didn't want to push the issue; eating quietly, he occasionally smiled at Robbie instead of talking to him. Matthew fought hard to eat his steak slowly. He would have loved to have eaten it three times over, but he slowed down to eat with company.

Robbie smiled at Ruthie often, and all times they were returned, but things were still awkward. With dinner coming to an end, Chloe started talking about the weather and whether it would affect his mining if it were to storm. Matthew told her it would be fine unless it rained very heavily for hours. Ruthie was finishing the last of her macaroni and cheese when between bites, she told everyone a powerful storm was coming.

"It's looking like the storm will arrive in the midafternoon and last into the early evening," Ruthie said.

Robbie listened to her speak of the storm and added, "It's probably going to dump a significant amount of rain, Dad, we're due for it."

Matthew looked at the kids briefly before turning to Chloe.

"I'll be safe, I always am," Matthew said seriously.

Ruthie and Robbie looked at each other and asked to be excused. Waiting several seconds before seeing no objection, they got up and walked into the living room to watch TV. Chloe made small talk while she finished her chicken with Matthew smiling on. They took turns talking about his recent mining experiences and totally avoided her recent shopping trip to town. It made Chloe laugh to hear him talk so passionately about rocks and dirt. She didn't hurt his feelings; she listened and nodded as the last of her dinner slowly disappeared.

"Thank you again. All of this was wonderful," Chloe said as she took hold of his wrist.

"All of this," she said, smiling while looking into his eyes.

"You are welcome. I know you would do the same for us," Matthew said to her.

"Robbie, are you already to go, son?" Matthew asked him, standing up.

"Sure thing, Dad," Robbie said as he squeezed Ruthie's hand before letting it go.

She smiled back and walked him to the door.

"Keep the rest for leftovers. I'll come over later on this weekend to get the bowls," he said.

"Thanks, Matthew, we appreciate that," Chloe said.

"See you at school, Ruthie," Robbie said with a glow.

"Yes, school will be fun," Ruthie replied.

Matthew followed Robbie out the door and turned to see Chloe wave good-bye. He returned her wave and smiled as Chloe closed the door. Robbie was tired by the time they arrived home and quickly went to bed. Matthew made a pot of coffee and opened his notebook to review his recent findings. He thought about Gwen while he sipped on his hot hazelnut flavored coffee.

The sex was absolutely great, incredible actually. Matthew smiled as he thought about treating her as someone you date as opposed to someone you marry. Matthew had been rough with her during sex, and if asked if he was acting out, he might have agreed. She still mattered to him, for now. He had to go and check on her tomorrow. First, he would call her and find out

how she was and where she was located and then check if she
needed anything. Matthew was confused; he did fuck Gwen, but
he cared for Chloe. The more he thought about it, he desired
or lusted for Gwen, but he loved Chloe. Wow, he said *loved*.
Matthew knew it was time to slow down on both women and to
spend more time in the mine . . .

Ruthie sat on the couch and continued watching TV as her
mom picked up the table.

"Do you need any help?" Ruthie asked.

"Nope, I'm good. You just relax, hon," Chloe said.

Ruthie stared at the TV as she focused on her mom's
mind. She read her feelings; she listened to her thoughts and
immediately she centered on her feelings for Matthew. Ruthie
also searched a little deeper and found memories of an ex-lover,
someone named Gwen. She occupied a lustful place in Chloe's
heart. Gwen also allocated room in her soul for hate, pain,
and anger for her; she had definitely wronged her. She was the
perfect woman for Chloe, if she could find her.

Looking over her shoulder, Ruthie sent the first of what
would be three thoughts about sex into her mom's head. They
were delivered along with warm, tingling sensations between
her legs and throughout her breasts. Ruthie had her think
about Matthew mining and then gave her the urge to pleasure
herself. Chloe stopped washing the dishes and placed both
hands on the sink for support. Chloe felt flush as several images
of Matthew holding her close and kissing her lips entered her
thoughts.

"I'm going to bed early, Ruthie," she told her as she headed
for her bedroom.

"Good night, Mom. Sweet dreams," Ruthie said quietly.

Chloe only heard the "good night" portion, so she nodded
her head and closed her bedroom door. Ruthie soon grew bored
of TV and soon followed Chloe's lead and went to bed herself.
Ruthie fell asleep with a very large smile on her face, just like
her mom did.

Matthew spent the next few days helping Chloe get back to a somewhat normal life. He prepared meals, visiting several times a day to check on her and helped to maintain her house. Robbie continued to spend time with Ruthie, referring to this with his dad as "doing his part." Chloe was a rock; each day she spent trying to understand, and each day Matthew tried to help her. She showed no weakness or worries in front of him and thanked him as always for helping her.

Back at school

Thomas turned the corner and looked down the hall before proceeding. He was to meet the guys for marbles before school today, and he wanted to practice shooting. Wearing his best overalls, he made a shuffling noise as he walked toward his destination. He wouldn't be sneaking up on anyone, Thomas knew that; he just wanted enough time to run away or duck into a nearby room and hide.

Nobody was supposed to be down in the boiler room, ever. This place was off limits, and everyone knew it; that's why it was perfect for playing marbles. One more turn and he would be at the door. Looking over his shoulder, he heard a noise, but scanning the hall, he saw no one. Smiling, Thomas turned right and walked to the boiler room door. He quickly ran up to it and pushed the door open. He wondered if maintenance knew that it could be kicked and then pushed open.

Thomas walked in and turned around to close the door behind him. He left it slightly ajar. He never told the others how he was able to get in, making sure no one saw him kick it. Turning to his right, he stepped forward into the room and ran right into Ruthie.

"Shit! Where did you come from?" Thomas shouted.

"Oh, Thomas, everyone knows you just have to kick the door. They were only being nice to you," Ruthie said, smiling.

"No girls allowed! We're playing marbles today," he said coldly.

"I'm here today to find out how you are cheating. How is it that you always win?" Ruthie asked as she stared at him.

"I said *no* girls allowed," Thomas said angrily as he pushed her several times.

"Too bad you didn't turn around to your left, Thomas. I gave you a fifty-fifty chance," Ruthie said as she pushed him back.

It was a hard push and one that almost sent him toppling over and onto his ass. Thomas went to his knees and pleaded to her.

"Don't hurt me, Ruthie. I didn't mean it," he said, trembling.

Ruthie watched as he repeated the words "I'm sorry" several times before lowering his head.

"Now back to your cheating, Thomas. How are you doing it?" she said with a smile.

"I don't cheat. I'm just a very good player, one who practices every day," Thomas replied.

Ruthie looked on with disdain and contempt; crossing her arms, she lost her smile and lowered her eyebrows.

"Do you really expect me to believe that, Thomas?" Ruthie said as she kicked his leg.

Thomas jumped but continued looking at her feet, not saying a word. He walked closer to her and stood motionless, awaiting judgment.

"Look, I'm sorry," Thomas said before Ruthie pressed a finger against his lips, interrupting him.

"A kiss, give me a kiss, that is your punishment, sir," Ruthie said, puckering up and closing her eyes.

Thomas stared at her, but he did not budge.

"A kiss, Thomas," Ruthie demanded as she listened for him to move closer.

Still only crickets; nothing more was heard by Ruthie; and her kiss never came. Ruthie opened her eyes and blinked them several times at Thomas, who still stood very close to her.

"Seriously, no kiss?" Ruthie remarked; an evil smile found its way across her face.

"Oh. I understand. I do," Ruthie said, paying particular attention to the I's.

Ruthie smiled one more time and walked to the back of the room and sat down on a chair, out of sight. The door opened, and Luke came inside. He took a step to Thomas and hit him squarely in the shoulder.

"Hope that ruins your game, you bastard," Luke said, laughing.

Thomas sat down, and both boys began setting up their game.

"You go first today, Luke. I'll be right back," Thomas told him.

Ruthie made eye contact as he approached her before he bent down to pick up a wrench that was leaning up against the corner of the wall. She stood up and walked past Luke, kicking his foot as she passed him.

"Watch it, Ruthie. Ruthie?" Luke said, confused.

"Good-bye, Luke. I hope he kills you," she said coldly.

"Fat chance, girlie, I've been practicing," he replied.

Ruthie closed the door behind her, and Luke resumed setting up his marbles. Thomas walked over and stopped with his feet only inches away from Luke's circle and his shooter. Ruthie paused on the other side of the door to give Thomas the last of his instructions.

Shouldn't it be Tomi with an i, *instead of Thomas?* Ruthie said in her mind.

Ruthie waited a moment before continuing.

"How long have you had doubts, Tomi? How long did you cry at night over who you were and what you looked like?" she said to Tomi.

Thomas looked down upon Luke with tearful eyes as she swung the weapon repeatedly in Luke's direction.

"Thomas! No! Stop! Thomas!" Luke cried out from behind Ruthie.

She gave Tomi one final command and headed off to English to meet up with Robbie; she took off at a brisk pace; she was already late for class.

Ruthie made the necessary turns down the hallway to reach her English class, sitting down beside Robbie.

"I missed you today," he said to her.

Ruthie looked at him and only smiled.

"Where were you?" he asked with a hurt voice.

Ruthie blinked her little girl eyes and made a small frown.

"I'm sorry. I'm all caught up now. I was running a little late today," she said to Robbie.

Class went on as expected; new homework was assigned and class discussions ensued from last night's work. The thing that was different was Thomas and Luke; they were absent. Robbie had seen both of them earlier today; he had assumed that they were playing marbles. Robbie was spending most of his time nowadays with Ruthie and not with the guys. He was crushed when he passed up marbles today to spend time with Ruthie and she didn't show.

"That's OK. I was just worried about you. I didn't know you had walked by yourself or if you were sick," Robbie said to her.

"Oh, I'm sorry, Robbie. I assure you, I've never felt better," she said, closing her book and giving him her complete attention.

"You know what, I feel bad that we missed each other earlier today, I really do. You could have played marbles with them," Ruthie said.

"It's no big deal, I'm still looking for more marbles anyway," he told her.

Ruthie smiled at him and reached inside her book bag. She produced a small leather pouch with a drawstring and placed it down on the desk in front of him.

"Here. I've been meaning to give these to you," Ruthie said with excitement.

"Pencil's down, everyone. Please pass your answers to your left, and I'll swing by and pick them up," the substitute teacher said.

It was times like this that Ruthie wished she could read the thoughts of men. Ruthie always tried; she never knew when she would be successful or if she could learn to access them. She always tried to read the thoughts of anyone nearby, such as the teacher on her left.

"Another week and I'll introduce myself to Chloe, I can't wait," Ruthie heard her say.

"Thanks, Robbie, Ruthie," Gwen said.

Robbie smiled at her briefly and turned back to the leather pouch and began opening it.

Ruthie smiled at Gwen and looked back to Robbie.

"Go on. Open it," she said.

Robbie felt them by squeezing the bag, but he opened it instead of commenting. Marbles!

"Really, marbles for me?" Robbie said.

"Yeah, some of them are actually yours, some I found," Ruthie told him.

"Awesome! How did you get mine back?" Robbie asked.

"One day I ran into Thomas, or actually he ran into me. I told him that I would turn him in if he didn't give them back. No one tattles better than a sixth grader," she said, laughing.

"Thank you! Thank you!" Robbie said as he emptied the contents into his hand.

"You should go and play during lunch. We'll catch up later on the way home," she said, smiling.

Robbie looked them over and placed them back inside the leather pouch, giving her a hug.

Why wait for next week? Come over tonight, Gwen thought.

"Yes, that's a good idea, a good idea indeed," Gwen said.

Be sure to wear a red dress, and be there around 7:00 p.m. Don't be late, she heard herself say in her head.

"Don't forget your homework tomorrow—there will be a quiz," Gwen said as the bell rang, and the kids all took off.

A few more classes and it was lunchtime, and then total marble carnage would ensue, Robbie thought. General math and science classes came and went with little interaction between him and Ruthie. A couple of times, Robbie thought about Thomas and Luke missing the morning's classes, but he knew they were having fun playing marbles down in the boiler room. He could barely concentrate on today's lessons because he thought of only marbles. Who knows—he might even take the rest of the day off after lunch; if they could get away with it, so could he.

"Remember chapters 10 through 14!" the substitute teacher shouted as the kids ran away to lunch.

Robbie hit the door running, dodging other kids along the way.

"Later, Ruthie!" he said, disappearing down the hall.

Ruthie watched as he hit the stairs and waved bye to her. It wouldn't be long now, she thought, before Tomi was discovered.

CHAPTER TWENTY-TWO

Sorry about the Door

Chloe had just put on a pot of coffee when she heard a knock at the door. It was early, she thought. Matthew had to be stopping by before he headed home to settle in with Robbie. *How wonderful to see him today,* she thought. She went to the door and opened it up, and Gwen stood there smiling with her hands outstretched. Gwen waited for her welcoming hug, and with a reflexive movement, Chloe moved to her and placed herself within Gwen's arms.

Gwen closed in upon Chloe and held her tight, burying her head between her neck and shoulders.

"It's so good to see you. How have you been?" Chloe asked.

"Wonderful, just wonderful. I've been teaching at the local school," Gwen said.

"Where are my manners—come in," Chloe said, smiling as she moved backward from her.

Gwen walked in and looked around at her small house. Chloe closed the door forcefully behind her and motioned for Gwen to sit on the couch.

"It's been a long time. How did you find me?" Chloe asked.

Gwen sat on the couch, smiling, as she continued to look around the room.

"Been following you for months now," Gwen confessed as Chloe looked on.

It had been months, six to be exact, since Gwen went to Chloe's business in Sacramento and saw the closed sign on the door; she was devastated. Gwen spent the next several months tracking her down and finally had a lucky break when she heard two women talking in a coffee shop one morning.

"I feel like we have unfinished business, my old friend. I feel drawn to you, as if I am told to be with you. For months I have done little more than teach and search for you—oh, that and fuck your boyfriend," Gwen said coldly.

Chloe felt the tension; the situation was rapidly going south, and she wanted her out of her house. Chloe used to be the one in charge, she was paid to be that way, but something felt different now; she no longer had the stomach for that sort of stuff. Matthew was hers; she would not share him with anyone, let alone some tramp from her past.

"Get out. Get out and don't come back. I'm not sure how you found me or how you found yourself into the arms of Matthew, and I don't care, just get out," Chloe said as she stood to lead Gwen out the front door.

She smiled and looked at the two of them. She did not wonder how things would turn out. She had a hand in the outcome; she wielded as much power as Peter Jackson at this point, and she knew it.

"On your knees, Chloe. I'm afraid that we have unfinished work. From what I can tell, our roles are reversed now," Gwen said with authority.

Chloe felt an all-too-familiar headache and confusion wash over her body. Her scalp tingled, her arms felt light, and her legs seemed as if they would give out. Chloe went to her knees not because she followed her commands; she did so because she would have fallen over if she didn't comply.

Ruthie watched on as Gwen stood over Chloe and the two women continued talking. Gwen started to undress as she told Chloe to do the same.

"Leave the panties on but remove everything else," Gwen said.

Chloe followed the simple instructions and looked at the floor as she awaited the next.

"You know the rules. Fold your clothes and place them to your right and then get up and sit on the couch beside me," Gwen told her.

Ruthie watched as her mom got naked and followed Gwen's instructions. Gwen was already sitting on the couch when Chloe finished folding. She watched her as Chloe crawled on the floor to the couch and then climbed up beside Gwen.

"Nice. Good job, my little whore. Now make love to your pussy with your fingers. I want to watch," Gwen demanded.

Chloe placed her right hand inside her panties and began pleasuring herself. Gwen watched as Chloe's hand moved around, disappearing down to her wrist inside those pretty pink panties.

"How lovely. Let me see the enjoyment on your face. Show me your smiles, hon," Gwen said.

Gwen watched as Chloe smiled and turned her head in response to her lovemaking.

"Sounds, you want to hear me too?" Chloe asked.

"Not until I tell you. This is good for now," Gwen said with a smirk.

"Faster, fuck yourself faster," Chloe heard someone say.

She looked down at her hand as she felt it come to life. Two sometimes three fingers entered her pussy roughly and pushed in as far as she hoped they would go. Her head pounded now, and as usual, closing her eyes did little to lessen the pain.

Gwen watched on and began to participate; Ruthie was amused by this, and she was doing that all on her own. Gwen was along for the ride, and she was enjoying it. She didn't care if she understood it or not; it was not the first time that she had been directed on a particular course of action. She loved the result and she cared not how she achieved it.

"Come closer, kiss me, pay me attention, my little whore," Gwen said.

Chloe removed her hand, which she was thankful for, and slid closer to Gwen. Placing her hands on her waist, she held on and leaned in for a kiss. Gwen felt the first of several sloppy kisses spread themselves over her lips, her cheeks, and her chin. She kissed Chloe very passionately several times and then continued masturbating.

Ruthie quickly grew tired of this; she wanted to finish everything. She wanted Matthew to suffer. She stepped out of her room and closed the door with a loud bang.

"Mom! Seriously?! You are with her again? I can't believe this!" Ruthie said loudly.

Chloe looked at her daughter and back at Gwen in shock. Gwen smiled and blew a kiss in her direction as she finished. Her eyes rolled back and she bit her lip as the last of her orgasms came and went. Chloe stood up and went for her clothes and then walked over to Ruthie.

"I'm so sorry, Ruthie. Gwen was just leaving," Chloe said.

Gwen removed her fingers and spread her legs wide before grabbing her breasts and pushing them up.

"Your mom's incredible, Ruthie—confused but incredible," Gwen told her as she stood up and grabbed her clothes.

"I'll be back soon for my girlfriend, you'll see," Gwen continued as she walked out of the front door naked.

Ruthie looked at her mom and frowned, she watched her lock the front door and then turn back to her.

"How could you, Mom?" Ruthie asked sadly, walking back into her room and closing her door.

Chloe stood there naked, holding her clothes. She was left wanting more, close to orgasm, and emotionally drained. She felt pain, anger, confusion, lust, and disappointment. She went into her bedroom and finished herself before falling off to sleep. She would have to talk to Ruthie about all of this later; she hoped she would understand.

The next morning

Ruthie was outside waiting for Robbie to get there when Chloe opened the front door.

"Ruthie, we have to talk," Chloe said.

"Hi, Ms. Narlst, how is your day?" Robbie asked as he walked up to the mailbox.

"Oh, it's just fine. You two have a wonderful day at school. Be safe," Chloe said to them as she walked over to Ruthie and kissed her good-bye.

The two walked to school quietly, not really talking about anything. Ruthie could not stand the silence, the not knowing, so she came right out with it.

"Yesterday when you played marbles with the guys, who won?" Ruthie asked.

"Nobody was there actually. I walked in, and the room was empty," Robbie replied.

"Oh, well, I guess it would have been boring anyway. If they weren't there, where were they?" Ruthie asked.

"I don't know. The place where we usually played had some blood on the ground, maybe Thomas cut himself," Robbie stated.

"Weird," Ruthie said.

"I know, right?" he said, smiling, as they continued walking.

Matthew spent as much time as possible mining. He had yet to find a large nugget, and although he had enough money to live comfortably with his son for the next several years, he wanted to get a sizeable return on his investment. The time he spent in the mine was not providing anything financially for his future. It helped to keep him in shape, mentally, and physically, but it provided no significant amount of gold.

He had to decide if his time was better spent getting to know Chloe and Ruthie, or if he should continue to exhaust his efforts in exploring the mine. The more he worked through expanding those two tunnels, the more material he had to go through. He was still waiting for the pieces that he ordered in town for his mini stamp mill. It would crush the rock and leave behind the heavies. It was a small one, but it was still too loud to be running in/around the mine; it would surely attract unwanted attention. Nor could he take large amounts of material out to his house to process there.

It was time for him to place an iron gate on this mine and to protect his interests. After he had that lockable gate in place, he could get earplugs and operate that device here in the mine. That gate would also give him more peace of mind that his mine would be safe and secure. *Not that they would get much out of here anyways*—he laughed—*but you never know,* he thought. It was time to get back at it; he had placed enough notes and thought long enough about what to do and where to place that gate; he had to keep expanding those tunnels.

Matthew wore his arms and back out as he drove that pickaxe into the wall time after time. Again he was getting cluttered up and making his surroundings dangerous with debris, it was time to clean up. He needed to get the bigger rocks back into the main processing room. He would spend the next several hours moving material and sorting it out into three areas by size and potential.

Having missed lunch, Matthew decided to spend another hour or two mining and then he would head back home to see his family. *Wow, family,* he thought. He was taking things slower now, maybe too slow. What if she thought he wasn't interested or if he didn't like her? Matthew made the last decision for the day; he would spend more time with Robbie, and with Chloe and Ruthie, and give this place a rest until he can get that stamp mill in place.

Packing up early, he headed home before going into town to purchase some steel and an acetylene torch. He would secure the gate this afternoon and then call Chloe later on this evening. Walking past the first of several hills, he ate his turkey sandwich and continued thinking about Chloe. He really enjoyed her company; he had to figure out a way to tell Gwen that he no longer needed *all* of her services . . .

A lovely picnic by the mine with both families; now that's exactly what Chloe needed. The next time she would talk to Matthew over the phone, she would try to arrange that. It was meant to be a convenient way for her to spend more time with Matthew and for her to continue her healing. Chloe was also curious on how Matthew was going to tell Robbie about the murder at school. She had fought off three attempts at conversations with Ruthie, biding her time until she would think of the proper way to present it. It wasn't easy for her to talk about death; she would do pretty much anything to avoid that topic.

Dinner came and went with Chloe and Ruthie doing their normal things, separate and together. They each had their own roles when it came to cooking and setting and cleaning the table, no confusion there. Tonight was a special treat for Ruthie; it was a bake of macaroni and cheese with small pieces of barbecue chicken mixed in. The chicken would be cooked by itself, pulled apart, and then mixed into macaroni and cheese before being baked with extra cheese on top.

It really was a wonderful dish that even Chloe liked. Chloe liked it because she was a picky eater, not just because it was easy to make. Both women ate like birds most of the time, but this meal was different. They sat at the table like a broken family should; eating their dinner as if it would be their last. Chloe laughed inside about that; Ruthie and she had a lot in common. Chloe had done her best to instill good moral values and kindness into Ruthie every day; and by speaking to Ruthie and having dinner with her afterward, one would know that to be evident.

The small talk was less than normal today, which gave a clue to Chloe that she should talk more to fill in the gaps and inquire on what was wrong.

"So I hear grizzly bears were seen near the market. Weird, huh?" Chloe said.

"Yeah?" Ruthie questioned as she shoved in another mouthful of cheesy goodness.

"It's time for the annual book drive to hit Arnold. Do you want to go and check it out this weekend?" Chloe said excitedly.

Ruthie loved books; Chloe was sure that she would be excited about this and even possibly already had plans for them to go.

"Oh, I had forgotten, but we can still go," Ruthie said politely.

Chloe watched as Ruthie's appetite tonight was a little less than normal. Ever since the shopping incident in town, things have been a little weird, but when Tommy was murdered in school, Ruthie withdrew. From what she knew from talking to the principal and Robbie, aside from class and an occasional game of marbles, they hardly knew each other.

Dinner came to a completion with both women filling up with cheesy goodness. Ruthie didn't eat that much and seemed distant. *Rightfully so,* Chloe thought. *She wasn't taking everything in the best of ways herself.* She had blocked out most of the painful memories of that day in town, but from time to time, a smell brought back images of sex, rape, and violence. There were even times where she would turn the corner and stop dead in her tracks and listen for anything out of the ordinary.

Ruthie enjoyed planting those thoughts; it was a way that she could have fun while she awaited their arrival; it was inevitable. She couldn't tell who or what they were, just that they were close now. They were very close on the airplane. *Too close,* she thought, but for now they were still miles away. She never really spent much time on thinking about the couple; she only concentrated on her end game. There was still a man with his son who breathed; and as long as they did, her personal goals were incomplete.

"May I be excused so I can work on my homework?" Ruthie asked.

"Sure. It won't take me long to clean this up. Go ahead, hon," Chloe said with a smile.

Ruthie returned her smile and then some; she walked over and hugged her mom, giving her a kiss. Chloe felt loved as Ruthie held on tightly to her. They parted ways, with Ruthie disappearing into her room, and Chloe working on clearing the table.

Ruthie sat on her bed, cracked her book, and stared out the window while dishes clanked together in the kitchen sink. Chloe became rougher and rougher with the dishes that she placed into the sink. Her trips to the table and back became quicker, as if moving with a purpose. She watched as she turned on the hot water and filled the sink halfway before adding liquid soap. The sink continued to fill as she watched the dishes fall victim to the suds and disappear under their white bubbles.

Chloe didn't know why she stared into the bubbles. She didn't know why she had turned on the hot water instead of making it warm for her dishes. Ruthie drew a large smile on her face as she told Chloe to reach for the butcher knife and run it across her arm.

"Why continue on? How can you live with what was done to you?" she heard in her head.

Tears filled her eyes, ruining most of her central vision, leaving only her peripheral vision intact. Looking down, she added her body's salt to the fresh water.

Chloe thought about being suspended from the general store counter and cringed when she felt their hands upon her. Ruthie smiled as she saw her pick up the butcher knife and pressed it to her arm. Chloe cleared the tears from her eyes and watched as she inserted the tip of the knife into her arm below her elbow and moved it to her wrist. A knock at the door distracted Chloe, and when she looked up to determine where the noise came from, she was told to look down and finish what she started.

Chloe looked down and concentrated on sliding the knife the rest of the way to her wrist. Another knock came, and this time it was much louder.

"Come on, Chloe, open up. You can't stay in there forever. Talk to me!" she heard Matthew yell.

Ruthie was annoyed by all of this and lost control of Chloe as more knocking pounded its way inside the room. Chloe looked at the door and dropped the knife on the floor as Matthew pushed his way inside, splintering the door in the process. Chloe looked down at her arm and noticed that it wasn't even scratched. She thought for sure that she had sliced deeply into her arm, trying to end her life.

"Sorry. The door can be fixed," Matthew said seriously, staring into her eyes.

Looking up at Matthew, she half smiled at him and moved away to avoid eye contact as she continued to cry. Matthew reached for Chloe and took her in his arms. Chloe began crying and leaned against him as he picked her up and turned her around. He passionately kissed her neck as he kept her immobile against his chest. Between whimpers and heavy breathing, she thanked him for coming and told him that she needed his help.

"I'm so glad you came. I've wanted to talk to you," Chloe said, crying.

Kiss after kiss showered her from her ear to her shoulder. Matthew held her loosely now, allowing Chloe to turn around to him and kiss him on the lips.

"You taste salty, baby," he said with broken kindness.

A few more soft kisses and Chloe leaned in against him and clung to his body. Matthew reached down and picked her up, walking her to the couch. He held her in front of him and sat down, resting her body against his. Chloe never let go of his neck; she had her eyes closed and buried against his chin when he sat down with her and placed her on his lap.

Ruthie watched on from a cracked bedroom door as the couple held on to each other and kissed. She grew tired of this charade; she could have easily ended this game last week, if she had wanted to. She could break out of this room and do it right now, she was sure of it.

"Damn those two," Ruthie said under her breath.

Ruthie opened the door all the way and interrupted their kissing. Chloe quickly slid off of Matthew and sat beside him, clearing her throat. Matthew smiled to Ruthie and removed his arm from behind Chloe's back.

"Good evening, Ruthie," Matthew said.

"Yes, apparently for some," she said, smiling, as she walked into the kitchen.

Chloe and Matthew looked at each other and laughed. They made small talk as Ruthie finished not one but two glasses of milk and then placed the empty glass in the sink.

"Good night, you guys," Ruthie said, smiling, as she closed her bedroom door rather firmly.

"Kids," Chloe said.

Matthew laughed and reached over to her, sliding her back on his lap, and reached in close.

"Where were we?" he said quietly into her ear as he sucked it into his mouth.

Matthew had every intention of spending the night over there to keep them safe; he had no time to fix their door before tonight. He held on to her tightly and talked to her in a calming voice.

"I'm staying tonight, Chloe. I'll sleep on the couch. I can't leave you without a front door," Matthew said.

"Yeah, let's talk about that door, shall we?" she asked, smiling.

He kissed her a final time and then carried her to her bed. Matthew tucked her in and kissed her good night. Matthew used her phone and called Robbie.

"I'm staying here with Chloe and Ruthie tonight. Their door's broken, so I'm going to stay the night," Matthew told him.

"Sure, Dad, I'll be fine. I'll see you tomorrow then?" he asked.

"Yes, we'll probably all have dinner tomorrow, not sure yet," Matthew said.

"Good night, Dad," Robbie said.

"Night, Robbie," he told him.

Matthew hung up the phone and turned around to walk over to the couch and almost ran right over Ruthie.

"Holy shit! Ruthie, you startled me. I'm sorry for that language," Matthew said with embarrassment.

"I'm sorry. I was hoping to talk to Robbie before I went to bed," Ruthie said, smiling.

"It's OK. The phone is yours," he said and sat down on the couch.

"Oh, I'll just call him tomorrow. Good night," Ruthie said as she closed her bedroom door.

Matthew made himself comfortable on the couch, setting his alarm to wake up around 5:00 a.m. He planned on getting up early, starting a cup of coffee, and writing a note before leaving. It was a cheesy way to invite them over for dinner. *But why not?* he thought.

The note read: Chloe, sorry about the door. I'll come over this afternoon and get it squared away for you. I was wondering if you both would like to come over for a simple dinner tomorrow evening. Please call me or tell me when I come back over to fix the door to let me know – Matthew.

Chloe woke up to the smell of coffee and quickly jumped out of bed to put on some shorts and a T-shirt. Going out to say hi to Matthew, she looked around, but he was gone. She turned her head to Ruthie's door, and it was still closed. She was still asleep; it was 5:30 after all. Chloe poured a cup of coffee and sat at the table to enjoy it when she saw the note. It made her smile, and getting out of the house would be good for them, she thought.

"Sure, we would be happy to come," she said to herself.

Taking a sip of coffee, she placed the cup on the table and turned her head to the living room. Ruthie was right in her face, only inches away.

"I heard you walk up. Did you think you would scare me?" Chloe said, smiling.

"No, I just heard you talking, and it woke me up. Did you sleep well?" Ruthie asked.

"Like an angel," Chloe said as she reached out to give Ruthie a hug.

Ruthie was smashed against her mom's body and returned the hug until she was allowed to escape.

"Mom, come on, I've got to get ready for school, you know," Ruthie said, laughing.

Chloe let her go and finished her coffee before going into the living room and turning on the news. Ruthie dismissed herself after reading the note and went to wash up before getting dressed. She came out of her room fully dressed and smelling good within fifteen minutes and walked straight to the fridge to grab a yogurt and an apple for her breakfast.

"Do you mind if I sit with you out there, Mom?" Ruthie asked.

"No problem, come and enjoy the news with me, it's almost over, though," Chloe replied.

The two finished the current news show and one other half-hour segment before Ruthie got up and placed her yogurt cup and what remained of her apple in the trash.

"Have a wonderful day, Mom. I'll be thinking of you today," Ruthie said with a crooked smile.

"I sure will. Have fun, hon. I love you," Chloe said.

"I love you too," Ruthie said with a pause as she left through the front door.

Chloe turned off the TV and got her computer booted up for today's work on her latest project, and thus her day began. A few minutes of verifying her latest proposal and she would prepare to go into town. Chloe didn't know if she would be home this afternoon before Matthew did, so she wanted to write her reply down on the note. She walked over to the kitchen table and looked around for it, but it was gone. Her cup of coffee was in the sink, along with Ruthie's yogurt spoon, but no paper note. No worries, she thought, she would just call him and leave a message.

Chloe had finished with her shower and was dressed shortly afterward. A few minutes later, she was checking her information for today's meeting and then she saved her work before shutting down her laptop. Peeking out the window, she saw that Ruthie and Robbie were nowhere in sight; they were probably up the first of several hills by this time. She reminded herself to talk to Matthew tonight about letting the kids walk versus driving them to school now.

There had been animal attacks, crazy happenings, unexplained murders; she wasn't sure what to think of that school anymore. Maybe Matthew thought the same, she thought as she left her house and drove to Murphys—who knows? The drive to town was as beautiful today as it ever was. The hills and sparse trees showed the lovely terrain of the area she called home.

A lot of what she immediately saw belonged to Matthew and her, a thought that had not escaped her earlier when she first thought about dating Matthew. *It was good for the kids,* she thought. *Maybe we are right for each other?* She had many thoughts about him, most were good, politically correct thoughts, some of a romantic nature. Chloe smiled as she drove past the last hill before she turned left onto what the locals called Main Street.

Soon, Chloe was in town, Matthew was mining away down another corridor that he thought had potential, and the kids were in school; all was right with the world. Later on in the day, Chloe stopped at the fresh market so she could pick up some items for the picnic and a dessert for tonight's dinner. Matthew had already left the mine early after getting the entrance organized so he could have enough time to repair her door. He also had to make it back to the house in time to get dinner started, although he had already left Robbie a note on what to start.

Robbie was walking Ruthie home from school when she told him about dinner at his house tonight.

"Yeah, I read a note your dad left. We are coming over tonight for dinner," Ruthie said coldly.

"I hope there's time for a movie too," Robbie said.

"I'm sure it will work out in the end," Ruthie said as she hugged him good-bye.

"I'll see you soon," Robbie said as he took off running.

Ruthie approached her house and saw that the door had been fixed.

"You sure are handy, I'll give you that," Ruthie said as she closed the door.

The rest of the afternoon passed with all four being very busy. Robbie started dinner for them as he was the first home. Ruthie worked on her homework, while Chloe baked a cake for dessert. Matthew arrived and carried in groceries so he could make the last of his Italian feast. Hours later, he was enjoying his success with both his and Chloe's families.

After dinner, Chloe thought long and hard about having a picnic. It was time to test the waters and ask. Chloe finished her spoonful of cheesy goodness and looked at Matthew.

"So, Matthew, how about we have a picnic at the mine sometime soon? I could prepare the food," Chloe said.

"That would be great. I might even help to carry it down there," he said with a smile.

Ruthie and Robbie didn't really care and showed little excitement when Chloe suggested it.

"I guess, just as long as you have dessert," Robbie said with a pout.

Ruthie leaned in close to him and whispered, "Be prepared for fresh fruit, and lots of it."

Chloe and Matthew finished their meals and began talking about their days when the kids became bored. After several glances at each other and occasional nods to their perspective parents, they nodded to each other.

"Can we be excused?" they said at the same time.

The kids were on their way to the living room before Matthew pulled out his notebook and started showing Chloe his maps.

"That's wonderful, let's go and see it!" Chloe said without blinking.

"Sure, sounds good. Get your stuff then," Matthew said, closing his notebook.

Chloe started laughing at him and told him she was kidding.

"It's too late tonight, but let's make plans the picnic for this weekend then?" Chloe said smiling.

Matthew laughed at the thought of dropping everything and taking her to the mine tonight.

"Sorry about that, I'm intense about that subject," he said.

Chloe looked over at the kids, and then she flipped her hair back over her shoulder, smiled, and asked if it could be everyone.

"How about the kids? Do you want to make it lunch for four?" Chloe asked.

"Oh, sure, that would be fine," Matthew said, showing as little disappointment as possible.

"I know what you were thinking, don't worry, we'll have our date night soon," Chloe said as she took his hand and held it.

Matthew smiled back at her and looked at the clock. He so wanted to mine tonight, or at least to get an early start tomorrow. A full day of mining would give him time to get organized and make it safe for them to take a peek at it.

"How about we have a small tour of the entrance after that picnic?" Matthew asked.

"Sounds like a plan. We'll meet you over here sometime Sunday afternoon then?" Chloe said.

Matthew looked at the kids who were talking to each other while they had the TV on to block out their conversation. He saw them as a nice pair, as brother and sister, actually.

"Sure, I'll be home around noon, so if you can be over here, I'll carry what I can and we'll walk to the mine," Matthew stated.

The evening ended on a positive note, and when the two kids were still busy talking and watching TV, Chloe leaned in for a kiss. A single kiss between them lasting no longer than a few seconds excited Matthew to his core; Chloe liked it too. It felt natural to her; it felt right. This time it was Chloe's turn to take a tired daughter home, and for him to extend an offer for them both to return.

"Good night, you guys. Drive safely, it's dangerous out there!" Matthew said as he hugged Chloe and let her go before patting Ruthie on her head.

Chloe mouthed the word "bye" as she smiled at him. Matthew stayed put until they made it to their car and left the property, heading home.

He closed the door and turned to help Robbie clean up. The dessert was hardly touched, probably because they all ate a heavy Italian meal. He made a note to take that for the picnic if there were any leftovers from Sunday. The house was back to normal, and Matthew and Robbie took a small break to relax in front of the TV before going to bed. All that reminded Robbie of tonight's dinner with the thick smell of meat sauce and grilled chicken that hung in the air. Matthew smelled that too, but his attention was on the kiss; both smiled as they relaxed and watched a bit of mindless TV.

Chapter Twenty-Three

Lovely Day for a Picnic

Matthew got an early start today because he had to be back around noon. He was to lead everyone back to the mine for the picnic; he couldn't be late. Matthew had been crawling around snake-like tunnels for several days now; he had to clean them up. Chloe and the kids could not be expected to safely navigate them on the tour. Matthew decided to only clean up a few of the closer rooms and corridors. He spent several hours regaining control of the entrance and then went deeper to mine down his hallway. He swung is pickaxe a few times and he just couldn't get into it; all he thought about was lunch with Chloe. A few swings more and he was on his way home to prepare.

Chloe and the kids returned from a quick trip to town content, all except Robbie. He had not found any marbles. Although he didn't play much anymore, he still practiced and tried to get better. At the very least, he wanted to win back all of his original ones from the guys. Taking the kids into town was what Chloe wanted to do. She knew Ruthie wanted a book, and Robbie, marbles. The disappointment in Robbie's voice and face was evident.

"It's OK, Robbie. Next time we'll go one town over and try again," Chloe said to him.

"You can read my book, Robbie," Ruthie said.

"It's OK. I don't play as much as I used to anyway," Robbie replied.

It was after 10:00 a.m. when they started to get ready to go to Matthew's house. Chloe smiled at the kids and went back to making lunch.

"Mom, it's ten till, we really need to be going," Ruthie said.

"OK. Let's go. Everyone please take a bag and we're on our way," Chloe said, opening the front door.

They all piled out, bags in hand and got into her truck. Matthew was waiting outside when they pulled up. He was their pack horse, their guide. He gave them all a bottle of water and thanked them for coming.

"Welcome one and all to Cougar Mountain Tours—where no one gets out alive!" Matthew said with a smile.

"Yeah, right, Dad. Good one," Robbie laughed.

They walked between the hills and the trees in the midday's sun. Ruthie remembered each landmark all the way leading up to the mine. Matthew and Robbie already knew them, while Chloe was oblivious; she was just along for the walk. Arriving at the boulders that protected the mine's entrance, they set up their lunch.

Dried cherries, raisins, and walnuts sat atop a large mound of leaf lettuce on the rock table in front of Robbie. He anxiously stared at it as he decided what he would do. Adjacent to it was a basket of vegetable chips ranging in color from green to yellow to red; all of which looked inedible to Robbie. He watched on as Chloe opened more containers and sat them on the ground beside their makeshift table. Some of them were left closed, leaving Robbie unable to guess their contents.

"Now it's not all that bad," Chloe said to Robbie, placing a bowl of strawberries just out of his reach.

Robbie smiled back politely and continued perusing their feast. The picnic was an impromptu meeting at the mine, involving great friends and, hopefully, good food. Ruthie looked around the area and took in her surroundings; she cared more for what was to happen afterward at the tour. Matthew had promised them a brief tour of the mine after their lunch. Matthew smiled and looked at the kids and then back to Chloe.

"What a nice lunch. Thanks for all the trouble you went through," he said to Chloe.

"Oh, not at all—it was fun. I have to pay for the mine tour some way," she replied, smiling back.

Ruthie and Robbie talked about school and ate fruit while Chloe handed out their plates. Matthew reached for the two sealed containers and opened them, exposing chicken wings and mozzarella sticks. An excited Robbie reached for them, placing several on his plate before returning to carrots and celery. Ruthie laughed at him; she had to remember to be a kid. Chloe made Matthew a plate with the remaining chicken wings and mozzarella sticks. Only after that did she give him a small amount of vegetables to fill the plate. They all ate their lunch slowly and as a whole quietly.

During the picnic, Chloe and Matthew took time to catch up on the local news and current events.

"What about the murder in the boiler room?" Matthew asked.

"Nothing for sure, nothing verified anyway, but . . ." Chloe said quietly.

Matthew leaned in close and, without trying, raised his eyebrows in anticipation.

"There was a large pool of blood in the center of the room. Inside of it were several small circles that were themselves arranged in a larger circle," Chloe spoke so quietly that not even Matthew had heard all of the words.

Looking at her, Matthew made a puzzled face, and it was her turn to lean in closely and say her last sentence again.

"A pentagram? Circles of protection? Demons? What's next?" Matthew said with a serious face.

Chloe looked at him and waited for a smile before continuing her story.

"So they never found them, and in the back corner leaning against the wall was a large bloody wrench," Chloe said.

"They never found them? *Them* who?" Matthew asked.

"Thomas Gruder and Luke Masters, the two boys in Ruthie and Robbie's classes, the missing boys presumed murdered in the boiler room," Chloe said.

"That's crazy. It sounds farfetched if you ask me, probably a prank by the two kids themselves," Matthew said.

"They've not ruled it out, not yet," said Ruthie.

They looked over at Robbie and Ruthie and saw the concern in their eyes.

"I'm worried, Dad. It's not like them to miss school," Robbie said.

"I'm sure it will all work out. They'll find those kids," Chloe said.

Matthew changed the subject and turned to Chloe and smiled.

"What a lovely summer day, and not too hot either," Matthew said.

Chloe smiled and finished the last of her salad before answering.

"Do you think we need to drive the kids to and from school now with all of the recent happenings over there?" Chloe asked.

"With the mountain lions, the recent disappearances, and possible deaths, is it safe to let them walk there and back?" Chloe added in support of her last statement.

"It's too soon, really. But if you want to take turns, we can revisit that in the near future. Don't worry, the police will figure this out," Matthew replied.

Ruthie had taken the last of the strawberries before standing up and asking Matthew to show them the mine.

"I'm ready. Let's go and check out the dark mine," she stated.

Matthew looked at everyone and stood up to stretch. An exaggerated motion from beginning to end was followed by a bear's growl and then he was ready to go.

"OK, everyone let's stay close to each other. I'll be in front with a light, and Robbie will have one in the rear," Matthew said as he motioned for the group to enter the mine.

"Yay! The mine tour begins!" yelled Chloe.

Robbie stood up and took his light and turned it on and waited for Chloe and Ruthie to pass him before entering. Matthew walked them down the main corridor for about fifty feet or so before they had options. There were openings to the left and right, as well as the option to continue on forward.

"We go left here, it's dangerous out that way," Matthew said, pointing to the right tunnel.

"Can't we go and just take a look?" Ruthie asked.

"Maybe later, but for now we go left and then come back to continue forward," Matthew said.

Later was as good as no, all kids knew that, so Ruthie stopped walking as Matthew and Chloe continued on ahead.

"Hey, we should come back one night soon and check out that right corridor; it could be interesting. Will you come out with me one night and check it out?" Ruthie quietly asked him.

"Sounds good to me, I like scary!" Robbie replied.

"Let's go kids, catch up, please," Matthew said over his shoulder.

Chloe was amazed at the size of the tunnels and the main room; it was unlike anything she had ever experienced before.

"You did all of this?" Chloe asked Matthew.

"Me? No, not all of this. Most of what you see here was done initially when the previous owner dug down deep. I have taken what he's done and expanded upon it," Matthew stated.

Chloe looked around and took in the size of the tunnel she walked through; she could outstretch her arms and not touch a wall or ceiling.

"Way too cool. Show me where you have dug then," she asked.

He led them into the main room and then into the corridor beyond it, reminding everyone to be careful and watch where they placed their feet.

"Remember to pick up your feet and not to drag them, there are lots of rocks here," Matthew said.

Matthew showed everyone where he was working now and what he swung his pickaxe into daily.

"The big room where we just came from is where I'm going to break up my rocks and then prepare the material for panning. I know, exciting, isn't it?" he said.

"It's very nice down here, relaxing and calming," Chloe said.

Matthew and Robbie knew otherwise, and Ruthie, well Ruthie knew it would be exciting very soon . . .

Matthew and Chloe were looking at a wall to the left of the last corridor when Ruthie took Robbie's hand, and they moved away toward the main room.

"We should sneak out and bring a flashlight and map it out. It's not too scary," Ruthie said to Robbie.

"After school then?" Robbie asked.

"No, nighttime, when it's dark," Ruthie replied.

Ruthie looked left and right and wrote into memory the room she was in and how she got there. Looking back at Chloe, she saw her lean in to Matthew.

"There are treasures within these walls," Chloe told Matthew as she kissed him.

Ruthie helped her go a little further to ensure he understood her meaning. She had Chloe use more tongue than she had intended on using and had her brushed her right hand against the front of his jeans. Robbie looked at what Ruthie was looking at and turned away.

"Gross. Come on, Ruthie, let's walk back to the entrance," Robbie told her.

After a few more minutes of kissing, Chloe stopped and apologized. Matthew smiled and told her they would come back here one day soon, when the kids were still in school. Chloe kissed him one more time and then she straightened her blond hair.

"Let's go find our kids," she said.

CHAPTER TWENTY-FOUR

Tainted, All Tainted

Outside Murphys

The old couple drove their SUV like a '70s station wagon, slowly and with purpose. The couple concentrated on their task at hand as they drove under the speed limit and obeyed all posted signs.

"Last reports say Murphys, but I feel something around Arnold. I'm confused," the old woman said.

"Murphys is close, so we'll check it out first," the old man said, smiling at the woman.

"Never fear, hon. I'm sure she'll find us before we find her," the old man said in a calming voice.

"I know dear. I wish I felt better about all of this," she said as they drove on.

The old couple drove through the night and pulled into Murphys at around 8:00 p.m. They kept going until they hit the outskirts of town and pulled over to prepare.

Ruthie appeared to hover slightly above the ground, seeming taller than Robbie knew her to be. He looked through the window as Ruthie tapped on it to get his attention. Robbie never thought of her that way, but he swore that her breasts were larger, possibly due to them being at eye level.

"Let's go. Let's go check out the mine," Ruthie said.

Robbie grabbed his flashlight and his book bag and climbed out the window. Ruthie and Robbie ran into the hills at a brisk pace.

"Hurry, I don't want to be late," Ruthie said.

"Late? late for what?" Robbie said to Ruthie's backside.

The old man and woman walked toward the mine hand in hand.

"Good memories," he said to her.

"Good memories, hon," she replied.

The woman carried an old lantern, and the man an old pickaxe and a burlap sack.

Matthew yawned, stretched, and walked through the hallway to the bathroom. He passed by the door to his son's room and felt a cold draft hit his toes. That chill was followed by the sound of crickets; Robbie was sneaking out! He threw open the door and saw Robbie's bed a mess, the window open, and when he stuck his head out, neither him nor Ruthie was in sight.

"Dammit, Robbie!" he yelled as he went to get a pair of pants. It was too close to the time that he had told the kids not to go to the mine. Matthew opened his door and found himself running through the field in a matter of minutes. Up ahead he saw that damn light again as it bounced through the air. "Fucking claim jumpers," he said under his breath as he continued to run. Seeing that light only made him run quicker, although his focus was on the kids.

It didn't take him long to realize things were wrong, they were seriously wrong. He received a call from Chloe and slowed down to take it.

"I'm on my way to the mine. Let me guess, Ruthie's gone, right?" Matthew managed to get out between dodging rocks as he ran.

"Yeah" came from a tired woman's voice.

"I'll be dressed in a minute and then I'm on my way," Chloe said.

"No, it's too dangerous. You stay put," Matthew said to a click on the phone; Chloe had hung up.

"Shit! Shit!" Matthew yelled as his pace again quickened.

Ruthie and Robbie entered the mine and made their way through the water.

"Don't go through the water, it's too dangerous," Ruthie said.

"Never tell a kid that," Robbie replied.

They trudged on through, laughing as they went along.

Chloe grabbed a nearby shirt and a pair of shorts and made her way to her front door. Upon arriving, her pants and shoes were on; her shirt was the last to go. She opened the door and slid her face into the shirt and fished her arms through. The door was closing behind her when Chloe's shirt was pulled tightly over her face. Her hands were still exiting their sleeves and were held upward, with her elbows against her sides.

"Breathe, dear. Breathe in deeply. It will all be over soon," an old voice said to her.

Chloe was now raised off the ground and leaned backward against the person who was holding her hostage. The old man held her tightly against his chest, pinning her arms to her body. As Chloe struggled, he held on tighter; soon she would not be able to breathe at all due to constriction. She tried to scream, but he shook her violently when he thought she was to try.

The older woman copped a feel; it was more for the shock and confusion of Chloe than it was for the old woman's pleasure. *But what the hay,* the old woman thought. The old man kept her off the ground and her arms immobile as he continued to crush the woman's ribs. The old woman hit Chloe in the stomach with a closed fists a few times, and then he lowered her feet to the ground. Turning her around to face the door, he slammed her head into it. Chloe saw stars and ceased to struggle as tears filled her eyes, and her legs would not support her.

Chloe saw blurred images as she was turned back around to face the old woman.

"You have lovely breasts, you know that, right?" the woman said to Chloe.

"Thank her," the old man said as he shook Chloe violently.

"Thank you," Chloe barely managed to get out.

The old woman picked up the pickaxe and raised it above her head. Chloe's vision returned just in time to see her swing it down with great force and plant it into her chest. Chloe stared at the woman and then looked down at her chest. Blood poured onto her front porch in torrents at her feet.

"Up here, hon, my eyes are up here," the old woman said as she removed the pickaxe.

The old man let her go, and the couple grabbed up their belongings and headed off to the mine.

"Sorry, hon, it was the only way to be sure," she said as she left Chloe bleeding out onto her front porch.

The couple had not taken two steps before Chloe fell lifeless to the ground, sending her blood into the air around her. Looking over his shoulder, the old man saw Chloe's head bounce once and then settle in the pool of blood. It made his heart sad as he turned back to follow his partner.

"I wish we had a way of knowing for sure," the old man said.

"Well, she was tainted, and recently too. At a minimum, it stops her from going into another's body," the old woman said.

"You're quite right, as always. You see the big picture," the old man said.

The couple moved faster to arrive at the mine as soon as possible. Had they been viewed from a distance, one might have thought it comical, or they would have not believed their eyes.

Robbie walked a little slower than Ruthie did, and as she turned another corner, she told him to hurry.

"Hurry up, Robbie. The water is foul here. We need to get past this," Ruthie said over her shoulder.

Robbie sped up and hit the next corner much faster to make up distance, and he plowed into a motionless Ruthie headfirst.

"I'm sorry, Ruthie. Take my hand," Robbie said sadly.

He pulled her up and noticed that she was crying.

"It happened here, you know. Old man Timmers," Ruthie stated.

Robbie listened as she explained what happened without saying a word.

"He had marbles, you know. He took them wherever he went. They never left his side. That's how we met actually. He asked me if I knew how to play. When I told him no, he spent time teaching me," Ruthie continued.

"I'm sure he knew some cool games and that he was a good shooter," Robbie replied.

"Oh, he was the best. He was the best. In town, he would buy me a malted shake, a chocolate one, and we would play right there. It wasn't safe in the mine, he would tell me. He found good gold you know. He was well off, that Mr. Timmers was. Some said that he mined often to defend, to protect his property, that he didn't need to mine for gold, he'd already found enough," Ruthie said then sighed.

Robbie took her hand and led Ruthie to a nearby rock where they both sat down. He was still holding on to her hand as he looked into her eyes and continued listening. It was during their walk to the rock that Matthew crept closer, keeping his distance, but staying close enough to listen to everything. Matthew looked around from time to time, thinking that he heard noises, but he knew they were in front of him.

"One day I followed old man Timmers. I snuck out and waited for hours through the night. Being very still and with great purpose, I hid along the tree line to the east of where I thought the mine was. I just wanted to say Hi. I just wanted to play marbles in the old mine," Ruthie said as she broke into tears.

Robbie continued to hold on to her hand, keeping her close.

"All of this is very interesting. It sounds like a wonderful time. Do you know if the man knew you were there or that you were following him?" Robbie asked.

"I had been there for so long, I had dew on my shoulders, on my hat—I don't think so. Once he started moving, he was quick. The old man traveled light—he was very quiet. He made no noise as he moved through the cover of darkness. If it were not for his labored breathing and sometimes his breath that hung in the cold, chilly air, I would have lost him, like the others had done so before me," Ruthie said with excitement.

Matthew listened on and he knew something spiritual, something supernatural was happening. As excited as Ruthie's voice carried those words around the corner, he found himself watching her, his concentration fell on each word she said. Ruthie paused before speaking again.

"They killed him. They hit him with a pickaxe. So I panicked and ran back through the water. The air became foul and I had trouble breathing. Before I could reach the entrance, I was overcome and fell forward. I was light-headed, confused. I could not think clearly, and I began crawling toward the light. I had almost made it when someone grabbed my ankle and pulled me back into the water. They held me down and pushed my lips into the stinking water. Every time they held my face in the water, I held my breath. I struggled, but I could not get free. They would pull me up and then I would breathe that foul air in, lungfuls of it at a time. I coughed and then it was back into the water for me," Ruthie said sadly.

Matthew was taken aback by her speech; he didn't know what to believe. He found himself with doubt, and as he remained motionless and concentrating on her every word, he heard more noise from behind. Robbie too sat mesmerized, listening to her as he rubbed away her tears with his thumb. He felt her emotion, and as the first of several tears came, his eyes watered. Ruthie looked past Robbie to his left and she knew it wouldn't be long now; they were close.

"I coughed and then it was back into the water for me. I passed out. I saw my body from above—they were still holding me down. I heard them say they wanted to be sure," Ruthie said.

"I can still feel her. She is still around," the old woman told the old man.

"We'll get you. Soon we'll find you resting and we'll finish this, I swear we'll find you," the old man whispered.

Robbie stood up and looked at Ruthie with very large eyes and let go of her hand.

"You're dead? They killed you?" How—" he asked, stopping abruptly.

"Robbie, I looked differently back then. My spirit is inside this little girl—I possess her body. Everything I have done up to this point was for a means to an end. I wanted people to know that old man Timmers did not kill me, like the newspapers said he did. They said he kidnapped me, that he did bad things to me, and then killed me. Some said he killed me and then did bad things to me. None of that was correct," Ruthie said sadly.

Robbie was confused and was having trouble taking all of that in; Matthew, however, understood it all. He was watching the kids when the old man and woman ran past him and confronted Ruthie. Robbie was startled and took a step backward, not knowing at first who had jumped around the corner.

"I'm sorry; it seems they have followed me here. They are always close by," Ruthie said to Matthew.

Matthew moved to the side and stood in front of Ruthie and Robbie, brandishing his pickaxe.

"Don't listen to it. It's pure evil. She's not to be trusted!" the old woman shouted.

Matthew looked as the old man moved to position himself closer to the kids, moving his pickaxe up and down in a slow, menacing rhythm.

"Now you guys let the kids go. We can talk about this," Matthew said to them.

Matthew watched on as the old woman circled them to the left, and the old man went right. He watched the man start to raise his pickaxe, and Matthew swung wildly at him. Matthew went a little sideways, and the man moved behind him.

"Tainted, all of them, they must all die," the old woman said.

Ruthie took off running down the side corridor with Robbie close behind. The old man dropped the pickaxe and took hold of Matthew. He raised him above the floor and shook him a few times before talking once again.

"Be still, stay still," Matthew heard, but it was in his head, and it was his own voice.

It was more of a suggestion or a thought than a command, and as he questioned what he had recently heard, the old woman picked up the pickaxe and raised it above her head. Again Matthew heard those words; he struggled against them and turned his body to the side as the lady swung the pickaxe violently toward them.

Matthew shook his body left and right to defy the man; it turned out to be just enough to position the old man's body in the path of the old woman's pickaxe. Matthew thought he was out of the way, but the pickaxe hit him in the side and took out an inch of flesh before tearing deep inside the old man's stomach. Both men screamed out in pain and moved backward from the old woman's damaging blow.

"Dammit, old woman!" the old man said as he let go of Matthew.

"Now look what you've done," he finished as his intestines fell upon the mine floor.

The old man fell to his knees from his wound and landed on his left side, facing Matthew. The old woman stepped to the old man and swung the pickaxe with the strength of ten men, burying it inside the old man's chest, killing him instantly. The look on her face was that of insanity. She smiled crazily as she looked directly at Matthew before removing the pickaxe.

"Run, Matthew. Run to your son. It's too late—she has him now," the old woman said to him as she raised the pickaxe above her head and stepped in his direction.

Matthew was bleeding pretty badly now and holding his side. It was done mainly out of one's reflex to protect a wound. Matthew continued walking after the kids, holding his side as he went. The pain in his head was worsening, but the thoughts telling him to stay put, placing him in danger were not present. He took off down the hallway fast enough to stay ahead of the pickaxe-wielding old woman who was close behind him.

Turning the corner, Matthew saw the two kids struggling in front of him. They rolled to and fro on the ground and over the rocks. Every time one wound up on top of the other, punches were thrown and landed against the person on their back. Both had bloody hands and black eyes. Matthew took a step toward them, and out of the corner of his eye, he saw the pickaxe. Holding his side, Matthew moved out of the way, and the pickaxe stuck in the cave wall. Matthew looked again at his son, who was still struggling with Ruthie, and did something he had not done in his life—he hit the old woman right between the eyes. He landed his closed fists twice against the old woman, knocking her backward with blood pouring from the corner of her eye.

Matthew felt crippling pain; it was worse than before. White explosions blurred his vision. He could not see shapes; he was effectively blind. A little girl's laugh came from somewhere on his left.

"Thanks for taking care of them for me. You dispatched them with ease. I've been looking for them for quite some time now, years actually," the little girl said.

It was clear to Matthew now that the thing he spoke with was not Ruthie; there was something else in there, something else inside of her.

"I don't understand, but you were the victim?' Matthew muttered.

"Yes, because my life force goes from one body to another, but only women, though. So, yes, I am the victim," the little girl replied.

Matthew's head hurt, and another attack of searing intense pain flooded his mind.

"Kill your son—it's the only way to stop her," he heard in his head.

Matthew yelled out, "No!" as more explosions and white light bombarded his mind, causing him to close his eyes reflexively.

Matthew took slow deliberate steps toward the last location that he remembered his son being. Ruthie watched him stagger and easily passed him by as she reached for the old woman.

"Consider your life forfeited, old woman," the little girl said as she twisted her neck clear around to the left.

Matthew leaned forward and fell over on the ground. He spread his hands out and felt for Robbie. He knew the little girl was on his right, so he moved slowly forward and slightly to the left, his hands outstretched and reaching for any part of Robbie.

"I could not have done all of this without you, Matthew. I remember the first day we met," the little girl said.

Matthew stopped crawling and listened to her as he stalled to regain his vision; he noticed that she was moving closer.

"I made the decision to insert myself into your life when I ran into you at the antique show. I read your thoughts, noticed the love you had for each other, as well as your darker sides," she continued.

"Who makes deals with strangers in exchange for sex? Seriously?" she laughed.

Matthew tried not to speak to her, but he felt the need to defend himself.

"You broke up my marriage!" he yelled.

"You broke us apart. I quit my job, I moved clear across the country to get away from it all," he slurred his words, half shouting.

"Yes, I orchestrated all of that. Once I found out you were coming here on vacation, I took an interest in you," she said as she followed his bloody trail.

Kicking his right foot, she continued to speak to him.

"It was you, Matthew. You were the reason for all of this. I have killed in your name. I made your plane crash in your own backyard. I had those men break into your room and violate your wife. I made you appear not to care, to sit back and watch, to do nothing to save her. You know she hated you for that; extreme hatred," she said softly, her voice trailing off as Matthew began to cry.

"Why? Why me?" he cried.

"Well, for starters, you had a strong will to resist me. I place my emphasis on *had,* Matthew," the little girl said coldly.

Matthew continued to listen and regain his strength.

"You would overcome almost every obstacle that I would throw at you. It just so turns out that you are a pleasant distraction for me, and I needed that distraction. Those two had found me again, and I needed to draw them in close. I knew that they would try to figure out how you fit into the puzzle, and when I threw your son in for good measure, the deal was sealed—they would come for me at once," she said.

Ruthie walked around to the other side of Matthew and kicked his other leg, just below the knee.

"Now, once and for all, you have helped to end their involvement with me and others in this world. There's no one else close enough for them to go into—they are finished," the little girl said with a small laugh that turned into a growl.

Ruthie took his ankle and pulled him backward, scraping his stomach and his wound over the rocky floor.

"It's a shame that the lovely lady had to die," Matthew said to her.

"Yes, but it was necessary, hon," Robbie replied.

Ruthie heard this, and before she could let go, Matthew kicked her with both of his feet, pushing her arm into her chest. Ruthie felt her arm break in several places, and it became unusable for what she had in store for these two. She was launched backward against the wall, with her back hitting before her head did. Robbie jumped over his dad and started wrestling with her again. Matthew hunted for his pickaxe, which he found about ten feet away between some small rocks.

"She's strong, very strong. Help me now. Leave the pickaxe," Robbie said.

Matthew turned to see Ruthie place Robbie in a headlock as he grappled for position. Ruthie let out an evil laugh as Robbie felt her applying pressure. Matthew took a step toward them and closed his fist around a handful of her hair, slamming her head onto the floor.

Ruthie saw something she had not seen happen in this mine in several years; she rose above her body, floating gently in place. Her life force hovered above the dead girl's body. She had lost control of the young girl. It was OK, though; there was someone else close by. Matthew stood beside Ruthie and looked in her direction of the evil spirit.

"Good luck finding another. We're out in the middle of nowhere," the old lady said through Matthew.

"Yes, it's too bad she had to die, your precious Chloe," the old man replied through Robbie.

The nightmare continues . . .

CHAPTER TWENTY-FIVE

Time for Meds

"I told you not to go directly to the final chapter; nothing good can come from this. If you are reading this because you finished the last chapter, you should know that this chapter of my story has already ended, and I'll be coming for you shortly. While you wait, how about a lovely Haiku to help you relax?" she says to you.

Wait for me to come
Look into the mirror now
Stare until I come

"If you want to learn more about me, please contact us through the author. We are conveniently located on social media, but more specifically from www.peggylanders.com. I'm afraid that he will require a bit of persuasion to continue my saga; it appears that he likes to read about those who read about him," she tells you.

"Oh, one last thing before I come for you. Do you have any ideas about that beige door in the olive-tasting bar?" she asked.

The end

Well, that all depends on you . . .

"Deirdre, it's time for your medicine . . ." the nurse said quietly.

Edwards Brothers Malloy
Oxnard, CA USA
March 1, 2016